OUT OF THE DARKNESS

OUT OF THE DARKNESS

The Phantom's Journey

A Novel

Sadie Montgomery

iUniverse, Inc.
New York Lincoln Shanghai

Out of the Darkness
The Phantom's Journey

Copyright © 2007 by Sadie Montgomery

All rights reserved. No part of this book may be used or reproduced by any means, graphic, electronic, or mechanical, including photocopying, recording, taping or by any information storage retrieval system without the written permission of the publisher except in the case of brief quotations embodied in critical articles and reviews.

iUniverse books may be ordered through booksellers or by contacting:

iUniverse
2021 Pine Lake Road, Suite 100
Lincoln, NE 68512
www.iuniverse.com
1-800-Authors (1-800-288-4677)

Because of the dynamic nature of the Internet, any Web addresses or links contained in this book may have changed since publication and may no longer be valid.

This is a work of fiction. All of the characters, names, incidents, organizations, and dialogue in this novel are either the products of the author's imagination or are used fictitiously.

ISBN: 978-0-595-45454-9 (pbk)
ISBN: 978-0-595-89765-0 (ebk)

Printed in the United States of America

To my family and friends, tarts and tartans, GALS, and all of those obsessed with the man behind the Phantom.

Remember that I am thy creature; I ought to be thy Adam, but I am rather the fallen angel, whom thou drivest from joy for no misdeed. Everywhere I see bliss, from which I alone am irrevocably excluded. I was benevolent and good; misery made me a fiend. Make me happy, and I shall again be virtuous.

—*Frankenstein* Mary Wollstonecraft Shelley

Prologue

The Phoenix of the Opera

Once upon a time a man haunted the underworld of the Opera Populaire. Outcast and disfigured, the Phantom of the Opera met life's cruelties with his own. Condemned to the shadows, his face hidden behind a mask, he dedicated himself to the pursuit of the beauty that he could not find in himself. Through illusion and deceit, he fashioned a world, a counterfeit of the one he dreamed. And then he fell in love.

But the woman he had nurtured and taught could not love him—after all he was a ghost—and he returned to the bowels of his illusory kingdom to die.

That was the tragic end of the Phantom of the Opera. He had given everything and had nothing left to give. He had gone mad and lashed out at the world that shunned him. But even as he had watched his beloved Christine, her friend Meg had watched him. As much as he loved Christine, Meg loved him. Only she knew the face behind the mask, only she understood the man behind the monster. But a broken heart does not easily mend. He could not forget his Christine. Meg dared to follow him to the depths of his misery and coaxed him slowly back to his music and his life. She became the pupil, and he taught her as he had Christine until she achieved the success that his former pupil had only tasted. But Meg wanted more than his music. She wanted the man imprisoned behind the mask.

Meg had saved Erik, but she had also exposed him to the world beyond the lair. Although she loved him, he was drawn to haunt his former pupil Christine. For a time, he was content to watch her from the crypt at the cemetery when she visited her father's grave or to observe her from the wooded park on the grounds of the estate. He did not seek her love as he once had, but he did seek her compassion and friendship.

Then one day tragedy struck the Chagnys. Christine and Raoul's son drowned. Christine sank into a world of grief from which Raoul could not save her. So even though Meg loved Erik, and he found himself irresistibly drawn to her, the Phantom would not leave Christine to her grief. In one last mad effort, he took her to his underground world and forced her to face the darkness. He dragged her to the cemetery and made her choose the light. And then when Christine was finally able to accept her own grief, Erik understood that he had lost her forever. Christine loved Raoul. The Phantom set her free.

Before he could release Christine into Raoul's care, the Parisian police descended upon his lair and captured him. When the Phantom was put on trial, it was Meg who stood beside him. Sentenced to be hanged, Erik was resigned to his death. But Meg would not allow him to face it alone. In a clandestine marriage, the two were wed. Moved by Erik's suffering, grateful for what he had done for Christine, Raoul devised an escape plan for the condemned man. The hanging was rigged, and Erik's body was hurried away to an unmarked grave. From the cemetery, Raoul and Christine rescued the Phantom from his living tomb and smuggled him to the border where Erik took his final leave of Christine. His obsessions lay behind him. Ahead, in Italy, was the hope of a future with Meg.

CHAPTER 1

Flight

*Like one, that on a lonesome road
Doth walk in fear and dread,
And having once turned round walks on,
And turns no more his head;
Because he knows, a frightful fiend
Doth close behind him tread.*

The Rime of the Ancient Mariner, Samuel Taylor Coleridge

The coachman warned him that he would drive the team into the ground if he did not relent and rein them in. They had traversed many miles since passing the border from France. Erik flicked the whip above the mane of the lead horse forcing it on down the road. Sorrow and anger spurred him on and left him no choice but to careen heedlessly toward his destiny. Behind him Christine. Behind him his life in the Paris opera house, his protective labyrinth of tunnels and vaults, his papier maché world among thespians and divas and the treasure of exotic and fabulous properties with which one could construct one's own world. Behind him his stage. And the gallows.

On and on the team carried him away from all he knew, threatening to abandon him in a world far beyond his grasp, a world he wouldn't understand or be capable of controlling. With him, a woman he had taken into his heart only to displace Christine whose power over him had led to madness and death. Behind him Christine. He fled like a thief in the night, repudiated, tortured, exhibited, and publicly hanged on the gallows in Paris. Meg told him he had escaped death, but he knew better. He lay in the coffin unable to breathe, buried under a mountain of churned earth, insects tumbled through crevices in the wood and crawled across his lips. He had not escaped death. They had hanged and buried him and brought him back, back to exile him from all the fortifications and defenses he had created, from the world of the opera house cellars that had nurtured him and protected him from emptiness. Hades sitting on his throne in the underworld was no more a god than the Phantom had been in his domain, among the multiple worlds played on his stage.

What mercy is this that spits him out on a desert shore like a broken timber from a shipwreck, bereft of home, of all he possessed, of meaning itself? What shelter was there for a ghost dispossessed, whose house had burnt to the ground?

The horses found themselves winded and exhausted in a small village at the skirt of the mountains as the sun began to set. The driver morosely accepted the reins from his mad passenger and waited for him to help the lady from the carriage. He noticed that not a word or look passed between them. It all struck him as strange—the masked traveler, the impetuous flight from the border, the detached reserve between the man and his new bride. Settling the reins in their place, he dismounted to bring in the sparse luggage his passengers had before he could brush down, feed, and bed his precious team.

The inn was small, inside a room with benches set on either side of a large, rustic table. A fire blazed in the hearth, and an old woman served stew from a huge black kettle suspended over the flames. A narrow wooden staircase led steeply to the guest accommodations above. An old man, as ancient and haggard as the old woman, sat by the fire smoking a pipe. Two guests, a young woman and older man, possibly her father, sat at the table having their evening meal. Another man, the innkeeper himself, Erik supposed, had lifted the valises and begun to escort Meg up the stairs toward the room. All glanced up to welcome the newly arrived traveler, but any word of welcome lodged unspoken as they noticed the unusually tall and imposing figure of a man whose face was concealed by a mask. They watched as he bowed his head and entered the inn.

Erik froze ominously just inside the doorway.

"Our rooms are all taken," said the man with the pipe gruffly without hesitation as he continued to stare at Erik suspiciously. "Luigi, tell the young lady we were mistaken."

Flushed, Meg was at a loss as to how to react. They had inquired about the accommodations upon entering the village and were told that few guests were currently lodged at the inn. Erik reached into his pocket, drew out several coins, and threw them disdainfully at the old man's feet. Taking the stairs two at a time, he pushed past the innkeeper to the rooms above. He opened the door to each room until he found one that was unoccupied. He called to Meg who uncomfortable as she was with the situation knew better than to ignore Erik's summons. She gathered her skirts, blushed apologetically, and climbed the stairs. The flustered innkeeper glared at his old father in silence and hurried with the guests' valises. Erik waited while the innkeeper placed them on a chair near the feather bed and backed out of the room closing the door behind him. Meg avoided Erik's intense scrutiny as she settled her articles on a small table by the window. Without a word, he opened the door as if to leave.

"Where are you going?"

"You should go down and have supper. I'll take my lodging somewhere else."

"But you can't leave me alone here. You're my husband."

"They've no room here for me!"

"Then we both go!"

She walked past Erik to the open door and gently pressed it shut with her palms. He didn't resist. She recognized his anger; she could see it in his scowl. Even though the mask covered his face, she knew the contours of his flesh and knew his brows were knit and heavy above his eyes. She knew because he wouldn't look at her lest his anger spill out and slam against her like the back of his hand. How fragile his control! A battle raged inside him to pacify this darkness, to keep it from swallowing them both alive.

"You're tired." She soothed him with her voice, the voice that he had trained and honed. The voice she had used each night at the opera to call him to her. "I'll go down and bring some supper up for us. Take off your coat and sit here while I help you off with your boots." She reached out and took his hand. And though he loomed over her, his eyes fixed on her face, she led him to a chair and knelt beside him to remove his boots. Then she took his hand again to lead him to the bed, but this time he refused to rise.

"Go. Have your supper. I'm not hungry."

She wanted to argue, but it was clear that he was sullen and on edge.

Just days ago he had heard the judge pronounce his sentence. The Phantom of the Opera captured, found guilty of murder, was to hang on the gallows. If Raoul hadn't helped them stage a false hanging, Erik would be dead now. Unfortunately something had gone awry, and Erik's body had been too hastily carried off to the paupers' field and buried. Raoul and his men had managed to find his grave and had exhumed him perhaps minutes before he would have expired in earnest from suffocation. Meg couldn't begin to imagine the terrors he must have suffered knowing he was buried alive and not knowing whether Raoul would find him in time. Yet he sat in the chair pretending that he was simply tired after a long day's journey.

She wouldn't argue with him. She slipped out the door, one glance back to see him slump forward in the chair and bury his face in his open palms.

When she returned to the chamber, she found him asleep in the chair. She had supped as quickly as she dared and asked to bring a carafe of wine, some bread and cheese, to the room for her husband. For one awkward moment she feared the old man and woman would refuse him even this modest repast, but the younger man, the innkeeper, apologized for his elderly parents and prepared a tray. As an excuse, he mumbled something about banditti and waited expectantly for Meg to return the gesture with some explanation for her companion's strange attire and aggressive behavior. But even though Meg saw that this was the moment yet again to create another fictive identity for the Phantom, she was too tired and her mind too addled to think. She simply accepted the tray along with his apologies and excused herself politely.

Erik had to have been incredibly fatigued to fall asleep in the uncomfortably straight-backed chair and not to rouse when she slipped into the room. In the past, he would never have been caught off guard by any disturbance however slight it might be. She took the moment to examine his physical condition. She noted the bruising along the side of his jaw from the guards' mistreatment in the last days of the trial. More disturbing were the raw tearing and bruising where the hangman's noose had clamped down on his throat. Very gingerly she drew back the edge of his shirt and found the band of dark black and purple from the harness that had saved his life. It crossed his chest and disappeared under each of his arms. The physical trauma was visible, but one could only guess what damage the last days of his ordeal had wrought on his mind and soul. She had never seen him so deep in sleep and hoped that it was his mind's way of healing those unseen wounds.

Reluctant to leave his side, Meg drew several cushions from the bed and piled them on the floor. There she sat to watch over him, her poor lost soul. As she sat and lay her head on his knee, she took up his hand. She felt rough, abraded skin along his finger tips. She bit her lip hard to stop from making a sound as she read the signs in the torn flesh of his fingers. The tips were raw, scoured, the skin scraped off, scabs crusting over the abrasions. Desperate to escape, before mercifully passing out, he had clawed at the inside surface of the closed coffin. His beautiful hands! The lacerated finger tips would eventually heal, but she could tell from the slight swell of the knuckles and the subtle bend to the four fingers that they had not mended and never would mend completely. One by one the Parisian inspector of police had broken his fingers, a musician's fingers. The inspector had known exactly what he was doing to his prisoner. Meg frowned to think that the joints would always bring him some discomfort and the fingers would surely have lost some of their delicate flexibility. Knowing what music meant to him, she prayed he would still be able to play.

she sleeps with her head lying on my lap like a spaniel next to his master, she's as close as if I had chosen to lie with her on the feather bed, her blond hair warms my thigh, I sit at my station by the door, to keep watch, to guard, to guard from what? from those downstairs that quaked with fear when they saw my masked face and wondered what secrets I hid, from those who prefer to kill what they don't understand, I felt their anger and fear the moment I crossed the threshold, it's always been thus, and it dripped like rain through the air saturating my clothes, covering my face and blocking my airways with its pestilence, their fear and anger and loathing evoked the same emotions in me and I wanted to draw my sword and strike them all, wash away the scent-laden air with the rain of blood, but Meg brushed by my side, her perfume wafted round me, a shield, her hair glowed like a torch in the gathering gloom of my rage, and I had to hide my monster's face behind even thicker layers of masks than before to act the gentleman, to play the husband ... the innkeeper had already offered to lead the young woman to the bridal room, smiling reassuringly at Meg's soft cheeks ablaze with a modest blush as she spoke of me, her husband, of our recent wedding, of a trip through the Italian Alps to celebrate our nuptials, only when he turned to watch the husband breech the doorway, steal into the warm enclosure of his inn, a man whose face must bear some evil sign to merit a mask, did the innkeeper pause on the staircase to wonder what monster is this who had ravaged the blonde cherub, how would such an angel wed herself to such as this man whose face must not see the light of day? gone all pretense of belonging to the common race of man, I must never forget that I'm not one of them! I rape one of their women, a monster doesn't take a bride, he takes a victim ...

When she woke, she lay on the bed, the coverlet draped over her. Momentarily disoriented, she stared at the wooden beams that bisected the ceiling and wondered why she still wore her chemise. Turning she saw a distorted image of a man's face next to her on the pillow. She quickly looked away, her heart beating like a startled dove from the unexpected sight. Next to her lay Erik. He must have carried her to the bed in the middle of the night and lain down beside her. He rested next to her, unmasked, a strange composite of beauty and horror. His presence had taken her by surprise. How could she react that way to his face? She had seen him without the mask, but she had forgotten how devastating that face could be! She couldn't control her initial reaction, but she must, she told herself. She turned again toward her sleeping husband and was startled to see his eyes open and fixed on her. He immediately turned his face away, sat up on the edge of the bed, and reached for the mask. Without a word, he put it on. Meg had no time to think of a way to smooth over the moment, her apparent rejection.

"Erik, I ..."

"We should prepare to leave," he hurried to interrupt her before she could make it worse. What could she say? As if he were weighing each word, he reluctantly started to explain, "The mask ... last night ... it was ... uncomfortable." He had forgotten, he was amazed to realize. In the prison they had taken his mask away. Without thinking about it, still overwhelmed by fatigue, he had brought Meg to the bed, taken off the mask, and collapsed in the bed next to her. Was it too much to expect—after all her protestations of love and reassurances that she saw beyond his ugliness to his soul—that Meg would wake and smile to find his naked face next to hers on the pillow?

Meg, ashamed and incapable of speaking baldly of what had transpired, rose and began to dress. She feared any excuse on her part would sound hollow and only serve to make him even more uncomfortable.

He thought he might say something to her to dispel the scent of betrayal that hung in the air between them, but he couldn't think of what that would be. So he merely let the words fade away ...

Shortly after they had dressed, there came a rude and loud knocking on the door. Erik pushed Meg aside into the corner of the room, as if to protect her, and called out to the intruder.

"What the blazes do you want?"

"Open up! We want to know what's happened to that little lady! We want to make sure she's all right!" came more than one man's voice on the other side of the heavy oak door.

Of course, they imagined he had torn her to pieces with his bare teeth in the middle of the night, Erik supposed. It was the same everywhere and would always be the same. He checked to see that his mask was firmly in place and slowly opened the door. Two men tried to push their way past him into the room, but they had no idea how strong Erik was. He blocked their way belligerently forcing them to look beyond him and around his shoulders to Meg in the opposite corner of the room.

"My wife is quite well as you can clearly see. May I ask the meaning of this?"

Meg rushed forward to assure the men that she was fine, and only then did they stand down, relax their aggressive positions, and edge slightly away from the doorway. The bigger of the two seemed to consider taking Erik on in spite of Meg's reassurance. When Meg spoke up, Erik gave her a look she didn't understand. He seemed upset with her as much as with the intruders.

"You see we were quite done in from the trip. We appreciate your concern."

She actually smiled at them, thought Erik. She deliberately misinterpreted their hysteria and turned it into concern for the both of them. Without another glance at the men standing in the passageway, Erik slammed the oak door closed. It narrowly missed crashing into the bigger man's face.

Meg jumped from the crack of wood against the doorframe.

"They thought I had done something to hurt you! And you make small talk as if ... as if they were concerned we were indisposed! How can I live like this, Meg? How am I going to live with their suspicions and their hate and their fear of me? How can I live this way when even you ..." His voice caught in his throat. His eyes darted away from her to rest on the rumpled bedding.

"I'm sorry, Erik. I ..."

"No, Meg. You've done nothing wrong. I'm the one who's sorry. I'm sorry that I've dragged you into this with me. It's not your destiny." He took the valise that Raoul had prepared for him. It included several changes of clothes, personal articles he would need, even several monetary securities that could be used in case of an emergency. He fastened it and opened the door. There still in the corridor waited the two men. They had been joined by two others on the stairs. One of these new men held an axe menacingly in his hand. They surely had heard the conversation that had just taken place between him and Meg. Erik pushed his way through the human barricade sending the first pair tumbling toward the walls of the corridor. As he descended the stairs the two who had stationed themselves along the narrow staircase tripped and fell backwards to land flustered at the bottom.

"Send for the driver and instruct him to take my wife back home to Paris." He threw several gold coins on the counter and went out into the street.

Dumbfounded, Meg watched as Erik descended the stairs, and when she heard the instructions he gave the innkeeper she called out to him to wait.

She would not go back. Not without him. He couldn't leave her!

She quickly gathered her bag throwing loose articles into it and slamming the clasp shut. She half dragged and half carried it through the hallway past the men, who were just then picking themselves up off the floor, and flew down the stairs and out the door after Erik.

He was already far ahead taking giant strides toward the livery stable. She cried out to him to stop, the panic obvious in her tone. The commotion was bringing the residents out to the street to watch. She paid them no attention. She recognized Erik's resolve in his stiff carriage and determined gait. He meant to leave her. Her coat was loosely pulled around her, and she was so bent at the hip from the weight of carrying the valise that her hem dragged along in the road. As she tried to pick up the pace, she caught her foot in the garment's hem. Although she struggled to regain her footing, she was off balance and careened face first onto the dusty road.

Her scream stopped Erik cold. He turned only in time to see Meg fall hard to the ground. Her valise flew open, and several articles of clothing as well as some of her toiletries rolled out onto the street. He paused a moment to see if she might get up by herself. But when he saw that she remained stretched out on the dusty pavement, he feared she might have seriously injured herself. Those near her stopped in their tracks as Erik rushed to her side.

He pulled her into his arms. There was a small gash on her forehead, and smudges of dirt on her cheek and nose, but her tears were fast washing these clean. She clung to him even as she berated him for being cruel and selfish. *How could he consider abandoning her in a foreign town or sending her packing as if she meant nothing to him?* Her words were in sharp contrast to the tight hold she had managed to gain on his neck. His hurt pride was mollified by her own humiliation and the vehemence of her desperation. He held her while she swore at him even through her tears.

She didn't understand. He was trying to leave her in order to protect her from a life of constant suffering, constant hiding, constant struggles to be left in peace if not accepted. For her world was never going to accept him. He belonged to another world, a world in the shadows, not this one.

"Please, Meg, calm down. Please, don't cry. It breaks my heart when you cry."

She lifted her face to look up at him, and he wiped her eyes, her cheeks, and her nose trying to find some way to make her stop crying. "Shhhhh. Don't.

Don't." His voice brushed over her face drying the tears. He flicked wild strands of blond hair away from her large, brown eyes. He could see her anger melt away leaving behind only the hurt.

"You won't leave me, will you?" Her voice was small and childlike, tears barely held in check. She waited for him to answer. When he didn't, she became frantic again. "Please, Erik. Please, take me with you! Whatever I did, I didn't mean to displease you. I promise I'll …"

He stopped her promise with a kiss. He didn't trust his voice.

Such childish bargains that one makes to keep disaster at bay! He had made many an oath himself in vain. But he couldn't say no to her. She seemed so small and fragile. He feared she might break in his arms.

No one approached the two lovers. It was clear to the onlookers that the beautiful young woman had chosen to be with this strange man. So no one thought to stop Erik when he easily lifted Meg into his arms, along with the contents of her valise, and marched down the street to the stable to hire the carriage that would complete their journey.

The next three nights were no easier than the first. So we came after dark. The driver was used to us and well paid, and he seemed relieved as well not to arrive in daylight where we attracted a good deal of attention. Coming upon the next village, we lingered a few miles away until just after the last rays of the sun flared and sank beyond the horizon. We didn't speak; I was too morose. Meg respected my black moods and let me be, but she watched me like I was some bizarre species of insect she was to study, describe, and classify. Her constant attentiveness annoyed me, but it proved useful. She was learning my ways. It was because she watched me so carefully that she knew not to speak to me in those last moments before darkness came to shelter us and as we stole into the village square in search of lodging. We waited while the driver made the arrangements, paid the innkeeper, took in the valises, and when all was ready escorted us to our rooms.

Each night I was locked away in our room—it was as if I had never escaped from prison! Each morning I was transferred from my comfortable cell in the inn to the box of the carriage. I thought I might go mad!

Like the canary that I sometimes thought her, Meg would chirp her happy plans for the country villa that awaited us in the sleepy, sunny village of Pianosa near the beautiful Lago di Bracciano. If we continued south from there, we wouldn't be too far from Rome. And directly west in a matter of several hours, we could bathe in the Tyrrhenian Sea. She had all the necessary papers and deeds to the villa and surrounding lands from Raoul's solicitor. There were also funds deposited in Civitavecchia, a nearby city on the coast. Our villa was nestled in a low rolling valley of vineyards; an olive grove flanked the western slopes of the hills. A handful of locals had been taking care of the villa for the past several years after the last member of the family, an elderly bachelor, had died with no one to inherit. These servants were under retainer and agreed to continue on with us. I could only hope that someone had the foresight to explain the eccentricities of their new employers!

Although Meg had not yet seen the villa Raoul's solicitor had secured for us, she had poured over the documents in which the grounds and structures were described. The manor itself boasted a grand hallway, a modest ballroom, two large parlors, a generous kitchen and servants' quarters on the first floor. On the second were ten lovely bedrooms, a library, a small parlor. But the feature that most enthralled Meg was a private, interior garden surrounded by stone walls and accessible from the smaller of two parlors.

As she described again and again the beauty of the villa I found it harder and harder to calm the rising panic I felt. I didn't dare ask her the one thing that I wanted to know, for even I understood the absurdity of my question. The only concern I had about the architectural wonders of the villa was did it have underground cellars and how deep did they go? Her descriptions of the rooms blinded me with light. The large windows and portals that let in the fresh breezes from the vineyards made me feel giddy and dizzy as if I were to be suspended in mid air! Finally she let slip a detail that I clutched at in desperation: There was a vast wine cellar under the villa. Even though I realized how simple and shallow this cellar must be, barely one floor underground, at least there was somewhere that I might hide away from the glare of daylight, some deep, dark, damp womb into which I could crawl when all my resources were drained. More and more I felt the need to find somewhere to hide for the sake of my fragile sanity.

Each night we spent at an inn I recalled that first night with the hostile residents just beneath us and the next morning the men who banged on our door demanding to see Meg, to check on her safety. There was merely the width of a good heavy door between them and us. I knew that these men presented little threat to me. I'm far too strong for them to do me any serious injury. But what if there had been ten? What if the entire town had stormed the inn with pitchforks and torches to save Meg from the monster? What if I had been forced to kill one of them?

I tire of death!

I've slept and eaten little these past few nights. Nor have I responded to Meg's modest efforts to entice me to her side of the bed. Each night I fall into bed and pretend to sleep before Meg pulls down the covers on her side. I'm too aware of the presence just on the other side of the doorway of strangers who would be frightened by my face, yet unsettled by my mask, and angry that I even existed. How easy it is to upset them! All you have to do is not be like them, and their every instinct is to eradicate you, to wipe you off the face of the planet, in their crusade to ensure their continued dominion over all.

As we go farther and farther into the countryside, the more I feel my heart break into smaller and smaller pieces. All the colors outside the carriage window dissolve into shades of gray. All tastes are bitter. The music is silent. The only sound that greets my ears are the thudding of horses' hooves, the mumble of strangers whispering behind our backs. All desire has melted away, and if I were alone I would weep until there were no more tears in the whole world!

Meg slept exhausted from the day's journey. After a few hours, Erik woke and found it impossible to go back to sleep. He felt trapped and breathless as if the air had been sucked out of the room. The walls tipped in toward the bed ready to crush him with their weight. He stood at the window for some time and was overwhelmed by the desire to be outside in the cool night air. Hastily he dressed and slipped out careful not to wake Meg and made his way across the road to the stables.

Not a horse among them, not even the pretty little chestnut mare, to compare to Caesar's august stature and equestrian grace. Full eighteen hands at the shoulder, a glorious white stallion, Caesar could out-prance, outpace, outshow any of these sad courier and carriage horses. After all, Caesar had starred at the opera in practically every production the Opera Populaire had staged. How Erik missed that horse! To many at the opera house, he had been just a horse, another stage prop, but Erik had spent most of his life in Caesar's company. When the singers and their entourage, the stagehands, and various managers, were gone or the chorus girls and dancers in their dormitories, Erik came quietly and stealthily up from the cellars and visited Caesar and the other company horses. The memory of those experiences drew him from the inn in the middle of the night to the stable.

It was comforting to share the warmth of these animals. The smells of hay, horse, sweat, and leather were familiar and calming to Erik; he welcomed them after having been closeted in tight quarters with the body odors of strangers, the reek of onions and cabbage, the competing fragrances of colognes and perfumes and powders, the smell of hickory smoke and damp cloth. Meg didn't seem to notice or to mind the assault on the senses that each sojourn at one of these country inns imposed!

He brushed the chestnut's tawny coat and leaned against its barrel chest to feel the fluttering vibrations of the animal's heartbeat against his own.

"You'll spoil that animal for work if you continue to brush her like that. She's practically in a trance from the pleasure."

Why hadn't he heard her slip up on him? He was unaccustomed to being startled, especially in the middle of the night, and much less by a woman! The horse had given him absolutely no warning, which was also puzzling. Chagrined by the failure of his usually acute instincts, he pretended that he had known she was there all the time.

"I wonder why a signorina would be out and about at this hour of the night in spite of the dangers." He continued to stroke the horse, thinking that the mask he wore might unsettle even this woman, as self-assured as her voice suggested she was, if he were to turn and face her now.

"Dangers? Should I be frightened? Are you perhaps one of the dangers to which you refer?"

She was playing with him! Her tone lay somewhere between teasing and flirting. Bewildered and at a complete loss as to how to respond to this stranger, Erik decided that she must surely be one of those gentlewomen who had never been disappointed and for whom the whole world bowed down in eager compliance. Spoiled and unaware of her own vulnerability, ignorant of what he could do to her, she felt safe to toy with him.

For one moment, a horrid thought crossed his mind. There was no one to save her, no one to witness. He might strangle her with his bare hands, and no one would know. What if he dragged her out into the nearby forest? The lust to control another human being, to have her at his mercy, sprang from some deep buried corner of his soul. Disturbed, he pushed it into the darkness. Even so the power of its desire lingered. Slowly he turned his head just enough to catch a glimpse at the woman who had unwisely stumbled across the Phantom's path.

She was dressed like a youth, but her long wavy auburn hair gave her sex away. The disguise apparently was not so much a disguise as a convenient outfit that suited her purposes whatever these may be. Her skin was olive colored, not the light freckled skin that usually accompanied women with her color hair. The dark eyebrows framed two almond shaped eyes of dark azure-green which seemed to burn with a light of their own in the dimly lit stables.

Erik couldn't take his eyes off her. Forgetting the chestnut, he stepped away from the horse and allowed himself to examine her with mounting pleasure, a mixture of excitement, curiosity, and arousal. She was tall for a woman, strong, and the young boy's attire couldn't hide the voluptuous nature of her body. Only the lower buttons of the vest were fastened, and even at the apex the material strained against her bosom. Her hips were rounded and generous while her waist was so small that he was sure he could encompass it with his two hands. Her fingers were long and tapered, the nails immaculately manicured. The oval lines of her face drew his gaze to her prominent cheek bones and subsequently down to her lips, full and shapely. But it was her eyes that intrigued him. Like jewels they shone. And they looked back at him with none of the reserve or fear that he was used to seeing in others'.

A curious expression brought her eyebrows together and her dark red lips into a pout as her eyes fell upon his masked face. "Why …?" she started to ask, but stopped. Perhaps she noticed how he stiffened slightly in anticipation of the question about the mask. Perhaps she preferred to discover answers more gradually and on her own. The previous expression gave way to a playful grin as she explained that she, too, had trouble sleeping in strange beds. She was on her way to the Adriatic coast. A shadow momentarily fell across her face, and she paused before continuing.

"I was sitting by the window when I saw you sneak out of the inn. When you headed toward the stables, I was curious and wondered if you were a horse thief. My Margarita is worth a good deal to me; I've had her since we were both foals, you see."

That was why the chestnut hadn't stirred when her mistress came into the stables. Now Erik understood how he could have been lulled into such an unguarded state that even he hadn't sensed her intrusion.

"I'm teasing you, Monsieur. You're from Paris, aren't you? Everyone was talking about you last night after you and your friend arrived."

"My wife," Erik corrected her. Meg lay asleep, her blond hair splayed across the pillow like golden threads. Erik refused to examine the confusing emotions that accompanied such an image.

"Your wife. Yes." And then she smirked.

Erik was astounded by the unexpected gesture and wondered what it could mean. Didn't she believe him?

"What would you say to a night ride?" Without waiting for a response, she began to saddle her chestnut. "I'm sure you could use that gray in the next stall." She ran her eyes up and down Erik's body as if gauging his height and weight. "He's a big, strong animal." Again Erik felt unsettled by her directness. It was as if she had touched him.

Cautiously curious, Erik chose not to speak. Instead, he dragged a saddle from the post and placed it on the gray's back in answer to the auburn beauty's suggestion.

"My name is Lucianna."

"Erik."

"Can you ride?"

Erik scowled.

"I'll take that as a yes." She laughed at him and led her mount through the stable doors out into the night.

They rode at a brisk canter down the path until well away from the village. The moon was high in the night sky and bright enough that the riders were easily able to make out the silhouette of each tree along the road. Suddenly Lucianna turned the chestnut sharply to the left and broke into the forest. Erik reined the gray in and hesitated only momentarily before he spurred his mount after hers.

Given the unknown terrain and the darkness, the speed with which she rode the mare was reckless. The moonbeams shone intermittently through the tree branches and illuminated only swatches of the forest bed. The trees were not densely packed, and Erik had the advantage of following the path blazed by the chestnut. Even so he was acutely aware that the woman was rash and foolhardy to careen through the woods in this fashion.

Suddenly, in a clearing just ahead, he saw her rein in the mare and dismount. Erik edged the gray to a nearby stand of trees and left him to inspect the chestnut. Lucianna stared up at the moon, her back to him. As if cold, she wrapped her arms around her body and hugged herself.

"Light can be so cold!" She seemed to be speaking to the moon.

He came up behind her and stopped. He was close enough to feel the loose strands of her hair flutter out and catch against his chin. She smelled of soap and lilacs.

"I know you're there. I feel you breathing," she whispered softly in anticipation as she imagined his arms wrapping around her, his warmth dispelling the coolness of the night. He was tall and dark, and his eyes had shone dark green with bottomless depths.

She waited. There was only silence. She heard the horse trod softly off into the distance. When she turned, she and the chestnut were alone.

CHAPTER 2

Pianosa

Thy lips are warm.
Romeo and Juliet, William Shakespeare

He had been so passionate. It was the last night of their journey. Until that night she had feared that he despised her and regretted they had ever fled Paris together. Perhaps it would have been best if he had escaped alone. He didn't love her, and she couldn't fault him for not having warned her several times. So she found herself lying next to a husband who couldn't bring himself to touch her. This was the life she had made for herself, but it wasn't what she had desired. She had wanted his passion! She was so sure that her desire and love for him would bring him to her. If she were patient, he would come to love her. Each night, after the long day's journey, she tried to show him her love in countless subtle ways. She didn't speak to him when she saw he was fraught with confusion and anger. She reached out and touched him at every opportunity, just so he would know that she desired his touch. She spoke of their future together hoping to inspire some enthusiasm and anticipation in him, but whenever she spoke of Pianosa and the beautiful villa that would be their home, he withered and shrank from her. So she stopped talking altogether. And even this did not please him!

That last night, she felt him slip from the covers, dress, and leave the room. She waited and when he didn't return she sat by the window and watched for him. That's when she saw someone mounted on horseback riding out of the stable, and close behind another rider. The first she couldn't recognize, but the second was unmistakably Erik. He had left her! What she most feared had finally happened. He had abandoned her to return perhaps to Paris, pulled like the opposite charge to a magnet back to Christine and the opera house. She knew it was too late to run after him. He had left the village at a canter and would be far away by the time she could hire someone to drive her or ready a mount and ride after him herself.

And to what purpose would she follow? If he didn't want to stay with her, nothing she could do would convince him! She would not beg him. She had her pride. Perhaps that was all she had. She collapsed in the chair near the window and sobbed hopelessly.

She must have cried herself to sleep, but something woke her. She opened her eyes just in time to see him cross the road on foot from the direction of the stable and slip inside the inn. She couldn't let him see that she had been spying on him and especially that she had been crying. Quickly just seconds before he slipped into the room she got into bed and turned away from the door to feign sleep. He delayed only the time it took to remove his boots and clothes; then he lifted the covers and slid into the bed beside her. She felt the bedding shift with his weight. Instead of staying on his side as he usually did, he nestled against Meg's back and pressed her against his naked body. His body was cold to the touch yet with the promise of heat. He was breathing heavily and whispered into her ear quite softly. The sound of his voice alone made her body perceptibly shudder. "Are you asleep, Meg?" was all he asked. Without answering, she rolled over in his embrace and kissed him passionately on the mouth, lips parted.

He was relentless, inexhaustible that night. They lay spent in each other's arms as the first rays of daylight filtered through the window. The birds began to chirp as they sighed and fell into a deep, satisfied slumber.

Today they would be home.

Dear Signorina,

You must forgive my impertinence since we are strangers, but last night you acted very unwisely. Your guardian would be distressed to know that you spent time in my company without any guarantees as to your honor or safety.

I apologize for leaving you in the woods. I left you at that moment because I wanted to avoid what was about to happen if I had stayed. You are playing a dangerous game, and I myself refuse to be a part of it. I sincerely hope that you'll desist from such wild behavior in the future. I have only your safety and honor in mind when I beg you to be careful.

Your humble servant,
The man in the stable

The sun was already high over the horizon when he gently but firmly woke me. I so wanted to linger in that sleep. He urged me to go down to arrange for some food to be packed for the journey. A boy would be sent ahead to make sure that the carriage was ready and to inform the driver that we were to leave within the hour.

When I returned to the room, he was sealing a note he had apparently been writing in an envelope. It may have been my imagination, but he seemed uncomfortable that I had found him doing so and the envelope disappeared inside his vest pocket as if he didn't want me to notice it. To whom would he be writing except Christine? I bit my lip in anger and pretended not to have noticed the envelope or his guilty air.

The driver soon arrived and hauled our valises down to the waiting carriage. Erik stood just inside our room holding the door open impatiently waiting for me to gather my purse and leave. I was thanking the innkeeper for his hospitality when Erik took me by the arm in mid-sentence and dragged me out to the carriage. I was of course surprised and not a little annoyed with his haste, and for the life of me I couldn't explain it.

For the first hour of the trip not one word passed between us. I was becoming more and more annoyed, and it was increasingly difficult for me to restrain my tongue. After the night we had spent together, I was completely confused. On the one hand I feared he wanted to be rid of me; on the other he had been incredibly passionate when he returned to the bedroom after his ride. How could he be so distant the very next morning? Unable to stand it any longer, I demanded that he tell me where he went last night. The moment I said the words, I desperately regretted them. I wanted to pull them back unspoken, but it was too late. The look he gave me left me without breath.

"You're not my jailer!"

No other explanation, but the coldness of his eyes froze me to the spot.

He must have regretted his sharpness, for eventually he reached across the way and gently took my hand. Why does it have to be so difficult? I was still angry, hurt, confused. I shouldn't have, but I took my hand away and refused to look at him.

In response to my refusal to be placated, he knocked roughly on the roof of the carriage for the driver to halt. Before I could think what to say or do, Erik left me alone and went to sit above with the driver for the rest of the journey.

Damn him! I wanted to be angry, not sad, not desperate. I was determined to stay angry; I would let this emotion build, and I would feed it until I didn't feel the pain anymore. Let him go! Why had I tied my destiny to this ugly, violent, emotionally crippled man?

The moment I put my feelings into words, when my anger took the particular form that it did, I was appalled at myself. How could I speak of Erik in that way? Was it so easy to kill love? But he was so cruel to me, so ungrateful. I had left everything to go with him. I was willing to build a new life, a home with him, in spite of his crimes, in spite of his not loving me the way I so needed him to love me. Yet he withheld that dear sweet part of himself, the deepest heart of hearts that I had glimpsed before and that I knew was there and wanted to be set free! What was I to do to make him love me?

The day passed miserably. I was hungry, yet the coach didn't stop. Erik could go without eating for days and not feel it. He had learned to ignore his bodily needs. He was indifferent to food! I wasn't! I hadn't had breakfast, and now I sat bored and anxious hoping the carriage would stop at least to give the horses a rest.

The sun had dipped well past its highest point in the sky when at last the carriage slowed to a stop on the roadway. I peeked out to find the driver coming to help me down. There was no sign of my husband.

As I stepped down from the carriage, I took the basket the driver had lowered from the bundles and thanked him politely. He was nervous and ill at ease, but he seemed to make a special effort to be kind to me. Of course he had spent the entire day so far sitting beside Erik, poor man. Then I caught sight of Erik. He was soothing the horses, speaking to them intimately as if he were one of them, not part of the human race at all. My anger stirred again, and I picked up my skirts and walked determinedly to an area off the road under a huge elm tree and spread my riding cloak upon the ground. Ignoring my husband, I called to the driver to share some bread and dried meat with me. I pretended to be enjoying the setting and chatted insanely to the driver who was even more uncomfortable given my preposterous behavior. But even though I could see myself and knew I was acting quite bizarrely, I couldn't stop.

After hastily eating the repast I offered him, the driver excused himself to find a place to rest well away from his strange passengers. I prayed that Erik would approach. I intended to remain aloof until he apologized properly. I waited and forced myself not to look in the direction of the horses. I glimpsed out of the corner of my eye that he was actually tending to them. Only after he had given water to all four of the animals did he casually saunter over to my "tea party."

His eyes were on me, and my cheeks flushed hot with blood! How accomplished an actress I was after all, for I didn't look up, not for the longest time.

It would have been better if he hadn't spoken at all. Quietly he said my name, and reluctantly I looked up at him. In spite of all my resolve, I know my eyes were damp. He paused as if judging whether or not to embark on the next step or to leave things as they were between us.

"Forgive me, Meg. Once you're settled in the villa, I plan to disappear."

"You mean you're going to abandon me here on foreign soil and go back to Paris?" I was dumbfounded that he would treat me this way. After all he had promised.

"No. You didn't hear me correctly. I plan to disappear. I can't go back to Paris. Although the idea appeals to me in a macabre way. I would indeed be a ghost, wouldn't I, if I returned to Paris. They pronounced me dead at my execution, didn't they?" His laugh didn't warm me. On the contrary, it frightened me. There was something final about his tone. "I won't be far. I'll find somewhere to live in the area, perhaps in Rome. You'll continue to be my widow and have full access to my accounts. The villa is already in your name, I imagine."

He could see that I was about to cry as I had so many times before when he hurt me, and he waited for me to compose myself before going on. "There's nothing more to be said, Meg."

"And this morning? When you returned from your ride? How could you …?"

If he hadn't had the mask over his features, I'm sure I would have seen signs of shame. He bowed his head and looked away in the distance before he answered. "I can offer no excuse. You should be angry with me. I'm selfish and cruel. Christine understood that and was wise not to love me. But you foolishly insist. I don't want the life you've imagined for us. It's not in my nature."

"It's not fair," I protested like a naughty child whose parents have punished her.

"You want me, but you shouldn't. You desire me because I'm dangerous. You think you can tame me. But I will not be tamed, not by you, not by anyone!" His tone had changed to one of anger and defiance. I felt him loom over me like a storm cloud, and knew that it would be dangerous to contradict him.

Suddenly I didn't care! I didn't care if he tore me to pieces or broke me in two. I was angrier than I had ever been in my life, and desperate at the same time. I got to my feet and slapped him hard with the palm of my hand. I raised the butter knife I had in the other to stab at him blindly. He grabbed my fist and squeezed hard until I dropped the silly knife. It most likely would have bruised him and little more. Then he let go my hand, and I resumed beating at his chest and face, whatever I could reach, with both fists clenched. I was yelling something, but I don't remember what it was. I expected any moment that he would strike me or shake me or strangle me. He simply took the blows as if they were nothing.

Then I ran. I ran away from the road into the forest. The branches of the trees caught in my hair and struck me across the arms and face as I raced heedlessly into the thicket. He was behind me and gaining fast when my foot caught on something, and I fell face forward and rolled down the side of the hill striking my head against the edge of a sharp rock jutting out of the ground. I felt dizzy and, before I slipped into darkness, heard his muffled voice call my name.

The blow was hard, and she lost consciousness almost immediately. Her whole body was bruised from the tumble down the steep slope. How reckless she had been to run wild through the forest. In his initial examination of her body, he was relieved to find no broken bones. Perhaps the knee was sprained on her left leg; there was a hideously vivid bruise forming around the knee cap. He carefully straightened her limbs and picked her up from the leaves and twigs and carried her to the carriage. The driver, pale and frightened, eyed him suspiciously. Erik imagined the man thought him to blame for Meg's accident. He hadn't followed them, and he may have even believed Erik had struck Meg. However, surely he knew better when he saw how anxious Erik was to get Meg to someone who could treat her wounds.

This time Meg didn't ride alone; her husband sat beside her cradling her so as to minimize the jarring of her body in the coach as the driver sped the horses on at full gallop. They weren't far from the villa itself. Once there Erik could send one of the servants for a doctor to attend Meg.

Having spied the advance of the carriage, the servants had assembled in front of the villa to greet the new owners. Without a word of greeting or explanation, Erik pushed past them and carried Meg into the central hallway.

"Where's the master bedroom? Quick, woman!"

"Follow me, Signore." The heavyset woman curtsied and led the way up the staircase to the second story.

Erik gently placed Meg on the bedcovers and ordered the woman to send someone immediately for a doctor.

When the woman made no sign to go, Erik turned toward her and saw that she was staring at him. The mask, of course! The driver had gotten used to him over the course of the journey, but all these servants were aghast at the strange appearance of the new master of the villa. If Meg hadn't injured herself, she would have reassured the servants with her smile and logical explanations. *Her husband had met with a serious accident and preferred to wear a mask to cover the scars.* Unfortunately, Meg lay injured on the bed, and it fell to Erik to explain and win over the good will of these superstitious and fearful peasants.

Summoning all his resolve and patience, Erik addressed the woman with a soft and kind voice. His voice often had a hypnotic effect on people, but not on everyone. If the person were very, very frightened or nervous, or if the person were adamantly ill disposed toward him, no amount of soothing tone could reverse those strong emotions. However, he found that those who were ambivalent or easily influenced often responded very well to a few melodic suggestions. Now he addressed this woman, who he imagined was the head servant, and willed her to calm down and listen to him carefully. "I'm very glad to have arrived at last at our new home. My wife has had an accident, and I need you to send for someone as quickly as possible to come attend to her wounds."

"Yes, Signore."

The doctor—a tall, gaunt, white-haired man—arrived within the hour from Pianosa carrying with him a black surgical bag. The heavy-set woman, Donna Annetta, ushered him quickly to the room where Erik sat holding Meg's hand, staring intently into her face as if willing her to wake. The doctor must have been prepared by the servants to find the husband hiding behind a mask for he made no indication that he noticed anything out of the ordinary when he greeted Erik. Asking the husband to step aside from the bed, the doctor examined Meg intently. After a few minutes, he sighed and turned to the strange new resident of the villa.

"I'm afraid that she might have sustained a severe concussion. Her pulse is weak."

Erik waited for the doctor to continue.

"She may not wake again, Signore. I'm sorry." Without waiting for a response, the doctor was replacing the instruments he had taken from the bag when Erik grabbed him by the collar and dragged him from the bed to a far corner of the room.

"No! No, no, no, no! You will save her!" The doctor's usual calm composure gave way to alarm as Erik shook him.

"Signore, there's nothing I can do for a brain injury. I can bind her knee, which is sprained. You have already cleaned the superficial wounds, but no one can do anything for her concussion."

Erik pushed the doctor out of his way and fell beside the bed on his knees. "No, no, no, no, no …" was all he could say as he buried his face in the covers by her side.

The doctor bandaged her knee, then slipped silently out of the room.

she's so small, so fragile, so weak, her pulse is irregular and fleeting, she's pale, there's no color in her lips, her eyes are strange when I lift the lids to see them, she's breathing but very shallowly, she might die, she might die, she might never wake up, like my sleeping beauty, I remember the story, like sleeping beauty waiting for her prince to come and kiss her, I would kiss her, but I'm not a prince, I'm the monster who put her under his spell, I'm the reason she lies here growing paler and colder each hour that passes, I wrap her in warm blankets and I sit beside her and I can't close my eyes because I might miss her if she wakes and I can't let her see me with my eyes closed, I must be there for her when she wakes, if I kiss her, I do kiss her, I kiss her eyes, I kiss her cheeks, I kiss her pale, pale lips and I know I'm crying because her face is wet and salty and these are my tears, my kiss won't wake her because I'm the monster and her prince is dead, her prince is somewhere else trapped in an enchantment of his own that nothing can break and I kiss her in vain and watch her fade before me like a plucked flower, each golden petal browns and falls to the pillow, and I would do anything to wake her

The new master didn't come out of that room for several days. We could hear him sing at night, a plaintive sound, beautiful and unlike anything we had ever heard before. Everything stilled when he sang: the crickets stopped their chittering, the night owl gave no sign of his vigilance. Giuseppe finally convinced me on the third day to go knock on the door. The only thing he had had was water, and I wasn't sure what was going on with the pale, blond wife he had carried up to their room. The doctor had told us that he feared the man had gone mad with grief and to watch him! The poor dear lady was on death's door, and there wasn't anything that could be done. If she came out of this, it would be because it was God's will and no one else's. So Giuseppe said to me that night that it was the Christian thing to do, to go to the room and ask the man to come have supper and offer myself to sit with his lady.

I wasn't too keen on facing him after what the doctor had said, and to be truthful his aspect made me nervous. What does he have hiding under that mask? I know the solicitor said something about an eccentric musician and his wife and that they would require respectful, discreet servants. But I don't remember him telling us the man wore disguises. He's a big man, too, a head taller than all the men I know and strong as an ox to have carried that child up the stairs that way, no matter how slight she was. So I came to the door—Giuseppe came with me—and I knocked most lightly and waited respectfully for him to answer. Nothing! Well, we waited and thought and spoke about what we should do. Giuseppe said I should open the door and go on in to see if they were both dead. I told him he was a fool! We knew the signore was alive; he had been singing to her. But Giuseppe reminded me that we didn't know if the lady was still breathing or if the man had gone completely mad and was singing lullabies to his dead wife! Now that sent chills down my back.

I knocked again, and when I got no answer, I raised my voice and told him I was coming in to check on him and the lady. I cracked open the door just a wee bit and in the dim candle light I saw that he was lying in bed next to her, his arms wrapped round her, her back against his chest. He was lying there facing the balcony, so I couldn't tell if he was asleep, awake, or dead. He must have heard the door open because he spoke up then and told me, nicely, that we could retire for the evening. He said his wife was still sleeping and that he needed to stay with her to be sure she slept peacefully. It almost made me cry right then and there. It sounded as if he meant to lie there beside her until they both passed on to the other side. I don't know where I got the nerve, but I told him he hadn't eaten in several days and that he wouldn't do her much good if he died of starvation. I told him my husband, Giuseppe, would show him the way down to the dining room to have just a bite and that I would stay with my lady and freshen her up with a warm bath and clean clothes. I think it was this that convinced him to agree. I think he thought she would rest better and that another woman's attentions might do her no small good.

He told me to go and that he'd come and join us after he dressed. I backed out of the room and in a few minutes I heard movement in the bedchamber, and then shortly after that he opened the door, and there he stood. Oh my, what a man! Tall and strong, but you could tell that he had already wasted. He had on the mask he was wearing when they arrived, and yet I could see so much in his eyes: weariness, sadness, a deep, deep sadness that made me want to comfort him. He made me promise that I would come for him immediately if she were to stir at all. He had to be there if she woke up. I told him I would straightaway and not to worry, that everything would be fine.

Meg was so cold, so I undressed and crawled under the covers and drew her close to me hoping my body would warm hers. She seemed to breathe better.

Every so often, she moves. Her hand turns or her shoulder rotates slightly. I lie with her cradled in my arms, and once I felt her nuzzle her head under my chin and her cheek graze against my neck. All these I take as signs that she'll eventually come back to me. I sing to her softly, and from time to time I doze off beside her giving no thought to the light or darkness outside our balcony window.

The old woman has come and told me to go down to eat. Why should I listen to her? Something about her makes me feel secure. She's right; I need to eat. I can't remember the last meal that I had. Thankfully Meg ate the day of the accident, but without water she'll surely die. I've given her the tiniest sip of water every few minutes, hoping that it might stave off thirst and death. If she dies …

The old woman's husband, Giuseppe, attends to me. I catch his expression reflected in a basin of water that he brings me to wash up. He stands behind me ignorant that I can see his entire face in the stillness of the unbroken surface of the water. He's waiting for me to remove the mask. There's curiosity and apprehension in his rapt attention. Perhaps there's also concern or even compassion. When I turn to look at him, he acts as if he has been folding my travel clothes. I ask him to leave me alone in the small room so that I can wash.

The water on my face is refreshing. The mask continues to cause soreness where the rough material rubs against my skin. It's served its purpose, but it's not nearly as fine a mask as those that I've collected over the years. The usual futile wish comes to the edge of my consciousness, the wish that I would never have to don a mask again!

Giuseppe waits on me at the mahogany table. He brings me wine, hard crusted bread, and fruit. He offers meat, but I wave it away. I nibble at the food without tasting it; all I can think of is returning to the room. I listen as if I might hear Meg breathe even from this distance. The room is warm and cozy, the curtains drawn, darkness outside. A deep wooziness descends upon me, and I relax against the soft cushion of the chair …

After a while, I came to check on the new master and found that he'd fallen asleep at the table. I had Manolo and Paolo carry him up the stairs. Strong ragazzos, the boys nevertheless strained to carry the gentleman to his room. They put him on the bed next to his wife, and Annetta and I sent them away. My wife and I looked at each other, puzzling over the same thing. How could he sleep so soundly, and how could he sleep with that mask on his face? Surely he would have removed it himself if he could have, said my Annetta. I argued that he kept it on whenever I was around and that he must have strong wishes concerning it, but she'd none of it. She insisted that it wasn't proper. We might leave him dressed, but we wouldn't leave his boots on or a hat on if he had one on, and we certainly shouldn't leave the mask on him. I sighed and gave up. She'll have her way, she will, I knew. Then she looked to me as if I would be the one to take it off. Nay, said I, I'll none of it. I'll take off his boots. You take off the mask.

I was struggling with his boots when I felt the bed shake and heard Annetta take in a great gulp of air and swallow it whole. She stood with the mask dangling from one hand and the other slapped across her mouth as if to keep her tongue from falling out. Her eyes were wide open and fixed on the master's face. And it was no wonder, for half of it was badly deformed and the other was normal, even handsome I'm sure my wife would say. Do you think I should put it back on? she asked me as if I knew what to do in these circumstances. Silly woman, you've done it now! You can't go putting it back on, can you? It's a miracle with all this fidgeting with him that he's not woke up. So, what do you think caused that? I asked pointing to the distorted features of one side. She crossed herself and shook her head. Seems as if God wanted to paint the battle between Lucifer and Gabriel right there on his face, doesn't it, Giuseppe?

Well, she's always seeing things as divine signs of something! We decided to leave him to sleep without the mask. I had work to do, so I left my wife there to keep vigil over the beautiful blond-haired mistress. Now that was another thing that struck me as curious. What the devil would a beautiful, angelic young woman like her be doing married to a man that has to cover his face to go out in public? Maybe he'd tricked her into marrying him or maybe he'd carried her off against her will.

After Giuseppe left, I sat next to the bed with the two of them sleeping. There I waited holding her tender little hand and staring at his face. It was like seeing two different men side by side on the same pillow. He'd turn his head slightly one way and I'd see an angel, two degrees the other way and it was Lucifer himself that lay there waiting to carry this beautiful young woman down to hell. I suppose I grew used to him, though, because I couldn't think ill of him like Giuseppe did. I kept thinking of how he carried her up the stairs and how he spent nearly two days trapped in this room with her trying to bring her back to the land of the living. And that was after the doctor had given little to no hope! What kind of monster would do that?

The more I looked at him, the less frightful and ugly he seemed. If things had been different, if the mistress hadn't had such a tragic accident and didn't lie at death's door, and if he hadn't been so sad and obsessed with her, and if he hadn't fallen into this deathlike sleep himself, I wouldn't have had the time to look on him and grow to sympathize with him as much as I did. But that's exactly what happened. There was no danger in him as he lay—big and strong as he was—on the bed exhausted and in grief. Each and every Sunday, I listen to Father Antonio describe Satan and all the demons of hell, and my new master surely has the mark of the beast on him, but that's where the likeness ends. I think I'd know if I were in the presence of evil. And I just can't believe he's evil.

Giuseppe would say to me, evil is as evil does. Well, by that standard, too, I can rightly say I see none of it in him.

I gave my mistress sips of water from a spoon. I imagined he had spent all the time doing the same, and no wonder he fell into such a deep sleep after two days keeping vigil. I noticed she was taking in more of the water as I offered it to her. I could see her throat working as she swallowed. Perhaps there was hope after all that she'd come out of this.

Annetta held her breath as she saw Erik turn in his sleep. He twisted his torso onto his side and brought his arm around and over his chest. A low groan vibrated in his throat, and he tossed his head several times back and forth as if struggling to swim to the surface from a deep dream. His breathing changed also, and his eyelids flickered open. For a moment he opened his eyes and stared straight ahead toward the ceiling; his brow knit as if he were confused. Then he turned toward Annetta and stared at her.

Suddenly aware, he pushed himself up in the bed to a sitting position and in the same instant brought his hand to his face finding it uncovered. He turned away from the old woman and scrambled from the bed reaching out to steady himself against the bedpost. There he froze wondering why the old woman hadn't screamed or run from the room. She had been there next to the bed while he slept and obviously had seen him all this time without his mask. Slowly he turned toward her, but he was still reluctant to remove his hand from the side of his face. She smiled at him kindly and nodded as if to encourage him to do something. Erik gradually lowered his hand from the disfigurement and waited for her reaction. Her smile simply grew bigger as if she were satisfied that he had accomplished some great feat of skill or daring.

"Would you like something to drink or eat, Signore?"

"No. No, thank you …?" If he had heard her name before, he didn't recall it

"Annetta, Signore. My husband is Giuseppe, and we're so sorry that your arrival has been under such tragic circumstances. We had assembled to greet you both when your coach arrived, but ..." She looked down at Meg who still lay white and motionless against the pillows.

Erik forgot about the old woman and rushed to the side of the bed to examine Meg. There appeared to be no change. His heart sank; a sharp pang of desperation struck him so deeply that he had to kneel down by the bed and grab hold of the covers to steady himself. "Oh, Meg!" He tried to swallow back the tears in his voice.

As Annetta told him what they had done, he stroked the sleeping woman's hair. The servant apologized that they had taken off the mask, assuming he wouldn't sleep comfortably with it on. She also told him she thought Meg was perhaps responding a bit since she was able to take in more of the water than before.

"You're able to look at me without ...?" he asked incredulously.

"I won't lie to you, Signore. It shocked both of us a bit at first, but we're used to it now." Annetta wanted so much to ask him about it. But she knew better than to let him see her curiosity. She sensed that it would appall him and any rapport they had at the moment would disintegrate. So she held her tongue, thinking it best to let him talk if he wanted to.

"I'm used to people ... The usual reaction is fear and disgust. These usually end with the person running away or trying to kill me. That's why I wear the mask, and that's why I would just as soon prefer to be alone."

"But your wife, she's different, isn't she, Signore?"

"Yes. Meg is different. She didn't run away except ..." There was a hint of regret in his tone.

Erik bent over Meg. His lips brushed against hers ever so slightly. As he drew back, he caught something out of the corner of his eye. Meg's eyelashes were fluttering almost imperceptibly at first. A faint rose color spread across her cheeks. He stood in anticipation as he noted signs that she was regaining consciousness. Annetta clapped her hands together in a joyful prayer as her mistress's eyes opened and settled on Erik.

And then she screamed.

As Erik loomed over her, Meg screamed and screamed.

He tried to calm her. He spoke to her softly and placed his hands on her shoulders tenderly to quiet her fears, to make her recognize him. But when he touched her, her screams rose to an unbearable pitch driving him back as surely as if she had pushed him away with all her strength. Her eyes were fixed on his face—his unmasked face! Reflexively he placed his hand over his deformity to shield her from it. She still looked at him wildly but no longer screamed.

"Meg!" The word came out as if his soul were in his mouth—a plea, a prayer. His body bent as if he were being scourged. She screamed again as he started to approach the bed. He stopped, frozen in his spot, a low moaning sound coming from behind his hand. She continued to look at him in wild panic, shaking her head vigorously from side to side as if willing him to disappear. Annetta stood amazed, trying to comfort her and yet wishing she could somehow help him, too.

Erik searched about the room for his mask, discovered it on the marble table by the door, grabbed it, and ran from the room.

CHAPTER 3

❈

The Fair

> *Arrived, before the lofty gates I stay'd;*
> *The lofty gates the goddess wide display'd;*
> *She leads before, and to the feast invites;*
> *I follow sadly to the magic rites.*
> *Radiant with starry studs, a silver seat*
> *Received my limbs: a footstool eased my feet,*
> *She mix'd the potion, fraudulent of soul;*
> *The poison mantled in the golden bowl.*
> *I took, and quaff'd it, confident in heaven.*
> *Then waved the wand, and then the word was given.*
> *'Hence to thy fellows! (dreadful she began:)*
> *Go, be a beast!'—I heard, and yet was man.*
> *The Odyssey, Homer, Alexander Pope*

He could hear her scream reverberating in his head long after the horse carried him far from the villa. He rode through the night, his only thought to get as far from that scream as possible, but he could not escape it. Over and over he saw her open her eyes and focus on him. Confusion had given way to terror, and she had let loose a soul-piercing shriek. Erik had tried to calm her, but when he reached out to touch her, she had become even more hysterical. It was as if she didn't know him! Or as if she finally saw him for what he was. He ran. His last tie to humanity was severed in that moment. He didn't belong to the race of humanity; he was something else, something other. So many years trying desperately to find his place among them; so many years yearning to be welcomed into their community; so many years believing he might love and be loved. She screamed at him, she who had followed him through the tunnels to save his soul. As long as she had loved him, there had been hope. When she screamed and looked at him in that way, he understood what he had lost. He had lost all rights to call her his beloved.

The horse was tiring. On and on he spurred the dark gelding. The road was well worn. Soon they'd meet others on the way to Rome. He reined the horse in and considered the dense woods on either side. Jerking the bridle to the left, he dug in his knees and directed his mount off the road and into the forest. The undergrowth was thick and the ground rocky as the grade slowly ascended. His gelding picked his way gingerly around the bushes and trees settling each hoof tentatively on rotten leaves and branches, twigs and loose rock. Erik sat in the saddle, hearing that scream, seeing those wild eyes, the realization slowly dawning that all that he had known before this moment was gone, and that he had absolutely nowhere to go. He had only the clothes on his back. He didn't notice the cold even though he had forgotten to take his riding cape. He had only a small amount of money on his person. Nor could he access his accounts without the proper documentation, all of which he had left behind him, like his very life, first in the opera house in Paris and now in the villa with his wife. At least he knew Meg would have the means to take care of herself.

He clicked at the horse, which had stopped to rest and munch on the vegetation in the forest. On they would go until they couldn't go any farther. He had no plan but flight, just as when Madeleine had helped him, a mere boy of ten or eleven, escape from his cage at the fair, just as when Raoul and Christine helped him escape his execution as the Phantom. His whole life had been a hopeless attempt to escape his fate. His fate was to be alone, to live as an outcast, to be hunted and despised. He didn't have the heart to fight it any longer.

The sun had risen, but the dense forest remained dark. The horse was tired and sweaty. Erik patted its neck tenderly and whispered his regret. He had pushed him hard, and they would stop now and wait for night. Erik dismounted and led the horse through the forest until he found a small patch of green next to a narrow creek running rapid, clear, and clean over a blanket of pebbles. There he let the horse wander and graze as he bent down at the water's edge to drink. On the surface of the running water, a demon with a mask raised his face toward Erik from the shallows of the stream. Why should he wear it even here, alone, with no one but the devil or God to see him? An anger beyond his grief filled him with a murderous desire that he turned upon his reflection in the stream. Only after a rain of futile blows that momentarily dispersed his image did he lay exhausted and gasping on the edge of the rivulet. He lifted the mask from his face and threw it to the side and waited for night.

Sunset had long passed when Erik was awakened by a gentle nudge from the gelding. The forest around him was an impenetrable wall of blackness. The clearing was canopied by the night sky ablaze with stars. No moon had risen. Erik listened to the random sounds of night creatures all about him. It was time to continue his journey. He would travel by night, rest by day. As long as there was a forest, wild and dense, he would continue. Eventually he would come to the end of his path, but he would deal with that when it happened. At the last moment, before he mounted, he remembered the mask and went to find it on the grass. In case he came upon someone in his path, he placed it in his pocket.

As they delved farther and farther into the forest, Erik dropped the reins and let the gelding decide their course. From time to time the horse would whinny and stop in his tracks, catching perhaps the scent of a predator or the scent of a fresh kill. There was no call to rush or to panic. Whatever came across their path, Erik decided, was meant to be. He would accept whatever his fate had in store for him. He hoped it might be sooner than later. He hoped that it might also be fatal.

Without the benefit of his anger, Erik began to feel the cold through the thin material of his shirt and breeches. With the cold came his old enemies, despair and sadness. He lay forward on the mount pressing his chest against the horse and wrapping his arms around his neck to share their warmth, his sole consolation the touch between this living animal and his own body. He listened to the sounds the horse made, snorts and whinnies, and wondered what music a horse would make if he could. There were sounds all around, a kind of nocturne of wood and wind combined with the death cries of a weasel and the triumphant hoot of the owl that caught it. Something else, something not right broke in among these notes. The horse pricked up his ears rotating them forward directly ahead of them. A theme—a musical theme on a flute—and the jumble of voices—human voices—came with the breeze from the general direction in which the horse was heading. As Erik recognized the human sounds, he also discerned the flickering of light through the trees.

Cautiously he let the gelding proceed toward the light and the sounds until at the edge of the woods, they both stopped and looked down a sloping grade toward a caravan of wagons and several campfires. Around the fires men and women and even children had gathered, talking and eating. Scattered along the meadow were carts and wagons on which were painted wild animals and fantastical creatures—mermaids and monsters, acrobats and clowns. A fair. A traveling fair.

Erik tilted his head back and laughed hysterically.

In my flight from sanity to madness, I had come full circle. My earliest memories came flooding in on me. The hem of my mother's dress clutched in my hands so that I might avoid stumbling and falling as we walked through the fair grounds. Organ music and the sounds of the crowd milling about me. Standing alone waiting for her to return. Many blank days. The cage, nowhere to hide from the jeering spectators pushing their bodies up against the bars to get a better look at the Devil's Child. The dirt, the filth, rough hands, and the sting of rawhide on my back. Bells tinkling on the ankles and wrists of the beautiful, young trapeze artist. Laughter, delicate and sweet. Laughter, harsh and wicked. His face forever looming over me, prodding and pushing me, tearing at the burlap sack that covered my ugly face. Punishment for the young lady who swoons, for the disgusted, pious, self-righteous who leave without throwing a few coins into the sawdust and straw, for the increase in the price of oats and horse meat. The hunger I ignored to train myself to eat little, the refusal to eat the meat he offered, and yet the continued growth and strengthening of my body. I grew, and I grew stronger everyday in spite of the lack of sunshine and fresh air, in spite of the sting of his lash.

Now I found myself leading the gelding behind me and of my own free will asking to sit among the carnival folk and share their meal, their wine. They stared at my mask but asked no questions. A midget dressed like a king handed me a cup of the stew. I ate around the fatty chunks of unidentifiable meat. A tall and obese woman with a full growth of facial hair and a soft soprano voice passed me the bottle of wine from which I, too, drank. Home, at last, I thought to myself with a bitter chuckle. How useless the pretense at beauty, the haughty illusions of grandeur, the yearning for the exquisite, the years masquerading as a fine gentleman in my underworld kingdom. All that was now gone. This is where I came from, the travesty of the bizarre, this home to monsters and aberrations, and I, the star attraction.

From behind me I heard him approach. Whether he meant to knife me or not made little difference to me, for I had given myself over to my fate. I longed for it! Instead of the sharp thrust of a blade, I felt his fingers reach around my face and rip the mask away.

Their stunned expressions soon gave way to a studied professional curiosity as they measured the commercial value of this new freak of nature—me. Was I looking for work? Did I need a place to stay? At long last to belong somewhere! Out of the corner of my eye, I glimpsed a very, very tall and thin old man—much taller even than I—examine me and then rush purposefully away. The man who removed my mask, Yayal, threw it at my feet in a careless fashion and told me Sabia would have to read my palm. Only she could determine whether or not I had a place among the Grotesques as they called themselves. Others scoffed at Yayal's hesitation. With a face like mine, they assured me, I'd certainly be welcome. The bearded woman stroked her mustachio and added that I'd likely attract a good crowd of both men and women. I gritted my teeth as they jeered and winked lasciviously. Yes, the price of acceptance was always high.

Yayal beckoned me to follow him to Sabia's tent. I reminded myself that I wasn't a child that they could manacle and lock away in a cage. I was a man, and they'd have to deal with me as such. They wouldn't need to chain me since I'd chosen to cast my lot with theirs. I'd come home, the prodigal son, to accept my fate, my long-delayed punishment for the murder of my keeper, my own brand of patricide. I had escaped sentencing for his death. But God must have given me this face because I was meant to suffer. It was only fitting that I found my way, guided by my fate, to this fair to take my place once more among the freaks and outcasts that made up this world. I had lived too long with illusion and lies. This world of the Grotesques was more real in its ugliness than the one I had abandoned.

Sabia's tent lay on the far edge of the compound. It was decorated with mystic symbols including a giant all-seeing eye. I followed Yayal into the tent. At the back, seated on cushions, was a mature disturbingly attractive woman with dark wavy hair that fell to her hips. Around her neck were multiple necklaces of silver and gold coins. Her wrists were likewise adorned with bracelets that jangled musically as she served me something hot to drink in a small china teacup. Her age was hard to fix, although the streak of gray in her coal black hair suggested she was no longer young.

"You're amazed that I showed no fear or revulsion when I looked at your face." She smiled. "I've seen your face before."

I interpreted this as an allusion to her powers as a seer. She indicated that I should drink. I took the teacup and drained the warm fragrant liquid. It was syrupy and left a bitter aftertaste on my tongue. It immediately occurred to me that it might be drugged.

She held her hand out to me in expectation. Hesitantly I placed mine in hers. She turned it palm up and brushed her long black nails across it. The sensation caused me to curl my fist shut, but she gently pried each finger back so that my palm lay flat and exposed. As she examined it, she knit her brows together at what she saw. She placed the flat of her finger just below my index finger and moved it along the crease of the line. She drew several shapes across the center of my palm before she looked up at me intently. She dropped my right hand and grabbed the left one and pressed it open as if looking for something she couldn't find in its mate. I sensed she found something strange in my reading.

"You were born in darkness and will end in darkness." I thought I had accepted my fate, but the sinking pain in my chest told me otherwise. I knew she would find darkness, but hoped against hope that there might be some release, some respite, some chance of peace. I told myself that I didn't have to believe her, but I knew I did. "You're very strong, a strength that is more than physical. But your way is troubled. There is blood. There is violence behind and before you on this path. There is guilt and anger. I cannot see the end of your days; they are clouded. Something keeps me from seeing them clearly." I jerked my hand away from her, wanting to stop her mouth. I knew better than to expect happiness, but I thought at least I'd have renounced violence.

"Wait. Give me your hand again."

"No. There's no need. I know my fate."

"No. There is something more. I saw something else. Give it back to me." She spoke with such confidence that I relented and placed my hand again in hers. I wanted her to see something else, perhaps something that would comfort me, some small forgiving sign. I found myself staring into her eyes as if willing her to give me a glimmer of hope. "Here. Yes, your path is darkness. In the darkness there will be a moment of light. I cannot say whether this is a turning point that might give you a different path or whether it is simply a respite from the darkness. But there is a light." Instead of giving me back my hand, she caressed it between her two palms.

We were alone in the tent. Her hands were warm and soft. A sensation of intimacy rose from this contact, and I felt suddenly stirred. My pulse increased, and my breathing along with it. She rubbed the fleshy tips of my fingers between hers rhythmically, and I puzzled that such a simple act would affect me as dramatically as it did. I slid my hand away from hers and waited for the excitement to dispel. I turned away to avoid facing her and tried to remember why I was here. I assumed that she would decide whether or not I could stay among them and perhaps what role I would play in their carnival. So I asked her if I could travel for a time with them. I offered my services as someone who could help keep order. I reminded her of the strength she saw in my reading. Surely, she'd want to put it to work in her service, I argued.

"No. I think you will have another job with us." I knew what she was thinking; I could hear it in her sardonic tone. Full circle, I murmured to myself. Of course she wanted me as an exhibit, the walking gargoyle, the hideous carcass.

"I'd prefer to do something less showy," I suggested, knowing she would persist in her own plans for me. "I'm a musician. I can play any instrument you have. I could also sing if there was interest."

"Music could be part of the show. But it's your face that the customers will come to see. It's extraordinary." She actually edged so close that I could feel her body heat. She brushed the side of my face with the back of her hand. The previous excitement fired up in my body again at this light caress! I fidgeted in my position and took in a deep, long breath and exhaled it audibly through my mouth. Although I avoided her eyes, I could feel them on me as if they were fingers traveling up and down my body. Why and how could she have this effect on me? There was something strange about it, about her. I felt, in that moment, that we had been here before, and that this intense intimacy between us had already happened. It was as if she and I knew each other. Rationally I tried to reason it out. Was it possible that some of the people working this small fair, including Sabia, were part of the fair where I spent my early childhood as a freak and prisoner? Sometimes people moved on from one fair to another. Sometimes exhibits were purchased by larger carnivals.

I examined her closely. Did we know each other? My keeper had kept me isolated. He wanted me wild and savage, like an animal. I was the Devil's Child, and he didn't want anyone treating me kindly or interfering with my handling. I had come into contact with only a select few of the other performers and hands in the company. I was no longer able to remember any of them, except my keeper and one other. After I escaped into the underground vaults of the opera house, I embarked on a campaign to forget all of the experiences I had suffered before. I blotted out as much of my childhood as I could; only shadows persisted in tormenting me. As much as I tried, I could never erase the face of my keeper. Especially in the first years at the opera house, I would wake drenched in sweat after nightmares where he would pursue me to the underground rooms and flay my skin from my body until I was raw meat. Even after all these years, he still appeared in my dreams. But most else was thankfully gone.

I drew close and looked into Sabia's eyes, a violet so dark it seemed black. Her lips were blood red and full. She stroked my hair, mistaking my approach for something else. Next to my ear the tinkle of her bracelet set off a flash of light in my mind's eye, and I saw a girl, older than myself but not yet married, with bells on her ankles and wrists. She was laughing as she performed contortions for me. I looked through the bars as she bent backwards and tucked her head and arms between her legs and walked toward me on hands and feet. An acrobat, a trapeze artist, she likened herself to a bell ringing out the glory of the morning from the heights of the main tent. I knew her!

Recognition in my eyes pleased her greatly, and she smiled at me as if in reward. "Do you remember me now, Devil's Child?"

"I remember your bells. And you gave me tiny cymbals." I waited for her to confirm my memory.

"I gave you more than that!" She arched her eyebrows meaningfully and pursed her lips together in a smile that made me suddenly queasy. "Don't you remember the key? I would sneak it from Abel's tent? You and me inside the cage?" Her hand now rested on my shirt and slowly penetrated the fabric to rub her palm along my bare chest. I couldn't move as she continued to talk about those late afternoons when all the others were busy preparing for the crowds. She whispered what she willed me to dredge up from long buried memories. Her hand dipped lower to my abdomen and then brushed across my groin. "You were frightened at first, but later I think you came to enjoy it."

The world went black. Her voice seemed far far away as the cage bars grew up around me, and I could see her face looming over me and feel her tugging at my clothes. The sound of bells and harsh laughter loud in my ears …

she lies sated on her cushions, her name used to be Belle, my head feels heavy, pain throbbing inside my skull, my mouth is stuffed with cotton, dry, I can't swallow, my clothes are strewn around the cushions, my bones feel bruised, I push out the flashes of images, her long, wavy hair falling over me as I lie, unable to move, next to her, the streak of gray shines in the dark, she wants me to remember her naked, laughing, demanding, the cage and the young girl taking my hands and placing them on her body, her voice harsh and domineering, telling me to do this, slapping me hard across the face, my burlap bag cast carelessly aside in the opposite corner of the cage, she has the key but she won't free me from the cage, he'll find out, he'll punish me, she holds the key above me and teases me, touch me here, not with your hand, you ugly monster, with your mouth, your tongue, she promises me a string of tinkling bells, if I'm good, I remember her, I remember her bringing me the tiny cymbals and helping me attach them to the stuffed burlap monkey that I always had, I promise I'll do what she wants if she'll take me out of the cage and away from him, she promises, she promises each time but she doesn't let me out, when I have done what she wants, she pushes me back, throws me my burlap sack to cover my head, and rushes from the cage laughing and locks it with the key, Abel will murder me if I let you go, she giggles, she gets angry when I cry, she shouts at me that she will tell Abel the wicked things I've done to her, she only came to bring me water, she won't bring me water, she'll spit in the water and leave it for me, she'll put dirt in the water and leave it for me, she'll tell Abel that I asked her to touch me, I clutch my stomach, I feel ill, she tinkles the bells, I try to hide in the corner, I tell her I don't want her to come back, she screams at me that I should die, that I should have died in my mother's womb, she says she'll never come to see me, to play again, I hate her, I hate her, but I want her to come back, I want her to steal the key and come inside the cage, her skin is soft and she smells like fresh cut flowers, recently cut hay, I want to touch her, I want her to touch me, one day we spilled the water, and it drenched the straw underneath us, we spilled the water, I don't want to think of that day, the water ran cold and wet under us, I push the image from my mind, I don't want to see the water spill over the rim of the bowl, she stole the key, she came and unlocked the door of the cage, she took the sack from my head and laughed at me, she opened her blouse and pulled my face toward her bare breasts, she sat across my lap and rubbed herself against my legs, I spilled the water, no, I didn't spill the water yet, I forced her back onto the straw—she pushed at me to let her go, but I was strong, much stronger than she—and pulled her skirts up, she wasn't laughing anymore, she clawed at my hands, I knelt between her legs, I wanted my flesh against hers, compelled, I did only what my body demanded, she tried to scream, her feet kicked out and struck the water bowl, the water spilled out over the metal rim, I felt wetness on my arms and legs as I continued to push, she dragged her nails over my face, I grabbed her hands again and pinned them to the wet straw, the lash struck me across the bare back and buttocks, it struck again and again, she crawled away from me, the water turned red at the edges of my body, the lash struck again and again, she brought me fresh water, she explained to Abel, I asked her to open the cage door, she felt sorry for me, she had never gone into the cage before, she knew I was dangerous so she never came inside the cage before, but she felt sorry for me, and I grabbed her like an animal and tore her dress, I lay in the water, my body convulsed, I lay in my own secretions and the spilt water and drowned ... I remembered her bells, I wiped out all else, her laughter, the touch of her, the pain, the humiliation, Madeleine saved me, not Belle, for that was her name then, I remembered I called her Belle for she was so beautiful, but Belle never brought the key to unlock the cage to set me free, Belle remained at a distance and never smiled at me again, Belle laughed scornfully with the others now, she lingered on the fringe of the crowd and threw insults at me, but Madeleine didn't laugh at me, she came the last time Abel whipped me with the lash, the crowd looked on and encouraged him, Madeleine cried for me, I saw her tears, she lingered even after the crowd disappeared, her eyes looked at me sorrowfully, Abel was wrong to whip me, to keep me in the cage, like an animal, Madeleine told me it was wrong, Abel crouched in the cage to collect the coins, I took the fragment of rope—my secret rope I had found and tied around one of the bars and hidden under the straw—and wrapped it around his filthy throat and pulled it taut and twisted the cords until it bit into his flesh and he began to bleed, Madeleine watched in horror, but her tears were for me, and as I knelt over Abel's body, incapable of thought or action, she was the one who broke the spell and called to me to follow her, to escape, she pulled me by the hand through the fairgrounds—slipping from tent to tent, crouching in the shadows—along the streets to the opera house and opened the window for me to crawl into the cellars, she saved me, she was my Belle, not the other one, the one with brass bells, I loved Madeleine, she brought me to a cold, hidden place that was safe and dark, she asked me how it was to be down in the deepest vaults of the opera house, she worried that the air was stagnant and vile, she feared I was lonely and would become ill, but no, the updrafts and ventilation shafts created a constant exchange of air, I'll show you, I told her, come with me, come down into the vaults to see the rooms I have decorated, I reached out my hand to take hers, to lead her down the stairs, but she drew back, she tucked her hands behind her to avoid touching mine, I insisted and grabbed her hand from behind her back and wouldn't let it go, she protested that she didn't have time to traipse around like a monkey, I knew she regretted the words the moment she said them, but I couldn't control how they made me feel, I dragged her down, I forced her to come to the vaults where I slept, the more she tried to get away the harder my grip on her, she was older than I, not a child, a young woman, beautiful, a shapely woman with firm bust and full hips, but I was taller and much stronger than she, as she struggled in my arms, she made me angrier, I felt powerful and aroused, she was small in my grasp, and warm and soft, and I wanted to press against her and touch her like Belle had taught me to touch softness like hers, suddenly she lay limp in my arms, and I saw how hard I was holding her and saw the look of fear and sadness in her eyes and released her ... I asked her to forgive me, but she repeated over and over again that nothing happened, there was nothing to forgive, she would abandon me completely to my loneliness if I ever spoke of it, I begged her to say the words, to release me from the guilt, but she threatened to go away forever so I promised, I promised ... she never asked about the vaults again, I never asked her to come with me, she avoided my touch, and I willed myself to forget, I knew Madeleine would never forgive me, I tried to make amends to her, I *brought her gifts, I protected her from the stage hands who leered at her, when she left me to marry, I thought I would die, but she found a way to write to me, when she returned a widow with little Meg in her arms, I sang to Meg and brought her gifts, when Meg entered the ballet I demanded that the manager give her a spot in the company, Madeleine accepted my gifts, but she would never want me to ..., I never approached Meg, it was Meg who sought me out, I was a fool to respond to her, how could I imagine that Madeleine would stand by when she found me with her daughter? ... so this was Belle cum Sabia's revenge, she would revenge them all—herself, Madeleine, and Meg—Sabia would own the key, she would once more have dominion over my body and soul ... the memories come flooding down on me and I swallow the bile and blood and filth in their waters ... I am destined to pain and suffering as my only escape from the horror of my own life ... I still hear Meg scream, her scream goes on and on ... I will submit to Sabia, I have no choice, I will pay for all my crimes ...*

The act was simple. Erik listened to Sabia and Yayal as they worked out the details of the lighting and the story. He marveled that he sat there, his face exposed, and that two people sat at the same table talking business. No one remarked on his disfigurement; no one cared. He was able to walk outside in the fresh air and pretend to be like everyone else. He was simply another freak at the freak show. Of course many who worked the fair were like Yayal, without any extraordinary or unique physical difference. There were those who had talents such as Belle when she was younger and before the tragic fall that left her incapable of working the high wire or performing the contortions of the acrobat. She limped now, her left leg stiff and weak, but as Erik had discovered, her injury didn't stop her from being a demanding and inventive lover.

The fair had nearly reached Brindisi when they launched the new exhibit, the "Angel in Hell." Word of mouth traveled fast, and the impressive crowds were eager to enter the tent to see the man on whom the battle between heaven and hell was visibly waged. "Within the same body, the demon and the angel fight," was one of the cries the barker proclaimed to the crowds to draw them in. Whenever they were within range of a town or city, Erik had to be careful and wear his mask even on the fair grounds. It would destroy the dramatic effect if anyone were to see him wandering about on the grounds as if he were nothing more than a man. No one was to talk about his face; no one was to see it until the show and only at the show. Sabia licked her lips as she thought of the profits Erik's show was bringing to the fair.

Indeed the fair had never prospered more. It had been months since they opened the show of the "Angel in Hell," and it was still the biggest draw at the fair. But Sabia was always thinking of better exhibits and larger profits. So one day she suggested that they'd rake in even more if Erik agreed to private shows for wealthy and eccentric patrons after the performance. She knew from experience that Erik's talent as a lover was second only to his voice. When she first mentioned her idea, he stiffened beside her in the bed and refused to speak or look at her. She dropped the subject immediately. Several days later, she whispered again to Erik that there would be other women who would enjoy the attentions of someone like him. He scowled at her and asked her to explain what she meant by someone like him. She smiled playfully—not without cruelty as Erik was aware—and traced her fingers over the deformed side of his face. Sickened by her suggestion, Erik withdrew from her room and again avoided her for several days. He was resigned to sharing her bed, but there had to be some limits to the humiliation he was meant to suffer.

Then one night near a small village dominated by a handful of noble personages, Sabia came into Erik's tent and congratulated him on a particularly intense performance. She reached behind her, outside the entrance flap, and ushered in a woman Erik didn't know.

Tense and alert, he knew immediately the trap Sabia had set for him.

"This is Signora de Mendoza, a widow of some ten years now. She wanted to express her admiration for your show in person. I'll leave you two alone. Signora, please be assured you are completely safe. No one will disturb you until you signal. I will have someone stand well off to the side to wait. Buonasera." Sabia smiled mockingly at Erik and closed the tent flap behind her.

Erik considered ignoring the woman and waiting for her to become flustered and simply leave. He also thought that he might get up and walk out of the tent, leaving the signora to her own devices. But as he fumed in silence he observed the young widow—she was still young, most likely in her late twenties—and felt moved by her awkward interest. She was nervous. A beaded reticule passed rhythmically from one gloved hand to the other. Her fingers, as if they had a life of their own, soothed the tiny pearl incrustations on the reticule's surface. He imagined the feel of running his own hands over the smooth pearls, but the sensation shifted to that of his fingers over the fabric of her white gloves and then to the tender skin of naked palms, to the pulse that beat close to the surface at the juncture of her wrist. He had thought perhaps she was anxious and fearful. Such was not the case, and the realization unsettled him. He didn't know whether or not to be flattered or appalled, titillated or nauseated. He was puzzled by her desire for him. His show had revealed his disfigured face to the audience, had allowed them to glimpse the incongruity, the bizarre nature he had always sought to hide, his very shame. For he had always felt ashamed to have been so cursed by God. It was unnatural, yet the young woman trembled visibly; her breathing rasped shallow and rapid. Her lips were swollen and moist. She parted them and sucked at the air as if starved. Color flooded her cheeks, and everything in her stance pulled at him.

Once upon a time he had learned to exert his will over that of another. He had done so through the artful manipulation of illusion and through the power of his voice. That had been deception, and in the end it had burned him. This time it was different. He had not deceived the young widow who had come to his tent, to his bed, to offer herself to him.

Even as he approached her and took her hand, he thought she might panic and flee. He refused to heed the echo of a distant scream. No, she had come to him. She had seen his face, and she had not run away. She had not screamed. He led her to the canopied bed that occupied the center of the tent. She followed. There were no mirrors, no tricks of the light, only the mask. There was only the mask between her desires and his.

She is not here for you. It is her need that brings her to you.

"You've been alone for some time?" he asked, knowing still the effect of his voice, but unable to give up all his former power.

"Yes." She blushed. "My husband was old; he died ten years ago."

"Why have you not remarried?"

"His family insisted that I not."

"That's wrong. Cruel. You should not have listened to them. You weren't meant be alone."

Her yearning for him was so intense that he sensed it as pain. He understood the longing she felt; he knew what it was to spend years and years without the touch of another human being. He felt his own desires stir, but held them in check. He would concentrate on her desires and needs, not his own. He would never again let his own desires outweigh his ability to sense another's.

"May I touch you?" he asked as he sat her on the edge of the bed.

She nodded shyly, her eyes downcast unable to meet his gaze. He gently lifted her chin and brushed his lips over her cheek, the touch of a feather, the whisper of a wing, down to her lips where he lingered and teased her mouth with his tongue.

"Would you prefer that I not remove my mask?"

Startled by the question, she looked up at him and hesitated. She scanned his face as if momentarily embarrassed to look at him so directly. The mask covered his face only partially. His lips and chin and the lower part of his cheeks were visible. The surface of the mask was smooth and soft, a layer of satin. The feel of skin and satin as he kissed her was not unpleasant.

"I … I think you should do what you wish," she stammered. "I think you're strangely handsome even without …"

He was touched by her attempt to be brave. He had no doubt that she'd prefer he wear the mask. If he were to remove it, she would try but fail to hide her disgust. She was intrigued by him, but she was mesmerized by the mask. The knowledge of what it hid perhaps stirred her, and it would only do so if the mask remained in place.

His lips traced a path across her face to her neck and down to the soft recess at the base of her throat. There he could feel the rapid thrum of her pulse. "Do you wish to disrobe or do you wish to remain clothed?"

Between deep intakes of breath, the young woman asked to keep most of her clothes on, but said that he could undo her stays if he liked. Rubbing his hands over her bodice, he whispered hoarsely that he would very much like to undo her stays. Excited more than he had anticipated, he opened her bodice. He caressed her, dipped and tasted her, suckled, teasing the sensitive dark brown tips. Gently he laid her back against the bedding and asked if she wanted him to remain dressed or if he should disrobe for her.

"Yes, yes," she answered eagerly, "I would like you to take your clothes off."

Erik drew back from the bed and took off his boots. Next he removed his jacket, then his vest, each of which he folded slowly and placed upon a chair, all the time watching the building excitement in her eyes. She left her bodice open, her breasts exposed, as he unfastened the clasps of his shirt and pulled it open to reveal his bare chest. Then he stopped.

"I would like you to help with my breeches, if you would be so kind?"

She brought her trembling fingers to the belt that circled his waist and unwrapped it, dropping it to the floor; then she unbuttoned each pearl button on his breeches until they hung loose around his hips. Then she hesitated.

"Could you pull them down?" he asked.

Her fingers no longer trembled as she placed both her hands on his hips. She pushed the breeches to the floor. The movement brought her to her knees before him. She fixed her gaze upon his groin.

They no longer worried about asking permission to do what they wished to do, both slaves to the same appetite. Erik quickly hoisted the woman's petticoats aside, up above her waist, and pulled her bloomers down to her ankles. Roughly he spread her knees apart, but on the verge of taking her, he forced himself to control his lust. Slowly, he filled her. She rotated her hips to take him yet deeper inside. He tasted her moans and knew she would not release him until she was sated.

After the young widow left, Erik lay exhausted amid the rumpled bedding. She had caught fire like dry timber and consumed him in the same blaze. What had transpired between them had not been sordid or disgusting. Quite the opposite. For the first time since he'd fallen into Sabia's snare, Erik felt clean. He had given of himself without thinking of his own desires. In return, the widow had made him not only desired, but whole. She had returned his pleasure and left him much more. She had freed him.

Moments later, Erik marched into Sabia's tent.

"I have more than made up for whatever grievance you may still bear me. Since you push me into other women's arms, I no longer intend to come to your bed." His tone was cold and assured. "I'm here to renegotiate our business arrangement."

"You forget that I'm the one who sets the conditions!"

"Not any longer. I will continue the show as long as it suits me. After hours, if I choose to entertain, it will be my choice, my decision. The profits for the show will be split evenly between us. I won't perform anywhere near Rome, and if the fair travels beyond the Italian border, it will go without me. Tell no one who I am or how we know each other."

"You forget that I know you're a murderer! I could turn you in."

"If I were you, I'd be careful who I threatened." Erik's gaze grew hostile and dark.

"What would you do?" Sabia tried to regain control of the situation. She smiled and laughed, but it was an artificial and unconvincing gesture.

"I'll kill you. I've murdered before to survive, to be free." Erik's voice remained eerily calm and even.

Unable to disguise her fear, Sabia swallowed audibly.

"I've nothing to lose, Belle. My debt is paid. I no longer feel the least guilt or obligation toward you. I can't bear the thought of touching you."

"Have I hurt your pride, Erik? Is that it?"

"I mean nothing to you, and you mean even less to me."

Sabia frowned, her dark brows ominous over deeply violet eyes. She berated him, reminded him that she knew every dirty thing about him that made the inside of him as ugly as his exterior. Erik stared at her in utter silence. His eyes flashed with rising fury, but his body remained tense and still. When he said nothing, when he continued to sustain her belligerent gaze, Sabia could sense the threat in the air between them as if a large wall were about to crash down upon her. She took several steps backward nearly toppling over a chair in her path. She recovered her balance at the last moment. When she looked over her shoulder, Erik had already gone.

The crowd pushed impatiently ahead toward the tent in the middle of the fairgrounds. The barker had promised a show that would both horrify and sadden the bravest and the hardest of hearts among them. This was the second or even third time for some who whispered with hushed, barely contained excitement to their friends and neighbors about the creature they had seen.

"A giant he is! I'm sure he could crush you in his bare hands."

"But the amazing thing is that he has a lovely voice."

"It's about a battle of some sort."

"They start in the dark, you see, and when a light comes on all you can see is …"

"Did you see it last night? The show?"

"The angel is so beautiful, and his voice is, too, but then the light goes off for just one second and …"

"Battle in heaven or some such nonsense."

"So beautiful."

"Angels and demons."

"No. He's not a real angel. Not now!"

"At first I thought it a trick because after all they light a candle and then blow it out and then light it again fast."

"I get dizzy when they turn out the lights too often."

"Let's not sit next to that man. Who knows what he might do when the light goes out."

"So the angel is ugly?"

"You're stepping on the hem of my gown."

"The devil part of the creature is frighteningly ugly, like garbled meat or something. And he looks at you as if he could kill you with that eye of his."

"Does he have wings or such?"

"Which one was it that wrestled the angel? Was it Julius Caesar or Jacob?"

"Do you think he really looks like that?"

"The man who tells the story says he's an angel that was damned. He used to be one of God's favorites, like Lucifer."

"Could we sit a little farther back? I don't know if I want to be in the front row."

"He was condemned to walk among us to remind us of ..."

"What did you say?"

"Isn't it supposed to start soon? Seems like we've been waiting for ..."

"I don't like war stories."

"It's about the double, no, the duality of good and evil that battle for men's souls. That's right. That's what his face tells us."

"I'm so hot I could die."

"But how can he sing so beautiful?"

"So there are two men? One ugly and one handsome?"

"After the story, you get to see his whole face and both sides are there at the same time so that you know it's not two people who are up there pretending to have one side of the same face."

"It's all a trick. These shows are all sham, illusion."

"Well, whatever he is, you know he must have done something horrible to be cursed like that!"

"It's no trick. You'll see."

"It's more frightening when you see him that way, the two sides together, 'cause it's just not natural!"

"Poor thing!"

"Can you ask the two young ladies to move over one seat so that we can sit together?"

"God doesn't make creatures like that and allow them to live unless it's a punishment."

"Evil, I'd say, pure evil."

"Wouldn't doubt that his voice is meant to tempt us!"

"They're not going to lecture us, are they?"

"I thought he looked sad."

"Do you think he's ugly all the way down his body on one side?"

"After he sings and you get to see the two sides of the face, the story is over, that's it."

"I heard that if you pay some extra you get to see more. I heard that the ladies in particular are encouraged to give up some coins, and they go back to his private tent. And you know what happens there!"

The last show of the evening was about to commence when Lucianna and her husband, Don Ponzio, were ushered to their front row seats next to Don Scevola and Donna Rosella. The riff raff were allowed to enter to find their spots only after the lords and ladies, and those with real money, were given preferential seating. There were only two shows a night. The very infrequency of the shows had increased the interest among the spectators who stood for hours on line to see the "Angel in Hell."

Lucianna had not wanted to come. Her husband insisted; he was excited by bizarre phenomena and had collected a number of oddities that he kept on the estate. The carnival owners would have swooned with envy to see his menagerie of monsters and misshapen creatures. Although he had a few that were alive, such as the two headed lamb, most were stuffed and preserved in jars and stored in glass cases. He had even suggested keeping their aborted fetus in a vinegar jar among the other exhibits until Lucianna, beside herself with grief and horror, took it from him and secretly buried it in the cemetery. That was the moment when Lucianna knew that she could hate with all her soul. The other torments had been nothing compared to that one.

Now they sat in the first row to see the exhibit the whole neighborhood was talking about. The fair had arrived several days ago and set up their tents in a meadow. They had requested permission from the church and the town council as well as Lord Scevola Stattore who allowed them to settle on his pasture. The church turned a blind eye on the fair while the council actually encouraged it because it brought business to the area. Lord Stattore thought it a wise decision to grant the local peasantry their entertainment a couple of times a year. Lucianna and Don Ponzio were visiting with the Stattore family for the month when the fair came to ask permission to set up their tents.

"I've heard that this 'Angel of Hell' is actually just a poor freak with a hideous deformity on one side of his face. They say that in recompense for the ugliness of his face he has a beautiful voice." Eyeing his wife and glancing at the others in the company he added with a lascivious arch to his eyebrows, "I've heard that his voice is not the only recompense God gave him!" The men chuckled, and Donna Rosella smiled behind her fan as Don Ponzio continued with a low growl, "I've heard his body is exquisite and that he is willing to entertain for a price!"

"Oh, Don Ponzio, you are such a rake. But if his face is so ugly, how could a woman want to dally with such a creature?"

"Well, Donna Rosella, in the dark, you wouldn't have to look at his face!" They all laughed, except Lucianna who was well aware that her husband was genuinely interested in experiences that would scandalize his peers. Since their marriage, Lucianna had been subjected to many humiliations so incredible that she was reluctant to confess them to the parish priest, for she knew he was dependent on Don Ponzio and would not believe the decadence and lasciviousness of the last son of such a noble family. The Stattores and Don Ponzio were friends of long standing, and although the month-long visit was still young, Lucianna had already seen signs that Don Scevola and his wife, Donna Rosella, were willing partners in her husband's games of decadence.

The lights in the tent dimmed, and a hush fell on the expectant crowd. Lucianna sighed as they were extinguished, submerging the entire space in a darkness so thick it weighed heavy on her. Suddenly, she felt panic. It was ridiculous! But she sensed something ominous in the dark and found herself looking blindly up toward the dais. She heard loud footsteps approach across the wooden floor, then silence. That was when he began to sing, a deep rich melody in a strong, virile voice. A single candle burst into flame and illuminated a man wearing a silver and gold mask.

Lucianna felt his voice as if it were hands moving over her body; a sensation of indescribable warmth rushed along her inner thighs and lodged itself in the secret recesses of her womb. A tingling pulse deepened and surged along her torso until she felt her breath quicken in tandem with the deep resonant beat of his song. As alien as the sensation was of this incorporeal touch, there was something strangely familiar. She felt drawn to that voice and that face. The eyes behind the mask slowly scanned the spectators, who were silently enraptured by his song, until they came to Lucianna, and there they fixed on her with sudden intensity. In the same moment, she realized why he seemed familiar. The mask and those eyes and even the tenor of the voice belonged to that man she had followed, in spite of herself, to the stable. It was the man in the mask that had ridden alongside her into the forest. She blushed as she remembered that night. She had been on her way to her wedding, her wedding to Don Ponzio, a marriage she had refused repeatedly until her father forced her to accept. When she followed the masked man to the stable, she knew she wanted him to be her first lover. She had felt compelled to give herself to him that night, a perfect stranger, even if it meant her death at Don Ponzio's hands. She had teased and led him to the forest, and in that forest she had waited for him to take her, but he didn't. He left her! The next morning, the innkeeper gave her a note the stranger had meant for her. She could find no other information, not even a name, for the man. It was as if he were a ghost; except for the note there was no evidence that the previous night had happened. Later that same morning, she continued her journey to her pre-arranged marriage. Yet, over the next several years, she often dreamed of him!

The man sang as if he sang only to her. Everyone around them disappeared in the darkness. As the final notes of the melody drifted away, she felt her entire body vibrate like a tightly wound string plucked by the expert hand of a violinist. The light became brighter on the dais, and he removed one side of the mask revealing a handsome face with strong cheek and jaw bones, deep and expressive eye—one moment green and the next blue. There were signs of the new growth of his dark, thick beard closely shaved earlier that day. His lips were full and shapely, and as he breathed he parted them slightly revealing beautiful, even white teeth. His eyebrow descended in a worried expression over his eye as he pondered her for a brief moment before the lights went out entirely. A woman screamed in the back of the tent, and several young children wailed. As suddenly as the light had been extinguished, it came on again, and on the stage the same man stood, the mask in place once more. Just as in the first case, the other side of the mask was removed. What the audience saw this time evoked a bevy of screams and gasps among adults and children alike, for as handsome as was the one side of the creature's face, the other was ugly.

Lucianna's heart sank to her stomach, and she covered her mouth to stop her own reaction, but she refused to close her eyes. She couldn't stop looking at him. Hidden by the twisted, reddened flesh was something familiar still. The mouth was the same, the line of the jaw the same, the eye although slightly lower than the other and surrounded by irregular, reddened tissue had the same deep, rich hue as the other. Her own lips began to tremble, and her eyes filled with tears as she realized that he, too, looked at her still. He knew her, and was anxiously watching her reaction. She lowered her trembling fingers from her mouth and smiled at him. The glint in his eyes sharpened as he saw her smile. The mask was removed from the other side, and Lucianna was aware that someone was telling the story of the Angel who defied God and was condemned to be both angel and demon for all eternity.

Lucianna glanced toward her husband. She didn't like the way he was looking at the "Angel in Hell." There was a glint of perverse pleasure mixed with cruelty in his leer. When she turned back to the dais, the lights went out once more, and when they came back on, the dais was empty.

CHAPTER 4

The Devil's Child

He had slavishly bound himself to Belle for the first of their more than two years together, but it had not been sufficient to appease her. His submission to her will had only been a sham. No matter how she degraded him, he reserved some core that she couldn't touch. She detested his ability to rise above the humiliation. His sudden refusal to come to her bed had shocked and angered her. How dare he!

He was hers, always had been, since she stole his innocence as a child. She had initiated him expecting that he would be grateful for her charity. No one else would ever touch him. He was deformed. At first she had even thought him an idiot, incapable of reason. Abel had kept him caged in his own filth. He would never have a normal life. No one would love him. From such a beginning, how had that pathetic, disfigured child grown into such a formidable man? Why did his eyes fill her with desire? His voice made her tremble. The touch of his hands, his lips on hers drove her mad with lust. The cowering, beaten, abused child had turned into a man that inspired both fear and passion. He exuded power, in every step he took, in every gesture and look, even as he slept. She could feel it in the room whenever he was present.

She had always been drawn to power. His was a rare animal energy, sexual, but more than sexual. Even silent he exerted a magnetism, but when he spoke he was like a force of nature. She saw that his effect was not unique to her. She saw it on men as well as on women. She wanted him in her bed. She needed him; she had become addicted to him. Though she had meant to chain him to herself through lust, she was the one now chained in the cage!

He had murdered his keeper Abel, but that was many years ago and in another country. Sabia knew the Italian police would be uninterested in a crime that took place in France some twenty or more years ago. But Erik was still indebted to her! Abel had been a powerful man as well as her lover. Once he was killed, she lost her position of power in the fair and had to rely on her skills as an entertainer like the rest of the performers. Then her accident left her unable to earn a living on the high wire. Still beautiful, she had gone from one man to another searching for one that could give her what she needed. One of them taught her the art of fortune telling, and she found that she had a talent for it that far exceeded her teacher's. This became her means of support, and soon the opportunity to start over again came her way. She snuck away in the dead of night, and fled to Italy where she convinced the owner of the Grotesques that she was a great seer, the "Great Sabia." She was still beautiful and charismatic. The owner of the fair was as easy to manipulate as the other men in her life had been. First he gave her a stall in the fair, then he made her his co-manager, and finally he signed over part interest in the fair itself. When he died, she inherited the remaining share of ownership. Erik was not going to use her and slip out from underneath her control. She'd see him dead first.

As long as he came to her bed, she knew she could control him. Her success as a seer was in part due to the fact that she understood human nature. In particular she understood its darker side, the way one deals with great sorrow and great shame. All around her as she grew up were examples of suffering humanity. She knew criminals and victims, the emotionally crippled and the emotionally perverse, the hopeless and the deluded. A man as powerful as Erik didn't fall into her trap and allow himself to be treated so shamefully if he didn't believe somewhere deep inside himself that he was unworthy of anything else. She used his guilt in Abel's murder for whatever value it had, but even she knew that he was more the victim than the criminal in that story. No, it wasn't Abel's murder alone that tormented and crippled him. The Angel in Hell suffered a deeply buried sorrow or shame other than the crime that he had committed as a child. There was something else, some horrible deed that he later committed as a man, for which he punished himself. To maintain her power over him, she must find out what tormented him. Why would he subject himself to her domination, if he weren't punishing himself for something he had done and for which he couldn't forgive himself? This was the key she had to find to control him.

Submission to humiliation and her control had been the punishment he inflicted on himself. She sensed that something had changed. He was resisting her. He was preparing to extricate himself from her. Somehow he had found the strength and the will to hope again.

Tonight I feel awkward and nervous. For the first time I'm anxious for the show to begin. I hope to see her there tonight. They say that she's an unhappy wife. I wonder if she was already married that night she followed me to the stable. Why would she have placed herself in such a scandalous situation? Meeting a stranger, alone and at that time of night? She could have been ruined. Perhaps that's what she hoped for, and I foiled her plans with my last minute attempt to be a gentleman, to protect her honor. But it was more than my concern for a seductive stranger. I had thought of Meg. She was asleep in our room where I had left her. I had awoken and had not been able to go back to sleep. I slipped from Meg's side to go to the stable. I had thought it would calm me to stand with the horses, to brush them, to listen to their tremendous hearts beating away. I might have held Meg in my arms. I might have sought comfort from her kisses. My Meg, so young and hopeful, so caring and so trusting. What did she see when she looked in my eyes? Why does it still pain me to think of the life that she had wanted for us? I was—I am—her husband, bound by holy vows, sanctified by rites of passion. Meg is still my wife. But I'm dead to her now. She's well rid of me. Wasn't that what I had wanted? Didn't I do everything to test her, to push her away from me, to make her see what I was and hate me? I should be glad that I succeeded. But why? Why did I treat her so abominably when she is the only one who has ever truly loved me?

A voice in the back of his mind answered him, *because you don't deserve to be loved!*

Erik had investigated Lucianna's situation as discreetly as he could. The rumors he collected were shocking, disturbing. She had refused to marry Don Ponzio Fiortino—his reputation in debauchery and cruelty was legendary—but he pressured her family until they agreed to betroth their youngest to him. Everyone whispered that he abused her, shared her sexual favors with friends, delighted in inventing ever more cruel torments to subject her to. Erik didn't believe these rumors to be idle speculation or exaggerations. During the performance, when he looked her way, Erik had seen the sadness and torment in her eyes; she was no longer that high spirited young woman who had dangerously flirted with him in the stable and had bid him chase her through the forest. But it was more than the passing of a few years that had changed her. Something darker had touched her and beat her down.

The Stattores and Fiortinos were in the audience again. Even though Erik wanted to look at no one else in the audience except Lucianna, he quickly understood from Lucianna's downcast eyes and surreptitious glances that he should not. He forced himself to look away from her, only occasionally darting sidelong glances at her to assure himself she was safe. He sensed her tension, her fear, and knew she didn't fear him, but feared for him and for herself. She sat in deadly panic of her husband whose leer disturbed Erik. Don Ponzio was obviously fascinated by him, and Erik wasn't sure he wanted to know the nature of his interest.

After the show, Erik put on his mask, donned the hooded cape that extended to mid-calf, and slipped out of the tent and into the crowds of villagers and performers. It was easy to merge with the faceless throng unnoticed and to follow the Stattores and Fiortinos through the campgrounds.

Too far from them to hear their conversations, Erik watched closely. At one point, Lucianna broke free of her husband's grip and turned to speak to him excitedly. They were arguing. The Stattores seemed slightly amused at first, then uncomfortable. Don Ponzio took a threatening step toward his wife, grabbed her forcefully with both his hands, and turned her sharply forward to walk purposefully toward Sabia's tent. Erik restrained his impulse to defend Lucianna. He easily might have dealt with Don Ponzio, who was a large man, but no match for him. Instead, he followed discreetly behind and when the two couples were invited inside Sabia's tent, he circled around to the side where he knew he could both listen and watch the encounter.

Sabia offered the couples refreshments and bid them sit. She asked them how they were enjoying the fair and thanked the Stattores again effusively for allowing them to set up their humble operations on their land. She repeated that they should come again and again as her guests to the fair to enjoy the exhibits and other entertainments. That was when Don Ponzio made clear his intentions.

"Yes, the other entertainments. That's why we're here, Donna Sabia. We're intrigued by the Angel or is it the Demon?" He smirked at the great Sabia, Seer of the Universe.

"I'm so pleased that you found our little morality play uplifting," she demurred.

"Uplifting? Well, you might tell the parish priest that drivel, but we all know better, don't we?" Erik could see that Sabia was uncomfortable with Don Ponzio's sarcasm. The patronizing note suggested that he was fully aware of the true nature of the entertainment and felt himself to be in a position to dictate to her.

"What did your lordship have in mind? Perhaps a private exhibition at the manor? An intimate and limited performance?"

"Something of that sort."

"I'm afraid that the Angel in Hell is very stubborn and insists on full control of his act. He only performs …"

"I've heard all this before. Yes, yes. He only performs twice a night and on his own terms. I've also heard that he entertains in his personal tent, after the show, certain patrons?"

"Patrons? No. Ladies, matrons, even the occasional signorina. Sometimes. And only of his choosing."

At this the nobleman frowned darkly. He tapped his fan repeatedly on the heel of his boot as if extremely annoyed and didn't speak for several moments. The tension in the tent was palpable, and Sabia knew instinctively to keep quiet until Don Ponzio decided to speak again.

The tone of his voice admitted of no disagreement. "I want him to spend a couple of months at my villa as my guest. I would expect him to be properly accommodating for the honor we would bestow on him. I know of many who would enjoy meeting him." Finally composed, Don Ponzio managed to give Sabia a cloying smile.

"I fear that he would refuse to …"

"I accept Don Ponzio's kind invitation," interrupted Erik as he stepped inside the tent and bowed low before the nobles. He pulled back the hood to reveal his masked face. "But I would establish some conditions."

Don Ponzio's smile flickered but remained. "Of course, er … I'm sorry, but I simply can't go about addressing you as Signore Angel in Hell, can I?"

"Erik should suffice, I expect."

"Well, then, Erik. What conditions would you wish to impose?" Erik was aware of the condescending tone the nobleman purposefully adopted.

"It's hard to say since I'm not quite sure why you're offering me this invitation or to what … purposes … you might put me."

Don Ponzio looked over to Lucianna whose pulse was beating wildly as she tried to keep her eyes focused on anything and anyone except Erik.

"I would hope that you could accompany my wife. You see, she's very lonely. I've not been the companion that she had longed for. Have I, my dear?" He reached over and took her limp hand in his and made a pouting face at her. She turned as far away from him as she might without moving from the chair itself. Erik bristled at the manner in which Don Ponzio treated Lucianna. Her discomfort greatly alarmed him. But he restrained himself so as to hide from Don Ponzio his urge to intercede.

The Italian nobleman proceeded to clarify his plans. "I would want you available at dinner parties and the like so that my friends could have the chance of making your acquaintance."

"I don't think that I would like being placed on exhibit during a dinner party, Signore. I'm sorry but I think I will have to decline your kind invitation." Coldly, Erik turned to go.

Don Ponzio, stunned, called after him.

"You misunderstand me, Don Erik. You would be one of my invited guests, like any invited guest. I meant you no disrespect." The words were gracious, but they sounded strained as if they caused Don Ponzio great pain.

"I wear a mask when it suits me, and I take it off when it suits me. That would be understood, even among your guests?"

"Of course. But surely you would gratify our curiosity from time to time?"

Erik hesitated, sensing the trap, but unable to avoid it if he meant to come to Lucianna's aid. "I will unmask myself under my own conditions so that your friends can see my face, if that's what you want."

"I've heard that you offer other entertainments of a more delicate nature to some …"

"No." Erik interrupted before Don Ponzio could finish. "This is not proper discourse among gentlemen in the presence of ladies."

"Gentlemen? Am I to understand that you consider yourself a gentleman?" Don Ponzio scoffed. He threw his companions a look of incredulity and encouraged them to laugh with him at the absurdity.

"Any man can assume the habits of a gentleman if he yearns to be better than he is."

"And you would aim so high, Signore Angel?"

"You misunderstand me, Signore. To be good is not always to change one's class but to improve one's soul."

Don Ponzio merely arched his eyebrow in response. "Well, let us assume that we can expect you within the fortnight as the fair closes?"

Erik merely inclined his head in agreement. Each held the other's gaze calculatingly. Before the two couples departed, Donna Rosella timidly reached out and touched Erik lightly along a crease in his cape and whispered, "Could I perhaps see you once more without your … you know, your …?"

"My mask? Anything to oblige you, Signora, but you must promise not to faint or to scream. Your heart is strong, I take it?"

Donna Rosella's eyes grew wide with fear.

"For women sometimes don't realize that seeing me this close is very different from seeing me on the dais at a safe distance. I wouldn't want to distress you or endanger your health." As he spoke to her, his voice low and hoarse, he drew even closer and bent down over her face to stare at her darkly.

Swallowing audibly, Donna Rosella quickly placed her hand on his as he reached toward his mask and said, "You might be right. Perhaps we should wait until another time."

As Lucianna followed her husband from the tent, she allowed herself to look up with grateful eyes at Erik.

Sabia rushed to bar Erik's path, her limp more pronounced than usual.

"You expect me to sit back and let you leave us at the end of our stay here?"

"You should rest your leg, Sabia. It's been a long day."

Sabia glared at Erik. "How dare you? How dare you even refer to my limp? You compare this to that face of yours?"

"Not at all," he answered. Although he pretended to be indifferent to her baiting, he couldn't mask the coldness in his eyes. He stepped around her as if to leave.

"You can't leave. We made a bargain."

She grabbed his cape. He ripped it from her hands.

"You read my palm when I first came upon the fair. Do you recall what you saw?" Seeing that she did, Erik continued, "I think I've seen the light you mentioned. I'm only following my destiny, Sabia." With that, he walked out of the tent, leaving Sabia fuming on her own.

"How do you expect to compensate me for the loss of your exhibit? They've been coming to see you!"

Erik had come to take his farewell of Belle. The carriage from Don Ponzio's manor had arrived and was waiting to take him to their villa on the eastern coast of the Adriatic. The journey would be several days, perhaps longer if they met with any obstacles.

Sabia paced back and forth ranting about profit and loss, debts owed, lost opportunities. He remained unmoved, enjoying her annoyance. She had made him remember the days of his childhood, the days locked away as a freak in a cage and tormented by a demon named Abel. She took from him the comfort of the one memory that he had rescued and preserved, that of a beautiful young girl with bells on her wrists and ankles who had brought him tiny brass cymbals, that had brought him music. For one moment he raised his hand, thinking to reach out and touch Belle's cheek, but he recoiled as he saw the hatred and venom in her dark violet eyes. The girl he imagined had never existed. He had invented her to shield himself from the young woman who had robbed him even of his innocence. There was no light in his childhood, only darkness, shame, and loss.

"That's a matter that doesn't concern me anymore. Your troupe thrived before I came; it will do well without me. If you wish, take it up with the Signore." Erik started toward the doorway.

"You monster! How dare you turn your back on me!"

"Don't tempt me, Belle, to show you the monster you think I am." His eyes bored into hers, his voice harsh and heavy in the tension between them.

"You don't think I know what a monster you really are? You make me sick—you pretend to be so fine. You're an ape dressed in gentlemen's clothes. Your pretense is pathetic. After what you've done, you think you can live free? You think you deserve to be happy?"

"You can't make me pay for his death. Not any more. He deserved a worse death than the one he earned at my hands. I've paid my debt. There's nothing more you can take from me that I haven't given up." He was finding it difficult to control his anger. He had expiated whatever guilt he might have had for the murder of his tormentor. He had lived a prisoner in the bowels of Paris his entire life. He had never been free. Abel had deserved to die. He had not been human and had taught Erik nothing but hate and violence. Erik refused to carry the burden of that demon's death.

"Is it so easy to discharge such a debt? Tell me, Erik, since you seem so wise and so able to judge the value of a man's life. How can a son pay back the death of a father?"

"What?"

"You heard me, Erik. Does it not bother you to know that you murdered your own father?" Sabia rose to her full height in triumph as she saw Erik's stricken face.

Stunned, he braced himself against a supporting beam. He thought to challenge her, to say that it was just a vicious lie, but once it had been spoken he knew it was the truth. Visibly shaken, he felt barraged by flashes of memory. Abel's eyes. His eyes full of cruelty and hatred. Why? Why did Erik's mere existence evoke such hatred in this man's eyes, eyes that were an eerie green and black, eyes that Erik found strangely familiar to his own? How could it be? No, his mind rebelled against the obscene idea, it must be a lie! Yet, he felt it in his bones as he remembered Abel's face, his father's face!

"Your mother left Abel when she found she was pregnant. Several years later she came back with you, a misshapen thing even she couldn't stand to look at, clinging to her skirts. Abel would have drowned you except for me. I saved your miserable life!" Sabia gloated as she watched Erik reel from the blow of the last weapon she had in her arsenal. She would at least have this revenge against him.

He staggered from the tent. He knew he had to get away before he did something horrible to stop Sabia's mouth. She had kept this last piece of his story to use against him. She knew that it would cut him to the quick. Over and over he could hear her repeating, "You killed your father. You murdered your father." His father had locked him in a cage like an animal, had beat him, left him without food, warmth, or kindness. He had listened unmoved to his tears. He had let the crowd torment him. But even though he had been but a child, what Erik had done was still an unnatural act. He had murdered his own father!

He stumbled behind the lions' cages and retched until the convulsions were dry and painful. The midget who always dressed like a king called out to him to ask if he was all right; other workers paused in their daily chores as they passed by and stared and murmured among themselves, but none but Yayal approached.

"Stay away," Erik managed to say before Yayal was within arm's reach. Yayal heeded the warning—there was menace in Erik's voice.

Erik pushed past him and through the small crowd of carnies to his own tent. Inside was Vosh, the tall, thin old man who used to work the high wire and now did odd jobs to set up the tents and help with the crowds at night. Sometimes he sold tickets; sometimes he performed as a clown with the midgets. Erik had avoided exchanging but a handful of words with him. Vosh, like Sabia, knew Erik's past; he had worked in Abel's fair. He had recognized Erik the night he wandered into their camp site and brought the news to Sabia.

Ignoring the odd presence of the old man, Erik went to gather the last remnants of his meager belongings in the tent. Behind him, he heard Vosh audibly sigh. The old man had overheard Sabia's harangue.

"She would do anything to keep you under her power. She told you about your father, didn't she?"

"Careful, old man." Erik's heart still raced from the shock of what he had just learned. Of course, Vosh would have known his story as well as anyone who worked that fair years and years ago. All of them had known that Abel was the Devil's Child's true father, and they had all sat back and let him cage and abuse his son.

"He was a cruel man."

"You knew him. You knew what he was doing."

Vosh understood the accusation. "Yes."

Several silent moments passed before the old man continued, "Your mother was ill. She had nowhere else to leave you." Although Erik didn't respond, the old man continued to speak. "She worked the horses. She was lovely. Had a lovely voice, too. None of us thought she went of her own free will to Abel's bed. When it became obvious she was with child, she packed up one night and left. Abel was furious."

"She was ill?" he barely whispered, his face hidden from the old man.

"She was dying. Consumption. But that's not what killed her in the end. She brought you one afternoon to your father's tent. She never came back. Later we learned that she was trampled to death by a carriage that same day."

Suddenly Erik turned on the old man and gathered his collar in his fists and pushed him roughly up against the support pole in the tent.

"No more, old man! No more mothers and fathers. I've had my fill of mothers and fathers! No more." Erik's eyes were wet and glistening, and his breath came in ragged gasps. As suddenly as he had taken hold of the old man, he let loose of his collar and backed away. "Please. No more. I can't."

Vosh stepped closer to Erik and very cautiously laid his hand on his shoulder. They remained silent for a moment. "Her name was Laurette, *une petite ange.*"

Erik took the bundle he had gathered and without so much as a glance backwards went out to the waiting carriage.

CHAPTER 5

❀

Awaken

Several nights had come and gone. Annetta and Giuseppe stood vigil on their mistress's uneasy sleep. In and out of consciousness, the young woman struggled to come back.

No one heard from the master. He had rushed so suddenly from the room that no one had had time to ask him where he was bound or when he might return. He had left his frantic wife in the care of the servants of the villa. By the time Giuseppe had reached the front courtyard the dust had settled on the path. There was no sign of the master. The stable boy attested to the master's state of mind. When Don Erik pushed him aside and mounted the horse, the stable boy had understood that the master would brook no interference. Without a single word, the strange man had sped the animal down the path at full gallop.

Even after her husband had gone, Meg opened her eyes wide in fright. Seeing no one, she called out for help and blindly flailed her arms. Annetta sat beside her and restrained her so that she would not injure herself. Although she appeared to have awoken, she was not conscious of her surroundings. She fled unseen monsters, careened down dark twisting stairways, struggled locked somewhere in the nightmare of her own mind.

Later in the evening, after she had fallen into a soft, natural sleep, Annetta soothed her forehead with cool water. She crooned to her in lilting tones a nursery song she had sung to her own children. When Meg's eyes fluttered open, the room was lit by a sole candle. Annetta had drifted off in the chair beside the bed, her hand softly poised over the young woman's arm.

Meg felt as if her mind drifted free of her body, searching the unfamiliar room for a solid shape, one that did not waver and melt as she lit on it, one that was anchored strongly in the earth and would keep her from flying away, lost in the night. She imagined his face bending toward her from the darkness, his eyes soft with concern, a gentle smile that was meant only for her.

As Meg moved her arm, Annetta woke with a start.

"Oh, milady. It's all right. Just lie back," she muttered half in sleep.

Meg's throat was so dry that the words she tried to utter stuck and shattered on her tongue.

Realizing that the young mistress was no longer delirious, Annetta calmed her. She told Meg where she was and briefly described the accident. She introduced herself and encouraged the young woman to take some water. All the while, Meg searched the room for Erik. Annetta sensed her anxiety but said nothing.

After taking several sips, Meg managed to ask, "Where is he?"

Meg was unwilling to believe that Erik had left her forever. Annetta and Giuseppe did their best to comfort her. The old man sent his grown sons, who lived in a neighboring town, to the coastal city of Civitavecchia to see if the master had gone to the city to withdraw funds from the accounts that the solicitors had set up. He also asked them to comb the area discreetly to see if any stranger matching the master's description had taken lodging on the night of his disappearance. They had found nothing. It was as if the man had vanished.

When a week had passed and Erik had not returned or sent word, Meg dragged herself, dizzy and weak, from the bed and insisted on traveling the few miles to Pianosa. Although Giuseppe told her that no one in the town had ever laid eyes on the master, Meg couldn't shake the idea that Erik must be somewhere in the town, perhaps in one of the inns, licking his wounds. She sat in the open carriage, wrapped in a woolen cloak in spite of the late afternoon warmth and watched Giuseppe trudge into every public establishment there was in the moderate sized town. Each time, Giuseppe came out shaking his head, casting a woeful glance up at the mistress, and sighing for the inevitable disappointment he knew he'd bring her.

Giuseppe insisted that they had stopped at every respectable establishment that offered temporary or permanent lodging in Pianosa. Unfortunately, Meg had latched onto the word "respectable" and immediately pressed her manservant to disclose that in another section of town there were houses of ill repute where a man might find a room by the month, the week, the day, or even the hour. Without hesitation, she urged Giuseppe to take her there posthaste. No matter how Giuseppe argued, Meg simply pulled the woolen cape more tightly around her and pushed her chin forward in the direction she assumed they would be heading.

The buildings along the road lost their freshly painted facades, the crisp bold lettering of their signs, the steady traffic of expensively clad patrons alighting from barouche and carriage, the servants weighed down by packages in intricately tied boxes and heavy paper. Instead they became squat, blind, dingy one-story buildings with this year's name scrawled over ghostly former designations.

Erik had detested the inns they had encountered en route to Pianosa. If he had come to town in search of somewhere to live, it stood to reason that he would have avoided the upscale hotel in the heart of town, as well as the comfortable inns that catered to the wealthier travelers, foreign and national alike. She could imagine Erik continuing down the path in search of something quiet and unpretentious, a place where they wouldn't remark on his mask, but calculate their profits based on the fine cut of his vest. He might well end up on the less respectable side of Pianosa.

Then Meg heard music, a gay and popular medley of tunes, coming from one of the buildings.

"Stop here!" she demanded.

Giuseppe barely pulled the horses to a standstill when his mistress clambered down from the carriage. He followed quickly behind, as quickly as his arthritis would allow, pleading with the young woman to wait.

"Donna Meg, you can't go in there!" He might not have moved as agilely as the young Frenchwoman, but his stride was longer. He made it just before she reached the door. The music was loud and tinny. Laughter, both male and female, competed with the piano.

"Giuseppe, please stand aside."

"Donna Meg, you don't know what kind of establishment this is." He dared to take her elbow to turn her back toward the carriage. "You wait here. Let Giuseppe go in and inquire. But I'm sure the signore would not have come here."

Meg scowled at the old man. She resisted the slight pressure on her elbow.

"You think I don't know what this place is?"

Giuseppe's chin dropped slightly, but he said not a word.

"It's a bordello, I would imagine. Is that not the case?" she asked. Giuseppe's uncomfortable silence was confirmation of her guess. "I'm not shocked, and I'm not intimidated. If my husband is here, I want to speak with him."

"But the signore …" Giuseppe wanted to defend the master against such slander. Even though he didn't know Don Erik, he recalled the state he was in when he ran from the manor. He did not strike Giuseppe as the kind of man who would seek rooms in a bordello.

"The music, Giuseppe. It's the music that might have brought him here." For the first time in several days, Meg felt overwhelmed by the impossibility of finding Erik. In addition she was annoyed. It was not Giuseppe who had annoyed her, but Erik's unreasonable behavior. Annetta had explained over and over what had happened. But Meg could not remember. She knew Annetta would not lie. She had no choice but to accept that she had screamed in terror at the presence of her husband. Yes, she could understand what Erik would have thought, how he would have reacted. Even so she had not meant to push him away. She'd been delirious. Surely he would come back. Annetta said that he had barely eaten, that he had kept vigil over her the entire time she lay unconscious, and that she had never seen a man so desperate for his wife to wake.

Meg was tired of explaining Erik to the world. She was tired because she needed someone to explain Erik to her. She had thought she understood him.

"But Donna Meg, a respectable woman like you can't go inside a …"

Meg stepped around the old man, pushed open the door, and went inside. Flustered, Giuseppe followed his mistress. The room was gaily lit with candles and oil lamps for there was no natural light in the large room. Along one wall there stretched a long bar, behind which several half-clad women served drinks to a handful of men whose backs were to the door. At the far side of the room a piano was being played by a tall, thin man while a small group of women in brightly colored undergarments looked over his shoulder and sang the words. Throughout the area were small arrangements of overstuffed divans and chairs, some of which were currently being used. Meg noted that Erik was not among those lounging among the cushions, so she immediately ignored them. A stairway led to the upper rooms. Descending at the exact moment that Meg was about to ask to see the proprietor of the establishment were two women in loosely fitting silk robes on either side of a young man impeccably dressed except for the fact that his cravat lay untied around his neck. The women eyed Meg as if assessing whether or not she was equipped for the job. However it was apparent to everyone that Meg didn't belong in the bordello.

"Are you lost, Signorina?" The woman who approached Meg and Giuseppe was a large, buxom woman, nearly as tall as Giuseppe, with unnaturally black hair that Meg knew was dyed. Meg would guess that the woman was forty-five or more. Even so, she was still handsome.

"Signora. I'm here looking for my husband."

The music continued to play, but those nearby stopped their conversation to eavesdrop on Meg and the proprietress.

"Perhaps he's here because he doesn't want to be found," the tall, statuesque woman retorted. She looked down on Meg with obvious scorn.

"That may be true, but nevertheless I'm looking for my husband, and I need to know if he's here. Do you have any gentlemen who rent rooms by the day or week?"

"If you want my advice, your husband won't be happy to know that you've come after him. Go home. He'll come home when he's ready to play the gentleman again." The proprietress made as if to walk away from Meg, but Meg stepped forward to block her retreat.

"My husband and I had a disagreement."

"Oh, as if I've not heard that before."

"Please, you don't understand. He's been gone for nearly two weeks. He's a tall man." Meg looked about her to see if she could find anyone near Erik's height. "That one over there, with his back to us." Meg pointed to a man whose build reminded her of Erik. She couldn't see his face, but he was dark like Erik. From her angle, he seemed nearly as tall. "My husband is a bit taller than he is. He's broad in the shoulders. He …" Meg's lower lip trembled, her skin grew hot, and she knew she was about to cry. She was embarrassed and ashamed that the next words were obviously the most important words in her description. She didn't want to say them, but it was foolish to leave them out. "He wears a mask." She managed to blink away the tears before they formed, and taking new courage she met the other woman's gaze.

"A mask? You mean all the time?"

"Yes. Has anyone of that description come asking for lodging?"

"Lodging?" The proprietress couldn't resist sarcasm. Yet something about the earnestness of the petite blond Parisian touched her. Although she had assumed the Frenchwoman was playing out the eternal cliché of the woman whose husband prefers to pay for his sexual gratification, there was something honest and sincere about her that was utterly unique. So the proprietress took pity on Meg and decided to allay her fears. "No, my dear. We've no lodgers at the moment. No one fitting that description has come asking for a room. In case he does come by, what's he like without the mask?"

Meg didn't answer. Instead she glanced once more about the room and nodded. "Thank you," she said, making her farewell.

Giuseppe breathed a great sigh of relief when his mistress hurried out the door into the bright light of the afternoon.

Neither of them saw the tall man in the back of the room catch the proprietress by the arm, exchange several quick words, and follow them out onto the street. Nor did they notice him lean against the doorjamb and watch them as they made their way by the same road they had come.

It took only a few more weeks for Meg to realize two truths. First she admitted that Erik was gone, perhaps for good. Second she had every proof she needed to conclude that she was pregnant. Annetta had fussed over her young charge in those first days bringing her rich broths and hard-crusted bread. Meg's lack of appetite didn't strike anyone as strange at the time. However, a week later, Meg was still unable to eat more than a modest bowl of broth without becoming violently ill. These bouts of nausea seemed restricted to the morning hours. In the afternoon, Meg was not only clear-eyed but ravenous. She managed to eat heartier meals to make up for her morning fast.

Annetta asked several discreet questions some time toward the end of the second week. Meg mentally made her calculations and realized that her condition was not a result of the fall.

It would be understandable to say that Meg was of two minds about her condition. On the one hand, she was amazed and in awe. On the other hand, she was terrified. She immediately posted a letter to her mother to ask her to take a respite from her teaching and come stay with her until she was out of danger.

Meg was unable to admit the fear that dogged her once she knew in no uncertain terms that she was with child. She pushed it aside each time it reared its head. After the first few weeks, her appetite and energy had returned. For most of the day she was occupied and confident. She found a thousand things to do at the villa to make it a home for her and for her child. Late at night, alone in her bed, she spoke to the unborn child, telling him about his father, about her life in the Opera Populaire, about the plans she had had for herself and Erik and now had for the child. Then as she was about to doze off the fear would taunt her; it always came in Erik's voice.

What if the child dies? What if the child is deformed?

Her mother's presence both allayed and exacerbated her fears. Madeleine promised that she would stay as long as Meg needed her. She calmed all Meg's fears, except the one that Meg would not admit to her mother. Yet Madeleine's silence regarding Erik troubled Meg, making it impossible for her to find peace. Her mother had discouraged her relationship with Erik from the start. It irked Meg to know that Madeleine felt her misgivings confirmed. Erik had left Meg, broken her heart, and left her with his child. The intimacy between mother and daughter was strained by the one theme they could not discuss: Erik. Between them there was an unspoken truce, but its effect was not always beneficial. Meg held back, knowing her mother would only pity her were she to admit that she was bereft by Erik's abandonment and anxious for the health of the child.

The idea of children had only come up once between Erik and Meg. It had been on the trip to Pianosa. Meg had been describing the villa and mentioned that one of the rooms sounded ideal for a nursery. Erik snapped at her that he did not expect to be a father. She had been stunned both by his tone and by the statement itself. As if he had regretted his sharp tongue and sought to soften the warning, he confessed to her that he thought he was incapable of siring a child. He was not like other men. The silence between them had been tense. He must have realized how hurt she was. His eyes, usually so direct and piercing, wavered and turned away to stare out the carriage window. She barely heard him when he said that he was sorry for her disappointment. She had not been clever enough to act as if it didn't matter. Instead she allowed the rocking motion of the carriage, the silence, and the passing of time to dissipate the unspoken concern that separated them.

He had been wrong. However it was another matter dreaming of a child and knowing that a child grew inside her. In his vehemence to deny his possible paternity was there also fear? Had Erik been reluctant to imagine a child of his flesh because he feared it would resemble him? If the child bore the same face as the father, how could she protect him from the pain that Erik had suffered?

Yet, if Erik were gone forever, this was all she would ever have of him.

Shortly after she learned she was pregnant, Meg accepted an invitation to a dinner party at the Tedescos, a wealthy family in the region. Both her mother and Annetta had encouraged her to attend some of the social activities in the community. Her isolation was not healthy, and she needed to make a place for herself in Pianosa. For the same reason, Meg had also begun to attend mass at the country church. She was still in the early months of her pregnancy so that her condition was not overtly evident. She chose her gowns to hide the thickening of her waist and the growing protuberance of her abdomen. Even so, Meg was annoyed and puzzled by the exuberance with which several of the unattached men of Pianosa pressed their attentions upon her. They seemed to have forgotten that she was a married woman.

There were a handful of single women at the dinner, but Meg was embarrassed to find that the men overwhelmingly sought her out over the local beauties. Perhaps it was genuine interest in her. Perhaps it was her exotic nature. After all she was a foreigner, a Frenchwoman. But she suspected that it had more to do with her property than her person. She had made the mistake of smiling, being kind and friendly to one particular gentleman, a Giordino Lacosta. Given what he thought was her encouragement, Lacosta pursued her doggedly through the rooms at the Tedesco mansion with the relentlessness of a bloodhound.

She had unwisely drifted away, at one point, from the party, feeling slightly lightheaded. She found her way to a side parlor and was leaning against the back of a settee, with her eyes closed, when a large, male arm wrapped itself round her waist and back. She opened her eyes wide in shock to see Giordino Lacosta's face coming down to hers. It was evident that he was about to kiss her. Meg let out a small cry of annoyance and brought her arm up sharply to fend him off. The side of her forearm struck Lacosta hard under his chin. As he fell backwards, cursing with a lisp—he seemed to have bitten his tongue—Meg scurried toward the exit only to run straight into a human wall.

The moment she touched him, the memory of another man's body came to mind. She looked up, almost believing she would find Erik, to see in his stead a handsome face, whole and unblemished, admiring her. Giovanni Cimino had dark eyes, full lips, sharp bones, and a square jaw. Except for the fact that he didn't really look at all like Erik, he reminded her of him. Cimino took the situation in at a glance, set Meg to the side, and in the next moment took Lacosta firmly by the arm and ushered him from the premises.

Meg held her disappointment in check and thanked Signore Cimino for having come to her rescue. From that day on, Giovanni Cimino's presence seemed to keep the other suitors at bay. Meg was relieved. She felt safe in Giovanni's company. Unlike the other men, he offered friendship. And although Meg would not admit it, even to herself on most occasions, it soothed her loneliness to have him visit. He brought with him the memory of another man, and that memory was all she had to live on.

Civitavecchia was one of the larger cities in the area. Here Raoul's solicitors had deposited more than enough funds to keep Meg and Erik comfortable for the rest of their lives. Signore Cimino had suggested that Meg open an account in Pianosa with a portion of the funds so that financial matters could be more conveniently handled. The vineyards were close to harvest. Meg would need to hire workers. If funds were available in Pianosa, Signore Cimino would be most willing to help with the administration.

Giuseppe drove Meg into the city to sign the necessary papers. She would take advantage of the trip and make some purchases that were not possible in the smaller town of Pianosa. Annetta and a young boy from the villa who came to help with the packages lagged behind as Meg went from shop to shop. She caught sight of the sign out of the corner of her eye. It was nailed to a wall of a barber shop. She stood as if the language were not one she could understand and read it over several times. Annetta drew up behind her mistress and read over her shoulder:

> Half Angel, Half Devil
> Come See the Bizarre Product of
> The Marriage of Heaven and Hell

"Get the carriage."

Annetta sent the boy for Giuseppe, but Meg was too excited to wait. She stopped several passersby before she got sufficiently clear directions to where the fair had staked its tents.

"But Donna Meg, the fair won't open until later this evening." Meg rushed by Annetta as if she hadn't spoken.

Within minutes, the tops of the tents were visible in the distance. Meg forced Giuseppe to whip the horses into a canter. Before he had even secured the reins, Meg was on the ground and heading for the thick of the tents.

She had to find him. What could have possessed him to join a fair? It made sense to her yet it was horrid. This was the life he had known as a child. This was the horror from which Madeleine had saved him. She ignored the curious stares of the men and women who, in the fallow hours of the day, attended the animals, practiced their acts, sat around playing at games of chance, lay on the ground soaking up the late rays of the afternoon sun. A man called out to her to ask her business. She ignored him and went on.

She passed wagons, each one announcing its act in garish painted images on its side. None among them seemed to promise the Devil's child. What would he call himself, this half demon, half angel? What would he call himself, her poor lost soul?

Rounding a corner she nearly tripped over several small figures. At first she thought they were children, but one was bearded and the other had small, firm breasts.

"Where is the exhibit of the half angel, half devil?" she asked.

The diminutive, but exquisite, woman spoke in a high pitched voice that reminded Meg of the upper notes of a flute. She indicated the tent just steps away. Meg barely nodded her thanks and went directly to the entrance. There were no paintings on the exterior, no signs to speak of. The tent itself was small, and Meg realized that it might well be private quarters. Seeing no way to announce herself, she pulled the tent flap aside and stepped into the dark interior. It was gloomy. Only a small lamp was lit on a table far from the entrance. She searched the dimness trying to make out the objects.

"Well, what do we have here?" A dark shadow separated itself from its darker surroundings and came forward into the path of the gloomy light.

Meg knew immediately. It was not his voice. It was not his body. It was not Erik. The shadow grew larger and took on color and depth. She could see the telltale signs of red paint in the corner of the creases round his nose and eyes. He was dressed only in large, baggy workpants, his dark shirt lay open to the waist. She could see that his chest was completely bare, as if he had shaven it. His face was long, and the goat-like beard made his chin incredibly sharp. She was amazed to see that he was even taller than Erik.

Meg took a step back as the man grew so large that he blotted out the dim rays of the lamp behind him. Cast in shadow, his features became indistinguishable, his silhouette sharply outlined. Meg thought she saw the points of two small horns sticking out of his short black hair.

She fell back out into the bright light of day. Erik was gone. He had disappeared like he had so often threatened. A ghost was what he had called himself. All she had was his child, a child sired by a ghost, a phantom.

As she turned and ran, she heard him laugh, a deep and wicked laugh that rang in her ears long after she passed the wagon with the picture of the same man on its side, long after she saw the red pointed face, two horns sticking incredibly far above the black hair, and a pair of beautiful white wings unfurled from somewhere behind his shoulders.

CHAPTER 6

❦

The Feast

In visions of the dark night
I have dreamed of joy departed—
But a waking dream of life and light
Hath left me broken-hearted.

"A Dream" Edgar Allan Poe

The view of the estate as the carriage came over the rise filled Erik with foreboding. The blackened stone and the exterior crenellation recalled a medieval fortress. The flying buttresses along one extreme of the building protected tall stained glass windows. The overall impression was one of time-consuming and labor-intensive work over the course of generations. Erik thought of the gothic romances so popular among the chorus girls at the Opera as he examined the rows of windows along the structure and wondered how many bedrooms the estate might have. He searched the ramparts for a gargoyle or two, but was disappointed. He laughed sardonically to himself as the carriage rolled in front of the huge wooden door framed by a stone archway. Perhaps he could haunt the estate for Don Ponzio! A footman came to open the door and welcome him to the Fiortino manor.

After several days on the road, days that recalled to him the discomfort and humiliation of his first journey into Italy with Meg nearly three years ago, Erik vowed he would never travel by means of carriage again. He would have much preferred riding by himself, on horseback, and sleeping in the woods to sitting inside the carriage and stopping at the inns along the way. His bones felt as if they had been disconnected and thrown into a bag and jostled.

He was shown into a large central hallway whose ceiling extended to the second floor. At the back of the space rose a marble staircase to an open gallery above; corridors branched out from the gallery in two separate and asymmetrical directions. Along the walls by the staircase were portraits of serious men with riding crops or swords or dressed in military uniforms and proud women boasting the fashions of the moment, Don Ponzio's ancestors no doubt. Most of the subjects had the same long sharp nose, the same narrow eyes and thin lips as Don Ponzio. Erik imagined that those who did not were relatives by marriage to the family. The manservant that escorted him into the hallway apologized for the absence of the master and mistress and begged Erik to follow him to his appointed chambers. He walked stiff-backed, his eyes never engaging Erik's, leading the newly arrived guest to the west wing. All the servants walked soundlessly across tile and wooden floors, not a sound issuing from their footfalls, and they wore serious, Erik thought gloomy, expressions. Not one looked him directly in the eye. He imagined that perhaps they had been instructed to avoid staring at the invited exhibit. Their disregard of him was so acute that he wondered if they would notice if he removed his mask.

Erik was impressed by the grandeur, the details of the columns and balustrades; he liked running his hand along the wood carvings. The manservant opened the door and invited Erik inside a huge, airy bedroom with a heavy, upholstered sofa near the windows. A wardrobe closet with full-length beveled mirror in the center stood opposite the four poster bed. A marble wash stand occupied the inner corner of the room, far from the windows and the draft, and next to it was a small dressing table. A writing desk was to the side of the window opposite the sofa. Large pillows and cushions decorated the sofa and bed in yellow ochre, terracotta and gray-green. The chest at the foot of the bed was open, and Erik saw within an array of bedding for the cold night's air.

"Signora Fiortino commends herself to you and expresses her hope that the journey has not been too taxing. She will await your company for dinner at nine, if that is agreeable with the gentleman?"

Erik turned and bowed graciously to the manservant and replied, "Please give your lady my thanks, and let her know that I will be happy to dine with her at her convenience." He was unfamiliar with such formality, but its very exaggeration allowed him to mimic scenes he recalled from operas performed at the Opera Populaire. Evidently, the quotations he employed seemed appropriate to the circumstances for the manservant accepted his courteous yet pompous reply without hesitation or remark and backed out of the room, closing the doors behind him.

Lucianna's auburn hair loose on her shoulders, ever so soft, she gallops in the moonlight, her slender form reclines against the horse's body, her skirt flaps at the side of her legs, she sits across the chestnut like a man, all power and grace, in the moonlight her hair is black, her face in shadows, her eyes shine, I take her face in my hands and stoop to taste her mouth, Don Ponzio's face leers at us from the darkness, the tent is empty except for Don Ponzio, I look for Lucianna but can't find her, I feel wrapped in darkness, Don Ponzio's lips, thin and cruel, his teeth red with blood, her auburn hair wet against my chest, her skin white alabaster, her eyes dead, blood drips down my body from a gaping wound in her throat, my hand bashes Don Ponzio's face, his eyes mock me, his head bounces away from me like a clown's face struck with a rubber stick, the tent is falling in on me, the tarp gags me, I push it away trying to breathe, someone pulls it away from my face, her hands small and white, such small fingers, they stroke my face, her voice coos at me words that make no sense, I lie in her arms, tender, thin arms that warm me, her blond hair falls across my throat as she kisses soft, wet caresses on my face, my mask is gone, she kisses my face, all my face, the soreness around my disfigured eye melts away, she calls me her love, her angel, her blond hair and her heart-shaped face, she smiles at me with her brown eyes, her mouth forms the sounds of my name, she asks me to teach her the melody, she asks if her voice is ready, I squeeze her hand, yes, Meg, your voice is glorious, you will delight them all as you have delighted me, she smiles but her smile disappears into a frown, I haven't told her that her voice is glorious, I have merely shrugged my shoulders and told her it's her decision, if she thinks she is ready to sing, then she should, I turn from her, she runs to me, and I push her away, she kisses me and I strike her, she cries and I laugh, Christine scolds me, she tells me that I lie, she knows that I am cruel to Meg for no reason except I fear she will reject me, I lie in my chamber under the opera house, all my music is around me, Meg lies beside me, I reach out to touch her but the bed becomes incredibly large, Meg is farther and farther away from my touch, Lucianna climbs into the bed from the foot, she drapes her auburn hair around me, it's long and covers me like a blanket, it ties me to her, I can't move, she is naked except for the cover of her hair, I hear Meg in the distance, she is telling me something, but Lucianna is talking to me and kissing my mouth, and she places her hands over my ears so I can't hear, something muffled, something tells me to wake up, there is a man's voice in the room . . .

I apologized for keeping her waiting. I had lain down only to rest for a moment before dinner and fell into a deep sleep. The servant came to wake me from my dream; I could remember only that Meg was in the dream. A tremendous sadness assailed me as I woke and recognized my surroundings. Even after all this time, I couldn't escape the sense of loss and regret when I thought of her. My only consolation was that I had set her free. I no longer plagued Meg's life.

I dressed quickly and descended the stairs to the main hall. Hearing my approach, Lucianna came from the conservatory and greeted me with a smile. She took my arm and led me to the dining room. The scent of her body—lilac and soap—wrapped around me like a gentle embrace. Her hair tightly coiled and pinned up off her long graceful neck seemed alive and poised to break loose from its pins and clasps so as to twist and twirl around her throat past the alabaster of her exposed shoulders. My lips tingled as my eye traced the path from the nape of her neck to the rise of her breasts. I became aware that I was staring at her when I noticed her cheeks were suffused with a deep red. I released her arm reluctantly so that she could take her seat at the opposite side of the table. I turned my gaze from the contours of her body to the bounteous display of food set out before us.

She remarked that the wine was from Don Ponzio's own vineyards and winery. It was quite light and refreshing. Evidently I drained the glass rather quickly, for Lucianna laughed at me as she sipped at hers. I promised I would be more careful to take the next one slowly. I hadn't had a good glass of wine in a long, long time. The second glass went down as easily as the first, but it left a strange aftertaste, and I refused a third. The warmth of the wine began to relax me, and after several courses I was sated and anxious for the servants to leave us so that we could talk.

Lucianna spoke with a gaiety that struck me as forced. She suggested we retire to the conservatory to have tea. She again took my arm, but this time she pressed her body against me in such a way that the intimacy aroused me greatly. Her hand squeezed my forearm tightly, and I sensed that she was afraid. She whispered as she pulled me down toward her, "We're not alone. We can talk in the conservatory."

The conservatory had high ceilings and a row of windows that opened onto a veranda. The view in the light of day must be spectacular—the blanket of meadows, the vineyard in the distance, the unobstructed panorama of the grounds. Without asking, Lucianna served me another glass of wine. Then she led me to the piano and invited me to sit beside her on the bench. She began to play a simple concerto which allowed us to talk quietly without being intelligible to anyone who might be listening.

"You should never have come. You don't know what my husband is capable of; he's a cruel man with no conscience. You must leave before he makes his presence known."

"Why do you stay with him?"

"You think I would be here if I had a choice? I only married him because he threatened my family, and my father was forced to give him my hand. Ponzio married me to get himself an heir. I've already lost two babies, and he blames me. He says I'm a barren field where he wastes his seed." She paused on the keyboard, embarrassed. "I'm sorry. Those are his words, you understand. I think he tires of me and wants to remarry. My presence makes that impossible. I fear he invited you because you are somehow a part of his plan." She made several mistakes in the performance of the concerto as she blinked to clear her vision. I stilled my hand against the urge to touch her.

"I'd never hurt you."

"Not willingly, not purposefully, not knowingly. My husband is a devious man." Her voice grew thin and high. She leaned over the keys as if to hide from me.

"I'd never hurt you. There's nothing he could do to make me harm you," I repeated. She was very afraid. I could feel her tremble.

"I want you to leave!" she insisted. "It's our only hope."

"You have little faith in me," I accused her. Why would she think her husband could so easily manipulate me? Did he know who I was? Did he know of the violence I had already committed? Sabia knew the story of my childhood, and if Ponzio had acquaintances in Paris, he might have heard the infamous story of the Phantom of the Opera. It would not take much for him to draw connections between the Phantom and the Angel in Hell. I vowed that I wouldn't let anyone have power over me again. Even if he threatened to turn me in to the police here or to have me dragged back to Paris to face the hangman's noose again, I would not be used to harm Lucianna. I would find some way to protect her from her husband.

It occurred to me that perhaps he had brought me here to be the scapegoat. I was simply the monster that would be accused of Lucianna's tragic end. It would make sense. I would be an easy suspect if Lucianna were murdered or died under mysterious circumstances. After all, I had murdered before.

"Play something if you like. It's a beautiful instrument." She slid over to allow me to occupy the center of the bench.

"The keys are a bit flat; the upper octave strings are fraying and should be replaced." Without waiting for a response, I drained the last of the wine she had served me and began to play a slow, haunting melody that didn't require great dexterity or rapidity of movement. Since Inspector Leroux and his men had broken my fingers in prison, I feared that I was no longer able to play like the virtuoso that I had once been. In spite of the slight imperfections of the instrument, I found myself lost in the music. I had forgotten Lucianna's presence as well as the threat of Ponzio. The melody changed, became something deeper, more disturbing, the notes complex and challenging. I pushed myself, testing my agility until the discomfort became acute. Slowly I brought the piece under gentle control, back to its melodic simplicity.

As my fingers hovered and stroked the keys, Lucianna rose and stood behind me. She leaned her body into mine. I stiffened my spine, but pushed back against her in response. She placed her hands lightly on my shoulders and gradually leaned her face close to mine. She slid her hands down my chest, I could feel her breasts pressed tightly against me through the fabric of our clothing. Suddenly, my head began to swim. I stopped in mid-phrase and rose from the bench. The air had gone stale, and I needed to get away. I latched onto the edge of the piano, but felt myself tilt precariously to the side. The room was spinning. The wine. There was an aftertaste. There was something in the wine, I thought. I saw regret in Lucianna's eyes as her hands reached out to me and the chandelier came dancing into the center of my vision …

When he woke and opened his eyes, the pain that seared across his forehead forced his eyes closed again and made him gasp audibly. Slowly he turned his head to accustom himself to the pain. Pain doesn't kill, he reminded himself. Pain is simply a mode of existence, a way of being. Once you know it can't kill you, you can bear it. He tried to bring his hand across his face to soothe his brow. Instantly he opened his eyes wide to verify the fact he already knew. His hands were restrained. He lay on the mattress, naked except for a blanket carelessly thrown across his body, his legs and arms manacled and secured to the posts at each end of the bed. Panic. A blinding white panic. His blood pumped so rapidly that he felt the rising pressure would burst his heart. The pain in his forehead and the tension at his temples pulsed in rhythm with his heart beat. He could reach the bed post with the pad of his foot. He stretched to the fullest extent the bondage allowed and kicked with the flat of his foot against the wooden post. A solid walnut, it didn't budge, not the first time, nor the second. Again he pounded it. Again. Again and this time he heard a distinct crack and saw the slightest tremble in the wood. He renewed his efforts trying to silence the rising scream of frustration and anger in his throat.

And then he woke up. The sunlight blinded him as it shone across the bed. He shielded his eyes reflexively drawing his hand to his face. He sat up in the bed. He found he was in a night shirt, not his own, and that he was twisted in this and the bed clothes themselves. He became aware of a gentle, but persistent, knocking at the bedroom door.

"Go away!" he yelled and immediately regretted it for the pain in his dream was also in his head and threatened to cleave his forehead in two.

"With all due respect, sir, will you need assistance in dressing? Don Ponzio hopes that you will join him in the smoking room."

He wanted to shout back that all he needed was to be left alone but restrained himself. Don Ponzio had returned. He cast his thoughts back to the previous evening. What had happened? He remembered the piano. Lucianna was pressed seductively against him. Nothing, nothing more.

"I've been dressing myself since ..." Raising his voice had set off several explosions behind his eyes. He groaned and held his balled fists against them. In a softer voice, so as to soothe the unforgiving pain in his head, he called out, "Never mind. Come in. At least you can bend over. I'm afraid my head will fall off if I attempt it."

He clenched his jaw tight in vexation when he realized that his wardrobe had been supplemented by several new articles of clothing that must have belonged to Don Ponzio. While Erik stood by, the valet laid them out carefully on the bed. Erik had always taken what he needed—and only what he needed—and was offended by Don Ponzio's assumption that his wardrobe was insufficient. He took each foreign article and tossed it in a heap to the floor for the valet to pick up and fold. Then he instructed the manservant to lay out his own garments in their place. Begrudgingly he allowed the valet to assist him as he dressed in the simple but elegant clothes that he himself had packed. After the man had helped Erik with his boots, he dismissed him. He had never been dressed by another man before, and it had not been pleasant.

As he left the room, he couldn't help but recall the dream. It had been so vivid that he almost rubbed at the skin about his wrists as if the rope had indeed left its mark.

I found myself the center of attention among Don Ponzio's guests. I recognized the Stattores immediately, but there were others, mostly couples, a few unattached women as well as some bachelors of varying ages that were clearly intimate friends of the host and little admired by his wife. I feared that I had made a tremendous mistake placing myself within Don Ponzio's sphere of influence. He was obviously displeased that I had not dressed in the attire that he had patronizingly placed at my disposal. The dream I had that morning flashed across my mind as I listened to the introductions and strove to ignore the naked fascination my presence stirred among this set of infinitely bored and deeply decadent aristocrats. I stiffened, wary of the expectations yet to be disclosed by my host. Trapped in his web, it was imperative that I remain aloof and alert or perhaps that dream would come true.

Over dinner Don Ponzio's guests bombarded me with questions, many of which bordered on the ridiculous but most of which insisted on the scandalous. The party struck me as an alternative stage, the social banter simply another version of the freak show. The only difference was that these spectators felt they had the right to interact with the freak, even to direct the show themselves instead of remaining attentive and passive in the audience. Don Ponzio had promised them a bizarre conversation with the monster himself, the "Angel in Hell." My mask afforded me protection for the moment and a certain amount of impunity. I answered some questions, ignored most—to Don Ponzio's sardonic delight and surprise—and retorted offensively in many cases when questions merited it. The ladies were more circumspect than the gentlemen, but were delighted to find that the men often voiced their unspoken desires for the titillating and outrageous. The conversation ranged from questions regarding my humanity—the very nature of my bodily functions were part and parcel of their scientific examination of me—to efforts to unravel my personal history.

As we retired to the conservatory for cognac and tea, the postprandial talk took a more philosophical turn. I had felt uncomfortable in the previous discussion, but the new tact was even more troubling. They had decided that I was human, a man of sorts, but there remained the question of my soul. Did I have one? I had skirted the issues of my past, refusing to answer most of their questions. I insisted on responding only to my given name, Erik, refusing to address the issue of my illegitimacy. I let them believe I simply withheld my surname because I wished to remain anonymous. They interpreted the apparent gaps in my narrative as an effort to protect my identity or my family's identity. It was clear that most of them thought this a confession of a life of perversion and crime. I let the assumption stand. After all it enhanced the illusion of power and danger that might protect me from them. The price, nonetheless, was that they thought me as depraved and wicked as they were.

A buxom, overly powdered and rouged matron that had taken every opportunity that presented itself during the evening to touch me strolled over to my chair and brushed up against my arm as closely as her petticoats would allow and asked, "Your face, Erik. Why do you think you have been marked in this way?"

She stood fanning herself as she examined the skin near the edge of the mask where it failed to cover completely my disfigurement. I had been unable to purchase masks specifically designed for my features, and the ones that I had selected served my purposes only imperfectly. She seemed excited by the discovery of a narrow slice of the red, uneven tissue of my deformity. Her curious stare burned like the flame of a candle brought too near my skin. I shifted away from her in my seat before I answered.

"Perhaps it is to remind others that the apparent world we inhabit is illusory. When people see my face they know the ugliness lying at the heart of material existence. They know death is their inevitable destiny. They know that under their finery, they are walking corruption."

"I cannot agree with you!" It was the first time in the entire evening that I had heard Lucianna's voice. "I think it is rather to force us to look beyond that surface to find that which is truly beautiful, to teach us that the material world is illusory, but that there is true beauty, hidden, in the soul, in art, in love."

I turned toward her as others became involved in the discussion. I didn't follow what they said, though, because I was transfixed by Lucianna's gaze. She looked at me with such earnest tenderness as if she were willing me to recognize that my deformity was only superficial, supremely unimportant.

I thought of the last time I had seen Meg, Meg who had loved me and had seen my soul.

"What if I could prove to you, Signora Fiortino, that the hideous stamp on my face has marked even my soul? That all that I am and that I've done arises inextricably from the ugliness of this face? That there is no beauty hidden by this face?" As I spoke I became increasingly angry and bitter. I wanted to destroy her! Why I addressed, in this way, the only person in the room who had shown me the least compassion, the least recognition of my dignity as a human being, I couldn't say. I was mercilessly cruel to myself, and I could see that this self loathing distressed Lucianna more than my vicious attack on her.

She audaciously retorted as if no one else but the two of us were in the room. "You couldn't prove that to me. Whatever you've done, it must arise as much or more from the cruel ways in which others have considered you because they have *not* seen you, really seen you. They saw your face, your unfortunate deformity, not *you!*"

I stood suddenly, angry beyond my control, my only desire to stop her from talking, to flee the room. I slammed my fist down onto the side table shattering my glass whose shards fell to the floor. I growled ominously at her, a sound deep in my chest. "I will *not* be pitied."

The others in the room froze in shock at my outburst. Only Don Ponzio seemed to be immune to the general astonishment my belligerent response wrought. His lips curled sardonically into a cold smile as he flicked the ash from the end of his cigar, his eyes darting back and forth between me and his wife.

I struggled to regain control of my anger. A servant silently came to brush up the shards of glass. Out of the corner of my eye, I saw the napkin he offered me. Wrapping the cloth around my bleeding hand gave me time to collect myself. No one spoke. Avoiding Lucianna as well as Don Ponzio, I straightened my pant leg and sat down as if nothing had happened.

"Bravo! Bravo, Erik! So I take it that you wish to offer proof?" Don Ponzio clapped his hands lightly together and encouraged the guests to do likewise. I bit the inside flesh of my lip to keep from reacting. "I never told you that my wife is a consummate artist, did I? She does portraits. A truly talented eye she has for her subjects. I have requested that she paint your portrait."

I felt ice course through my veins, and a pain sharp and piercing sliced through my gut. I willed myself not to look over to Lucianna. It wasn't necessary for I heard the sharp intake of air that she made.

"You will make such an interesting subject. Don't you agree?" He addressed this to his guests who made several indications of their agreement and delight. "Well, as we discussed before you accepted my invitation to spend time with us in my home, I hope you will do us the favor of unmasking yourself."

The excitement in the room nauseated me. "As we discussed, I decide when and when not to remove my mask. I choose not to." Don Ponzio's smile slipped only momentarily, but his eyes were like flint.

"May I ask when we will have the privilege of seeing you without it?" He barely disguised the impatience in his voice.

"We will have a double unveiling. When Signora Fiortino unveils her portrait, I will unmask so that you can all judge how well she has captured my soul."

CHAPTER 7

❦

The Portrait

move him to the sofa, leave us, footsteps, someone tugs at him, he feels as if the room were moving underneath him, the pull of the fabric along his skin, the coolness of air hitting uncovered flesh, his skin tingles, his body hair stands on end, sensations of coolness on his stomach, his groin, his thighs, shadows shift and float over his face, *are his eyes open?* he groans, he pushes his eyebrows up on his forehead to force his eyelids to move, a soft cascade of curls brushes across his face, he tastes a strand that drops across his parted lips, he hears a woman's voice, Meg's voice? no, someone else's voice asks in fear, *are his eyes supposed to be open like that?* another voice mumbles, a woman's voice comforts him or her? *he can't see anything* the voice answers, a weight presses against his groin, he is aroused, he must be dreaming, dreaming of Meg, her small lithe body, a body made to dance on the stage, a body made to please a man, her body claims him, possesses him, wraps around him, he is incredibly warm, flushed with blood rising to the surface, the weight shifts deliciously, pressing and releasing and squeezing and rubbing, his breathing follows the rhythm, increasing its speed as the movement along his groin, along his hips, grows more earnest, harder, more intense, he squeezes his eyes shut with the sudden pleasure that erupts along his body, he tenses and jerks with the pleasure and yet the weight shifting, the rhythmic moving and kneading across his body persists insistent, driving, demanding and abruptly grinds into him, a soft wetness spreads out across his abdomen and along his inner thighs, the dream is intense, too intense, it leaves an ache where his pleasure should be, his arms are heavy, he feels like wet clay, unformed, immobile, waiting to be shaped and molded, he thinks, no, he can't think, he dreams of Meg who wipes the semen away from his body and dries his skin, hands cover him, the friction of the fabric too soon drags across his sensitive flesh, he waits for her to lie beside him, to place her head on his shoulder, he waits to feel her cheek on his chest, her hair against his throat, he must be dreaming, he must be asleep in the villa, Meg will come in with cut flowers from her garden, she opens the drapes and the southern sun fills the bedroom, their bedroom, with a bright warm light, a breeze gently touches his face, Meg sings a country song she's learned from the villagers near Pianosa, they will walk through the vineyard, she holds his hand and points with delight to the improvements she's made to the retaining wall, the growth of the blueberry bushes she planted with his help last season, their hands sank deep into the black soil crumbling the clots, freeing the cold, slick worms wriggling to be free, they laughed as they set the roots of the bushes and covered them, tamping down the moistened earth around the young plants, they will eat blueberries, the cook will make blueberry muffins, blueberry pies, they will sit in the arbor of their home and eat the sweet pulp, Meg will laugh, her lips stained with the juice of the berries, her fingers blackened by the dark purple stain, her hands push at him, he hears her call him, she says his name over and over, she tells him to wake up, her finger tips stained by paint, the smudge of ochre and scarlet along the soft fleshy sides of her hand, a paint brush sticks out from her auburn hair, she jostles him softly, he blinks several times trying to focus on the auburn hair tied up off her neck, her brow heavy with concern, her eyes showing relief as he stares back at her in recognition, Lucianna leans in towards him and asks if he's all right, the words break the crystal of his dream, he starts at the sound of its crash and the sudden movement in the chair sets off a wave of pain in his temples, across the dome of his skull, he grimaces at the pain, pushes away the confusion to find himself seated in the chair opposite Lucianna's easel, Lucianna leaning toward him solicitously asking if he is awake, telling him he dozed as she was drafting the preliminary sketches for the portrait, he trembles and holds back the desire to howl in grief as the images of Meg and their villa recede into the emptiness of wishes, he focuses on Lucianna's stained fingers and takes a deep breath to clear his mind, his eyes glisten with unshed tears, Lucianna expresses her concern and suggests they resume the pose tomorrow

"Who's Meg," Lucianna asked as she mixed the colors on the palette.
"How do you know that name?" Erik asked, suddenly on guard.

"You spoke it several times in your sleep the other day when I was sketching you."

"A character in a bad French opera I once saw."

"Really? And what made it so bad?"

"The hero was also the villain. He threw away his only chance for happiness to wallow in self pity."

"It was a tragedy, I see."

"No. It was actually a farce. You had to laugh at the poor fool."

"And he was in love with this Meg?"

"He was. But he didn't know it until it was too late."

Lucianna stopped mixing the paints and studied Erik. He stared out the window, but she could tell he was seeing only what was in his mind.

"Has your headache gone away?"

"Yes, it has."

"I hope you're not coming down with anything. Your sleep habits are quite strange. I heard you up last night pacing back and forth in your room."

"I want to leave. I'm restless."

Lucianna looked away when Erik turned suddenly to meet her gaze. He needed to see her reaction to his announcement. She had turned incredibly pale, her cheeks a stark white against the darkening hues of auburn hair that framed her face.

"Don't worry, Lucianna. I won't leave you until we've found a solution for your situation."

She hid her face behind the easel and murmured her relief. Erik rose and came toward her. She quickly brought the drop cloth down over the canvas on which she was working before Erik could catch a glimpse of the progress she was making. She smelled fresh and vibrant like a ride on a cold morning. He so longed to see the brash, willful creature he had met that night in the stable. Don Ponzio had nearly broken her spirit. He prayed that he had not been completely successful.

"Is Don Ponzio away again this afternoon?" Erik returned to the sofa and assumed the pose she had placed him in every day for the past several weeks.

"Yes, I believe he has just left a half an hour ago." She dropped her brush on the floor and nearly toppled the canvas from its stand as she bent to pick it up. Erik noted a slight tremble in her voice as she asked if he would like a glass of port.

He paused before replying. He watched her cross to the cabinet and take down the decanter. He noticed that she placed it on the buffet table and stepped between him and the bottle so that he could only see her back as she served out the liquor. He studied her as she turned and walked toward him. A strained smile spread across her lips as she nervously offered him the drink that he had not requested.

"Thank you," he said as he took the crystal glass. She stood as if to watch him drink. Erik simply held the glass in his hand and waited for her to return to the easel. The moment she turned away from him, Erik drained half of the glass into the potted fern beside the chair.

Within minutes Erik's head lolled back on the chair, and his eyes closed. The glass began to tip over, but Lucianna caught it before its contents spilled on the carpet beneath his feet.

"Greta, come help me," she whispered at the doorway. A large servant came in wiping her hands on the half apron tied around her waist. She took Erik under the arms and pulled him as Lucianna grabbed on to his feet. The sofa was directly behind the chair, a very short distance fortunately for the two of them. Without speaking, they unfastened his breeches and pulled them down. Greta turned, now that her job was done, and left the room. Lucianna took several moments to admire Erik as he lay asleep on the sofa before she hiked up her skirts and sat across his hips. She had not put on her underclothing that morning in preparation for this. She noticed Erik's eyes slowly open, but Greta had assured her that he was unaware of her presence or her actions in this drugged state. His ability to open his eyes without necessarily understanding what he was seeing as well as his ability to react to her physical demand were all part of the benefits of this particular brew. The only drawback that she found was that it left Erik with a severe headache and in some discomfort after it wore off. Greta said this, too, was normal and that the headaches and malaise were transitory and would cause no permanent damage.

She had come to look forward to these interludes even though she felt incredibly wicked and guilty afterwards. She had found it nearly impossible to look Erik in the eye after the first time, without blushing or begging for his forgiveness. She had initiated this plan as a last desperate effort to provide Don Ponzio with an heir. She was convinced that Ponzio was incapable of siring a healthy offspring.

She had only two fears. One, she feared Erik would find out. She couldn't imagine how he might react or what he might do. Her second fear was the child. He might inherit Erik's disfigurement. If all his positive characteristics were inheritable, couldn't his deformity also be passed on to his child? If this were to happen, she and the infant would most probably be murdered by

Ponzio. But it was a risk she would take. If she did not produce a healthy heir soon, she knew what her husband was capable of doing. She had faith that Erik would inseminate her with a robust child. Aside from his face, he was a marvelous example of manhood, strong and virile, and his mind was exceptional. She prayed that his offspring would be strong and intelligent and artistic like the two of them.

She had stirred Erik sufficiently to begin to enjoy her position. She moved with no thought but her own pleasure, knowing that Erik's body would respond in kind. Her eyes closed, her lips partially opened, she tilted her head toward the ceiling and arched her back gently to catch the rhythm of her desire. She became aware that his hands had reached up to caress her breasts through the fabric of her bodice. Startled she began to rise from his lap, but he grabbed her firmly and brought her hips down again in place. She started to panic, but he held her tightly against him. He moved deep inside her, gently grinding and pressing upward, and she no longer resisted. He rubbed his hands along the sides of her torso, over the taut firm muscle of her abdomen, over her breasts, along her throat, behind her neck under her hair and brought her down until her lips rested against his mouth. The intense culmination of the act that she had experienced with Erik before was surpassed by several moments of intense convulsions, ripples of pleasure, throughout her body. Time and time again, she felt she had arrived at the apex of this pleasure only to climb and climb again to reach a further peak. They remained locked together until both were carried away by increasingly intense waves of ecstasy that left them depleted.

She lay across his chest until they began to breathe again at a normal rate. He resisted only momentarily when she lifted herself from him and straightened the folds of her skirt. She went to the door and whispered something to someone on the other side. Within moments, a warm basin of water and several towels were delivered to Lucianna who brought them to a table near Erik. He lay there watching her. When he didn't rise, she moistened one edge of a towel and handed it to him. He didn't take it, so she gently washed him herself as she had done the other times. He lifted his hips, pulled his breeches up, and fastened them himself. She gnawed at her lower lip, frantic for him to say something so that she would know where they now stood. Finally exasperated, she demanded in a tone that was somewhere between frantic and annoyed, "Well, say something. Call me a whore! Slap me. Do something. Say something!"

"I thought you preferred me silent and immobile," Erik said quietly with only a slight edge of sarcasm.

"No, not at all," she answered him breathlessly. "I much prefer what just happened."

"Needless to say, so do I."

"How long have you known?"

"Not long. The last time you served me a cognac, I was on the edge of consciousness. I thought I was dreaming, but some things broke through. I was beginning to think I was seriously ill, that I had a brain tumor; the headaches are extremely painful, like glass cutting across one's brain."

"I'm sorry." Erik saw that she was sincere. She backed away from him taking refuge behind her easel. "I was worried. I planned to stop as soon as …"

Puzzled, Erik asked her to go on.

At that moment, Don Ponzio came into the workshop and demanded to see the portrait. Lucianna, surprised by his early return, blushed violently for one moment and then turned to greet her husband.

"You know that I don't like anyone seeing my work until it's finished." Lucianna smiled brightly as she took Don Ponzio's arm and steered him toward the door.

"Erik." Don Ponzio brushed her hand away from his arm and approached Erik. "You are wearing your mask! But I thought my wife was painting the true Angel in Hell. Surely it's not fair for you to wear your mask and at the same time dare my wife to paint your soul?"

"He needn't take it off until next week. At the moment I am working on general contours." Her explanation struck Erik as a half truth. It left a bitter taste in his mouth as if he had indeed drunk the drugged port.

"How do you like the Arabian, Erik? You seem to know your horse flesh among other things." Don Ponzio mounted a black stallion, Charlemagne, that was a direct descendent of full-blooded Arabians his father had personally brought back from his travels in the East. Erik sat on the next generation, a young stallion still temperamental, not quite broken to the bit. He allowed the young stud to stamp and drag his hooves. He loosened his grip on the reins and gave him room to buck his head and shake his mane at will. Don Ponzio eyed him carefully. He could tell that Erik had a master's way with the horse, but he used none of the accepted styles of handling the animal. Lord and Lady Da Luca were spending the fortnight with the Fiortinos, and Don Pietro was having a devil of a time with a feisty mare. Erik trotted gingerly up to the mare and took a handful of her mane in his hand and spoke to her gently as if he knew her. Immediately, the mare stopped snorting and settled into a calm stance. Erik patted her softly and led his stallion off to the side to wait for the hunt to begin.

"The horses are wonderful animals," was the only response Erik gave his host. He hadn't wanted to participate today, but it was obvious that Don Ponzio was ready to take it as a personal insult if he refused yet again.

He had no desire to hunt or torment a dumb beast, but at least he'd get an invigorating ride through the countryside. He would have much preferred to sit for Lucianna while her husband worked out his blood lust.

Don Ponzio had drawn his firearm to shoot the animal when Erik knocked it out of his hands and went to inspect the horse's injury. His host had pursued the fox into the thickest part of the woods, and the stallion's hoof had gotten caught in a hole, and both horse and rider had fallen. Erik regretted that it hadn't been Don Ponzio who had broken something rather than Charlemagne. When Erik bent to inspect the animal's front leg, Don Ponzio lost his patience. He took Erik's mount and sped off in pursuit of the hunting party, leaving Erik on foot to deal with the injured animal.

As he had thought, the injury was not severe; it certainly didn't require putting the stallion down. After making a provisional splint for Charlemagne, Erik slowly led him back the long march to the manor house. They had gone a couple of miles and were within range of the estate when Erik saw one rider and one horse without rider fast approaching over the meadow. It was Lucianna. She had brought Erik a mount.

"I can't believe my husband left you out here without a mount! Is he all right?"

"He's annoyed. He doesn't like the splint, but he isn't in much pain. Any fool could see that it was a minor dislocation. I don't believe the tendons are torn."

"You love horses, don't you?" She smiled at him.

"Animals don't see things the way we do. They're pure." He said it guilelessly.

"I haven't seen this side of you before, Erik. You should show it more often."

He ignored her remark and mounted the bay. Taking Charlemagne by the bit, they set a slow, easy pace to lead the injured animal to the stables.

Once they arrived, Erik examined the horse's joint again and decided that he should be sure that it was properly set before leaving it to heal.

"Whoa. Whoa. You'll be all right." Erik spoke gently and softly to the stallion as he secured the forearm and knee between his legs firmly with both hands and inspected the flexor tendons of the animal's leg. Digging in his heels, he wrenched the lower limb until he felt sure that the ball of the joint had easily slipped back in place almost immediately after the fall. No permanent damage had been done. The stallion jerked and neighed, but Erik managed to retain his hold on the injured limb.

Lucianna watched as Erik splinted the leg afresh, wrapping it repeatedly with strips of cloth. The stallion nuzzled his back, poking at Erik to finish.

"Ponzio is furious, you know. You made him look bad."

"Your husband didn't need my help for that. He pushed the beast over dangerous terrain at an unacceptable clip. It's a miracle he didn't tumble and break his neck."

"You were concerned for my husband?"

"No, I was speaking of the stallion."

"He says Charlemagne will never recover. It's a waste of time, according to his expert knowledge of horseflesh."

"He's wrong about that, too." Erik leaned against the stallion and placed his head against his broad barrel and sweaty shoulder. His heartbeat was strong and steady. Erik began to wipe the coat down with a soft, dry cloth.

"The groom will finish, Erik. He'll wipe him down and make sure he's carefully watched." Lucianna patted the Arabian familiarly on the crest. The horse snorted peevishly, but turned his wet brown eyes toward his mistress in gratitude. "Where did you learn to handle horses like this?"

Before he could stop himself, Erik answered truthfully, "The opera house had stables. I grew up …"

"You grew up in an opera house or in their stables?" She eyed him curiously.

"It's nearly time for dinner. You should join your guests. I have to clean up." With that, he turned his back on her unceremoniously and went off to his room.

Lucianna had asked him to remove his mask in the last sittings. At first he did so with some trepidation sensing that she would not be comfortable staring at him without the protection of the mask between them. She was nervous, but after a few minutes Erik could see that she was so deeply immersed in her craft that he could tell no difference in the way she looked at him with or without the mask. He had also begun to get more comfortable removing it in her presence.

Then, one afternoon, the opportunity presented itself for them to lie with each other again. Don Ponzio and the Da Lucas planned an all-day excursion to the coast to bathe. Neither Lucianna nor Erik wished to accompany them. Annoyed, Don Ponzio thought to cancel the expedition altogether except that Signora Da Luca had become quite fond of the idea of dipping her toes in the Adriatic, so Don Ponzio felt obliged to go through with the original plans. Erik had taken up his usual pose, removed the mask, and Lucianna had already been working for an hour when Don Ponzio and his guests set off for the coast.

Lucianna laid her palette down and timidly advanced toward Erik. Aware of her intention, Erik reached for the mask to put it on, but she stayed his hand and with a quizzical look asked him why he would think to put the mask on again? Wouldn't he be much more comfortable without? To that, Erik had nothing to say. He simply assumed she'd prefer not to see his face while they were intimately embraced. Then he asked her if his deformity itself excited her. She remembered that at the fair wealthy, important women paid Erik handsomely to have sex with them after the show. The attraction was in large part his monstrous nature. She tried to reassure Erik that it was not that she was attracted to him because of his disfigurement, but rather that the disfigurement was simply not significant to her. It did not disgust her, nor did it titillate.

"What is it that draws you to me?" There was genuine curiosity in his question. He truly didn't know why she should be excited by him.

"I don't know how to answer that. I … I really don't know … I could definitely say that your body—the way you stand, the way you carry yourself—is beautiful. You exude raw energy, power, strength, and something else. I think you radiate health. Your body is substantial and whole and clean and right. And you know how to touch a woman. I don't know what you do that is so vastly different from what any man does with a woman, but you touch me and my body hums as if you were a tuning fork and I was a musical note."

Erik felt a myriad of emotions: he was amused and embarrassed, touched and skeptical. He wanted to believe her. But at the same time he sensed she was holding something back, and he couldn't tell what it might be that she was not telling him.

Don Ponzio was tiring of Erik's refusal to cooperate with his diversions. He watched the two of them closely, enjoying the fact that they thought they were being so clever, so discreet. He would have every opportunity to revenge himself on them whenever he liked. But Erik intrigued him. Oh how he'd like to have *him* in his collection, but then again if everything worked out well, he'd have his offspring. At this rate, it would be no time before the bitch would become pregnant.

Don Ponzio considered himself a amateur scientist of the abnormal, an aficionado of the bizarre. All the best authorities asserted that deformities, such as the one his guest suffered, were dominantly transmitted from one generation to the next. He had no doubt that Lucianna's and Erik's child would have the same features as the father. After Lucianna's confinement, she would only be an obstacle. He would find someway to rid himself of her. He remembered how she had carried on when she lost the last fetus. Stupid cow, she had insisted on burying it in the church cemetery; she had even named it—Rafael.

"Let's see if she can bear a monster's child better than mine!"

Tonight he would plan an entertainment for Don Pietro and Don Scevola. They were becoming impatient as well, and Don Ponzio had a reputation to uphold. His friends esteemed him a connoisseur of the bizarre. First they would take a trip to his menagerie. This would put that freak in his place. Later he would insist that Lucianna fulfill her duty. He was fed up with her coy ways. She could no longer insist on playing the prude, not now that she was conducting her own affair with Erik right under everyone's nose. He was going to enjoy accusing her and watching her squirm, she who had been so sanctimonious with him!

The underground vaults were much more modest than those that I had called home for so many years at the opera house, but nonetheless I was comforted the minute we descended to the floors below. The coolness hit me like the embrace of an old friend, the darkness calmed me, the heavy stone walls infused me with a sense of wellbeing and strength. That was until we reached the heavy door at the end of a narrow passage and I could sense the despair and loneliness on the other side. There was a residue of pain that haunted these rooms and something worse. Something alive was trapped down here.

Don Ponzio reminded me of the barker at the fair. He rubbed his hands together in gleeful anticipation of our wonder and delight as he prepared to show us his collection. He extracted a large skeleton key that turned easily in the lock—evidently he was a frequent visitor to these rooms—and the door opened smoothly on its hinges. Along each wall was a row of glass cabinets. They lined the entire lateral edges of the space, ending in the depths where I cringed to see a row of four cages like those at a zoological park or like those at a fair, the only difference being that these were set within the stone, permanent, and without wheels. I turned to leave, but Lucianna grabbed my sleeve and pleaded silently for me to stay by her side. I swallowed my desire to scream and held my hands tightly by my side in fists to control my urge to strike Don

Ponzio or to flee the horror chamber he had brought us to. He explained his acquisitions as we passed the glass cabinets. Out of the corner of my eye I saw white gelatinous objects in glass jars that I couldn't and didn't wish to identify. My attention was fixed on the cages at the end of the gallery. A voice inside was yelling at me to run now before Don Ponzio locked me away for the rest of my life like one of the other exhibits. I so wanted to listen to that voice but for Lucianna. The skeleton of a full grown man or woman caught my unwilling eye as I tried to decide where I should be in relationship to the others so that I could get away if I needed to. The skeleton was that of a hunchback, the spine bent and twisted, the collar bone and shoulder caved in upon themselves. Otherwise it seemed the remains of a normal person. Next to it was a small skeleton, that of a child whose limbs had obviously not grown properly. There were no hands or feet, and it was clear that they were not just missing, but had not developed. I was becoming queasy as Don Ponzio brought us closer to the depths of his chamber of anomalies.

In one of the cages, a lamb bent to eat at the grass, oats, and hay mixture left for it. Don Ponzio was delighted to see that we were puzzled by its presence. It was simply a lamb. Only when it turned to take the treat Don Ponzio held out to it did we see why it was one of his most prized possession—it approached Don Ponzio's hand and licked the sweet cane he held with one of its heads while the other dangled, unseeing, unresponsive to the side. He explained that on occasion such animals are born—and then he looked directly at me—but nature usually has the good sense to let them die.

"It's rare to have one survive birth, more so to survive as long as this one." The Stattores and Da Lucas glanced over at me to see my reaction. A wave of intense hatred rose in my throat threatening to strangle me. If Lucianna had not drawn close enough for me to feel her by my side, I would have thrown myself on her husband then and there.

The next cell was empty. I couldn't help but think it might be reserved for me in the near future. Beside that one was an albino monkey that sat forlornly in a corner pulling out the hair on its leg. Great bald patches spread across its body. When we approached, it didn't even look our way. I couldn't stay any longer. It was as if I were in that cage, in the corner, with that monkey. I felt his hopelessness grab my heart and squeeze it tight. I turned and walked as calmly as I could out of the room and out of the cellar, but I couldn't get the sight of that animal out of my mind.

Later that night Lucianna slipped into my room. I had not been able to sleep. I was sitting by the window in the dark when I heard the door handle turn. I rose quickly and went to open the door and strangle the intruder. In my mind, I could only imagine that it was one of the servants sent by Don Ponzio to carry me off to occupy the empty cell next to the monkey. Lucianna nearly screamed from the shock when I grabbed her roughly by the throat. I immediately released her, worried that I might have injured her. She rubbed her throat and coughed several times to open her windpipe.

"What are you doing? Are you insane?" I gripped her too tightly by the arm, and she winced. I released her and went to light a candle on the dressing table. In the semi-darkness I could see that she was scantily clad. It was incredibly foolish for her to risk coming to me in the middle of the night with her husband at home. Although they slept in separate bedrooms, he might come to hers at any moment of the night. We had been discreet until now. It wasn't that I feared Don Ponzio on my account, but I knew he was a twisted individual and feared what he might do to Lucianna. I wouldn't be able to protect her every minute of the day, and her husband was quite capable of avenging himself through devious and secret means. "Go back to your room, Lucianna. This is madness."

Instead of obeying me, she dropped her robe to the ground and stood naked in the dim glow of the candle. When I did not come to her, she walked over to where I stood and wrapped her arms around me. I thought to push her away, but once I felt her come into my arms, I knew I would not. I picked her up to carry her to the bed, but she protested that she wanted me to lay her on the sofa instead. I placed her on the cushions and let my nightshirt drop to the floor. Beside the sofa I knelt. I began to kiss her body, teasing and licking at her soft, firm flesh. One of my hands reached upward toward her breasts while the other was free to explore her inner thigh. With my fingers I cupped the intimate depths of her. I parted her lips, delved deep inside, and withdrew, trailing behind a path of slick warmth. I wanted to enjoy touching her, but she seemed anxious, impatient. Instead of relaxing while I had my way with her, she pulled my face up toward hers and urged me to come to her then and there. She asked me if I would make love to her, and in reply I knelt between her legs and slipped inside her. Her breasts pressed warm and soft against my chest. I wanted to bury my face in the curve of her neck and nuzzle the soft salty skin, but she kept lifting my head as if to look into my eyes. At that moment, I wanted nothing more than to please her. I took her slowly at first, but she rocked insistently and rapidly against me, urging me to increase the speed of my movements until I felt that I would not be able to control myself. But she had not yet come, and I refused to do so until I had pleasured her.

In spite of her protests, I withdrew from her and lowered my mouth to the heat between her thighs; I licked and kissed at the most secret and sensitive part of her body. Within moments she tensed deliciously under my mouth, and I knew she was on the edge. I quickly entered her again. All gentleness gone, we both rode the sensations to their limits, collapsing exhausted in each other's arms. We hadn't been as quiet as we should have been. But I listened and heard nothing. I prayed we had disturbed no one, for I was in no condition to meet a threat at that moment. As I was still catching my breath, Lucianna whispered to me that she must go. I released her. She slid from my arms. I watched her as she took her robe and without a glance in my direction left the room. She had never acted this way before, and it left me feeling cold inside and bewildered.

I rose slowly and walked to the basin in the far corner of the room. I washed myself and blew out the one candle in the room. For an instant, as I turned toward the bed, I saw a glimmer of light on the wall opposite the sofa. In the next second it was gone. My feet turned to lead. As I realized what had just happened, I couldn't move.

She had wanted me to take her to the sofa. She had wanted me to keep my face raised above hers, raised and facing the wall opposite the sofa where I had just seen through a small crack in the plaster and wood another candle being extinguished. She had not wanted me to linger in my lovemaking but did everything she could to make it all happen in the briefest time possible. She had even been willing to forego her own pleasure so that it would end quickly.

Don Ponzio had managed at last to have his show, and its only cost was his wife's honor and my dignity.

Relations between me and Don Ponzio have continued to deteriorate. He finds every chance possible to irritate me, to goad me into some kind of reaction. It's as if he wants me to lose control. That would certainly be entertaining, even if he underestimates the danger of facing my wrath. He also persists in making me the center of attention at his now infamous dinner parties. If at one point I might have obliged him out of respect for his hospitality, I have become as obdurate as he is insistent in refusing every and any request he makes of me. I tend to accompany him and his guests, but mostly as a passive member of the party. I leave untouched the wine he has poured in my glass and pick at the elaborate and wasteful bounty placed before me. It gives me a priceless feeling of self satisfaction to refuse his largesse. The dinner conversation ranges from the insipid to the perverse. What doesn't bore me to tears simply nauseates me.

Lately I've sensed that Don Ponzio knows more about me than is safe for him to know. Although it pains me to admit it, I worry that Lucianna has betrayed me even in this. She knows little of my past, but enough to serve Don Ponzio as a start from which he might manage to unravel my origins.

The other night, after dinner, the talk turned to music. As the others chatted, Don Ponzio kept his eyes on me as if waiting to hear me expound on Gounod's *Faust* or Verdi's *Il Trovatore* or Mozart's *Don Giovanni*. I was tempted to claim ignorance. He already knows that I sing, but the music I chose for the fair was often either one of my own compositions or a variation on a popular, folk song of the region. Yet he seemed to know that I have an extensive repertoire and requested that I sing for them. Even so, I was about to refuse when I noticed a pained expression on Lucianna's face. Don Ponzio's arm was behind her back, and I was convinced that he was hurting her. Lucianna seconded her husband's request that I sing. Reluctantly I agreed if she would accompany me in a duet. I offered to play. Don Ponzio was pleased, which also puzzled me. Lucianna rose stiffly from her place and came to sit beside me at the piano.

As we sang, I observed Lucianna's gown. It had a high lace collar that hid her lovely, long neck, and long sleeves in spite of the balmy heat of the midsummer's eve. In contrast Donna Rosella was practically falling out of her gown, her arms bare, her bosom amply displayed. A young man, Don Pietro's nephew or cousin—I had paid little attention to the introductions made—had unbuttoned his vest he was so warm. I couldn't shake the suspicion that Don Ponzio had vilely abused his wife, that he had beaten her. The choice of gown was to hide the contusions his cruelty had left on her body.

Outrage and concern competed in me as I tried to stay focused on the music we were performing. Lucianna wouldn't meet my gaze. Since the night, more than a week ago, when she slipped into my room, I have also avoided meeting her gaze. We had normally met daily for the portrait, but the day after our performance the time came and went with neither of us seeking out the other. Of course, this confirmed my intuition that Lucianna had knowingly played her role in the humiliating show we gave Don Ponzio and his select guests. I supposed her too embarrassed to face me, and I certainly felt too betrayed to wish to be with her. Nevertheless, whatever her role in that perverted exhibition—willing or unwilling—I couldn't condone her mistreatment.

I assumed it would be safer for Lucianna if I were not available for Don Ponzio's parlor tricks. After the duet, I excused myself from the company to retire to my room.

Erik selected a rapier tipped for safety and held it stretched out in his hand to feel the weight and balance. He had removed his mask and replaced it with the safety visor. Don Ponzio was likewise engaged in selecting his weapon and performing certain exercises to prepare for the sword practice. This had become the one and only activity that met both men's approval. Erik had learned to spar, certain classic fencing stances, and a limited number of combinations from the instructors hired by the opera management to train the actors for the frequent sword fight scenes that were popular with the public. He knew he was woefully unprepared to meet Don Ponzio in a contest of styles just as he had been when he faced Raoul in the cemetery and fought what seemed to be a lifetime ago. That fight he had lost, although he managed to wound Raoul and nearly upset him on several occasions due to his unorthodox handling of the blade. His reflexes and his physical strength made him a formidable opponent, but Don Ponzio had the advantage of years of training and was an expert swordsman.

Their previous encounters had been instructive to both. As they engaged each other, they kept track of the other's style and weaknesses. Erik imagined that Don Ponzio, like himself, was being rather guarded about the true extent of his mastery of strokes and strategies. He noticed that his host was much less aggressive than his nature would suggest and knew that he was trying to lull Erik into overconfidence. Of course he, too, was withholding some aspects of his skills such as the fact that he was in effect ambidextrous.

"En garde." Don Ponzio gave the signal to begin. Each of the previous occasions they had fenced, Don Ponzio had begun with a series of classic moves to test his opponent. This time was different. Don Ponzio launched into an aggressive assault that Erik fought off with some difficulty. From the start, Erik was forced into a defensive stance that put him at a serious disadvantage.

The ladies and lords in Don Ponzio's party applauded at the completion of the first set which ended in a point for the host when his rapier pierced Erik's defenses and would have pierced his shoulder if not for the button placed at the rapier's point and the padded protective clothing they wore.

"We will be celebrating the unveiling of the portrait within the next few days, Erik. Are you looking forward to seeing your soul on my wife's canvas?"

When Erik made no reply, Don Ponzio resumed the stance for the next set. "En garde."

Again Don Ponzio lunged forward, pressing Erik back in a set of reactions to fend off the attack. This time his host whipped the sword upward in a slice that Erik successfully countered. The force of Erik's downward blow must have sent a painful wave of vibrations up the length of Don Ponzio's arm because he lost the advantage in the few seconds that it took him to recover, time that Erik used to go on the offensive.

"We look forward to seeing your unveiling, too. That was the contract, wasn't it, Erik? We will all get to see your face, to see who you really are." Erik was sure that Don Ponzio really meant "what" instead of "who."

The next sets were intense. Both men seemed to have abandoned the idea of practice in favor of fighting in earnest in spite of the protective gear and the capped tips of their rapiers. Erik was sure that any connoisseur of the art would give Don Ponzio the victory hands down, but he was also sure that if the object were to maim or kill, he might well be the one to walk away alive.

As they finished and returned the equipment to their cases, Don Ponzio praised Erik on his unorthodox swordsmanship and in passing commented, "My wife looks a bit peaked, does she not?"

"I hadn't noticed, Don Ponzio," Erik cautiously answered.

"I'm afraid our attempts to have a child have ended once more in failure."

I couldn't remain indifferent to Lucianna's obvious suffering. If indeed Don Ponzio was telling the truth, she had lost our child. At the same time, I was shocked because I had never considered the possibility that she would become pregnant. We had not exchanged two words for well over a week. She had not come to my room again, for which I was thankful. I don't think I could have borne another betrayal. But she had also avoided me and had not asked me to pose for the portrait.

The next day, Don Ponzio took his guests, leaving Lucianna behind again, on one of his interminable hunts in the nearby woods—deer this time. Lucianna was in the studio, perhaps working on the portrait without me. I resolved we must clear the air, so I knocked lightly to announce my presence and came into the room. She was indeed concentratedly working on the canvas. Evidently my services as model, among others, were no longer needed. I felt a twinge of bitterness to see that she and the portrait were now completely independent of me.

She stopped when she heard me come in and as usual concealed the canvas. I went directly to the matter and asked why she had betrayed me. She didn't argue, deny, or defend herself. She simply asked for forgiveness. Even though I knew she had been a party to the lurid display of our intimacy for her husband's perverse pleasure, I irrationally wanted her to prove to me that it was all in my imagination. For a moment, I felt completely devoid of all emotion and incapable of action. But when she moved to leave me in the room, I reached out to stop her. As I took hold of her upper arm, she cried out in pain. I had not meant to harm her, and although I had been brusque I had not done anything to merit such a strong reaction.

"I knew it. He's hurt you!" I raised the sleeve of her gown and found huge purple and black contusions. Further examination revealed she had also been lashed across the back of her shoulders most pitifully. I saw red. If she hadn't begged me to stop, I would have tracked him down then and there and gutted him like the pig he was.

Instead I let her collapse against me in tears, and I kissed her tears away telling her I'd do anything to help her. Although she protested that there was little I could do, I didn't believe her.

"Why did he beat you? You did what he wanted."

"Please, don't. Don't talk about that night."

"Why did he do this?"

She couldn't or wouldn't give me a reason, but I insisted.

"I haven't gotten pregnant yet. My time of month has come."

Erik paused as he considered this. So she hadn't lost a child; she hadn't conceived. As he had thought, he was incapable of that kind of creation.

"He knows that we have been together, and he would be glad to see you pregnant with another man's child?" Confused, I looked to her to explain, but she just returned my gaze as if it should all be clear. "He wants a bastard?"

"He wants me to bear your child."

"I don't understand. He wants you to have my child, a bastard? He put you up to seducing me? The drugged wine?" I felt the room slip and lean to the left and wondered how it was that I could still stand. How could I have thought that she desired me? I searched along the walls of the room looking for the secret peep holes I knew must be there. "You have been performing for your twisted husband and his sycophants? You used me! You used me and degraded yourself for that monster's pleasure? And then you pretend to see my soul? I ask myself, Lucianna, do you have a soul? Tell me, do you?" Lucianna cowered, a look of pure animal fear on her face as I gave up my search along the walls and approached her.

"Why? Why does he want my child?"

Lucianna stuttered incomprehensibly for a moment until I impatiently cut her off. Then the truth hit me, and I thought I would go mad. "The menagerie. He wants an exhibit for the menagerie. Oh, merciful …"

Lucianna sat trembling on the sofa as I grappled with the horror of Don Ponzio's plan. I couldn't speak for some time. All I could do was stare at the wall. I clenched and unclenched my fists trying to regain some control over my wild thoughts.

Finally, in a small voice, she spoke. "When he found out about us, he …"

I snapped toward her voice and growled, "When he found out what?"

"My husband found out that we were having an affair. It wasn't his plan from the beginning. When he realized you and I were intimate, he told me that I was to continue meeting you and that I was to do everything within my power to become pregnant."

"And what had your plan been, my sweet?" I hated her at that moment, her softness, her beauty, her apparent innocence.

"What do you mean?"

"Why did you drug me? What was the original plan, your plan?" I watched her as she stared wide-eyed and pale like an animal caught in a trap. "If you wanted me, if you were attracted to me, why didn't you simply seduce me? You had no reason to drug me to get me to make love to you, Lucianna. I refused to face it at the time, but there must have been some ulterior motive. What did *you* want from me?"

Quietly she confessed that she, too, had wanted to become pregnant. She had hoped it would save her from further abuse from Don Ponzio. If she could give him an heir, one that he would assume was his child, then perhaps she would be safe.

"You expect me to believe that the two of you have not been using me when you both have the same goals?"

"No! I want a child. He wants …"

She couldn't say it, so I finished it for her. "An exhibit for his menagerie. He's convinced that my child would be disfigured like me. Had you thought of that, Lucianna? What if the child looked like this?" I ripped my mask off and dared her to turn away from me. I wanted her to see the father of the child she sought, to think of passing my curse on to an innocent soul.

"I didn't care! I think your child would be a healthy, beautiful child! I think whatever happened to you must be unique to your unfortunate destiny. And if it was … if it did have a deformity like yours, I suppose my husband would kill both me and the child and put us out of our misery. It never occurred to me that he knew and that he wanted it for his collection."

"And it would have been acceptable to you if he had murdered our child? You stupid woman! You stupid and cruel woman!"

Lucianna cried softly into her hands.

Suddenly I felt nothing. Not anger, not pity, just a deep coldness creeping through my gut. "Well, no harm done, I suppose. After all, you have not conceived. As I thought, I'm incapable of siring a child. So you and your husband will have to find some other helpless creature to torment."

"That's not true. I may have miscarried. It was too early to tell."

"Why would you think that?"

"Because you've already sired a child!"

I couldn't help but look at her as if she were deranged. But the next thing she said left me dazed and bewildered. "I've made inquiries. It has taken weeks to track down any information, but I've learned that your wife gave birth seven or eight months after she was abandoned."

How can I believe what Lucianna said? Meg would have conceived the night Raoul snuck her into my prison cell just before the end of the trial. She would have been carrying when we crossed the border from France. If Meg had been with child, if I had known … But she didn't tell me; she didn't want me. She screamed in terror when she woke and saw me beside her. Perhaps she didn't even want the child, my child. What was it? A boy or a girl. Or simply another monster? Lucianna had no details, just the bare information that Meg had given birth. The reports were vague, but several repeated the same story. Did the child live? Perhaps my child had died. I have to know. I have to leave here and find Meg.

Don Ponzio insists that the portrait is ready. He says Lucianna is simply stalling. Tonight is the unveiling. I owe these people nothing, but I can't leave Lucianna in that man's grip. Tonight it must all end, one way or another. If the only way to extricate myself from their sordid lives is to kill again, then so be it. She'll unveil her portrait; I'll unmask the monster.

CHAPTER 8

Behind the Veil

> *There was much of the beautiful, much of the wanton, much of the bizarre, something of the terrible, and not a little of that which might have excited disgust.*
>
> *"The Masque of the Red Death" Edgar Allan Poe*

A child. Meg had given birth to his child. It couldn't be! His mind rebelled against it. He had so long thought that he was not a man, but some monster, a freak of nature. Madeleine had tried to prove to him that he was human. She had taught him to read, to write. She brought him books—philosophy, science, architecture. She kept novels from him, but he found these in the dormitories. When Madeleine married and left to set up her new home, the steady stream of books dried up, the infrequent conversations and exchanges evaporated. Having no direct contact with any living soul, he lived for her letters. He read the novels the young girls carelessly left beside their dormitory beds, at first as if they were bizarre, incomprehensible nonsense. Eventually, he came to realize that the stories he watched and listened to on the stage were more like in kind to these popular novels than to the grand aspirations he found in the books Madeleine had given him. He returned again and again to those Madeleine had chosen for him, but they didn't lessen his loneliness. For that he turned to the novels, the stories of disinherited heiresses and dark heroes on the moors, thieves and kidnapped damsels, the betrayed man locked away in an island prison who returns years later to wreak his revenge against the love who forgot him and the man that had sent him unjustly to die in his cell, the stories of the crusades and the evil Knight Templar who redeemed himself through sacrifice for the beautiful Jewess. These stories he read as if they could teach him about the world from which he'd been exiled, and he imagined himself in them, and their characters kept him company while he hoped that eventually something tremendous would happen to rescue him. When Madeleine returned, a young widow with a baby in her arms, he thought his loneliness was finally to end, but she had changed. Although she resumed her role as his warden, all those tender ties he had imagined between them were frayed and broken.

Erik didn't complain. He knew he had been a monster and would always be one. But then each night he watched common, garish men and women don wigs and apply their make-up to cover their mundane nature and transform into princes and magicians, beautiful maidens and tragic kings. If they could do this, why couldn't he? So his world was ultimately a fiction not unlike those in the cheap novels or in the operas staged in the theater. It made the loneliness bearable. It helped him forget that he didn't belong to the human race. So how could he now have a child? How was it possible that he had—out of that fantasy—created something real?

He remembered once asking Madeleine—on a rare occasion when she was alone and hadn't found an excuse to leave his company—what love was, what it was like when she was married. All the books he'd read talked about sighs and swoons and deep longings, but aside from the kisses which he'd seen faked on stage, the rest was hidden from him under a veil of words.

Now he understood that he had already buried—in a deep, locked part of his mind—Sabia's visits to his cage, the degradation of those lurid experiences, the loss of his innocence. He had also forgotten the shameful occasion when he frightened Madeleine. He led her down to the vaults under the opera house. She didn't want to accompany him. She feared that he meant to abuse her. He still wasn't sure what his true intentions had been. He thought, he hoped, that he simply longed for another's companionship, another's touch. Madeleine had pitied him; she protected him. He believed that he could reach out to her. When she struggled, he became angry and held her even more tightly. Only when she began to cry did he realize that he was hurting her and that he had to let her go. Now he understood why Madeleine's behavior changed toward him, why she became cautious, why she avoided being alone in his company and slipped notes to him or met him on the other side of a secret passage, why she had insisted on keeping from him the novels that entertained so many of the young men and women in their leisure time, and why she looked at him the way she did when he had asked her about love.

She didn't understand, wouldn't understand, that Erik meant something different from what she imagined he desired. He had seen the more experienced divas and chorus girls giving in to young suitors in the dark corners of the opera's backstage passageways. He even came upon a particularly ardent couple in the chapel once. But this was not love. This was not the longing and transcendence the novels spoke of again and again.

When he asked Madeleine to explain what love was, she had snapped angrily. Erik still remembered how devastated he had felt that even those experiences were forbidden to him. She cautioned that he should never seek to touch another person *in that way*. He understood what she meant by "*that way*." He must control his urges; the pleasures of the flesh were not for him. He was too ashamed to tell her that each night he already lay tortured by them. He was perhaps fifteen, as physically mature and as tall as or taller than most full-grown men. He swallowed any other questions that had been circling in his mind and realized that his Madeleine, his savior, was lost to him from that day forward. She expected him to bury himself in the vaults. Erik recalled trying to say something to her, but he choked it back instead. There was nothing he could ask from her or give her. That day he began to live as the Phantom—to her, to everyone, even to himself.

Could he risk returning to Meg? Could he bear to expose himself again to that pain? He had to. He needed to know. He had a child. If the child had survived, he must know him. He must find out if he'd been capable of creating even one thing that was whole, that was good. A child, their child! It might be his only salvation.

Erik was dressed for dinner in his best clothes. The coat was a tad shiny, the fabric a little frayed at the edges, but it was still elegant, and he wore it as if it were new. The vest was in better condition, and Greta had bleached and pressed his shirt. A simple cummerbund of burgundy and brown with gold filigree picked up subtle lights of the same hue from the embroidered vest. His tapered breeches were dark like the coat. He had polished his black boots to a high gloss himself earlier that day. He had allowed his hair—which he had always hated and disguised by wigs—to grow, and he could now tie it behind at the nape of his neck. He had used wigs to hide the extent of the deformity that stretched past his hairline and above his right ear. His hair grew sparse on the rough skin of his disfigurement.

Tonight was the unveiling, and it would be complete. He examined himself in the mirror, something he rarely did. His practice was to don his wig and mask blindly and finish his disguise with carefully selected make-up before a discreet mirror that reflected only small portions of his face at any one time. Now he stood without defenses. The full-length mirror on the wardrobe door was unforgiving. He saw himself whole, from head to foot, if he stood back from its surface. The trick was to carry himself as if he still wore his disguises and as if he were still the Phantom, still visible only when he chose to be so.

Tonight it would end. Tonight he was resigned to shed blood again: His or someone else's, it didn't matter which. It was the only way to free Lucianna from her husband. He told himself that he was only ridding the world of a monster worse than himself.

Prepared, he put the mask and wig in the travel satchel he had packed and left the room to go down to dinner. The other guests were disappearing around the corner into the dining room as Erik reached the landing. No one saw him until they chose their seats at the table and were about to sit. The air in the room seemed to have been sucked into an audible gasp of shock as all eyes turned to the tall imposing figure of a man in the doorway, a man with only half a face. No one moved as Erik apologized for arriving late and walked to the chair at the end of the table opposite his host. At Don Ponzio's side sat Lucianna who looked at him with a warm, concerned smile. Erik stood, like the other men, and waited for the ladies to take their seats. Seeing no one attending to the young lady on his right, Signorina Regina, he held the back of her chair for her. Slowly she slid onto the seat and quietly thanked him. Once all the ladies were seated, Erik and the other gentlemen took their seats as well.

"Bravo, Erik. A toast to our Angel in Hell. Or do you have other equally fantastic names?" Don Ponzio raised his wine glass to salute from across the room. The insinuation was not lost on Erik. Lucianna was not the only one who had been investigating his past. He was more and more convinced that Don Ponzio had discovered his previous identity. Perhaps through hearsay he had caught a detail or two that struck him as too coincidental not to be pertinent. One piece of the puzzle had led to another until Ponzio had concluded that Erik was the infamous Opera Ghost. Of course, it was still largely conjecture on his host's part. Whatever people whispered, there was no proof.

"As I've said on other occasions, Erik will suffice."

"It's yet to be seen whether you are an angel or demon, is it not? Although with your face," he laughed inviting his guests to join in with him, "it is hard to see what there is of angel about you."

"Please," begged Lucianna barely audibly. Erik glared at her. Her distress was more offensive to him than her husband's cruel effort to humiliate him.

"I'm afraid I've known more of darkness than of light. The only light I've ever seen has been illusory—in dreams or my imagination." Erik pointedly looked toward Lucianna.

"Oh dear. I sense some disappointment. Surely in our society you've found acceptance and proof of the existence of goodness and charity." Erik was sickened by Don Ponzio's cynicism.

"What was your favorite opera at the Opera Populaire?" Don Ponzio directed the question, not to Erik, to his surprise, but to his nephew, Carlo, a young man who had spent a number of wasted years studying in Paris.

"The last season they were open they did *Hannibal*, always popular with the public. But of course the most incredible piece was the famous one that led to the disaster, *Don Juan Triumphant*." The young man swallowed a piece of the venison and drowned it in wine before continuing his account. Erik studiously engaged himself in moving the venison on his plate from one side to the other. The young dandy delighted in telling in detail how a monster had cut the lines causing the regal chandelier that had graced the central chamber to plummet, crashing down in the crowded auditorium. Warming to his subject, enjoying the guests' rapt attention, Carlo went on to describe how the madman had kidnapped the ingénue and dragged her down into his lair.

Erik felt the rush of blood to his face and hoped it wasn't apparent at this distance from Don Ponzio.

Wiping a crumb from the corner of his mouth, Carlo described the tumultuous last days of the Opera Populaire leading up to the final disaster explaining that it had all begun with the scandal of an upstart chorus girl who dethroned the Italian diva, Carlotta, from her position in the opera.

One of the other guests snickered and said that he knew how an ingénue could use her charms with the managers to steal the role of an older woman on stage. Erik was about to snap at the slander of Christine's name when the young man himself interrupted in order to put the record straight. "No, no, no. It was much more interesting than that." He paused dramatically to insure that he had everyone's attention. "It seems a ghost had been haunting the opera house for quite some time, a ghost who had very specific tastes in music."

Don Ponzio kept his eyes on Erik. "Go on, Carlo. Tell us about this ghost. Was he really a ghost?"

"No! That's where it gets quite strange. He was some recluse who lived in the sewers under the opera. He was a rapist and murderer who liked opera! Can you imagine?"

All, except Lucianna and Erik, laughed.

"How awful! To live in the sewer!" volunteered one of the ladies with a look of disgust on her face. "I can't imagine the filth, the vermin, the rats."

"In point of fact," Erik spoke before he could restrain himself. "I've been told that under the opera house there are several layers of vaults. It's hardly a sewer."

"How authoritative you sound, Erik!" replied Don Ponzio.

"The Opera Populaire is a famous architectural treasure. What I say is common knowledge."

"To any Frenchman, I suppose. Your accent has always intrigued me, Erik. Is it Parisian?"

"No, not exactly. But we've interrupted Don Carlo's amusing story." There was little Erik could do to steer the conversation away from their discussion of his past, but it was at least easier to have them listen to Carlo than for him to field pointed questions from Don Ponzio.

"Yes, do go on. Who was this murderer? Why did they think he was a ghost?" Donna Rosella was so excited that her breasts seemed to quiver like the aspic in the middle of the table.

"He circulated like a ghost around the opera house for years through hidden doors and secret passageways, and until it was sold to the last owners—I can't remember their names—he supposedly had everyone under his thumb. To hear tell, he was the real managing director, decided what would be performed and who did what. He even received a monthly salary. Well, the last season, he evidently went quite mad! He became obsessed with this young singer in the chorus. You must remember Carlotta when she debuted in '65 in Rome. He demanded that she step down and give this girl her part in the opera!"

"Was she good?"

"Oh, I suppose."

Erik dropped his fork noisily on the plate and gnawed on his lip in an effort to avoid reaching for the knife and hurling it at the stupid young oaf.

"Anyway, it seems that a count or duke or something also had his eye on this same girl. She was quite beautiful, if you know what I mean." The men all leered, and their ladies chuckled knowingly into their perfumed handkerchiefs.

"May I interrupt, Don Carlo?" Erik was breathing hard; his mouth was pulled into a grimace as he addressed the entire party. Carlo's entertaining story had distracted them momentarily from the hideous face of their dinner companion. Now they turned toward him aghast at the effect of the grimace. He was ugly before; now he was frightening.

"Well …" The young man was loath to give up the party's attention.

Don Ponzio silenced him with barely a gesture. "No, not at all, Erik. I'm sure Carlo would enjoy hearing another version of the story."

Erik took the untouched glass of wine by his plate and drained it in one gulp. "It is rare to find true beauty in this world. If I didn't know that before, I do now. The young chanteuse was the daughter of a talented violinist, Gustave Daaé. When he died, she was a child, an orphan, and she was brought to be trained in the ballet at the opera. She was protected and trained by an honorable woman who thought of her as another daughter. She was beautiful, but it was her voice that was exceptional.… May I have another glass of wine?" He held the empty glass up in a demanding way and when the servant filled it, he drained it again before continuing. "Every good story has a monster. Ours was a man who lived in the bowels of the opera house. He had known nothing but ugliness except in music, on the stage, and in Christine's voice."

"The young lady's name?" asked Lucianna.

"Yes." Erik had not wanted to say her name among these swine, but it had slipped out. The wine was infusing him with a warm, dangerous glow. "The monster became her confidant, her companion, her tutor in music, her teacher. He was quite gifted evidently, and she was an exceptional student. He fell in love with her. But she never loved him; she thought he was a ghost her father had sent to her or her father's spirit that had come to protect her. You see, *he* didn't really exist for her at all."

"But why would she think this man was a ghost?" asked the young lady he had seated to his right.

"Because she never saw him. She only heard him."

"Why didn't he appear to her?"

"Because he …" In this moment he knew Don Ponzio would triumph. "Because he was a monster."

"What do you mean? Did he have horns and cloven hooves for feet?" asked Don Pietro, a smirk twisting his features.

Here Carlo intervened as if suddenly he had seen a ghost himself. He stared at Erik in shocked recognition. "They said he was ugly, hideously deformed, and wore a mask whenever he came up from the bowels of the opera house."

Erik refused to lower his eyes. He stared directly ahead, down the long dining room table, at Don Ponzio. The others began to murmur among themselves, casting furtive glances at the disfigured man who sat and dined with them. Lucianna pushed her seat back and started to rise, but her husband took hold of her forearm and forced her to remain seated.

"Go on, Erik, with your story. It sounds tragic. Or is it a horror story?"

"Is there a difference? I wonder." The guests listened attentively for Erik to resume his tale.

Instead of proceeding, he raised his wine goblet high over his head in a crass gesture toward the servant. As the servant began to move forward to fill Erik's glass yet again, Lucianna caught his eye and indicated that he should not. Awkwardly the servant returned to his position along the wall of the dining room. Erik rose from the table and strode over to him in three long paces and took the bottle forcefully from his grasp. He poured the wine himself, disregarding the slosh of the red liquid onto the linen tablecloth. He poured it to the brim and brought the goblet to his mouth and drained it in one gulp.

"She was ungrateful, you see. She was seduced by the charm and beauty and power of a young suitor. The monster had waited too long to seize his prize. He tried to keep her. He tried in vain to win her back. She had been his. And in one brief moment, he had lost her forever." Erik felt his control slipping away as the emotions of loss and self pity washed over him. He stared around the room at the frightened, distorted faces of Don Ponzio's realm. Lucianna was the only face he could bear to look at.

"But what happened?" asked Regina. Erik looked down at her young face and wondered if perhaps she was badly placed among this company.

"Your Carlo was telling the story. Perhaps he should enlighten us all." Why not let the young man spew out the gory details? At least Erik would know what the rest of them saw when they looked at him.

"Well, I don't know if I have all the details straight." Carlo was definitely struck with dread at having to go on narrating a story that he now realized belonged to the Angel in Hell. "They say the Phantom—he was called the Phantom by some and the Opera Ghost by others—went mad with grief when he learned that his protégée was in love with this other man. He killed someone just so that the managers would put the chorus girl—I mean, Mlle. Christine—in the star role of a play. Anyway, the Phantom had written an opera for her and insisted on its performance. The count or duke had the girl play the lead role to act as bait for the Phantom. The night of the performance, the Phantom attacked and almost killed the singer who was playing Don Juan and then came out on stage to play opposite this Christine. She betrayed him to all. She unmasked him on the stage."

Erik threw the crystal wine goblet against the wall where it shattered into a million pieces. The crash startled the party who looked again at the disfigured man. Erik snapped his fingers at the servant. "I seem to need another glass." This time the servant disregarded whatever sign his mistress might have made and brought the requested item directly to Erik who filled the new goblet once more but sipped at its contents. "Let's summarize, Carlo. The story's already too long. The Phantom stole Christine from the stage, and her lover followed them to the depths of the opera house vaults braving traps and the monster's fury. When this hideous creature had both in his clutches, he realized that he could only earn Christine's hatred if he forced her to stay with him or if he killed his rival. He had no choice but to let them both go. They left him there, and he disappeared."

"That's not the whole story, Erik. There's more." Don Ponzio eagerly waited for Erik to continue.

"Such as?" Erik decided to test Don Ponzio. What exactly did he know?

"The Phantom was eventually caught. There was a trial."

"If you know that, then you also know that he was hanged by the neck until dead and buried in an unmarked and unhallowed grave like the monster he was." He challenged his host to finish the mockery.

Don Ponzio didn't respond. The guests looked incredulously at Erik convinced that here before them was the Phantom in the flesh or his ghost.

Lucianna brusquely suggested that they would be more comfortable in the conservatory and rose to indicate that they should all follow her. Don Ponzio agreed and reminded them that they were going to see the unveiling of his wife's latest work, the portrait of the soul of the Angel in Hell.

I brought the wine with me to the conservatory where we were finally to see Lucianna's masterpiece! Everyone gave me a wide berth as if I were contagious. All of a sudden I burst out laughing. Although I wasn't wearing my costume of the Red Death, I realized that my presence among Don Ponzio's party was analogous to that of the walking death, the plague, that assailed Don Prospero's macabre asylum. I walked among them, and they were beginning to realize what I was! Don Ponzio would be the last to fall, hopefully victim of an agonizing death. I would reach out and touch each of them, and my disfigurement would spread across their faces. They would clutch their throats and crumple to the ground. None would survive. All would perish! I must have spoken out loud because those closest to me grew wide-eyed and shrank even farther from me.

I knew that I was out of control. I hadn't expected to be unmasked so effectively by my host. There are so many layers to our disguises! Lucianna was worried; she wasn't able to help me. She was supposed to be the light, my light, the one to lead me through the darkness. What had Sabia read in my palm? I looked at my hands. There was nothing there but blood. I wiped them on my vest, but they wouldn't come clean. Lucianna tried to come to me, but Don Ponzio held her tightly by his side. Such conjugal concern! It was touching!

I should not be here. My glee turned sour as I thought of Meg. I should leave now. I had no business among these vile leeches. I must see Meg, even if she didn't wish to see me. I wanted to see our child. I needed to know that Meg was well.

Lucianna was about to unveil her portrait of the monster. What was the challenge? I couldn't recall. Was she to show my soul and prove to me that it wasn't black as pitch, as hideous as my face? Was that her purpose?

I unbuttoned my vest and slumped in a chair near the canvas so that the audience might better compare the artist's conceit to the model. Don Ponzio was talking, but I wasn't listening. I poured another glass of wine—a truly dry, full bodied vintage—and started to drink it. The wine had drowned my inhibitions, but I was still lucid.

Lucianna lifted the linen covering from the canvas and stood to the side so all could see the portrait. Everyone gasped at the image she had rendered in pigment. Only one among the intimate crowd of guests seemed unimpressed. Don Ponzio fumed. His sardonic smile had fallen into a grimace. His composure, lost. I turned to look at the cause of such consternation on the part of my host. What I saw painted across the surface of the canvas stunned me. I let drop the wine glass and grabbed the arm of the chair to settle my lurch as I rose to give it a closer look.

The man in the portrait was not me. It was a man who shared my features as if he had stolen from me only a part of my face. He sat tall and elegant in the chair, his face in three quarters profile, two healthy intensely dark green eyes set in a handsome face, a face in which each side was complementary, not symmetrical, yet strangely handsome. His cheeks were smooth with a hint of a beard; he had a broad forehead, dark slightly arched eyebrows over his intense eyes, a long straight nose, full lips turned slightly up in the left corner. This would be my twin, my handsome and healthy twin. She had drawn me as I'd never been, but as I might have been if God hadn't cursed me. I raised my hand to my face to convince myself that my deformity was still there. I wanted to reach out and touch the pigment of the face that stared back at me, mockingly.

How could she paint this? Why would she do this to me? Its beauty pierced me with a painful longing to be that man. She had painted the impossible divide between what I was and what I wanted to be, making me appear even more monstrous than I was!

I turned to accuse her, but Don Ponzio was as dissatisfied as I was with the results. This was not the record that he had eagerly awaited. He had made his desires explicit: a faithful depiction of my monstrosity to hang among his freakish collection. Lucianna started as if to step away. Before I could act, Ponzio reached out and grabbed a fistful of her hair and threw her to the ground. I stepped between them and rammed my shoulder into Don Ponzio's chest with all my strength. He tumbled backwards over a divan and fell hard to the floor. I helped Lucianna to her feet and told her to go. As his servants assisted Don Ponzio, I skirted the divan and lunged for the man. My hands grappled at his neck. If they hadn't pulled me away, I would have crushed his throat.

"I challenge you, Ponzio. Pick your weapon."

Several guests restrained me as Don Ponzio rubbed at the reddening marks around his throat. In a strange attempt to recover his equanimity, he brushed himself off and straightened his cravat.

"I'd only have to call the police in, and you'd be carried off to face your execution a second time." He cleared his throat and fought the choking sensation.

Lucianna had not left the room. Her face smudged with tears, she was angry and determined to confront her husband. "The Italian police can do nothing to him. He's safe as long as he doesn't venture over the border to France."

I wondered if what she said was true. Judging from Don Ponzio's expression, it was. As long as I never ventured to return to Paris, I was safe from prosecution.

"Swords," Don Ponzio said. He snarled that he would be waiting for me in the fencing hall.

The men who had restrained me released me as they realized that I had calmed down. Lucianna argued that any challenge should be postponed until the next day when the proper preparations could be made.

"I need no preparation," I answered her. She had no idea how determined I was to wipe Don Ponzio off the face of the planet. "Don't interfere. Within the hour, you'll be a wealthy widow!"

Don Ponzio made as if to approach Lucianna, but I pushed her protectively behind me. He hesitated only a moment then went off to the hall to pick his weapon. I set off after him, the effects of the wine had completely disappeared.

Everyone eagerly followed to watch. They took up their positions on either side of the hall while Ponzio and I tested and flexed our blades.

Don Pietro, who had studied law, drew up a rapid declaration to be signed by both of us exonerating whoever survived from the death of the other. Although duels were still legal in Italy, it was a practice that was fast falling out of favor. The legal writ we signed was a precaution that might save the survivor from nasty legal battles in court. I had no worries. I intended to destroy Don Ponzio even if I perished in the act. If I survived, I would disappear as I had done in the past. After all, I was the Phantom.

Don Ponzio and Erik assumed the classic stance, and the duel began. Although fencing was a highly structured sport in which the rules were of long standing tradition, in this case there'd be no rules other than to maim and kill. As Erik expected, all the practice sessions they had done were carefully misleading examples of what they would not do if they were fighting in earnest. Don Ponzio charged unrelentingly, forcing Erik to parry and dodge on a continuing retreat across the floor. Don Ponzio varied his strokes easily, with the fluidity of a dancer. Erik had no choice but to defend himself, countering each assault and waiting for an opening or a mistake. In a daring move, risking a severe wound, Erik twisted away from Don Ponzio, exposing his back to his rival and obliging him to turn and follow. In the split second gained, Erik managed to attack with several intimidating thrusts. Don Ponzio stepped back quickly revising his approach. As he managed to deflect Erik's strike toward the left, discovering an opening in his defense, Don Ponzio thrust directly in and pierced his opponent's right shoulder. He expected, with this blow, to cripple Erik's sword arm.

Enjoying his imminent victory, Don Ponzio drew back, wiped Erik's blood from the tip, and paused. Erik examined the wound. Dangerously deep, it was bleeding freely. His right hand lay loose on the pummel of the sword. Before coming in to strike again, Don Ponzio called out to Carlo among the spectators. "Carlo, what ever happened to that chorus girl?"

Carlo, assuming like everyone else that Erik was finished, was delighted to have the guests' attention once more on him. "I heard she died in childbirth."

Dead! Erik dropped heavily to his knees, unable to silence the pain that overwhelmed him. Christine cold and alone in the grave! Her voice forever silenced; her eyes forever blind. His mind could not accept it.

Don Ponzio was glad that he had saved this piece of news for last. He drew close to Erik and whispered in his ear, "I'll let you live if you agree to be one of my exhibits. If not, I'll simply kill you now and have you stuffed and preserved in glass. It's your choice."

Erik swallowed his sorrow as if about to speak. Shakily he pushed himself off the floor and stood. He blotted the image of Christine's dead body from his mind and focused his hatred and anger on Don Ponzio.

His opponent cautiously backed away as he saw the fierce determination in Erik's eyes. Before Don Ponzio could shift his balance, Erik switched the sword to his left hand and attacked with a series of slices and thrusts that took his enemy off guard. Don Ponzio was forced to concentrate his efforts on fending off Erik's onslaught, but at the last moment stumbled precariously to the side. In the same instant, Erik's sword sliced across Don Ponzio's face leaving a hideous slash that ran from above his left eye across his nose to the man's right jaw. He screamed from the pain, but Erik didn't pause in his charge and caught his enemy's left ear, severing it clean from the side of his head. The spectators gasped as the piece of flesh flew across the room and landed on the floor. Don Ponzio was blinded by the blood oozing from the gash across his face and crippled by the pain on the side of his head. Erik easily deflected his weakened thrusts, came in close to Don Ponzio, and taunted him, "Your widow will not mourn you. The world will not cry for your loss. You will be dust. It will be as if you had never been."

Don Ponzio slipped back and away from Erik. In a desperate attempt to turn the tables on the Phantom, Don Ponzio rallied, employing a combination that he had wisely never demonstrated during their practice sessions. Erik, who had continued to bleed severely from his shoulder wound, was taxed to fend off the elaborate and rapid changes in Don Ponzio's assault. He stumbled, and in that opening Ponzio drove his sword into Erik's side just above the hip bone. The point went through the soft tissue and passed out through an exit wound in the back. The Italian's smile of triumph was prematurely erased when he saw Erik's steely eyes.

Intense pain along the side of his torso had given rise almost immediately to a dark, insane determination. Still pinned by Don Ponzio's blade, Erik didn't pull away. Instead, he held his breath and wrenched himself forward, the blade of the rapier disappearing inch by inch inside the bloody wound. Ponzio watched in fascination and disbelief. Within reach of Ponzio's hand, Erik seized it, locking its hold on the pummel of the weapon and making his opponent's retreat impossible. Ponzio could not withdraw his blade or step back from his intimately close adversary. Slowly and deliberately, Erik raised his own rapier in his left hand and swung it around in front of the man's face until its edge lay under his opponent's chin and along the soft flesh of his throat. Taking one moment to smile wickedly, Erik sliced Ponzio's throat the length of the blade. Horror filled the dead man's eyes. His mouth opened and shut, a wet froth leaking from its corners, as he drowned in his own blood. Erik let him fall crumpled at his feet.

Incredibly, Erik remained standing, Ponzio's sword still embedded in his wound. At first no one moved. Then chaos broke out among the guests who scattered from the room. Luciana ran to Erik. In labored phrases, he instructed her.

"Pull it out … straight. Keep it as straight as you can. The entry was straight. Don't let it turn."

"I can't," she exclaimed, her hands trembling at the thought.

"Then I'll die," Erik answered in a neutral matter-of-fact tone. His skin was ashen, his forehead covered by a film of sweat, his breathing rapid and shallow. She could hear the sound of his blood dripping against the marble floor.

She had to act. Time was precious. If he passed out, he'd force the weapon through healthy tissue, causing further damage. While Erik balanced himself by placing his hand on her shoulder, Lucianna took hold of the pummel. Slowly she began to withdraw the sword blade.

She stopped when he groaned in pain.

"Quickly, please," he barely managed to say.

Taking a deep breath, Lucianna pulled the sword with all her strength until the end came free of the wound and fell heavily to the ground. Blood spurted from both sides of Erik's torso. She ripped a swatch of material from the bottom of her petticoat to stanch the flow of blood. Before she could act, Erik stumbled to his knees and then fell, unconscious, to the floor.

CHAPTER 9

❀

The Gift

Lucianna had told her husband's guests that they were no longer welcome at the estate and to prepare to leave at first light. Don Pietro urged her to reconsider. Surely she didn't want to be alone with the man who had killed her husband, especially after what they had learned about him. He was obviously a lunatic, a known murderer who had somehow escaped justice in Paris. At least she should allow Don Pietro to stay as her legal counsel. There'd be an inquiry, arrangements for the funeral, the testament would need to be examined and read. Lucianna assured Don Pietro that she would engage legal representation of her own to handle the issues of the estate.

Her first concern was to keep Erik alive. He had lost a great deal of blood. No one but Lucianna felt he had a chance of survival. The servants carried him to his room. One was dispatched for the surgeon, another for the undertaker, a third for the magistrate. A priest was mentioned, but Lucianna explained that Don Ponzio had forfeited salvation a long time ago, and she hoped that Erik would have no call for one just yet. Greta prepared a poultice to apply to his wounds to stop the bleeding. Erik was propped up in the bed to immobilize him as much as possible as well as to allow access to both the entry and exit wounds. When the surgeon came, he explained that even if the patient survived the initial crisis, such wounds—punctures of even a modest depth—often led to infections that carried off the unfortunate even several weeks later.

Lucianna asked him to do whatever he could to save Erik's life. He suggested a rather daring new procedure he had seen in Germany, a transfusion. The blood had to be replenished; otherwise the patient would surely slide further and further into shock and eventually a coma and death. The transfer of blood from a donor to the patient, however, was still risky. In many cases, the patient died from the transfusion itself. Was she willing to risk it? She was.

cold, cold and damp, heavy, my body sinks into blood soaked earth, the muddy liquid covers my chest, my ears, it seeps into my mouth, my nose, my eyes, my arms lie leaden by my side, the mud stops my screams, Christine's voice, a long dark tunnel, she sings to me, someone pulls me from the mud, my body makes a sucking noise as it comes free, Christine holds a newborn infant dressed in a white lace baptismal dress, I reach out to touch the hem, Christine smiles at me, Christine falls back upon a satin cushion, her eyes are closed, she lies still, a baby cries, his cries are unanswered, Raoul lifts her and places her inside the wooden coffin

"It's all right, Erik. It's all right. Rest. It was just a nightmare." Lucianna called the servant over to help her return him to the bed. He had awoken crying out, distressed, babbling nonsense. Lucianna could only catch the meaning of a few words spattered here and there. In spite of the fever, he was incredibly strong, especially after the last blood transfusion. "... wasn't ... Christine ... not dead ... told me ... go before me ... forgives ... be my angel ... forgiveness ... so much blood, so much death ... no, you don't understand ... she ... promised ... not now, not so for a long, long time ... not until ... would be ... salvation ... my salvation ... ask God ... the guilt ... take the guilt ... don't want her to die ..."

She required the servant to push him gently back against the pillows. Unintentionally, the servant pressed the wounded shoulder, and Erik groaned with the pain. "You're all right, Erik. It will be all right." She repeated over and over the same things as she listened and tried to understand what he was talking about. He finally relaxed, lying back on the bed, among the cushions. His breathing slowed and deepened as he fell back to sleep.

"Send for Don Carlo Benedetti. Tell him I urgently request his presence."

Don Carlo expected to inherit a sizable income from his uncle's estate. He was, after all, the only living blood relative. He had every reason to believe his uncle favored him; he had paid for his education in Paris for the past seven years. Unfortunately Don Carlo did not enjoy the scholar's life, and what was supposed to be a four or five year residence turned into seven as he continued to do poorly at university. When Don Ponzio invited him for a holiday, he was pleased to leave his books and come to protect his investment in the future.

Now that Don Ponzio was dead, things had changed dramatically. If he couldn't finish his career in Paris, he would become dependent on the good wishes of the widow. Unfortunately he had done nothing to ingratiate himself to Lucianna. After all she was his uncle's third wife! And although, thankfully, she seemed to be as barren as the previous two, she had managed to outlive Don Ponzio and would now decide the future of his estate. When the widow sent for him to return to the manor house, he took it as an encouraging sign.

She received him in the studio-workshop where she had painted Erik's portrait. She offered him a libation and asked him to sit. Without preamble she went directly to the point. "Carlo, I know that this must be painful for you. Ponzio was, after all, your uncle, a blood relative. Even so I've had the impression that your ties were more pragmatic than those of true affection. Please, don't pretend. You've been away a good portion of your life. You're young, with few prospects except for a possible inheritance from my husband."

Don Carlo tried to object and profess a deep loyalty to his uncle, but he could see that Lucianna was not fooled.

"The inquiry into my husband's death is going smoothly. Don Pietro's writ has made it rather cut and dry. It was a duel. The police are not happy that such an important member of society has died at the hands of a man no one knows much about. But that's where it will end. I want your oath that you won't provide the inspector with any information regarding Erik's background. In exchange, I'm willing to settle a sum of 10,000 lire annually on you in addition to whatever provision my husband may have made specifically for you."

Thrilled with the turn of events, Don Carlo was more than obliging.

"Without your corroboration, I don't think anything the others could say will weigh heavily against Erik."

"You may count on me, Aunt Lucianna."

"Donna Lucianna." She corrected him.

"Quite right. Donna Lucianna."

"I wanted to see you for another reason. I need to know everything you know about his past. Then you are to forget you've ever heard of him. Is that clear?"

"Yes, yes. I completely understand. You can count on me. I am at your service. Whatever you wish, just let me know. I will do my best to satisfy you. Just ask."

"That's quite enough, Carlo. Answer my questions. Who was Christine?"

"Well, I think I said everything I knew. I exaggerated, perhaps, the inappropriate implications of her involvement in the opera. In point of fact, she's respectably married into the Chagny family. They retired from Paris after the trial and are living in the country."

"You said she's married. You used the present tense. I thought you said she died in childbirth."

Carlo turned a bright red and began to fidget with the chain of his pocket watch. He had been uncomfortable from the very start with the whole affair. He was a philanderer, a bit of a cheat, but he wasn't a bad fellow. He was just a poor relation after all and couldn't help but respect the wishes of his uncle. He was dependent on his uncle's good opinion, and if this other man his uncle disliked was a murderer, was it really all that cruel to treat him badly? If he was a criminal, he couldn't expect people to treat him nicely or compassionately, could he? He tried to put it in the best light, but there was no avoiding telling Lucianna the truth.

"We were talking about Paris and scandals, and I mentioned the Phantom story. Immediately Uncle became intrigued and demanded I tell him everything, which I did. But it was his idea to say that Christine had died in childbirth. He told me that when he asked about the fate of the young lovers, I was to report her tragic death. I didn't know why until I realized at dinner that your … friend … must have something to do with the Phantom story. I put two and two together."

"And when Ponzio asked you to lie, you did. You knew that it was a lie. You must have seen how important this woman was to Erik! And you must also have realized that blurting that out at the moment you did would severely handicap his chances in the duel!"

Carlo considered her accusations and uncomfortably admitted that he had certainly played a cruel role in the whole affair. "But, Lucianna, I mean Donna Lucianna, forgive me. It wasn't my idea!"

As cruel and egotistical as his uncle, Lucianna thought. However, he might still be of use to her.

"I want you to tell Erik to his face that you lied when you said that she died. Do you hear me? If you refuse or if he doesn't believe you, you won't get a cent of your uncle's estate. Is that perfectly clear?"

"Yes. Yes, I don't see how you could make it any clearer than that! Anything you say, Aunt … Donna Lucianna. But he must be in pretty bad condition and won't be up for a visit for a while, will he? I could always come back when he's well. Although, honestly, Donna Lucianna, is there actually any chance that he'll survive? The doctor doesn't give him very good odds, and it would probably be best not to disturb him with all this. Let sleeping dogs lie, as the British say."

Dear Madame Chagny,

I haven't had the pleasure of your acquaintance, but we have mutual friends, evidently, who have given me the means to contact you. The reason that I write you involves another mutual friend who is in dire need of your assistance. It's unwise for me to make it too clear of whom I speak, but it's a person whose very survival depends on your continued good thoughts. An unfortunate series of events have led him erroneously, I'm glad to say, to believe that you have met with tragedy. Indeed, there is nothing that can dissuade him that you are not dead. Forgive my bluntness.

If you know of whom I speak, you will certainly find it within your Christian charity to send him some proof of your continued well-being. He has suffered a near fatal injury, and has resisted recovery due to the despair that he experiences, believing that you have died in childbirth.

He has been of great service to me during a troubled time for the both of us, and I will do anything to see him recover.

The courier has been instructed to bring your reply. At this time our mutual friend does not wish for his whereabouts to fall into the wrong hands.

Your humble servant,
Donna Lucianna Fiortino

Dear Signora Fiortino,

I was distressed to receive your letter. I do indeed understand of whom you speak and cannot tell you how glad I was to receive your letter until I read the contents. I don't know if you are aware of Erik's situation. I feel it necessary to tell you that he is married and that his wife has frantically searched for him for these several years. I include herein her information and beg that you contact her directly so that she might come to her husband's side. I intend to write her and share this information with her as soon as I post this letter to you.

You are vague about Erik's current location, what has happened to him, as well as the nature of your relationship to him. However, I read in your letter a true concern for him and thank you with all my heart that you are doing what you can. I will also include herein a note that you can give him that should prove that I am well.

Why would he have thought that I had died?

I wish that circumstances were other than what they are so that I could immediately come to be with him myself. If this is needed, please do not hesitate to send word. My husband is adamantly opposed to my traveling, but if Erik's life is at risk, I will dare to disobey.

Your indebted friend,
Christine, Countess de Chagny

Inside the letter was folded another sheet addressed to Erik. Lucianna turned it round and round between her fingers. She had wanted proof. She hadn't expected that the countess would write so warmly. The story of their tragic encounter had suggested that there would no longer be any ties between them. She had expected a cold reply, one that she could still share with Erik to prove that the woman had not perished. She expected that the countess would be distressed to know that someone was trying to contact her on behalf of the man who had kidnapped her. There had been deaths involved. Yet the woman wrote with true affection and concern for Erik. Of equal surprise was the fact that she knew Erik's wife. Lucianna was glad that she had not included an address or instructions on how to find Erik. The only solid information the countess had was Lucianna's name and the fact that Erik was still in Italy.

The personal missive enclosed in the letter was addressed in the same elegant hand. Lucianna turned the sheet over and ran her fingers along the edge.

She could resist no longer. She unfolded the sheet and read:

My dearest Erik,

I have been in contact with Meg since the two of you crossed the border into Italy. I have been so worried for you. Meg wrote to me telling me what happened. She was frantic to find you. Even after that first year, she continued to wait hoping that she'd hear from you and praying that you could forgive her and would return. I wish I could tell you more, but it's not my place to do so. You must get well and return to your wife. She confided that the last time you were together she was not herself. Although she didn't give me the particulars, she said that she panicked. She deeply regrets what she did to drive you away.

I'm so glad that Signora Fiortino succeeded in contacting us. She says that you have been near death's door and that somehow you thought I had died. I can't shake my concern for you. I am deeply worried for your health and safety. I am well. Raoul and I have a little boy named Victor and a recently born baby girl, Elise. Victor is quite a handful, bright and happy. Elise is sweet tempered and gives us nothing but joy. I am well. Raoul is beside himself with pride. Raoul and I are very happy.

You are in my thoughts. Whenever I sing, I think of you and how much you taught me. Please make every effort to get well and to return to Meg. I know she waits for you even now after all this time.

Your truest friend,
Christine

Lucianna was not fooled by the friendly tone of the letter. There was something stronger than friendship that bound Erik to his Christine. In each line, she sensed a studied reserve, the effort to find something warm without giving away the true depths of attachment. Yet she spoke of children and insisted she was happy in her marriage. Clearly something held them together, but whatever it was, it had been safely contained and guarded.

What disturbed Lucianna more were the references to Meg, Erik's wife. She recalled Erik murmuring the name in the throes of passion, in the semi-consciousness of his drugged stupor. When she had asked him who Meg was, he had not told her the truth. Was it because he no longer loved Meg or because he loved her all too well?

Lucianna is there every time I open my eyes. I've vague memories of lying in her arms. I was so cold, I could not stop shaking. Her body warmed me wherever we touched. I dreamed and dreamed of blood and graves and of Christine. The obnoxious dandy who told my story came and confessed that he had lied about Christine's death. It was Ponzio's idea to unsettle me once he knew who I was and how much she meant to me. He was right that it would unsettle me, but I believe he had expected the consequences to be different from what they were. Hearing that Christine died drove me over the edge. It didn't matter to me in that moment whether I lived or died. Instead of succumbing to his attack, I pressed on like a madman. The only thing that saved me was my desire to kill Ponzio. I don't even remember the pain. Lucianna tells me that I was insane. She scolded me severely for the risk I took. It was no risk. I didn't care at that moment; I only wanted to see him die. It's always been like that. I have always let myself be consumed by passions that have led to pain for me and for others.

Lucianna thinks that I should be happy now that I know Christine is alive. Yet I can't shake the feeling of her loss. It's not that I don't believe Carlo. I pray that he's telling me the truth now. But my heart bleeds when I think of her. I can't stop feeling that she has died. When he said she died in childbirth, it did something to me that I can't reverse.

I lie here thinking of her, but strangely my thoughts keep drifting away and back to Meg, *ma petite danseuse*. Christine didn't choose me, but Meg did. In the dark, when I know Lucianna sleeps in the chair next to the bed, I cry. I can't stop the tears. I stuff my hand in my mouth so that I don't wake her. If only Meg could find her way to me now like she did that night of despair when I released my hold on Christine and decided to bury myself alive deeper and deeper under the streets of Paris. I went to my death. And Meg came after me and reached out and dragged me back to the light.

The light! Meg is the light. It has always been Meg. She is my star, my compass, my light in the darkness. If only I could trust Christine's words. If only it were true that Meg still loved me.

And the child? Was that, like Christine's death, a lie? If I languish here, I'll never know. I'll never know my child. I'll never know if Meg forgives me, if she still loves me. If only I could …

Perhaps Lucianna can still be the light Sabia foretold. If she were to help me find my way back … If she could help me get home …

Lucianna insisted that Erik come down each day and walk the short distance to the chaise lounge on the veranda to sit in the warm sunshine. He at first refused, like the petulant child she realized he still was in many, many ways. Frustrated with his resistance to exercise to regain his strength, she asked him if it was his plan to continue to live like an invalid with her at his beck and call. Gleefully, she faced his wrath. Not only did he snarl at her, but he sat up on his own in the bed and pushed himself to his feet. The moment the soles of his feet touched the floor the shifting of his weight must have sent waves of pain along his side. Breathing like a baited bull in the ring, he sucked in several deep gulps of air and took his first steps forward since the night of the duel.

The doctor was astounded at his recuperation. Although his wounds did become infected, his system fought the infection off, and they were nicely healing. Within another fortnight, the surgeon told Erik he'd be able to travel.

Lucianna had delayed giving him the letter from Christine. When she finally brought it to the veranda and placed it in his hands, he was puzzled and considered it apprehensively. She didn't explain; she just waited for him to unfold the letter and read. Slowly he fingered the edge of the paper and spread it open on his lap. As he realized who had written it, his hands began to tremble perceptibly. Lucianna watched him read and reread each line before continuing to the next. When he arrived at the end, he began to read it once more from the beginning. She turned away when she noticed that he was fighting to recover his composure. She heard him fold the sheet and slip it inside his vest, next to his heart. This was the moment she had dreaded.

"It arrived several weeks ago."

Erik waited for her to explain.

"I wanted you to be well," she lied. "I thought it might upset you."

Erik stared at her, and she realized he didn't believe her.

"You're right. I kept it from you for my own reasons."

"You've misunderstood everything, Lucianna." His tone was not angry, but grave. "Christine is part of my soul. I could as well live without my heart as live without her. But I can survive as long as she lives and as long as I know she cares for me. I expect nothing from her. I know that if I can be saved, it will be because she finds something in me that's worth saving. It's a strange love that exists between us, one that feeds on air and nothingness."

"You love her?" Lucianna had hoped this question would not arise. She had never felt as comfortable with another human being as she felt with Erik. When she was painting his portrait, she came to realize that she had fallen deeply in love with him. It was hard for her to believe that he felt nothing for her. The way he touched her, the sacrifice he made when he faced her husband were because he loved her; of this she was convinced.

"You still haven't understood me. Yes, I love Christine, but it's a love that is different from the love you ask of me."

"Is it so obvious?" She smiled ironically.

"How could you paint me the way you did if you didn't love me?" She didn't answer, and both watched the interweaving pattern of light and shadow sweep across the meadows in the distance.

"What about Meg?" She had to know it all, no matter what.

"What you'd ask of me, I can't give you. It belongs to Meg."

"Because she's your wife, and you feel obligated?"

"No. Because I love her. Because until Meg, I lived like a freak, alone, tormented by my obsessions, afraid of my body and its needs. I love her."

"Then it's simply gratitude you feel toward her. That's not love, Erik." Lucianna knelt beside his chair and grabbed his hands in hers earnestly entreating him to see that he was free to love her instead.

"No, you're wrong." Erik shook her hands off brusquely and pushed himself from the chair. He barely limped from the pain in his wound. When she started to come to him protesting her love, he pushed her gently away. "I don't love you, Lucianna. I never have. I wanted to free you from that monster. You intrigued me, excited me. I remember the first night we met. Then when I saw you with him at the fair, you were different; you were wounded, in pain, lost. I mourned the death of that high-spirited woman. I wanted you to find her again."

Lucianna now gave free vent to her tears.

"Don't. Don't cry, Lucianna. I care for you. But I can't love you. You used me. You both used me. You seduced me so that you could have a child."

"You were unfaithful to both of these women when you let me seduce you. Am I the only one guilty here?"

"No, but when I made love to you, it was because I wanted you. I didn't do it to get something from you or to bend you to my will. I have been unfaithful to Christine, but Christine belongs to another man. I have also been unfaithful to Meg, because I thought she no longer loved me and that I had no hope of ever being with her again."

"Erik, you have to believe that I would never have slept with just anyone! I wanted your child because I love you."

"I have a child, Lucianna. At least that is what you told me." Suddenly Erik feared that he had imagined it all. Perhaps there was no child or if there had been a child he had died. "It wasn't a lie, was it? Christine never mentioned the child in her letter."

"I would never lie to you about something that important, Erik. Your wife was with child when you left her. She had a child."

"What if something has happened? What if the child was sickly, deformed even more than I am? How could I leave Meg alone to deal with that?"

"I understand that you feel responsible, even guilty, because you …"

Erik interrupted her. "You can never understand what I feel for Meg. *I* barely do. Only recently I have thought it over again and again, and I've seen that I have failed to understand."

Lucianna wondered why he stopped suddenly. He had turned his back on her so that she couldn't see his distress. He loved Meg and desperately ached to return to her. This realization cut her to the quick, but she controlled the disappointment. She couldn't force him to feel something he didn't feel for her.

"Erik, the doctor says you can travel soon. You should go back to Pianosa, to find her."

"What if … what if it's too late? Or what if I've destroyed any love she's ever felt for me? What if she didn't want the child and … and … No, not Meg. She could never despise a child." Turning to Lucianna, he pleaded for her to understand the jumble of fears and emotions that tormented him. "Lucianna, I don't know what to do. I need to be with Meg. I want to go home, to find a home with Meg, but I'm afraid. I can't face her."

It took every ounce of courage she had in her to make the suggestion she was about to make. "Then don't. You don't have to face her, not alone. I'll go with you. We'll travel together, and I'll go to Meg."

"No, no, no, no. You can't tell her …"

"I won't. Hush. Listen to me. We'll take rooms nearby. You decide when and how to face her. You can wait and watch from the shadows. I'll introduce myself to Meg and seek her friendship. I'll earn her trust, and I'll find out what her heart says. I'll see what has changed and what has remained the same. When the time is right, I can tell her I met you and that if she wants I can get in touch with you. Nothing has to happen unless both of you are ready and want it to."

Erik took her hand in his and whispered, "You'd do this for me? You'd help me return to Meg? You love me that much?"

"Yes." She squeezed his hand and brushed aside the hair that had fallen across his eyes. She loved him more than she ever had, even though she knew he was not hers.

CHAPTER 10

❈

The Return

But lo! an ambush waits his passage o'er;
Fierce foes insidious intercept the shore.

Odyssey, Homer, Alexander Pope

As impatient as Erik was to return to Pianosa, it was a matter of several more weeks before Lucianna had finalized the reading of the testament and the arrangements necessary to leave the manor house. She charged Carlo to oversee the property while she was away and told him that any correspondence that arrived for her should be forwarded to Beatrice Fusco in the town of Pianosa. Without further explanation, she and Erik departed.

Erik was impressed with Lucianna's planning. The apartments that she rented for the two of them and several trustworthy servants were comfortable and discreet. He was explained as her French cousin, Pierre Fusco, a wealthy recluse who had been injured in his travels through Peru. Although Lucianna cautioned Erik to be patient, he insisted that she find out as much as she could immediately. She told him these things take time and proper preparation, but he warned her that he would go out and interrogate the first person he came upon by force if need be, so she relented.

After what seemed to Erik an eternity, Lucianna—or Beatrice as she encouraged him to call her—returned with the essential details, some of which she feared would not please Erik.

"How is Meg? How is the child? Do I have a son or a daughter? Is it … healthy?" He accosted her with a barrage of questions before she could remove her overcoat and sit down.

"Meg is in good health. You have a son, and he's quite healthy aside from …"

Before she could finish, Erik clutched the back of the chair to steady himself and interrupted her, "Yes, of course! He's …"

"No, no, no, no! Let me finish, for goodness sake, Erik. He's beautiful. There is no disfigurement. I was about to say that he has had the same childhood ailments all healthy children have, the sniffles, colic, rashes that come and go."

Erik's relief was palpable. He sat heavily in the chair as if dazed. The release of tension momentarily threatened to overwhelm him, but he struggled to remain composed. Lucianna had known that he was concerned, but she hadn't understood the depth of his fears for the child. She waited until the storm of emotions subsided and Erik was once again focused and intent on information. A new light shone in his eyes, a light of hope.

"What's his name?"

"François."

"That's good. That's a very strong name." As suddenly as a rain cloud crosses before the sun, a look of gloom swept over Erik's face erasing his brief smile.

"What's the matter?"

"I wish I could see him. Now. This moment!"

"Patience, Erik. You'll see him soon enough."

"Patience! You always say that as if it were a magic word that could take the sting out of disappointment and delay!"

"Can you wait at least until tomorrow? Meg takes François with her to the chapel during the week on Wednesdays to bring fresh flowers for the shrines. She seems to be rather devout."

"I hadn't known her to be religious. But how can I visit her there without her recognizing me?"

"There must be small chapels from which you can spy on her. Or perhaps we can sneak you up to the organ, and you can play!"

"What else have you found out, Lucianna?"

She shifted in her seat. The room seemed to chill. "No one around here, except a few of the household staff, had the chance to meet you before you fled. You seem insubstantial to them. Everyone expects Meg to ask for an annulment from the priest and to remarry. Even before François's birth there had been a steady stream of suitors at her door."

"Well, she's a beautiful young woman." Erik kept his gaze on Lucianna, knowing that there was more to it than that from her expression.

"It appears that one of the suitors has caught her attention."

The next day Erik and Lucianna arrived at the church well before Meg was expected. Lucianna introduced herself to the parish priest and asked if her cousin might have the use of the grand organ in the balcony. She explained that Pierre, the name she had chosen for Erik, was very private and only spoke with her. The small, round man scratched his bald pate as he peered around Signorina Beatrice Fusco's shoulder at the hooded and cloaked man standing in the shadow of the atrium. Lucianna added that he had suffered a horrible accident while exploring the jungles of Peru and that his only solace was music. They had heard that this particular organ was quite a marvel.

"Of course, he's most welcome any time. May I at least greet him?" Without waiting for Lucianna's reply, the jovial old priest walked over to the silent, dark figure in the shadows. Noticing that Erik had turned as if to leave, the priest stopped at a discreet distance and addressed him in a soft, fatherly tone. "You're welcome to come any time, my son. If you ever want to share a cup of tea or a drop of wine and a bit of conversation, I'd be glad for the company."

Erik inclined his head in response and turned to climb the stairs to the organ.

The music that filled the church was of such a sweet quality that the few parishioners who were bent in prayer turned their ears to the balcony in wonder at its source. The priest, too, paused in his instructions to the new altar boy as he caught the first notes of the music Erik played. He had never heard the organ sound so wonderfully subtle and rich. Lucianna withdrew to a discreet corner to wait for Meg.

She didn't have to wait for long. Meg and an older woman entered pulling behind them a cart filled with flowers—roses and carnations—to be placed at the shrines. Among the flowers sat a child, between two and three years old, who helped hand the flowers one by one to his mother. The organ music changed to a gay melody that delighted the child who laughed loudly and scrambled out of the wagon. He called out in a sweet voice to her, "Maman, the angels are playing for the baby!" Meg grinned at François's glee.

The music abruptly stopped. The air weighed heavily among columns and stained glass windows.

"Why did the pretty music stop, Maman?" the child asked, plaintively.

Just as suddenly as the music had stopped, it resumed. If before, it was lovely, it now held an amazing note of passion. No longer the whimsical theme of a childish song, it was a complex and dramatic composition that Luciana didn't know.

For an instant, Lucianna saw a puzzled expression on Meg's face, but it vanished when the older woman, Annetta, asked her if the roses were for the saint or for the Virgin Maria.

The child skipped along the aisle toward the music. Lucianna watched with her heart in her throat as the little boy began to climb the stairs in search of the source of the sounds. How would he react if he saw Erik at the organ?

Erik had seen them enter the vestibule of the church. Meg was a vision of light. Her hair was pulled back, revealing the gentle curve of her long neck. Several golden strands had escaped the pins and floated like ribbons down her back. She glided across the floor with her dancer's body. When she turned, he glimpsed her face. He sucked in his breath sharply. He had thought he remembered her, but his memory was a pale reflection of her true beauty. Her brown eyes, large and soft, dominated her heart-shaped face; her mouth small, but deliciously curved stirred desires that he found pleasantly familiar. And beside her in the cart was his son! He could see even from this distance his joyful face. He was perfect! He had her perfection, but he didn't really look like his mother. He had features that were vaguely familiar to Erik, but he couldn't identify them until he recalled the features of the man Lucianna had painted. The child looked like that man in the portrait, the one without the disfigured face. His child looked like him, but without blemish as he would like to have been himself. He watched the child come his way across the stone floor until he disappeared below the balcony out of Erik's view.

He heard Lucianna's voice. "Signora. Your child is very ambitious and daring. He was about to climb the stairs. I wasn't sure if you wanted him out of your sight."

Lucianna stepped into view, holding the child's hand, and led him back to the center of the church aisle where Meg went to meet them. In spite of the fact that he was a big child, Meg lifted him up and placed him on her hip as she thanked Lucianna. "He's bolder and braver every day. He's perfectly able to climb the stairs, but you're right to have stopped him. I prefer to have him where I can keep an eye on him. Not because he can't climb stairs, but because who knows what mischief he might get up to in the loft. You see, he likes to play the organ." She tweaked his nose and kissed his forehead as she teased him.

"The organ?" Lucianna asked skeptically.

"Yes, he's rather precocious. You think I'm joking. I know it's hard to believe that a two-year-old …"

"I'm not two; I'm two and four months old, Maman. You keep forgetting!"

"Well, anyway, it's still rather remarkable how he can play at two and four months."

"Are you a musician?" Lucianna asked.

"I performed as first soprano for several seasons in Paris at the opera. My first love was dance. But I was never proficient at an instrument. That talent François got from his father. A composer as well as a musician, he was a true genius." Lucianna sensed that Meg was uncomfortable talking about Erik.

Father Antonio took this opportunity to introduce the two women to each other. As he was about to mention Beatrice's cousin, Lucianna interrupted him and suggested perhaps they might visit each other. The priest recalled Pierre's reticence and decided to let Signorina Fusco decide when and if she should present her cousin to Meg.

Erik was mesmerized by the view of his son held against Meg's body, his legs dangling on either side of her hip as she rocked unconsciously back and forth from habit, he imagined. Watching her, he understood the iconography of the Virgin and baby Jesus. There was nothing short of the divine in the scene he saw of his wife and child.

Why wait? he thought. Where better than a church for him to make his presence known to his wife and son? Here she couldn't fear him. She'd realize that he had come to make amends. Wouldn't she have to forgive him and give him a second chance? The priest and Lucianna might intercede on his behalf. Even the old woman—he recognized her as one of the servants at the manor—would surely urge Meg to have compassion.

Erik had convinced himself that this could be the moment to reveal himself when a tall, broad-shouldered young man with light brown hair and a martial air about him came over to Meg and in a familiar tone that drove a hot spike of anger through Erik's gut reminded Meg that she had promised to accompany him on a stroll through the glen. Erik's heart fell, and his knees began to buckle when he saw that Meg smiled sweetly at this interloper. Taking her leave of Lucianna and the priest, she signaled to Annetta to take charge of their child and left with the stranger.

Erik anchored himself to the organ, fighting the urge to careen down the stairs and challenge Meg's suitor to a duel to the death. He had just managed to stifle the impulse when Lucianna emerged at the head of the stairs and called to him to return with her to the apartments.

I slip among her guests unseen, my mask being one of many in this banquet hall that I remember seeing only once before. Harlequins and priests, devils and jesters, Caesars and Cleopatras, mill about me as I search for her. She is dressed as a simple milk maid. No one remarks on my disguise; I come as a monk. I watch her waltz with a tall broad shouldered young man who places his hand upon her lower back as if he claimed her with that touch. His half mask doesn't hide the self-satisfied grin that dominates the unmasked expanse of his face. He struts around the dance floor knowing himself to be the center of attention dragging Meg along with him. She falls easily in step. She, too, is comfortable with his hands on her body. This must be the young Giovanni they all talk about, the man who whisked her away from the church on that first day.

I wait for her to disengage herself from this swain, this interloper who courts another man's wife. I avoid the eyes of those near me who furtively stare my way trying to guess my identity. A woman tries to involve me in a coquettish tête-à-tête, but I turn on my heels and disappear into the river of dancers.

She is surrounded by men. Giovanni disappears for an instant, and a bevy of young gallants assail her with offers of sweets and liquors. She smiles politely, but she shakes her head at their offers. They move in closer; she is anxious. I see her breathing increase. I set off across the wide space that lies between us, and before I can reach out to protect her, Giovanni is there at her side. In a glance he sweeps the pack of baying hounds away. She relaxes, relieved, onto the arm he has offered to her. I curse him that he does what only I should be doing! She has found her knight, her protector. She has forgotten her monster.

Dance after dance she weaves around the hall with her proud swain. I have retreated to the shadows to avoid the attention of the other guests. They begin to notice the stranger among them who doesn't speak, doesn't drink, doesn't dance, but obsessively follows the comings and goings of the hostess. From the shadows I stalk her.

Giovanni stops in the middle of the waltz and leads my Meg by the hand to the veranda, through the portico doors that are open to allow the cool night air to enter and refresh the revelers. My heart threatens to burst through my chest. Where is he taking her? I'm fully aware of his intentions. The young lovers swept up in the heat of the moment leave the crowded ballroom to find a dark corner in the garden to be alone, to exchange favors. He took her by the hand. I remember the night long ago when she took me by the hand and drew me out of the crowded ballroom to a private rendezvous. I rush to follow, inadvertently smashing into several of the guests, drawing unwanted attention to myself in my anxiety to impede what I imagine will happen between Meg and her confident suitor.

In the garden I see what I expect to see—a number of couples have escaped the vigilance of their society and are in various stages of love making. But I don't see Meg and her suitor until I round a corner of the veranda by the high walled garden at the rear of the manor. They are very close. The darkness hides their faces better than their masks, and I can't hear their whispers. He presses against her, and I start to approach to drag him away from her when she steps back. I almost sigh with relief that she resists! They remain like this for what seems an eternity. When he turns and walks back to the house, she remains behind. She faces away from the manor, toward the darkness, and into the night sky. The stars' cold light mocks us both.

I come behind her quietly. I stop her mouth with one hand and wrap the other forcefully around her waist. She is startled and would cry out, but she mustn't. She is afraid because she doesn't know who I am. I will her to know. I will her to say my name, but of course she can't. I drag her back farther into the pitch of the walled garden until I'm sure no one can see us if they come around the corner as I have.

I drag her back and hold her hard, tight, wedged inside the hollow of my embrace. I burn to feel her in my arms pressing, writhing against my body. She is small and delicate. I had forgotten how small she is and how sweet she smells. Her hair is soft under my chin as I bend to brush my cheek against it. At first stunned, she made no move to escape me. Now she struggles. Her hands scratch at my hand, the one that lies across her mouth. My palm is warm and wet from her mouth, and I so wish to place my mouth where it lies, to taste, to drink her. I don't speak. I simply wait until she calms. I wait until I feel her body soften and lean into me. I wait until her body finds the places it knows so well. I wait for her to sense me, to remember me. I am enthralled, and it takes every ounce of my strength not to reveal myself to her now. I am panting from desire for her. But in my desire there is also fear. Were I to take my hand from her mouth, would she not scream? Why doesn't she sense me? And if she were to know that it is I who hold her, would she still scream?

I have to go. I can't bear to put it to the test. I barely brush my lips across her cheek and release her. I run away into the shadows.

"We worked this all out before, Erik. You wanted me to meet Meg and to speak with her so that I could learn her heart. Do you want to throw all that away now and burst into the manor and make your presence known to her?"

Erik paced the floor. He had returned from the masquerade ball, disheveled and wild eyed. Lucianna, who had also gone to the ball but as an invited guest, had returned hours before. Not finding Erik in the apartments they had rented, she sat beside the door waiting. She had told him that it was a bad idea for him to sneak into the ball. What did he expect to find? Meg sitting alone and forlorn pining away for him?

"I held her in my arms!" Erik spoke this as if it were an accusation of some sort. "I saw all those men surrounding her, hounding her, and I was about to go to her when he came between us." Lucianna tried to follow Erik's train of thought, but it changed suddenly and unexpectedly as he tried to tell her what had happened at the ball. "I held her, and she didn't know me."

"Did you say anything to her? How did you manage to hold her if she didn't know it was you?"

"I grabbed her from behind. I didn't say anything. I wanted her to sense that it was me! There was a time that she would have known me even if I were across the room, without a touch or a word." He balled his hands into fists as he paced again the length of the room. "She's forgotten me. He's taken my place!"

Lucianna reached out to touch his shoulder. When he didn't move away from her, she slipped her arms around his waist and leaned her head against his back. She could feel his heart pound through several layers of fabric. The anger was dissipating, replaced by a sad melancholy. She saw it in the way his shoulders slumped and his head fell slightly forward. She released her embrace and circled around to face him. His frustration and sadness squeezed at her heart. He let her embrace him, lowering his head to her shoulder; slowly he encircled her body with his arms. Gradually, he released his hold on her and left her embrace.

Above them, over the mantel, hung the portrait of an unmasked man with dark hair and green eyes. For one moment, Erik glanced at his false twin. Then he turned his back to the image, away from Lucianna, to disguise his jealousy of oil and canvas.

"I'm sorry, Lucianna. You were right. She's had to make a life for herself without me. It will take time to see what room, if any, there might be for me."

"Erik, you must be more positive than that. I expect that soon we'll be able to arrange a meeting, and we'll be able to let her know you're back. I have just begun to win her confidence. She keeps mostly to herself so it's been rather difficult to have anything more than superficial conversations with her. I will find out what she feels for you. But you have to be patient."

"I've never been patient. Why would you expect me to be so now?"

"Because you don't have any choice. Unless you want to risk showing up on Meg's doorstep and just see what happens?"

"No."

"Erik? What is it that you're afraid of?"

"I told you how we parted. Isn't that enough reason to be cautious? I don't know if she really wants me to come back into her life. All I have is what Christine says."

"Why isn't that enough? She says Meg searched for you and has been waiting for you ever since you left. There must be something more that keeps you back."

Erik hesitated before he answered, "I don't know if I can do this."

"Do what?"

"Be with Meg. Live a normal existence."

"You have a child, Erik. You have a wife who loves you."

"That remains to be seen."

"Still you come back again and again to your doubts."

"I've been betrayed before!"

"I understand." She reached out to him, but he brushed her hand away brusquely.

"I don't think you do. You've never had to run from someone only because they've seen your face. You've not spent years in the shadows watching the person you love only to have her turn away from you and run into someone else's arms just when you finally had the courage to declare your love to her. You've not lived cut off from everything human, lived in fear and dread that they might find you, knowing that they wouldn't give you the mercy or compassion they'd give a stray dog."

What kind of life had he lived, wondered Lucianna, hidden away in the shadows? How difficult it must seem to him to think of carrying out a normal life with Meg! She had observed him with others at the fair and at the manor. She could tell that he shrank from contact with everyone. He had found ways to protect himself. The mask he placed on his face was not the only one he wore. Joining them at the dinner table was like walking onto a stage for him. He would assume a character, approach those around him as if they were simply players on the same stage. But this wouldn't be possible in day-to-day life with Meg. To live with Meg would require that he live in the world. How was he going to manage that day in and day out? How could he protect himself?

Suddenly Erik took her hands in his. He seemed to struggle with some inner demon as he began to speak. "The child." His eyes said it all. They traveled, against his will, to the portrait and back to Lucianna. How would his child react to a father who hid half his face behind a mask? And if he were to take the mask off?

"Erik, we need to take one step at a time. Meg has invited me to tea. I'll be able to see the boy, too. I'll come back and tell you everything."

At the end of the day, after riding beyond the narrow confines of the village into the countryside and walking aimlessly for miles, Erik would wait for dusk and gallop at breakneck speed to Meg's manor, his manor, he reminded himself time and time again to no avail. It didn't feel like his, and every sign around him told him he had no place there. Even so he couldn't keep away.

He had found an elm that spread across the enclosed garden wall on the north side where it didn't interfere with the southern sun the plants so needed. Under its branches Meg would come in the evening and sit watching the fireflies and enjoying the cooling breeze. He never failed to be there when she came out, and he never left until she began to shiver with the night air and finally rose to enter the warm safety of her home, their home, he whispered to himself unconvincingly. At least he could admire Meg from afar, and sometimes he caught glimpses of his son playing on the stone patio, if it was a warm night, just outside the house.

Tonight he sat and waited, but Meg didn't come out alone as she normally did. The young man he had come to loathe, Giovanni, accompanied her. Erik drew back into the dense shadow and held his breath as he watched the young suitor brush the bench off, unnecessarily since Meg always kept it scrupulously clean, and invite her to sit. She seemed uneasy to Erik, or perhaps he wanted to believe so. Yet she did fidget with the tassels on her shawl and stare out away from Giovanni as they spoke. At first he had difficulty hearing their conversation, but soon he caught the rhythm of their words and could make out most of what they were saying. He was relieved to hear that most of it was insipid small talk, the kind he remembered from Don Ponzio's dinner parties, about friends and neighbors in the area. But then the conversation took a decidedly bad turn as far as Erik was concerned.

"I was speaking with Father Antonio the other day, and he remarked that cases such as yours are easily resolved, Meg. You must give it serious thought. I can't bear the idea of you walling yourself up in this house as if it were a tomb.

You're a young woman." Here he edged so close that Erik thought they must be kissing, but Meg's voice proved that this was not the case.

"You promised you wouldn't talk about this again, Giovanni. I can't."

"It's beyond me," Giovanni rose from the bench, and his tone barely veiled his annoyance, "why you would wait for that monster. You can't believe your marriage was real, Meg."

"Stop!"

Erik clenched the branch of the tree so hard that he felt the bark cut into his palm. *So she had told her lover about the monster she had married.*

"He's left you, and I say good riddance. Now you can marry and lead a normal life. Thankfully the child ..."

Meg rose in one movement and slapped Giovanni hard across the face with the flat of her hand. She didn't say another word, but marched off to the house. Giovanni remained outside stunned momentarily by the blow. He cursed under his breath before straightening his vest and jacket and following Meg into the manor.

Erik waited until the lights in the facing rooms were extinguished and even longer past the rise of the moon before he carefully climbed down the elm and walked to the tree where he had tethered Charlemagne. He circled stealthily around the manor to make sure that Giovanni's mount was gone before he set off himself for Lucianna's and his apartments.

He went straight to the servant's room and asked Luigi to prepare a bath. His whole body ached.

Erik lay back in the great tub filled to overflowing with hot oil-scented water. He soaked his body deep in the healing, soothing warmth and breathed in the vapors. Old wounds ached and threatened to plague him more and more as time passed. He was perhaps nearing forty he calculated according to his best estimates, although to look at him one would never guess his age. "Monster" Giovanni had called him. Yes, Meg must have told him their story; she must have described him to the young suitor.

He didn't hear Lucianna approach until she bent down behind him, picked up the soapy sponge, and began to rub it along his back. He leaned forward so that she could reach his lower back and at the same time he could modestly conceal his nakedness. But the touch of her fingers along his neck relaxed him so much that he felt his inhibitions melt away in the water. She whispered softly that she heard him come in. She waited for him to talk, but he didn't say a word. He let his head fall forward on his chest and closed his eyes as he felt her hands moving all along his body. Bending over him, her nightdress dipped into the water, and regardless of the dampness she lowered her hands deep into the soapy depths of the metal tub.

The world began to dissolve for a moment until he desperately dragged himself back to reality and opening his eyes he took her hand and brought it to the surface of the water. "Please, Lucianna. I'm having a difficult enough time resisting you."

"Why should you try so hard? What harm could it do?"

She bent forward, oblivious to the fact that she was more and more drenched by the bath water, and kissed him hard and long on the mouth. Her taste filled him with longing, and he brought her down into the water without thinking. The tub overflowed, the water splashing out onto the floor, but the two of them were too intensely clasped in each other's embrace to care.

CHAPTER 11

❀

The Graveyard

it wasn't that Giovanni hadn't been kind and solicitous, it wasn't that she didn't find him attractive, quite the contrary, she had yearned to touch and be touched, she dreamed of Erik returning to her, climbing into her bed, lifting her up in his arms and scalding her with his warmth, she dreamed so often that she had begun to relish the strike of ten o'clock, the earliest she could reasonably dismiss her maid, check on François and climb between the cool sheets naked and wait to dream, it wasn't that she felt she had no right to ask the priest for the annulment as Giovanni had urged, only then could she start afresh, marry, live like a normal person, it wasn't that a new life didn't call out to her with reassuring comfort, and Giovanni had many of the same charms that Erik had, he was tall, perhaps not as tall, he was darkly handsome, although Meg studied his face for scars and small blemishes in a perverse desire to find some hint of Erik, when she found herself doing this one afternoon when he was particularly amorous insisting on touching her hand, on sitting so close that she felt his breath on her face, on trying to kiss her on the mouth, she was horribly confused and wondered at it, why would she seek imperfection in her lover? and why would that sign of imperfection be considered a mark of some higher quality? what quality lay in imperfection that was superior to those handsome traits that made her feel giddy when she was too close to Giovanni? she had loved Erik, not because of his hideous deformity, but in spite of it, hadn't she? and here was a man who insisted that he would always be constant on whom she could not find the least blemish and it bothered her to distraction, it bothered her so much that on occasion she found herself looking away from him as if he were not handsome but rather ugly, perhaps she felt herself unworthy of such a perfect suitor? after all Erik had abandoned her and her child, Erik who had half a face had never loved her the way she wanted to be loved, she had pursued him, she had comforted him even when he was most beastly and pushed her away, she had tied herself to him, he had never wanted her! so why did she still dream at night of Erik, not Giovanni? she even tried to imagine Giovanni in her bed as she lay on the edge of slumber only for him to turn toward her in her dreams with Erik's face and body, there was no real hope that Erik would ever return to her, she had read Christine's letters and the vague encouragement she offered, she had begun to hope when the first of these arrived informing her that some noblewoman in the east had written to her of Erik's whereabouts and suggested that he would soon come back to Pianosa, but Christine had lost contact with the lady and could find no more information about Erik, she continued to write encouraging notes full of lies, saying that Erik loved Meg and had come to realize it in his absence, but Meg clung to those lies until they were so worn and ragged that she knew she had to toss them away, he hadn't come, and he wouldn't come, and she would be wise to mend her heart and find a proper father for François, but something was wrong, she sensed that something hung in the air that wouldn't let her give her heart to Giovanni, something made her skin prickle and her ears twitch as if she were a stag in the forest and a wolf were drawing down on her, it was a mixture of fear and excitement that she couldn't shake

"So the priest is prone to lengthy sermons, and this past Sunday was not exceptional?" Lucianna laughed as Meg served her another cup of tea with milk.

"I'm afraid Father Antonio enjoys the pulpit a great deal. But he's a kind, old man. He's helped me a great deal."

Here Lucianna finally found the opening that she had been waiting for after several visits in which small talk of a rather impersonal nature had dominated. "Meg, I'm sorry. I hadn't realized. I hope it's not indelicate of me considering our rather recent friendship to tell you that you can confide in me if you need a friend. I myself have been through a rather traumatic experience recently."

"Yes, please forgive me. I know you're a widow. I'm sorry for the loss of your husband. I didn't realize it was recent." Meg blushed.

"You wonder why I don't wear mourning for him. That's quite reasonable. I should have thought! I don't wear mourning because my husband was a sadistic monster, and his death was a relief to me."

Meg was mildly shocked at Lucianna's frankness, but it immediately made her trust her new found friend. "I have to confess that when we spoke the other day, I hoped we might become friends. All my acquaintances here have long practiced a patronizing compassion for me since Erik, my husband, left me. They mean well, but I find them difficult to be with sometimes. When they aren't being overly sympathetic, they enjoy talking ill of my husband or they feel they have the right to tell me what I should do or should not do."

"I've heard a little about your situation, Meg."

"Signore Cimino, Giovanni, wants me to ask for an annulment." Meg was uncomfortable when she spoke of this. Lucianna sat and listened, careful not to indicate one way or the other what she thought. "I've been successful fending off many of the other young suitors in the area. I don't know why they've been so persistent."

Lucianna knew Meg was not fishing for compliments, so she felt quite justified in reminding her how beautiful she was, and that she was well situated besides. She would be a wonderful match for many a young man in the area. Lucianna let her talk about the past years since the birth of her son and the onslaught of men who had hounded her before she steered the conversation back to Erik.

"What was your husband like?"

Meg looked at her surprised and asked if she hadn't heard all the gossip in Pianosa about Erik already? Lucianna admitted to having heard some details but thought they were too bizarre to be believed. Here she knew she was lying and that eventually she'd have to confess to Meg, but it was the only way to let Meg express herself sincerely.

"He was intense and haunted. A tall, imposing man, he was strong yet vulnerable, quick to temper, outwardly severe but sweet and kind inside, passionate, above all else, passionate. He was many things, but tortured most of all. You must have heard that he wore a mask?"

"I did hear something to that effect. Was he disfigured?" Again she adopted a level, neutral tone so as not to affect Meg's responses.

"Yes, one side of his face was partially disfigured. You probably find it strange that I could have been attracted to him. Everyone else does, except Annetta and Giuseppe. They've been more like family than servants to me. They were here when we both arrived, and they came to know Erik, even though it was only a few days. They got a glimpse into his true nature before he left."

"Why did he leave you? Surely he didn't know you were with child?"

A look of shame flashed across Meg's face, and she turned away for a moment before responding to Lucianna. "I don't think I want to talk about it."

"Of course. Please, I shouldn't have asked. I understand how difficult these things can be. I still have a very hard time talking about my married life. You see, I didn't love my husband. I was forced to marry him. I lost two babies within a very short period of time and fear that I'll never be able to have any more."

"Why should you think that? You're young and healthy. When you remarry, you …"

"I doubt that I'll remarry."

"But why?"

"I'm in love with someone who doesn't return my affections. It will take a long time for me to get beyond it. I'm determined to do so, but in the meantime I can't imagine marriage, family. I also seriously believe that my experience with my husband has made me physically incapable of bearing any more children." Lucianna hadn't meant to reveal so much of her own anguish. Meg left her chair and came to sit beside Lucianna on the sofa. The two women sat silent for a time.

"Beatrice, please tell me you won't repeat what I'm about to say to you."

"You can count on my discretion, Meg."

"Erik and I had argued. We actually argued a great deal. Life with him wasn't going to be easy, I know that now. I was rather naïve when we crossed the border into Italy. I was full of plans for a new life together. I didn't take into account how drastic a change it would be for him. I expected everything would be easy. We had already passed through the bad part, I thought. Ahead of us was happiness. On the road, we had this disagreement as I was saying. Actually it was a rather heated argument. Erik's temper can be violent, and he's an intimidating man. Like an idiot, I ran. He chased me through the woods. At the time I panicked and simply wanted to get away from him. Even though he had never harmed me, I think in a corner of my mind I was afraid of him at that moment. I fell and lost consciousness. Anyway, he brought me to the manor, and he took care of me. That was when Annetta and Giuseppe came to know him. When I awoke from the concussion, evidently it was as if no time had passed, as if I were still running away from him in the forest. He had been incredibly angry with me. I do that to him. I can make him so angry! When I saw him sitting beside me on the bed, I screamed in pure terror. Even though he tried to soothe me, I couldn't stop. At least that's what Annetta told me because I was completely irrational. I don't even remember what happened. I just know I screamed, and he ran from the room and from the house. That was the last time I saw him." Meg turned away for a moment to compose herself. Lucianna placed an arm tenderly around her shoulders and comforted her.

"It sounds as if you still have feelings for him," Lucianna suggested quietly as Meg dried her eyes and sighed.

"Of course I do. But …"

Hearing a note of reservation, Lucianna cocked her head to one side and considered the woman. "Go on, Meg."

"I wonder if Erik and I could ever have lived together. He's made his choice. Apparently he prefers to live without me. In all this time, not a note, not a word!"

"You've no idea of where he is?"

"Some time ago a friend of mine wrote me that she had received a strange letter from a Signora Fiortino who had news of my husband. My friend was vague, had no particulars except to say that she thought my husband would soon be home."

"Isn't that good news, Meg?"

"It was. At the time."

"But?"

Meg had been twisting her wedding ring round her finger. The flesh was red and swollen near the band. She stopped and closed her hands into two tight fists. They nestled in her lap. When she looked up, there was nothing but coldness in her eyes.

"That was over two months ago. He's not come home. Not one word. He's had more than enough time. I can't be expected to wait forever. I won't. That's why I've agreed to ask Father Antonio about the procedures for an annulment. François seems comfortable with Giovanni. My son needs a father, not a ghost. Erik has made his choice, and it's about time that I made mine and got on with my life."

Lucianna wasn't sure whether Meg was sincere. Her words were filled with hurt and anger. The fact that even now after so much time Erik could stir such strong passions suggested that Meg still loved him.

Even so it would be hard to tell Erik this news. For whatever she felt inside, Meg had obviously decided on a course of action that no longer included him.

"Father Antonio, I need to speak with you." Meg waited for the priest to invite her into the kitchen where he usually visited casually with his flock. She dismissed Annetta who scooted François out to the cemetery grounds so she could keep an eye on him while she weeded around the flower beds and gravestones.

Father Antonio pitied Meg. She was too young to have led such a tragic life. In confession she had confided her past with the Phantom. However he had to be careful when she came for these little "talks" to avoid mention of any of her soul's secrets unless she herself brought them up. What was said in the confessional stayed in the confessional. Even so, Meg didn't need to explain much for the old priest to know her current heartache.

"Giovanni has proposed. He's anxious that we investigate the possibility of an annulment. I know that it can sometimes take months or even years. He also wishes to adopt François and raise him as his own."

The priest listened for her to continue, knowing that there was something more. When Meg began to worry the scratches on her hands from the roses she had been pruning, he knew she needed him to prompt her with some well placed questions. He decided on the direct approach. There was as much information in what she had not said as in what she had said.

"Is that young bull pushing you into this?"

Meg had only to blush to answer the question.

"Are you as anxious as Giovanni to start the annulment procedures and set a wedding?" She had not mentioned her agreement.

Again her reaction was revealing. This time she laughed too loudly and too long and shifted nervously in her seat before answering. "Of course. I wouldn't be here if I wasn't. I've given it a lot of thought, and I think this is the best solution."

Father Antonio started mildly in his chair and knit his brows at her as if she had done something wrong. "Solution? Are you broken, and Giovanni a tool to fix you? Is that the way to talk about the sanctity of marriage? Is that the way a woman in love talks about the man she wants to spend the rest of her life with?"

Words were never more poorly—or more effectively—chosen. Meg's eyes opened in shocked pain, which immediately gave way to embarrassed consternation.

"Well, there's something not quite right about all this, isn't there?" continued the priest patting her lightly on the shoulder. "It's him, the other one, isn't it?"

Meg chewed nervously on her lower lip and lowered her eyes.

"Oh, this is so difficult, my child. He's gone. How long has it been? Years!"

"But that's it, Father, he's not gone!" She spoke so vehemently that the priest was somewhat surprised. "He's always in my thoughts, always has been, even when I curse him. And for the last year, I've cursed him almost daily. But lately it's more than that. I can't shake the feeling that he's here—really here in Pianosa. I've felt him. And there have been moments when I thought if I turn around right now I'll catch him there by the window or in the garden or even here in the church as if he were waiting and watching me."

"Tricks of the imagination, Meg. Why wouldn't he reveal himself to you if he were here?" Meg could see the doubt in the priest's eyes. She knew he thought it was only her own fears conjuring up an obstacle to Giovanni's designs, a reason to demur.

"Father Antonio, the night of the ball, I argued with Giovanni. He stormed off leaving me alone by the garden wall. Moments later someone—a man—grabbed me from behind in a tight embrace. I struggled. Then I thought it might be Giovanni, but he simply held me. It was Erik. My body, my soul screams it. I even asked Giovanni later if he had played a trick on me in the garden. It wasn't him." Almost in a whisper as if to herself alone she repeated, "It was *his* body, Erik's."

The priest found this disturbing. What if this man had returned? Unfortunately knowing what he knew about him, Father Antonio wasn't sure that it was safe having someone like the Phantom living among them. Then again, if this was Meg's fevered imagination, the poor child was in danger of losing her mind.

"You know what happens at these parties when the young men drink too much, Meg. You've broken many a young fool's heart with your aloofness. Perhaps it was Albertino or even Michaelo. I've seen how they look at you. They like causing trouble when they've had a few drinks."

"No! It had to be Erik. Several of the guests remarked that there was a stranger at the dance. No one could place him. They said he followed my every movement."

"If you truly believe he's here, why are you so frantic? What is it that you really want, Meg?"

"Oh God, if I only knew! You don't know him, Father," she said. "He's had to be so careful." Her eyes were wide and glistening. She was sitting forward on her seat, and the priest feared she might begin to cry. "He doesn't even trust me anymore. He's punishing me. I know it."

"For what, my child?"

"Please don't make me talk about it. I hurt him. I didn't mean to, but I did."

"Would he harm you or the child, Meg?"

"Harm us? No. But what if he's come to steal François from me? What does he want? Why hasn't he come to me? Why won't he talk to me? Sometimes I think I'll go mad trying to understand him! He's cruel and ..." Before she could finish her thought, she stopped and clasped her hand over her mouth as if the words had had a life of their own.

"Then it's not fear of him?"

"No! I'm not afraid of him. But how long can this go on?"

"Meg, calm down. Drink your tea. I'm only a simple priest with modest understanding of canon law and even less of human nature. The Church might grant an annulment if you were to explain what your husband has done, his past, the abandonment, and perhaps your fears for the child. But I can't help thinking that an annulment is not a wise decision. At least not until you sort out your feelings. No matter what this man is or what he has done, you and he are husband and wife. If you still love him, you can't ask the Church to dissolve the vows you both have made. After all, God has blessed your union with a beautiful child." Father Antonio realized his intuition was correct. Meg was not only calmer, but seemed to be relieved that he was advising against the annulment. "Giovanni is a headstrong lad. I've known him since he was no bigger than a gnat. He can be difficult, willful. Don't let him push you into anything you don't want."

"Thank you, Father."

"Does he know that you think Erik is back?"

"I've hinted at it."

"Does he know everything about Erik? About Paris?"

"No! I would never betray Erik. What I've said has been in confession to you alone. The only thing I've shared with Giovanni is that Erik avoids society because of his disfigurement. I spoke only in vague terms so that he might understand a little of my situation."

"Of course. It's best that Giovanni not know the details for now. After all it's your husband's life and his sins. We should leave his judgment to God."

Meg snapped at the priest. "He's more than paid for those sins!"

Soothingly, the priest reminded her that as a priest he was concerned with the man's soul and until he confessed his sins could not truly be forgiven. "His soul is in grave peril, Meg. Maybe that's what keeps him away from you."

Annetta called out from the cemetery for Meg to come quickly.

Erik had come early as usual to play the organ and wait for Meg's visit. About the time that she was expected, he stopped playing and waited in the dim balcony for her to enter. He didn't need to wait for long. Meg, François, and Annetta entered the vestibule, but instead of occupying themselves with the flowers, as they had done on other occasions, Meg spoke quietly with Annetta and then went directly to the back of the church, to the priest's rooms. When Annetta and François left through a lateral portal which opened out onto the cemetery, Erik came down from the balcony and left by the opposite door to circle around toward the back of the church. There he crouched next to a window through which he could hear Meg and the priest in conversation. The caretaker was off in the catacombs, and Annetta and the child were on the other side of the church at a safe distance.

He heard Meg ask the priest to go forward with the annulment so that she and Giovanni could marry. He listened as she laughed and told the priest that she was as anxious as Giovanni to get on with her life. Erik tried to slow the beating of his heart; the sound threatened to drown out everything else around him. He felt nauseous and physically weakened. When he turned his ear again to the conversation, he was incredulous to overhear Meg reveal that she knew he had come back! She told the old priest that she knew he had returned to Pianosa. She had sensed his presence! Yet it made no difference. It couldn't, for here she was in the priest's rooms arranging to dissolve their union so that she could marry another man. He stumbled away from the window, oblivious to the need to remain unseen. He wandered among the tombstones until he collapsed by an old rectangular granite stone behind which he knew no one from the church could spy him. There he sat, his knees drawn to his chest. His breath came in ragged gasps, but he could not cry.

He would go away, go away forever. He'd forget Meg and the child, her child, if he had to rip his eyes from their sockets. He'd haunt her no more. It had been a mistake to return.

His eyes stung, and he squeezed them tightly shut. He sat, his cheek against the cold stone of the tomb, waiting for the pain to subside, when he felt several soft pats on his arm. He jerked away and turned to see the child François staring at him with a pout on his face. Without thinking, Erik held out his arms to the boy who came into them as if he had always done so. Erik hugged his son, holding him to his breast, and swallowed his tears.

For a brief moment, the child let the sad man hold him. Then he pushed himself away, but he did not bolt and run. Instead he sat upon his father's lap and pointed at the mask. "Are you a banditti? Have you come to rob the church?"

Still not trusting his voice, so in awe of the moment was he, Erik could only shake his head no.

"Do you always wear it? Can I wear it?" The child brought his fingers to the edge of the mask, but Erik took his hand in his and kissed his fingers. "You've got tears on your cheek. Did you hurt yourself? I can call Maman. She can fix it."

"No. I'm all right. I wear the mask because I'm very ugly underneath it."

"Can I see?"

"I don't think it would be a good idea."

"I don't care if you're ugly."

"Can you be very brave?" Erik smiled as his son shook his head so vigorously that his dark curls bounced like ribbons across his forehead. "I'll lift a corner, and you can tell me to stop if you don't like what you see. I promise I won't mind." The child nodded in agreement with the plan. But Erik didn't move, couldn't lift his hand. He didn't want the moment to end. It might be all he'd ever have. He looked at his son's face intently as if trying to memorize every line, every shadow, every hue of color that crossed his cheek.

Impatient, François raised his hand and pushed the mask up and out of his way. Unflinchingly he studied the formerly hidden side of his father's face. He placed his soft hand on the irregular skin and asked if it hurt.

"No, it doesn't hurt." Erik bit his lip to keep it from trembling as he resisted pulling the child to him again.

Lifting the edge of his short pants just over his knee cap, the child showed him a jagged little scar from a recent fall. "I didn't cry. Maman said I was brave, just like my father."

"I'm sure you were. You are." Erik wanted to ask François what he knew of his father, but he heard Annetta calling for the child. There was a rising note of panic in her voice. She had lost sight of him while weeding the graves. Refusing to allow the tone of regret to enter his voice, Erik pointed toward the far side of the graveyard. "Go to her. She's worried."

As his son rose to leave, Erik reached out and stopped him. "May I give you a kiss?"

The child stood hesitant.

"Never mind, François. You must go quickly." Erik swallowed hard but smiled at the little boy. The child turned toward the increasingly frantic sound of his nursemaid's voice and yelled that he was coming. Then abruptly he rushed into Erik's arms and kissed him on the cheek before scrambling away from the tombstone.

Erik watched him run to Annetta. Lightly he touched the spot where his son had kissed him. When Annetta led the child toward the church, Erik replaced his mask and silently crept away.

He couldn't hide any longer. Meg knew he was back. She still planned to annul their marriage and marry that smug dandy, Giovanni. He couldn't hide any longer—like a coward—in the shadows and allow this to go on. He'd fight for Meg, for his son.

Lucianna noticed something had changed the moment Erik returned from the church. He took off the mask, throwing it to the divan as if it were loathsome, and stood in front of the mirror inspecting his reflection.

"Send a note to Meg inviting her to dine with you here, tonight. Tell her to bring François."

"Erik, that wouldn't be a good idea." Lucianna started to argue that it was risky bringing Meg to their very rooms. She might snoop around, put things together, see something she shouldn't. "What if she happens into the library and sees your portrait."

"Never mind all that. Do as I ask. Please." There was a new determination in his voice.

"Erik, if Meg is determined to go through with the annulment, we could go back home." He understood the implication of her offer. And it was his own fault that Lucianna held on to false hope. He regretted that he had been weak the night he had spied on Meg and her suitor in the garden. Licking his wounds, angry and hurt, he had allowed himself to succumb to Lucianna. Even now he was ashamed that he was too cowardly to accept the full responsibility of what he had done. She had tempted him—yes, that was true—but he was no fool. He was a grown man, capable of self-restraint. He had not wanted Lucianna. He had wanted Meg.

Since that night, Erik had taken precautions so that the event would not happen again. He locked his room at night and kept his distance in the day. He was grateful to Lucianna for her help, but he didn't trust her. He sensed that she wanted more from him than he was willing to give. He suspected that she didn't always advocate for his success and that she wanted him to fail in winning back Meg's love.

"My son," he said. A surge of emotion made it difficult to speak. "My son came upon me in the cemetery. He asked to see me without my mask. He let me hold him. He wasn't frightened or repulsed by me. Lucianna, I can't give them up. I want my son. I want Meg back. I want her to love me again the way she did before I ruined everything."

Lucianna sighed in resignation and assured Erik that she would write the note and send it posthaste to his wife.

CHAPTER 12

❃

Home

> *Amazed she sate, and impotent to speak;*
> *O'er all the man her eyes she rolls in vain,*
> *Now hopes, now fears, now knows, then*
> *doubts again.*
>
> *Odyssey, Homer, Alexander Pope*

"What do you intend to do when Meg and François arrive?"

"I think it's time that Meg know the truth. I want you to tell her."

"Tell her what? You mean about the freak show at the fair and the after-show performances? The duel? Our affair? What do I tell her, Erik?"

"Don't do this to me, not now, Lucianna." Erik struggled to contain his anger, lowered his voice, and pleaded with her. "Please don't frighten her away. I'll tell her everything eventually, but what she needs to know now is that you're Lucianna Fiortino, the woman who wrote Christine. Tell her that I'm alive and I want to come home if she'll accept me back. I need to know her answer to this before I take the next step."

Lucianna wrung her hands and walked over to the window to look out. She kept her back to Erik and didn't answer. They hadn't spoken of the night they made love, the night he came back sore and dejected after spying on Meg and Giovanni. She knew it was a gamble to go to him like that. She counted on his pain to allow her in. When he slipped away from her that night and avoided her for the next few days, she understood that she had lost. Their affair had ended long ago, at the estate. No matter how much she tried to explain to him her genuine feelings for him, he wouldn't forgive her for using him the way she had. Foolish woman, she had hoped perhaps he would turn to her if he saw that Meg was making a new life for herself. Hadn't she proved her love for him in countless selfless acts ever since? How could she convince him that she loved him?

"Will you do this for me?" His soft voice startled her from her thoughts.

Luigi tapped on the door to announce the arrival of the guests. Lucianna told him to show them into the parlor. Erik waited for an answer which never came. He was at Lucianna's mercy. She could tell Meg the lurid truth of his experiences since he fled Pianosa; she had the power to confirm all of Meg's worst nightmares. There was so much that he had done. There was no way he could make Meg understand.

"Lucianna?" Erik whispered, but she stood coldly silent. "I beg you. Please let me have this chance," he urged.

As if he weren't there, Lucianna turned to meet her guests in the adjoining salon. He reached out and took her hand just as she was about to leave the room. She paused and glanced over her shoulder at his compelling eyes, knowing that his heart was in her hands, and silently, slowly withdrew her hand from his. The door closed, and Erik leaned his forehead against the wood panel. His heart pounded feverishly, and his palms were clammy with sweat as he listened at the door to their movements on the other side.

The minute Annetta let go of François, he ran around the room exploring every nook and cranny, picking up objects and putting them down in new places. Lucianna's servants brought tea and pastries for the ladies as they exchanged greetings and settled on the sofa by the fireplace. François soon took advantage of the open door and slipped outside the room to find other interesting areas to investigate. Meg called out to him to be careful and to stay close by. Lucianna reassured her that there wasn't much he could get into. Once the servants had withdrawn, Meg dropped the courteous artificiality and asked, in a concerned tone, what was so urgent.

"Your note puzzled me, Beatrice. It seemed as if there might be a problem. Is there something I can do?"

Meg's concern was sincere. Lucianna considered her options. On the other side of the door she knew Erik was in agony. She had the power to end his suffering or to seal his doom. Meg was on the verge of creating a new life for herself. She had every right to know what Erik had been doing all this time. Yet Lucianna recognized that it wasn't the love of the truth or her friendship with Meg that was influencing her, but her desire to keep Erik for herself.

On the other side of the door, Erik held his breath as he waited for Lucianna's answer.

"My name is not Beatrice, Meg. It's Lucianna Fiortino."

The name snapped into place, but Meg didn't have time to react for François was calling excitedly for his mother to come quickly to see what he had found. He was so excited that he came to the door and called repeatedly for her to come see, to come see the sad man. When Meg saw the look in Lucianna's eyes, she realized the woman would try to stop her. But she was too late. Meg rose and followed François into the foyer, across the way, and into the library. The door had not been locked. The child went to the center of the room and pointed with his finger up at the portrait that hung over the mantel. "Look, Maman. That's the man I saw. He was so sad, Maman. I gave him a big hug to make it better."

Meg stared in amazement. Above her, imprisoned by a gilt-edged frame, his unmarked face, turned slightly to the side, stared down at her. His beauty confounded her. His eyes were the intense, proud eyes she knew, the contour of the face was so accurate that she could imagine brushing her hand along the side of his cheek to feel the roughness of his beard. It was Erik, and yet it was cruelly deceptive.

"He wore a mask, Maman, over a big booboo."

"What's the meaning of this?" she demanded.

Lucianna stood in the doorway.

Meg grabbed her son so suddenly that he was startled and began to wail.

Hearing his son cry out, Erik came through the doorway from the adjoining room where he had been waiting.

Meg stared at her husband in disbelief. Fiortino had been the woman Christine had mentioned. Beatrice and Erik had come to take her son from her. As Meg backed away from him, she dragged François against the folds of her skirt. The child began to cry more fiercely than before.

"François, you told me you were brave. Remember?" Erik stepped slowly toward Meg and held out his arms as if to take his son.

"No!" shrieked Meg. "You can't have him!"

Erik scowled. "Please, Meg, calm down. You're frightening the boy. I've no intention of trying to take a child away from his mother!"

Immediately she loosened her strangle hold on her child and began to speak soothingly to him. But François was overexcited and afraid because everyone was acting so strangely. He continued to sob even as he watched the sad man in the mask.

"François, I have a gift for you." Erik drew closer, but seeing Meg stiffen he retreated a half step.

Lucianna didn't know what to do. She stood frozen, her heart in her mouth as she watched Erik. She was amazed at his calm, and then she realized that this was the behavior she had witnessed when Erik dealt with a frightened horse. He kept his eyes focused on Meg and the child. His voice was low and soothing. He waited for the two of them to calm down.

The boy rubbed his eyes with the balls of his fists and looked inquisitively at the man with the mask, the man from the portrait. He nodded his head eagerly and hiccupped.

"Would you like a mask like mine?"

Again the child nodded, this time smiling and hiccupping simultaneously.

"Lucianna, could you go to my room and bring me the mask on the bureau, the one just like this one?" His gaze never left the two of them. Lucianna was eager to help smooth things out. She had thought she wanted the encounter to fail, but that had been selfish. She didn't want to be selfish. She went quickly and returned with a simple white mask similar to the one Erik now wore. She gave it to Erik, knowing that he should be the one to offer it to his son. Slowly he approached within reach of the child and stretched the offering out to him. François tried to put the mask on, but it was very large for his face. Erik took advantage of his difficulty and stepped closer, took the mask, and fixed it to the little boy's face. "See? You look very mysterious."

Lucianna called for Annetta to take the boy, who was now anxious to see himself in a mirror, into the kitchen where he could pick out some caramels to eat. She asked to go with them and left Meg and Erik alone in the library.

The moment the doors closed, Erik reached out and took Meg into his arms. She resisted at first but soon melted into his embrace. They remained that way for a long time without speaking. Meg pulled away gently and stepped back.

"Are you and Lucianna happy together?"

"What?" Erik was confused by the question and then he realized what Meg had assumed. "No. It's not what you think. Lucianna is a friend who offered to help."

"To help you lie? What game have you been playing with us, Erik? You've been gone for a long time. Now you come with this other woman who lies about her identity. You stay hidden, spying on me. At the masquerade, it was you in the garden, wasn't it?"

"Yes."

"And at the churchyard. Tell me, Erik, did you drill a hole in the wall to listen to my confessions?"

"I couldn't stay away. I was waiting for the right time to tell you I was back."

"What stopped you from coming to the manor and telling me directly to my face the day you arrived in town?" Meg's voice was rising in anger.

Erik was losing his patience, too. Instead of answering her question, he snapped at her, "You asked for an annulment. Do you intend to marry that smug braggart?"

"What concern is it of yours if I do plan to marry Giovanni?"

"I'm your husband! We have a child!"

"He's *my* child! Mine alone! You weren't here. You left us!" Instead of cringing from him, Meg squared her shoulders and spoke defiantly. If she had learned anything from this man, it was to fight back. Giving into fear is what had placed her in this situation in the first place. She wouldn't be afraid, not anymore. She was angry, angrier than she had ever been in her life. All of a sudden the burden of the past several years crashed down upon her, and she asked herself why she had waited and for what? She was a young, beautiful woman. Her reluctant husband had abandoned her, and she had waited like a love-sick school girl for him to tire of his adventures and come home. Why?

Erik's anger dissipated. She was slipping away from him. She was seriously thinking of ending their marriage, casting him out of her life and away from his son forever. She hadn't ever really loved him. She was in love with the danger, the mystery, not him, not the reality of him.

"Please, Meg, listen to me. I didn't know you were with child. I thought you wanted me to go."

When he thought of that day, he wanted to collapse before her and beg for her to take back the screams. They still echoed in his mind. When she had awoken from her unnatural sleep, he had been so relieved, so relieved that she was alive and would recover. They would have another chance; *he* would have another chance. But her eyes, when he came into her line of vision, had bored into his soul, and her scream told him that she saw he was a monster. It had been unbearable to stand naked before her and to hear those screams.

"You were frightened of me. A wife shouldn't be frightened of her husband."

"You're right! A wife shouldn't be afraid of her husband. And you *do* frighten me!" The moment she said it, she saw its effect on Erik. All the blood drained from his face, his eyes squinted in pain, and his shoulders sagged perceptibly. He lowered his head so that she couldn't see his face and turned to leave.

"Wait!" Meg called to him. "Don't go. I didn't mean to say that. I was angry."

Erik paused, his hand on the doorknob. Hesitantly, he glanced back over his shoulder for only an instant, unable to hold her gaze, afraid of what he'd see there. Was there any hope?

"Do you love him?" He spoke to the door, but his voice was clear and even, almost without emotion.

Meg swallowed hard as she seriously thought the question over. "I have only loved one man."

Erik turned quickly toward her. He came to her and placed his large, square hands upon her shoulders. He bent so that his eyes could look into hers. "Do you still love that man?" His voice was urgent. His breath, warm and moist, broke against her face as he drew intimately close.

"Yes," was all she managed to say.

Erik didn't want her to say more. He wanted to cling to that one truth as long as he had breath in his body. He wanted the sound of that word to deafen the screams. He pressed his lips to hers. When their lips parted, Erik whispered in a low rumble deep in his throat, his face pressed against hers, that he had never forgotten the taste of her.

When Lucianna entered, Meg took the opportunity to extricate herself from Erik's hold.

"I have to think." She kept her eyes averted from his face. She wouldn't give him time to react, to stop her. She swept her child up in her arms and fled through the doors.

"Give her some time, Erik." Lucianna placed her hand consolingly on his shoulder. Erik stood, frozen, stunned, his eyes locked on the empty passageway just beyond the threshold of the room. The air had thinned, as if it too had abandoned him. Lucianna continued to speak, but he couldn't hear her. Instead, he heard the footsteps receding down the stairs, the door open and close with a soft shudder, sounds in the street, the clip clop of hooves on cobblestones and the sharp sound of metal as the carriage whisked his Meg and their child down the road.

"She's had more than enough time to think. There's been too much time for thinking." He strode out of the room barking orders to have Charlemagne saddled and brought round immediately.

In the next several minutes the entire staff was in a dither, and Lucianna watched from the second story window as Erik mounted the Arabian—her gift to him—and galloped off in the direction Meg's coach had taken just minutes before.

Hearing the advance of hooves quickly gaining on them from behind, the driver feared it was a highwayman and urged the team on at a dangerous pace. Inside the carriage Meg and Annetta were apprehensive, but the child was thrilled at the speed by which the images from the window were careening past them. The sound of the hooves was louder and louder until Meg saw a streak of black pass the window and heard someone reining in the horses. Meg brought her son protectively to her breast and leaned over to look out to see what was happening. There she saw a man mounted on an expensive saddle atop a staggeringly sleek Arabian stallion. The animal was barely breathing hard after the race it had just won. The man was no less impressive than his animal.

Astride the horse Erik sat regal and imposing. It was as if they were one magnificent beast. She had forgotten how powerful he was. One touch of his hand on the horse's flank, and it bent its head to his will. Meg felt as if his hand had stroked along her body instead. He pressed his knees against the Arabian's barrel urging the stallion to sidle up along the carriage door where he stared in at the window at Meg. He seemed as struck by Meg as she was with him because he didn't speak.

Finally, Annetta broke the silence. "Signora, we left without dinner. I can put together a nice cold meal for the two of you in the garden. It's going to be a lovely sunset." When Meg gave her an annoyed look, she feared she had overstepped her bounds. She apologized quietly, but Meg squeezed her hand. However, Meg didn't contradict Annetta's suggestion, and Erik understanding the silence as acquiescence accepted the invitation to dine. He spurred the Arabian forward to the lead horse and led the team to the manor.

Not only was the dinner a veritable masterpiece of colors, textures, and tastes—elegant finger sized meat pies, fruit compote, salads, cold fillet of fish surrounded by slices of lemons, oranges, tomatoes, artichoke hearts and olives—but Annetta had sent Giuseppe to run a line of lanterns along the pathways to light the garden in a warm orange glow. One of the young staff played a flute softly in the background. Erik and Meg sat at the table; neither one of them did much more than nibble at the banquet prepared for them. Nor did they speak much. Erik knew that if they really talked, it would take them hours to sort out the years they'd been apart. He dreaded the lurid confession, and asked for this one evening before they both had to face the realities of the past three years. They would talk, but not tonight. Tonight was made for other things.

After the meal had been cleared and Erik had downed the last drops of port in his glass, Meg awkwardly rose and hinted that she was tired. Without further ado, she said goodnight and walked into the house leaving Erik behind in the garden. He hesitated not knowing exactly what to do but refusing to let the evening end this way. God help him if he was wrong! It was a risk.

He followed after Meg and climbed the steps taking them two at a time catching up to her at the landing on the second floor. She didn't run from him, but she did stop and turn slightly in his direction. In her eyes, there was a question. Without a word, he lifted her into his arms and carried her to their bedroom. He carefully set her down inside the chamber and kissed her gently on the forehead, on the cheeks, and ever so softly on the lips. Taking his time, he took out the pins that held her blond hair up and off her neck and ran his fingers through the silky tresses as they fell about her shoulders. He paused only a moment more and slowly removed his mask. He placed it on the table next to the bed, his fingers lingering on the sculpted features of its material. Slowly he turned toward Meg, but he still hesitated before his eyes met hers. His heart beat fiercely in his chest, and he thought he might not be breathing. She reached up and placed her hands on either side of his face and looked at him with the same desire as before. He felt as if his knees would fold under him as she brought his face down to hers. He kissed her slightly parted lips; his tongue hesitantly explored the curve of her mouth and dipped shyly inside. She tasted of vanilla and cloves. He was only mildly aware that he was moaning softly.

They drew apart only long enough to remove their clothes. Childbirth had rounded her body, filled in her form so that her bust was full and heavy, her hips broader, a small protuberance of her abdomen added greater depths to her waist. He wrapped his arms around her, and bending his knees he drew her body tightly against his.

"Meg, I can't be gentle. Can you forgive me? I want you so desperately." His whole body tensed against hers; his breathing was loud and rapid against her throat as his hands gripped her tightly.

"I want you. I want you now," she urged. Her own passion, so long dormant, shocked her. If he waited any longer, she thought she'd go mad.

She led him to the bed and pulled him down heavy upon her. He brought her knee up against his hip and sank deep inside her, withdrawing only to thrust again, impossible to control the rawness of his desire for her. Her legs wound around his hips, her heals digging into his flesh, urging him on. Meg ground against him seeking to take him deeper yet inside her, shocked by the fullness of him. The sudden waves of pleasure took them both by surprise. As

Meg cried out, Erik buried his head deep into the curve of her shoulder, his lips against the side of her throat, and shook with the intensity of his own release.

They lay in each other's arms gasping for air; the sweat gluing their skins together. Eventually Erik pushed himself away from Meg's body and lay beside her on the bed. She curled to his side. They remained clasped tightly, their arms around each other, their heads side by side. Slowly they reached out to caress each other's body. Erik nuzzled against Meg's throat and traced the line of her chin, kissed her lips long and deeply, teased his tongue softly along the depression at the base of her throat where he found her brown mole. He cupped the soft contours of her breast in his hand as she ran her hand down his belly toward his groin. She pulled him even closer, and they entwined their bodies again, but this time slowly and languorously, until the world around them melted away and there was never a thought of separation.

CHAPTER 13

❀

Trials

> *Bless'd in thy queen! bless'd in thy blooming heir!*
>
> *Odyssey, Homer, Alexander Pope*

The light shone in on the two of them wrapped in each other's arms. As it slid across Meg's face, she began to stir. The birds were loudly twittering on the balcony pecking at the seeds that she always left for them. Her head lay on Erik's chest which rose and fell rhythmically in deep sleep. She lifted herself onto one elbow and looked at him lying beside her. She stroked his light brown hair, his cheek. A dark shadow of stubble defined his jaw and the side of his face down along his chin. Sadly she allowed herself to linger on the side of his face which was deformed. It broke her heart to know how much grief he had experienced for this alone. She stretched her body up along his chest so that she could kiss this tortured landscape; lovingly she placed her hand along the side of his head and then brought her lips down onto his mouth teasing the parted lips with her tongue. He stirred at her touch. One of his hands by chance came up and rested on her back as he shifted slightly under her weight.

He had never slept this profoundly before to her knowledge except when he was ill. The least noise, the slightest movement, in her past experience, would wake him. He was always alert, watchful, expectant, ready to fight or flee at any hint of danger. It touched her deeply that he lay here with her for perhaps the first time in his life safe.

Suddenly his body tensed, his back arched nearly throwing her clear, and his arms rose over his head stretched out across the pillows in a tremendous yawn. His eyes struggled to open, and when they did, they lighted on Meg's smile. He smiled in turn and grabbed her in a tight embrace.

"Then it was real?" His voice was scratchy and deep. He turned his lips to Meg's and kissed her passionately.

She managed to respond, the sound merely disappearing inside his mouth. His hands glided down her body and over her hips. She felt his sudden desire and gasped at its intensity. Just moments before they had both been lazily asleep, their bodies soft and fuzzy. Now their muscles were taut and tight as they sought each other out again.

Erik wouldn't stop until Meg collapsed in exhaustion onto her side, their chests pounding, their lungs dragging in air, sweat covering them both. At one point, just before she cried out in the throes of her pleasure, she had thought she'd heard footsteps in the hallway. Now, as they recovered from the excitement and exertion, she again heard someone approach the door.

"Annetta? Is that you?" she called out. Erik had dropped off to sleep again, but her voice roused him slightly. Even so, he refused to open his eyes or change his position.

"Yes, madam. I'm sorry to disturb you. Would you want breakfast soon or should we wait a bit and serve lunch?"

"Breakfast would be nice. We'll eat in the garden. Is François up?"

Erik shifted slightly, annoyed by the noise. Meg rose from the bed and put on her dressing gown and went to the door. She opened it just wide enough to slip through into the passageway.

"Yes, Signora. He's playing in the orchard with the puppies. He wanted to come in to greet you, but we mentioned you had stayed up late and wanted to rest." Annetta couldn't help but smile knowingly at her young mistress. They had been together long enough that there was a bond of true affection between them. Meg hugged Annetta in her joy. "So everything is good?"

"More than good, Annetta. Much more." She turned back toward the door and peeked inside to find Erik on his side and fast asleep. "Let him rest. I'll be down in a bit."

Shortly after noon Erik came down the stairs completely dressed, his mask in place, looking for Meg. Annetta offered to prepare him a lunch. At first he was about to say there was no need when suddenly he noticed that he was famished.

"Where's Meg?"

"She's in the orchard with François, milord."

Erik turned quizzically toward her at this appellation. He asked if the food could be taken down to the orchard itself. Annetta left to prepare a basket.

François was playing with several puppies on the grass under the apricot trees. Meg sat on a bench nearby with a sewing basket by her side. However, at the precise moment when Erik was coming down the path, she was simply sitting and watching her son and enjoying the fresh breeze crossing through the fruit trees. She saw him just as he was drawing near. So did François, who left the puppies biting their tails to skip up towards him.

"Maman says you're home now. Why didn't you tell me you were my father?" The little boy didn't wait for an answer but grabbed Erik by the hand and dragged him to where the black puppies were playing. "This is Gabriel. That's Olivia. And this one is my favorite." He tried to pick the puppy up by the wrong end, and Erik quickly took the pup and righted him in his son's arms. The puppy's front legs dangled over the sides of François's arms and his bottom hung down low so that at any moment the puppy would easily slide out of the child's embrace and fall safely to the ground to join his litter mates.

"What's his name?"

"Swiggles."

Erik laughed out loud. Meg gasped in shock. She had never heard him laugh like that. It was a joyful sound, not the bitter and cynical laugh she had on occasion heard him make when he was locked away under the opera house or in the prison cell. She motioned for him to come and sit by her, but François wanted him to stay and play with the puppies.

All afternoon Erik followed his son around the grounds. They chased the puppies, played at hide and seek, picked fruit to bring back to the house, dug channels in the dirt, and built a stick town for the ants. As the afternoon came to a close, Erik reached out to pick François up and placed him on his shoulders to carry home.

As they rounded the corner in the path, the three of them stopped. They noticed the horse tethered near the door and a tall figure standing just outside. Giovanni had come to pay Meg a call.

Meg went to greet him, while Erik and François hesitated and remained slightly behind.

"Giovanni, welcome. I'm pleased to have this chance to introduce you to someone very important to me. Would you like to come in and have some tea?"

Giovanni eyed Erik from head to toe in a barely veiled assessment of the competition. Erik stood a few inches taller than Giovanni; however, in every other way their builds were quite similar. Both were slim yet muscular with broad shoulders and long legs. Both were imposing. Giovanni was used to towering over men; it was a strange sensation to meet this masked stranger who looked at him eye to eye. Of course Giovanni knew instantly who this must be. Meg had told him enough about her husband for him to recognize that the mask was more than a coincidence. This was Erik, his rival. Even so, he let Meg usher him into the parlor where tea was served, and the three of them sat and exchanged pleasantries as if Meg had not been on the verge of accepting Giovanni's proposal of marriage just days before.

The young Italian mustered all his good breeding and a good deal of will power to maintain a tone of cordiality with Erik that he was far from feeling. He was not used to having his desires thwarted. Erik, too, sat stiffly and cautiously studied the young dandy. No one was comfortable or fooled by the smiles and compliments, especially Meg. She knew Giovanni was tempestuous in nature. It struck her suddenly as she saw both men on either side of her now in the same room that she had been drawn to Giovanni for those characteristics that she remembered from Erik, even the ones that were problematic. Was his fiery character, his proud demeanor one of the aspects that perhaps attracted her to him? And yet these characteristics, which in Erik were born of his need to survive in a hostile environment, were flaws in this young man who unwisely failed to temper them.

François had always seemed to like Giovanni, but Meg observed that he stayed close to Erik, even held his hand on several occasions, and avoided approaching Giovanni. Perhaps he sensed Erik's discomfort and knew his allegiance was owed to his father and not to their guest. Perhaps when Giovanni was placed alongside Erik, his inadequacies seemed glaring to him as they did now to her. For whatever cause, it was certainly apparent to their guest that the three of them had drawn together as a family and that there was no longer any place for him in Meg's life.

"I hope that we will have the honor of your presence from time to time in the gaming rooms in town, Signore …?" Giovanni waited for the man to supply a last name, but Erik stared at him in silence. Meg had used her maiden name since Erik had no name to give her. The funds that Raoul had transferred from Paris for the couples' needs were also in Meg's name for this same reason.

The Italian shifted uncomfortably in his seat. "Pianosa is not Paris, but I believe you'll find our society engaging."

"I may on occasion drop by, Signore Cimino, but I am a retiring man who looks forward to enjoying the calm pursuits of my family life from now on." He bowed slightly toward the young dandy.

When Giovanni finally rode off down the path, Erik studied his wife. The sun was just beginning to set and the orange glow of its light fell across her face, making its expression difficult for him to read. She turned to find his eyes on her and saw the question they held. In answer she wrapped her arms around him and buried her face in his shirt squeezing him as hard as she could. He returned the embrace, but gently, and lowered his mouth to her ear, where he whispered, "Meg, I love you with all my soul."

Before they were to retire that night, Erik followed Meg into François's bedroom where she sang the child a lullaby and kissed him goodnight. Erik lingered to watch his son close his eyes and drift off to sleep. Ever so softly he bent to kiss his eyes and stroke his hair. Meg waited outside the door and took his hand to lead him to the bedroom, but Erik stopped her.

"We must talk."

"Not tonight. Not ever unless you insist. Whatever happened during those three years, it won't change how I feel this moment or what I want for us."

"How do you know?"

"I won't let it change anything. I can't do anything about the past, but I have the present. I loved you since I first saw you in the opera house rummaging around the wardrobe rooms for your masks and clothes, since I heard you sing."

"To Christine."

"Yes," Meg responded cautiously. "Since you sang to Christine because she was crying for her father. I loved you then, and I love you now. Can't that be enough?"

"It's more than I deserve."

She stepped into his arms again and roughly clapped her hands around his face to bring his mouth to hers. She kissed him hard and angrily as if to prove to him that she would love him in spite of everything. When she finished, they were both somewhat breathless, and she could tell that he was deeply stirred. But he took her by the elbow and led her to the upstairs library. There he forced her to sit, and he stood before her and began to tell her what he had done since that day he ran from their bedroom.

he was in a cage, a cage like the ones at a fair for the lions, but he was not a child, he was a grown man, a face of a woman surrounded by dark hair loomed over him, there were cards floating in the air, special cards, she thought they were called tarot cards, the ones the gypsies used to tell fortunes and that silly old women in search of the exotic liked to play with at parties, men were laughing, women whis-

pering behind fans in baroque drawing rooms, images of gaiety and festivities flashed across her mind's eye, François playing with Erik's white mask, no, she didn't want François in this dream, she didn't want anything to happen to him, even if it was a dream, it felt like a dream, but she couldn't wake up, Erik unmasked kissing someone, not her, naked limbs intertwining on a bare floor, carnival music, Lucianna, Erik takes Lucianna by the hand and brings her to their bedroom, Erik's and her own bedroom, Erik sits in a chair, Lucianna, naked, paints him, as she paints him, she only has red on her palette, his disfigurement melts away, but on the canvas, no matter what she does, it grows and encompasses the entire side of his face, but it's the wrong side of the face, Meg realizes, Erik laughs as he wipes blood that oozes from his shoulder, someone is sneaking up behind him, Meg tries to see, but can't, the shadow grows larger and larger behind Erik, she yells a warning to him, they lie in each other's arms in the garden under a tree, leaves drop one by one on them both, he brushes them aside, he kisses the spot where the leaf landed on Meg's belly, Annetta comes and says someone is waiting for him, she leads Erik, they're both naked, to the parlor where the townspeople all have gathered, they have angry faces, she steps in front of Erik to protect him, his nakedness, she screams at them to leave him alone, but they have weapons and someone pulls her by her hair away from Erik who stands there taking the blows, the cuts, his body is awash in blood, and she knows he'll die ...

"You've been sleeping. You had a bad dream." Erik cradled her close to him and gently hummed to calm her. Meg sobbed, shaken to the core by the images in her nightmare, and buried her face in his shoulder.

"I dreamed they were hurting you. You were covered in blood!"

"It was only that—a dream. No one's hurting me. I'm here. I'm safe. Look. Look at me, Meg." He took her face from his shoulder and forced her to look up at him. "Whatever they can do, they've already done, and I'm still here."

She brushed her fingers across his chest, lingering on the scar Don Ponzio's rapier had left on his shoulder. She knew it was a dream, but it still frightened her. Slowly the images coalesced, and she realized that she was worried for Erik. She had drawn him back into the world that had shunned him. Thinking back on the previous night, she realized that there was something disturbing in the way Giovanni had looked at Erik. He was not just jealous or disappointed. He stared belligerently at Erik's mask. There it was: the obverse side of the coin. What was safe and tantalizing in the freak show was monstrous and threatening in the real world. They would not abide anyone who was not like them. His mask alerted them to his alien nature. His existence called into question the nature of their well-ordered universe. And if they were to see him unmasked?

She knew they could pity him if he were weak, crippled, and pathetic. But they would fear and reject him if he were strong, independent, proud, and seemingly uninterested in their acceptance. In short, Erik could ask for their pity but not their respect. How was she to protect him, to keep him by her side, in this world?

Overwhelmed by anguish, she blurted out, "What are we to do, Erik?"

He squeezed her close again, worried that he didn't understand exactly what was troubling her. He pulled her with him from the bed and out onto the balcony. The night was warm, the moon full, and he sat her on his lap and held her in his arms. He sang her the lullaby he used to sing to Christine when she was but a child all alone and forlorn in the opera house dormitories. Slowly Meg's shudders subsided, and she relaxed completely against his body.

"Is it what I told you about the past three years?" He dreaded that she was appalled at his infidelities, the violence and the humiliation he confessed to her the night before, but he sensed that even if it were his past that disturbed her, she wouldn't let it come between them. There was nothing, he was certain now, that could ever come between them, not the past, not even Christine. That realization had released him as if chains had been removed from his heart. He was free to love Meg and to accept her love.

He waited for her to answer and thought she'd fallen asleep she took so long to reply. "Not exactly. It's just that in those three years you were treated so abominably. Now you're home, and I so want us to be able to lead a normal life."

"You worry that it's not possible?"

"Yes."

It wasn't as if Erik hadn't asked himself the same question, but his doubts seemed more real now that Meg had expressed similar fears. He had no words to comfort her or himself for that matter. She clung to him, perhaps sensing that he might misunderstand her. As she was on the verge of assuring him that she never wished to live again without him, he spoke up. "Our son doesn't mind my face. I don't think strangers and acquaintances would feel the same. I'll have to wear my mask."

She started to speak, but he hushed her.

"It's simpler that way. I don't mind. I'd miss my mask. It's my second skin. I'll wear it whenever we ..." He struggled to imagine himself among Meg's friends and acquaintances or simply walking about the small town of Pianosa with Meg. He couldn't. He felt her turn her face toward his, so he hurried to fill the silence. "Don't worry, Meg. I won't go, not unless you tell me to."

"I won't."

"You say that now. If you ever change your mind ..."

She interrupted, "I would never want you to leave us again!"

"Even so," he insisted, "if you want me to go all you have to do is tell me."

"You must promise me that you won't go, even if I tell you to, if I say it in anger! You must wait and talk with me when our tempers have cooled. Promise me!"

"I promise." He brushed aside the hair a light breeze had fanned across her face. "You never had such a bad temper until you met me."

They both laughed softly.

"By the way, François lost the mask. Do you have another you can give him?"

"Maybe I'll make one just for him, one that actually fits his face."

"He'd love that. He liked that it was exactly like the one you usually wear."

Erik told Meg to listen. There was a fox barking out in the copse of trees over the crest of the park. Crickets were working to drown out any other ambient sound.

"Will you come with me tomorrow to church? I want you and Father Antonio to meet. I usually go and work in the garden with Annetta."

Erik's smile fell away, and he shifted slightly under Meg's body. A long moment passed between them in complete silence. Meg felt that she had stopped breathing, worried that she had pushed him too far.

"Would you be disappointed if I refused to go?"

Meg's heart sank. If she could be sure that anyone would be willing to consider and accept Erik with an open mind and heart, it was Father Antonio. If they couldn't start here, they wouldn't be able to start anywhere. She almost lied, but decided that they must be truthful with each other, even if it hurt. "Yes, I would be." She said it softly, barely as a whisper against his throat, her face nestled under his chin.

She felt him swallow hard before he spoke. "Then we must go."

The plans lay on Father Antonio's table—architectural designs and blueprints for the school. Erik found his eye drawn to them over and over again as Meg and the old priest discussed the recent events, in particular Erik's return. The plans were simple, well designed but modest, and he immediately made mental notes on what he would change if he had any say. The priest had been mildly shocked to find that Meg's long lost husband had returned, but he felt rather silly not having recognized that the reclusive cousin of Beatrice Fusco was none other than the same man. Given that he fancied himself an astute judge of character and having already embraced the tragic Pierre Fusco as part of his 'flock,' the priest couldn't very well act as if Erik were a complete stranger much less a dangerous character. Yet the priest was uncomfortable, and Meg could see this in his unusually jittery way of serving the tea and the way he talked nonstop and to no end for several minutes at a time. He knew more than he wanted to know about Erik. Sinners he had plenty among his flock, but mad killers, as far as he knew, none. It was one thing for this woman who loved Erik to make excuses for his past crimes, but he was a priest and couldn't ignore the enormity of Erik's sins. Yet he had no first-hand knowledge—only Meg's confession—so he could hardly accuse him or throw him out or call for the authorities. There had been something—a debate in the seminary—about breaking with the sanctity of the confessional if there was a crime about to be committed, particularly a heinous crime such as rape or murder, that might be avoided. However, he thought he remembered that the Church remained firm against disclosure even in such dire circumstances. Of course, that had been a hypothetical case, and his years in the seminary were ages ago. Anyway there was no reason to believe that Erik was a threat now.

"Well your cousin left you this note. She left the day before yesterday." Erik was confused momentarily by the priest's mention of a cousin before he realized that Father Antonio still believed that Lucianna was a relative. The priest handed Erik a folded piece of paper which the latter folded yet again and tucked away in an inside pocket of his vest to read later.

"She's not my cousin. Meg and François are my only family."

The priest raised an eyebrow and glanced at Meg. Evidently she already knew of this. So whatever the relationship between this man and the other woman had been it was an issue best dealt with in the privacy of their marriage.

Pointing at the plans, Erik asked if the priest had considered alternative designs. The priest who knew next to nothing about architecture or construction shook his head and sighed in disappointment. "We had hoped to have the edifice ready for the next school session, but I lost the foreman to a larger and better paid project in Rome."

Erik turned quickly in his seat and leaned excitedly over the plans studying them in earnest. "Do you have the materials?"

"Why, yes. We gathered all we needed, at least to start and according to the foreman to frame it. More are promised by donation from the lumber yard and nearby quarry."

"Men? Do you have masons and carpenters as well as some men with strong backs? Is the stone granite or limestone?"

Erik was not just curious but intensely interested in the project. "Yes, I think we have an adequate crew, many are willing to work for half pay since it's for the children and the Church. The quarry is limestone. You sound like you know something about construction."

"I've studied architecture. I've done some construction on my own. Small jobs." He paused and seemed to be debating something with himself.

"Erik, are you considering offering to help with the plans?" Meg pulled gently on his sleeve to get his attention.

"Not just help. He needs someone to supervise the construction."

"Would you be able to do it?" The priest was now intrigued and excited, having forgotten all about Erik's shady past.

"I'm capable, but will your crew follow my orders?" He held the priest's gaze.

Father Antonio felt as if he could see into the man's very soul. Erik's eyes were intense and unguarded, and in them the priest saw the question. There was anxiety and hesitation. Yet what most struck the priest was the faint glimmer of hope and a sincere eagerness to take on the challenge.

"We can only try and see," was the priest's honest answer. For as much as he wanted his school, he wasn't sure his crew would take orders from a foreigner who hid behind a mask, a foreigner who had been the subject of much gossip over the past three years.

❦

Dearest Erik,

Forgive me for not taking leave of you in person. When you failed to return the next day and the day after that, I surmised that our mission had succeeded. I had to remind myself that this reunion between you and your family had, after all, been the purpose of our journey and our masquerade, my dearest cousin Pierre. Since you have no more need of me, I've decided it's time I returned to my home.

I had considered leaving you the portrait, but I know it never met with your approval. And more selfishly I couldn't part with it. I may have lost the original, but I can retain a humble copy. I hope it makes our parting more bearable. In defense of my rendering of you in oil, it was your soul that I labored to reveal and on that score I could find no blemish in the model or fault with my attempt to capture it.

I intend to find that high-spirited girl you met once on a midnight ride. If our paths were ever to cross again, I would consider myself fortunate. My solace is to know you are happily reunited with your family. I will always be indebted to you for being my champion and freeing me from my husband as well as for your gentleness and companionship over the past months.

Your servant and friend,
Lucianna

Erik reread the note once more and placed it in the top drawer of the desk he had taken as his own in the library. Meg was standing in the doorway as he did so. She didn't ask, but Erik volunteered that Lucianna had returned to her estate and wished them well. When Meg asked if he planned to write, he hesitated and replied that he should at least acknowledge receipt of the note and express his gratitude. Meg smiled and said that would be the right thing to do.

Construction began on the school within the week. The priest introduced the new foreman to the men who stood indecisive while Erik gave the first orders. However seeing that the priest had put this stranger with a mask in charge, they concluded that he must know what he was doing. After the first several days the men had made a good deal of progress, but Signore Erik—for that's the only name he'd give them—insisted on pushing them to get the retaining wall up to the most exact measurement. A few of the workers were beginning to grumble about his pickiness—especially when he berated the carpenter for approximating the plumb line for the struts and beams and made him do it over to the exact measurement. The grumbles turned to outright rebellion when Erik ordered a partially built wall demolished and rebuilt because it didn't meet his specifications. Bruno stood, like a brick wall himself, his arms akimbo on his hips and defiantly challenged Erik to take the wall down himself and put it together the way he wanted if he wasn't satisfied with their work.

Erik stripped down to shirt and breeches, carelessly laying his vest and coat on a pile of discarded rubble. He lifted the mallet and swung it at the wall. No one thought he'd actually do it. The wall immediately buckled and began to crumble. He raised the mallet again and blasted through the wall. He didn't look at the men who had all stopped in the middle of their tasks to watch him.

Erik salvaged the unbroken stones for reuse and cleared away the rubble. He took the broom and cleaned the base. Without a word to the masons, he poured the water and mixed the mortar which he began to apply in an even layer. There he fixed the stones to the new plumb line that he had checked for accuracy to make sure the wall would be aligned the precise way it was supposed to be.

The sun had already begun to sink in the late afternoon, and Erik was the only man working on the site. He had run out of stone and took the wheel barrow and rolled it to the deposit where he loaded as many of the stones as he could manage to transport. He had broken a sweat transporting the stones to the site of the wall. No one moved to help, but all seemed to be transfixed to the spot. As Erik carried and placed the rough hewn stone, the skin of his hands began to blister and bleed. Simon took off his heavy work gloves and put them on the half wall as Erik went to prepare more mortar. When Erik came back to the wall and saw the gloves left obviously for his use, he paused only long enough to put them on. He was almost out of mortar again but one of the other men had prepared some in the interim. He brought it over in a bucket and placed it by Erik's side. Bruno watched as one by one each of his co-workers took up tasks to assist Erik in the construction of the wall. Then Simon took up a place farther along the wall itself and began to lay mortar and place stones. Erik noticed his bare hands, took off the gloves, and offered them to him.

"No need, sir. My hands are already leather." He displayed proudly the calloused hide of each hand to Erik and gave him a toothy grin.

Bruno kicked the rubble at his feet and began transporting stone from the deposit. By sunset, the wall was more than half finished. Erik stopped and went to wash off with the rest of the workmen. As he put on his coat and vest, Simon gave him a hard pat on the back and said he'd see him first thing the next morning.

Meg cleaned the blisters of Erik's hands and applied a soothing ointment. He didn't complain even though they had burst and revealed raw flesh underneath. She had demanded details, but Erik just said that the men were resentful since he didn't do the work himself yet complained that they didn't do it properly. So he had shown them how to do it. She was somewhat reassured by the matter-of-fact way he told her of the day's events, but she worried that Father Antonio's idea of exposing Erik to this group of workers was hopelessly naïve.

After she applied the ointment, she wrapped his hands loosely in soft gauze.

"How am I supposed to use my hands like this?" He lifted both in what appeared to be white snow gloves.

"You're not. You can take them off in the morning." She gathered her medicinal tools and placed them on a shelf in the wardrobe and began to undress. Erik stood still in the center of the bedroom, his eyebrows knit in consternation.

"And how am I supposed to get undressed?"

She laughed at him. She laughed louder when his face turned red. "I'll help you. Just wait a minute. She let the last of her undergarments slip to the floor. The effect successfully took his mind off his bandages. She slowly unfastened his buttons and gently pulled his shirt from the waist of his breeches and slid it off his shoulders and arms, taking special care to avoid undoing the wrappings on his hands. Then she dropped to her knees and pulled his breeches to the floor. When she didn't rise, Erik took in a sharp gasp of air and closed his eyes savoring the pleasure.

They had both underestimated the toll of physical work Erik had done that day, and as Meg continued in her lustful appreciation of her husband's body, Erik's legs began to tremble from excitement and fatigue. He begged Meg to let him take the bandages off, but she held him to the spot until she knew that they were fast approaching the point of no return. She brought him to the bed, leading him by the elbow, and had him lie down. From that point on, she took it upon herself to proceed with the evening's festivities.

It was an experiment.

"I'll take five meters of the taffeta." Meg turned the fabric over in her fingers and placed it on the side to browse through the other bolts of heavier material, the cottons and wools, for Erik's new trousers and a dinner jacket which he badly needed. It had been years since he robbed the wardrobe rooms of the opera. It was a miracle that he wasn't in tatters and rags, but his wardrobe was woefully out of fashion at this point.

They had to test the waters, she had argued over and over with him.

"What good is having money if one can't send a servant to do the errands?" he had retorted when she announced their shopping trip to Pianosa.

Now he stood next to her in the shop as she examined the fabrics. He could feel everyone's eyes upon him. Why should he care? Why should he be here?

Why couldn't he stay at the villa? A thousand years might have passed before he would have felt the need to seek out society in the town!

"I want them to get used to having you about." She paused and looked at how he was fidgeting next to her at the counter and added, "You need some practice, too."

He frowned at her. She insisted on trying to act as if he were not who he was, what he was, and as if they could lead a normal life within society.

The travesty of it! Here she stood over the greens, blues, yellows, ochres, and browns—all he could see were the colors—and her fingers rubbed and stroked the fabric, cream on a sea of rust. So hopeful she looked as she smiled up at him. How could he destroy her fantasy? He could hear the matrons behind him whispering. He saw the mother grab her daughter and pull her close as Erik came through the doorway. He smelled the fear on the shopkeeper's hands as he wrapped the cut cloth in brown paper and tied it with string. Out of the corner of his eyes he saw several curious onlookers sneak inside the shop and draw back together to watch him. He tried to stop his blood from racing as he felt closed in, trapped. Meg was thankfully oblivious to it all as she counted out the coins and made small talk with the polite, but wary, clerk.

"Can we go now?" he hissed at her as she gathered her purse and he picked up the packages.

"I just need to stop at the dry goods shop for some flour and yeast." She began to list the ingredients on the list of paper she had hidden away in the many pockets of her skirts when he took her firmly by the elbow and ushered her toward the door. Only on the street did he exhale and feel that perhaps the worst had passed.

That was when he saw a short, beefy man with a handlebar mustachio grab a little boy's arm and shake him angrily. Erik held his breath as everything around him melted away except the look of terror on the child's face. The boy must have been no more than five or six years old. His lips were trembling and a line of snot dribbled down his face. The man was yelling something, but Erik couldn't hear the words. He saw the beefy arm rise above the man's head, his fingers splayed. Time had broken. The man's hand came down in what seemed to Erik a slow arc and slapped the child across the face!

Meg tried to hold him back, but Erik walked straight down a tunnel that led him inexorably to the man's side. Before the short and stocky man could raise his arm yet again, Erik grabbed his forearm tightly in his fist and brought it savagely down.

"What the hell!" the man gurgled as Erik's other hand came to his throat. Meg was at Erik's side in the next second, her hands pulling at his arm. Several passersby stopped in shock on the sidewalk and in the street as they witnessed the stranger accost Pietro Santini, the butcher. The child had picked up the brown package from the ground and run off to disappear around the corner of the building.

Erik became aware of Meg's frantic pulling, and suddenly the tunnel disappeared leaving him standing in a wash of strange faces surrounded by a cacophony of noise. He pushed the man to the wall of the shop releasing him now that the child was safe. The butcher rubbed his throat and coughed several times before he could speak. Meg grabbed Erik's sleeve and led him hurriedly toward their carriage. Their manservant rushed to take the packages and to escort his mistress and her husband into the safety of the box. As he was leaving, Erik could hear the butcher behind him curse. The boy was a thief. He had stolen, right from the counter, a leg of lamb that was meant for a paying customer.

Just when Meg thought they were safe, Erik wrenched away from her and strode purposefully back toward the butcher. The man, who just moments before was cursing Erik at the top of his lungs, cringed and quieted in shock as the tall, imposing gentleman loomed over him.

"He was just a child! Did it occur to you that he might be hungry?" Erik stared in the little man's eyes and thought that it probably did occur to him that the child was stealing because he was hungry but that he didn't care. A thief was a thief!

Erik scanned the crowd that had gathered about them and saw only scowls and disapproving looks. They were meant for him, not for the butcher. Taking several coins from his purse, he threw them on the ground at the butcher's feet.

What did she want from him? Wasn't it enough that he had nearly gotten them lynched in town? Wasn't it enough that he was doing rather well with the men at the construction site? Couldn't she be content with that minor triumph? He had never worked with anyone, never lived with anyone. He certainly had depended on Madeleine's help at the opera house, but essentially he had led a solitary life. He had come and gone, had slipped among the singers and technicians, had watched from his hiding places, looked down on the amphitheater and stage from the catwalks, but he had never really been with them.

Since the incident in town, Meg had backed off a bit. She had dropped several hints that she might invite some of her acquaintances and friends for a modest dinner party some night. Erik held his tongue, terrified at the idea, but unwilling to confront Meg at the moment. He couldn't do it, not again. Memories of Don Ponzio's dinner parties filled his mind.

Wasn't it enough that he agreed to visit Father Antonio's rooms three times a week after working on the construction site to talk? No one had made it clear, but he was no fool. He knew that the purpose of these meetings was to prepare him to join the church, Meg's church. She had already expressed a desire that he attend mass with her and his son. He had resolutely refused. He agreed to the visits to keep her from insisting on the other.

As much as Erik tried to steer the conversation toward the subject of church music or the school construction, Father Antonio kept shifting back to the distinctions between venial sins and mortal sins. Perhaps he did lack a soul, thought Erik. He simply couldn't retain the subtleties in his mind. He grew quiet as the priest spoke of hell, a subject to which he returned again and again. What did this sweet old man know of hell? Erik, on the other hand, had been there already. He feared Don Ponzio would reach through the fissures in the earth's crust and drag him down into the fire with him.

He preferred to remember the soothing words of the Prioress of St. Isidore's. It must have been God's will that he took refuge in her cell that night years ago now when he fled the police. Her message had always been one of love and forgiveness. This priest, unlike the nun, was obsessed with a seemingly unending list of requirements and duties upon which God's love was evidently dependent. He would forgive Erik's sins if … There was always the "if." And uncomfortably Erik realized the priest knew just how black his soul was.

Meg pushed, lovingly but insistently. She quizzed him after each visit to the priest's apartments about their "conversations." He answered in monosyllables, unwilling to let her know his resistance to the old priest's catechism and even more his fear that he was beyond redemption. In particular he was despondent given the incident in town and the conversation he had had this very day with the priest. It was more and more evident to Erik that whatever happiness he would have must be sought on this side of the grave or never. And he had his doubts that he would even find it here when he saw the elaborate dreams Meg still seemed to harbor that their life together would be like that of any other married couple in Pianosa.

"Do you think you might be ready soon to make your first confession?" Meg had just assumed that Erik would eventually come to the church. She knew that he hadn't been raised in any faith, but they were a family now, and if he joined the church with her and François, the congregation would welcome him she was sure.

Erik stared at her in horror. Seeing his face Meg bit her lip and held her tongue. She continued folding the cloth she had embroidered and only when she saw Erik's shoulders relax as he resumed reading the latest gazette from Paris did she speak again, gently and softly. "He'll forgive anything you confess, Erik. He will."

She meant to be reassuring, but he didn't move or speak. Only the slight stiffening of his back suggested he had indeed heard her.

"Father Antonio already knows what you …"

Erik threw the gazette to the ground and whirled around to loom darkly over her. His eyes glistened like steel, and he barely unclenched his teeth to speak. "He knows that I've murdered innocents. He knows that I …" His voice broke, and he collapsed at her knees, his head in her lap, his arms wrapped tightly around her hips. She held back her own tears as she stroked his hair. She couldn't think why he was not comforted. Why would he despair knowing that redemption was so within reach? She spoke nonsense sounds like those she used with their son, but grew panicked as she saw no abatement of his grief. Finally she drew his head from her lap and looked into his face. "What is it, Erik?"

"There's too much …" were the only words he managed to express.

"You must trust that His love is greater than your sin."

Erik twisted his face away from her hands and buried it again in her lap. His sobs had slowly lessened, and now he was only occasionally shuddering.

"I love you, Erik." Meg didn't know what else to say.

"I … I … can confess, but I won't be forgiven if I'm not truly repentant."

Meg's hand stilled. She waited for him to continue.

"I don't repent. I … I can't repent them all. Meg, I killed my … father." The tears and sobs erupted again. Through them he managed to repeat that he would not repent the murder of his father.

She couldn't stop her own tears now as she drew him up into her arms so that his face rested on her shoulder and they could wrap their arms around each other. "Erik?" She controlled her voice with some difficulty. "Erik? Do you wish you had been able to love your father and have his love?"

He pushed away from her angrily. "I hated him! I still hate him. He deserved to die!"

"Yes, but can't you see that it's God's place to pass judgment?"

Erik rose quickly to his feet and stumbled backwards several paces until his back hit the wall opposite Meg's chair. She saw the look of betrayal on his face and understood his pain at her words. He thought she was judging him. "Erik, do you wish things had been different? That you would have been loved?" She saw in his eyes that this he understood. Her heart threatened to bleed as she saw for one brief moment that the child Erik had been was still trapped inside him, hidden ever so deeply in a dark corner. She wasn't sure whether it was to punish that child or to keep him safe or both. "Then you can repent that you were driven to violence and admit that violence is bad?"

The nod he gave was nearly imperceptible. "Go to Father Antonio tomorrow. Ask to confess. Tell him you confess that you have committed murder, that you have felt forced into a life of violence in order to survive. God knows it all already, Erik. Ask for forgiveness. That's all you need do."

He swallowed hard. He still looked at her as if somehow he had been flayed alive and every inch of his body and soul had been laid open and bleeding. She lifted her arms out toward him, and like a child he came into them burying his face against the curve of her neck, his shoulders shaking with the force of his tears.

Sunday morning. The music coming from the loft was inconsistent and irritating to Erik. He grimaced at Meg who knew that her husband would rather climb to the loft and kill the organist than walk down the church aisle among all these strangers. He'd be so much more comfortable playing the music for the congregation than being a part of the congregation.

Father Antonio had expected Erik's confession to be long and detailed, but he used his discretion as a priest and absolved the man of his many sins without forcing him to enumerate and describe each and every instance. Even so, the old man was shaken when he left the confessional. He fervently prayed that Erik was enlightened by the Holy Ghost and understood the true nature of his sins and repented sincerely. Yet he wondered if there wasn't still some aspect of his sinful nature that Erik clung to and refused to see for what it was. He decided to leave it in God's hands. It was perhaps more important to bring the prodigal son back to the fold even if his understanding was still imperfect.

Today would be Erik's first mass, and he would be able to join the faithful at the communion rail and accept the sacrament of the holy Eucharist. The priest was delighted.

Several small groups of friends and family lingered outside as Erik, Meg, and François walked up the steps to the church entrance. A heavy silence fell on each gathering as Erik passed them, and the memory of the Red Death flashed unbidden across his mind. They were all looking at him as if he were the plague itself! Inside many of the congregation had already taken their stations; most of the parishioners had attended this same church just like their fathers and their fathers' fathers before them and occupied the same pews, the same side, Sunday after Sunday. Meg and François had found a corner of the church unoccupied by the others and had established it as theirs over the past several years. Everyone knew Meg and the child. Normally they would have greeted her, but today they turned as if they hadn't seen her and remained silent. Erik glimpsed the shock and disappointment on his wife's face, and it made him angry. He was angry with the hypocrites around him, but he was equally angry with Meg. She should have known! He knew! He had told her, but she refused to accept it.

The three of them approached the basin of holy water and dipped their fingers lightly, made the sign of the cross and genuflected before going to their usual spot. Erik forced his mind to focus on the altar, the flowers, the music which he had to admit was not really so atrociously played as he had originally thought, the altar boys in their white vestments. He dropped Meg's hand as she knelt and indicated that he should do the same. His heart was thumping painfully against his rib cage as he bent his knees. Only the presence of François next to him, fidgeting, gave him any relief. He brought the boy close to his side and squeezed him lovingly. His son immediately responded to his father's caress by wrapping his arms around his neck and laying his face on his shoulder. Unlike his parents, François remained standing so that he could see over the back of the pew. The few parishioners in the same pew edged quietly and slowly away from Meg and her family. Meg tried to focus on the prayers, but her face was scarlet and hot with shame and bewilderment at the hostility she felt from the people among whom she had spent each Sunday and many holy days the past several years.

Everything seemed to pass as if in a blur for Erik until suddenly everyone was rising and pouring out into the main passageway. Meg placed François on the seat and motioned for Erik to follow her out into the queue that was forming for communion. He looked at her as if he didn't know who she was. The smile on her face began to fade as he stared at her. He blinked several times, and she realized that he was close to panic. She edged back into the pew and took his hand in hers and held it very, very tightly. She could hear his breathing; it was rapid and shallow. His color was pale. She knew he was no coward, but in this moment she saw that this is what he would look like if he were. Suddenly he took an enormous breath and gently pushed her out toward the queue. She stepped out among the others and felt him follow close behind. Again it was painfully evident to the two of them that those around Erik were distancing themselves as much as they could without it appearing too heinous and too obvious.

Meg knelt before Father Antonio and accepted the wafer on her tongue as the priest gave the blessing in Latin. She moved to the side and glanced back to watch Erik kneel. She held her breath as she saw the wafer disappear inside his mouth. He made the sign of the cross as he had been taught, and rose to follow her back to the pew. There the two of them knelt and prayed. She couldn't see Erik's face; he had dropped his head low between his arms as he prayed. She edged close enough to him so that he could feel her beside him. He straightened his back and looked directly ahead. She could tell that his eyes were moist, but he was holding himself erect and proud for her.

After the service, he held her back until most of the congregation had left. Then they rose and went out to the front of the church. Erik had expected that most would have already departed, but a crowd of people lingered on the steps and along the grounds of the churchyard as if they might return for a second mass. The curious had lagged behind to watch them leave. Father Antonio greeted each member of his parish as they left. When Erik and Meg appeared with their son in the doorway, he made it a point to greet them exuberantly. He shook Erik's hand and patted him on the back saying loudly that the church was glad to welcome him into the congregation. Drawing nearer to Erik's ear, he whispered just so he could hear, "God loves you, Erik. The rest will follow."

The priest's acceptance of the stranger in the mask seemed to calm some of the parishioners. Several who were particularly friendly to Meg went as far as to smile and nod at Meg, but they didn't come to chat. Simon and a handful of the workers from the construction site nodded discreetly at Erik but also remained huddled together in quiet conversation. Erik felt his insides shiver in anger as he discerned Giovanni amid a group of young dandies in the distance snickering among themselves as they watched Erik and his family leave the church. He pulled Meg along to the carriage, anxious to get away.

"Why don't you say it?" Erik growled at Meg. "You're ashamed of me!"
Meg reddened to a deep scarlet as she looked at him in shock.
"I won't go back!" He slammed the prayer book down on the bureau. She had meant it as a present to commemorate his first communion. He was angry. He wouldn't calm down. He would yell and rant because it felt good to yell and

rant! He had spent several hours holding himself in check, letting those people snicker and sneer. He knew that Meg had fallen under his contagion, as well. Thank God François was oblivious to it all.

"Why are you so angry with me?" Meg cried out at him, deeply offended by his accusations.

"I told you! I told you that they're all alike! It was useless. I felt like hot pokers were being shoved up …"

"Stop it! You're not the only one who suffered today!"

Erik grabbed her roughly by the arm and drew her close to him. "Don't you think that I don't know that? If it were only me, I would have marched out of there! It was the way they looked at *you* that made me want to set fire to the church and destroy them all!"

"You wouldn't!" Meg pulled roughly away from him and glared at him. Her lips were set in a grim line, and she straightened herself up to her full height even though it was woefully inadequate compared to her husband's.

"You looked at me as if you were ashamed, Meg." Erik's voice had become soft and still; a slight plaintive note crept into his complaint.

Her lips trembled and buckled as she broke into tears and struck him hard with her closed fist across his chest. "I was NOT ashamed of you! I was ashamed of all of them! Those were supposed to be my friends and neighbors. They were supposed to believe the same things that I believe, and they looked at you as if …" She covered her face momentarily as she cried. Erik reached out to her, but she backed away and spoke again. "I was so proud of you!"

Erik stared at her in shock. He dug his nails into the palm of his hand to keep back the tears that threatened to break through yet again.

"I was so proud of you because I know this was harder than almost anything you've ever done, and I know you did it mostly for me, for François. When you followed me for communion and when you walked out of that church beside me, you were so brave. And I thought to myself how I might never have found you! If I hadn't followed you that day down under the opera, if I hadn't tricked you the night of the masquerade, so many 'ifs' that I am terrified that this won't last."

Erik grabbed her into his arms and squeezed her close to his chest. He was unable to speak himself, for he was so surprised and so moved by what she was saying. But she wriggled away from him, determined to finish what she had to say.

"I don't care what happens. I don't care if we wall ourselves up alone in this villa for the rest of our lives as long as you're with me. I love you, Erik, so terribly much, so much that it hurts." She pounded her heart with her closed fist to emphasize the words.

This time she let Erik wrap her in his arms. She nearly swooned into his embrace as he picked her up and carried her to the bed. All he wanted to do was hold her. He set her on the edge of the bed and helped her out of her Sunday frock until she lay back upon the blanket, a thin chemise covering her body. He removed his coat and vest and took off his boots, and clothed solely in his shirt and breeches he lay down beside her. Only then was he aware that he had been repeating over and over that he loved her, that she was more important than anyone or anything in the world to him. She turned in his embrace so that they lay face to face. His mask sat forgotten on the table near the door. He kissed her gently along her cheeks while she caressed his face, brushing the hair from his eyes, softly tracing his lips with her finger tips, grazing the back of her hand across his chin. Then her hands wrapped round his shoulders and glided down his back, across his shoulder blades and along his taut muscles. They nestled closer and closer until she lay on his arm and they tasted each other's breath. He stroked her hair, and she squeezed his shoulder and pulled him tighter.

"I love you, Meg," he repeated again and again as he kissed her, as he buried his face in her blond hair, as he searched for her mouth and tasted her. Her lips were soft and moist. Her tongue moved to meet his, flicking along the tender inside of his mouth, across the rough surface of his tongue.

Slowly, ever so slowly, they found themselves touching, caressing, rubbing together, their hands delving and pulling and squeezing until the surface of their bodies grew hot and sweaty with arousal. Meg slid her knee up along Erik's side and hooked her calf round his hip. She pressed her heel into his muscle as if she would draw him into her body by force. Erik slipped his hand over her hip, along her long sleek thigh. *He imagined watching her dance. She danced only for him. On the stage, she balanced on tiptoe and thrust her leg high toward the ceiling, her arms raised in graceful arcs over her head, every muscle in her body alive with music. He imagined cupping the bottom of her thigh and lifting her into the air.* He wanted nothing between her body and his touch. He took the edge of her chemise and pushed the fabric out of his way. He squeezed the supple, naked flesh of her bottom and cupped her sleek firmness in his broad hand. His hand glided along the length of her thigh. Gradually his fingers slid between their bodies. First one, then two buried themselves deeply inside her. They deftly caressed her, warm and moist, as his mouth sought her parted lips, teased her tongue, buried itself inside. As his fingers entered her again and again, she teased his tongue, drawing it deep inside her mouth. Eventually, his kisses moved to her breasts, pulling the fabric of the chemise away from her, and Meg's back arched, urging him to deepen his kisses, to suckle and tease and bite at her. Anxious to touch him, Meg fumbled with the button on his breeches, pushed her fingers inside, and grasped him firmly in her hand. She caressed and stroked him, enjoying his arousal, delighting in the velvety feel of him until he begged her to stop. He breathed hot words in her ears, telling her of his desires. She guided him between her thighs until they were deeply joined. They moved slowly and gently, relishing each stroke, each moment of suction, friction, and pressure. He kept his mouth sealed to hers and with his hands, as the urgency reached its fullness, he grabbed her buttocks and pulled her up against his hardness until they both cried out and clutched at each other savagely in their pleasure.

He came out of the shadows as Lady Tedesco was about to get into the barouche outside the mayor's house. The driver thought to call out a warning when he saw the ominous form approach, the silhouette of a tall, imposing man with a flourishing cape that nearly reached mid-calf. As he drew near, under the gas lamp on the corner of the lane, the small group of guests who were departing glimpsed his masked face. In the next instant, the stranger had brushed past Lady Tedesco and torn the diamond necklace from her throat.

Although one of the younger gentlemen gave pursuit, the thief had disappeared as if by magic in the darkness of the alleyways.

CHAPTER 14

The Necklace

François was playing the melody his father taught him on the piano. It was supposed to be a surprise, but the little boy was too eager to show how well he could play. Meg recognized it as a piece Erik had composed in those mad, tormented days after Christine and Raoul married. It had been modified; a clear strain of incredible beauty dominated the slightly ominous background. She had remembered Erik playing it fortissimo with a heavy dose of anger. Now in the child's delicate touch it held a sweet, melancholic allure she had not heard before.

"You shouldn't tell your father that you played it for me. Let's keep it a secret so that he can enjoy his surprise when he asks you to play. I'll act very, very surprised. All right?"

"Yes! And then you can see the secret gift Signore Cimino left in father's desk."

"What secret gift? When did you see Giovanni?"

"This morning." The child got down from the piano bench and ran to his special box where he kept his treasures—a handful of lead soldiers, marbles, broken springs, a few coins, and a ball of coarse twine. He pulled out the white mask she thought had been lost.

"Where'd you find your father's mask?" asked Meg, drawing near. Why would Giovanni come by and not announce himself? What had François found in Erik's desk?

"I found it in the bushes outside the front door." He took each treasure out and placed it on the bench to show his mother.

Annetta came in to dust. Meg turned away just as François took his latest treasure out and put it in the center among the others.

"Why didn't you inform me that Giovanni had come by?" Meg felt queasy. She recalled the way Giovanni had looked at Erik.

"I didn't know, Signora, until I saw him ride away. It was a little after Don Erik left. I thought …" Annetta stopped in mid-sentence and furrowed her brow in curiosity as she stared at the child and his collection. Meg's gaze followed Annetta's to the display François had carefully arranged on the piano bench. Among the odds and ends sparkled a stunning diamond necklace.

Before she could ask her son the origin of the piece of jewelry—which was not hers and was obviously quite expensive—she heard a tremendous din coming from the hallway foyer. Giuseppe opened the door unceremoniously and was pushed to the side by several armed police officers. Behind them, Meg could see others climbing the stairs to the second story, rifles cocked and ready. In a panic, she reached for the piece of jewelry, but not before the officer in charge glimpsed Lady Tedesco's stolen diamond necklace.

"I'll take that, Signora." One of the officers took it from her. "Where is the man who wears the mask? Your husband, I believe?"

François, sensing his mother's panic, grabbed her skirt and burst into tears. As she put the pieces together, Meg's legs began to tremble. It was as if her bones had turned to pudding. They were here to arrest Erik for some crime involving this expensive necklace. She had no doubt whatsoever that Giovanni had somehow orchestrated all of this to place the blame on her husband. She also realized no one would take her or her son's word in defense of Erik. He was doomed to go to prison, and there he would most surely die. She remembered his ordeal in Paris, and she knew in her heart that he would not be able to bear imprisonment again.

The officers came down the stairs reporting that Erik was not on the premises. They had brought along with them several of Erik's masks as if these were valuable evidence.

Although Meg refused to speak, as did Annetta and Giuseppe, it was evident that the police knew about the construction site. The officer in charge, a thin man with large ears and arms too long for his height, assigned a detachment to remain at the house and left with the remaining men for the construction site. Knowing it was probably futile, Meg shouted out to the captain that Erik was innocent.

"Signora, do you even know what he's accused of? How do you protest his innocence when the spoils of the crime are found here under your very nose?"

"It was Giovanni Cimino. He left the necklace with my son to incriminate my husband."

"That's ridiculous. How dare you, a foreigner, come here and accuse the son of one of the most respectable families in the area? We have witnesses, Signora. Your husband is a thief." Without a further word, he marched out the door.

There was no way to get a message to Erik in time.

"He went to the quarry to supervise a transfer of newly cut stone."

"Is he returning to the site?" asked the captain.

Bruno looked past the captain's shoulder toward Simon who signaled him as if to say, 'keep your tongue.' Something was wrong. Shifting uncomfortably from foot to foot the burly man shrugged his massive shoulders and said, "Don Erik doesn't tell us his business. We just do the work."

Simon snuck off and circled around the piles of materials to see if he could get to the road without being seen by the patrol. Erik had told them he might stop off at his home and not return until quite late in the day. Unfortunately there was no way Simon or any of them could warn Erik. The quarry was on the opposite side of Erik's manor, and he would not pass by the construction site on his way home.

Erik encouraged Charlemagne to slow to a trot across the open meadow now that they were within sight of the stable. Since he had ridden as the crow flies cross country and off the path, he had gained a bit more time, time he hoped to spend with Meg and François. He took Charlemagne into the stable and settled the horse in his stall, curious not to find the stable boy. He went toward the house through the garden instead of the front entrance. He was pleased that his conflict with the workers had resolved itself well. The blisters had been worth it. Since that episode, each morning when he arrived the men were already busy organizing the materials and waiting for orders. Even Bruno seemed compliant and eager to show his mettle. So he felt quite at ease leaving them to it and traveling to the quarry to check on the stone cutting.

Preoccupied as he was, he still wondered at the silence and the lack of usual activity around the grounds. He opened the veranda door wide and strode in eager to greet Meg. He immediately took in the scene: An officer had his wife clenched in one arm, her mouth stopped with his free hand. Another restrained his son. Several other police officers were stationed in the room. Enraged Erik took one step forward when someone behind him slammed the butt of his rifle across his head. He fell heavily to the floor.

First I heard strange men's voices, boots marching in and out, someone crying. My body told me I was on the floor. There was pain. Something wet dripped down along my cheek and nose into my mouth—salty. Crying, it was François who was crying. I forced my eyes open, and dancing lights and shadows condensed gradually into recognizable forms. As I noticed that Meg and François were being restrained by several uniformed men, someone on either side of me twisted my arms behind me and secured my wrists with a strap. They hauled me to my feet with some effort since I was still dead weight.

No one had to tell me what was happening. These were gendarmes. They'd found me and were taking me back to face my sentence. I was unable to staunch the sickening panic that overwhelmed me. I struggled to twist and pull away from my captors. Several other officers came to assist them. Only the escalating cries of my son broke through my fear and anguish to some conscious level. He was frightened, and my desperate struggle scared him even more. Meg was soundlessly holding him, tears streaming down her face. I forced myself to calm down. I stopped struggling, but remained tense in the policemen's grip. I slowed my breathing and tried to look reassuringly at my son and wife. Their grief broke my heart, for I knew there was no way to save them from this.

I managed to blurt out to Meg that she should take care of our son. So much more I wanted to say and wondered if I'd ever have the chance to say to my loved ones.

A thin man with long arms ordered me to be taken away. I asked them to mount me on my own horse Charlemagne. I had only a moment to glance back at Meg, hoping she would know what I couldn't say to her. I couldn't go back to prison. I was a dead man, my fate having been sealed long ago in Paris. Fortunately, the captain agreed to have Charlemagne saddled for me. Hearing this, I was able to stand on my own two feet, to control the panic, to think, to calm the shaking of my limbs, to block out the pain and fear I saw on Meg's face, to set my own into a mask of stoic resignation. Two men helped me gain the saddle. Meg and François had come out to the yard to follow my departure. Charlemagne stood—as glorious and dignified as ever—and I dared to call back to my family that I loved them. The captain reprimanded one of the men who snickered.

The officers crowded around me as we set off at a canter for Pianosa, my life sinking away farther and farther behind me. My house was soon out of sight; we were approaching the fork in the path where the road branched to the right for Pianosa and to the left for Rome. The woods here were thick, impassable for a posse in hot pursuit unless they were expert horsemen and knew the forest well. I tightened the grip of my knees on Charlemagne's sides, leaned in toward his crest in preparation. The worst that would happen was that they'd subdue Charlemagne before we could get away, and we'd arrive in Pianosa as they planned. My other options were to break my neck in a fall from my mount, to be shot in the back as I tried to escape, or to be caught after a harrowing and useless flight through the woods. The options leading to death were far more desirable to me than the possibility of recapture and imprisonment. The most optimistic outcome would be a successful escape through the woods. I tried not to think beyond that.

Alternately applying pressure from my knees, I edged Charlemagne close to the mare on my left. Annoyed, the officer led his mare slightly away from me to avoid his mount rubbing up against my stallion. A very narrow aperture was created. The mare was no match for Charlemagne. I was sure that she'd rear up and give way. Just before we reached the fork in the road—several in the party had already turned to the right and were disappearing around the bend—I squeezed my knees and dug my heels into Charlemagne and gave a loud shout. The Arabian bolted forward crossing directly in front of the startled mare who reared onto her back haunches throwing her rider clear of the saddle. Before the patrol knew what had happened, we were in the woods.

As Charlemagne bolted through the dense growth of the forest, I held desperately with thighs and knees to the saddle. My head pounded, but the rhythm of my heart was far more urgent. Precariously, I centered my weight as best I could over the stallion's back. I nearly fell from the saddle more than once as we careened at full gallop, weaving round the trees, across rotted trunks, along terrain that was both slippery with dead leaves and uneven. In the back of my mind, I understood that a fall here, at this speed, would most likely leave me crippled or dead. However, the other choice appalled me even more. I could not survive the cage. I let the Arabian run his race, trusting to his agility and intelligence.

I could hear the shouts of the men as the posse gave pursuit. The thunder of their hooves sounded to me like the very hounds of hell were on my heels. Renewed panic made me spur Charlemagne on to even more reckless speed. For several moments, the woods flew past my eyes as a blinding blur of greens and browns. I heard nothing but the rapid, powerful breathing of my mount and the rush of my own blood in my ears. Soon the terrain became unfamiliar, and I thought to listen for the approach of the posse. But Charlemagne continued to gallop, the sound drowning out all others. Somehow I sensed we were no longer being chased with the same fervor. I imagined the gendarmes far behind us cautiously picking their way through the woods.

Eventually, Charlemagne showed signs of fatigue and slowed his pace. I listened. Nothing but the ambient sounds of the forest hit my ears. Softly I urged my stallion toward a grassy patch among large cedars and oaks where I hoped he would halt. I was sure the posse had been left far behind. They would perhaps continue, but they would track us slowly and carefully. After several unsuccessful attempts to stop Charlemagne I was about to despair that he would ever come to a complete standstill. Finally, exhausted, he slowed. As he wandered about munching at the short grasses amid the roots and leaves, I swung my leg over and slid off the saddle. I landed hard on my knees and rolled to my side. Charlemagne looked down at me as if disgruntled by my unorthodox dismount. My hands were still fastened behind me. I tucked my legs up to my chest and managed to slide my arms under my body bringing my hands to the front where I worked away with my teeth at the leather straps until eventually the knot came loose, and I was able to free myself.

Exhausted, I sat for a moment on the ground to assess my situation while Charlemagne grazed nearby on the scrubby vegetation.

Blood had long ago crusted on my face and mask. My shirt was stained, too. My head throbbed worse by the minute. I had no cloak, and without that or some other way of covering the fact that I wore a mask and was wounded, I would easily be thought a highwayman or the fugitive that I was. I had no money. My only asset was Charlemagne.

I could not return home.

Ahead of me lay Rome. There, among the urban throng, I would be able to disappear. Perhaps I could find a way to get word to Meg, to let her know that I had survived. That was as far as I could make myself think. Thoughts of Meg and my son overwhelmed me with anger and despair.

Don't look back, I warned myself. *Don't think of them. Don't think of what you've lost. Not if you wish to live.* That was a life I could never go back to.

Erik managed to steal a peasant coat along the way which covered his blood-stained shirt. The hood draped over his face and shielded him from unwanted stares. It was sufficient to pass along the streets of Rome without attracting too much attention. No one seemed interested in asking about the incongruous cut of the breeches as opposed to the rough fabric and stitch of the coat, nor to ask why a "peasant" was mounted on a horse of obvious breeding. It was a city, and its inhabitants learned to look without seeing, to pass among the masses without knowing them.

There was no recourse for Erik but to sell Charlemagne. He took the time, even though he and the animal were both tired and hungry, to inspect several stables in the wealthier section of the city in order to pick the one he judged would treat the Arabian with the kindness and respect he deserved. The farrier was gruff at first, and Erik thought he might wish to take advantage of a traveler like himself who was obviously in desperate straits. Much to his surprise, the man softened as if he sensed the fondness Erik had for the animal and regretted parting them. Erik kept his face as concealed as he could, but caught the man's eye as it perhaps lit on the mask. He asked no questions, though. The price he gave was more than Erik had any hope of getting under these adverse circumstances, so he was emboldened to ask a favor of the owner of the stable. He asked if some word might be sent to a lady in the environs of Pianosa, a Signora Giry, and that she be informed that a Signore Fusco had sold him the stallion. He added that he thought the signora would be pleased to find the whereabouts of the Arabian and would pay handsomely for him since she had expressed interest in buying the stallion some time back when his fortunes had been better and he had not been willing to sell. He knew the explanation was elaborate and full of inconsistencies, but the farrier accepted it and said that he'd post a letter the very next day.

Before Erik left, he asked to bed down the horse himself. The man gave him leave to do so, if it pleased him. Erik removed the saddle and bridle and began to wipe the horse down. All the time he whispered to the animal, told him Meg would surely send someone to purchase him back, that he had saved his life, and he was forever grateful. He brushed him with the curry comb until he knew that he was only doing so in order to avoid taking his last farewell. The man had given him the name of an inn nearby that was modest and quiet. Erik patted Charlemagne, nuzzled his nose, thanked the farrier, and left to find the inn. He'd stay a night or two at most, then try to find more permanent arrangements. He needed to rebuild his shattered life yet again. This time he would choose something more familiar. Since the age of ten or eleven he had lived in the Paris Opera House. He would find somewhere similar where he could spend the remaining years of his life, if need be alone. He couldn't allow himself to think about Meg and François. Without him, they were safe. That was all that mattered.

My esteemed Count Chagny,

It is with difficulty that I put myself at your mercy and beg your help. Although I am not able to explain to you the nature of my current situation, I ask you to please send a note to Meg and tell her that I am safe. She is not to worry. I've done only what I felt I had to do. You must refer to me in the note not by my true identity but by a false one, Pierre Fusco, whom she will understand to be me. It's also urgent that you ascertain Meg's situation and that you come to her assistance since I can't. Whatever she needs, I'm sure Christine would not withhold it.

In addition, I'm embarrassed that I must ask you for some financial assistance. A draft of money in the amount of 17,000 lire would be sufficient. Meg can reimburse you from our accounts. I cannot ask Meg for the money—she is not to come into direct contact with me—and unfortunately I need it urgently.

Communication with me can be directed to the same name as above and at the Teatro Argentina in Rome. It is crucial that my whereabouts and identity be kept secret. Meg will be able to inform you of the cause. I swear to you that this situation is not of my own doing. Unfortunately, as I have feared, my attempts to live a normal life have failed. I have sincerely tried to make my life with Meg succeed, but it simply was not meant to be.

In your debt, your humble servant,
O.G.

CHAPTER 15

Teatro Argentina

"Please, do continue."

Erik stiffened at the voice from behind him. He made as if to rise but the voice again came from somewhere at his back.

"I'm sorry to startle you. I came to pick up some papers that I left behind this evening."

The voice was drawing nearer. Erik considered bolting for the trap door under the stage. The man—his voice that of an older gentleman—would not be able to follow quickly enough to catch him. Even so he'd most certainly set off an alarm bringing in the police to search the premises. Although Erik had found a storeroom apparently abandoned and forgotten in the cellars, the underground levels in the Teatro Argentina were quite simple and modest. There were few places he could hide in safety if a concerted search were undertaken. In the flash of an eye he considered other options, one of which was unfortunately that of killing the man and dumping his body somewhere far from the theater.

Before he could act on any option, the man came alongside the piano. Erik heard the sudden intake of air, recognized the jolt of shock, as the stranger came into a position from which he unavoidably saw Erik's unmasked face. Erik resisted turning his head away. He had become careless, leaving the mask in the storeroom on the nights when he came up, undisturbed, from the cellars to wander through the dressing rooms and auditorium. At these early hours between midnight and morning, not even guards or custodial workers were about.

He might still have escaped. Why didn't he? he asked himself. Perhaps it was for the same reason that he stayed buried in the storeroom for hours on end without food or drink only to come up after all had departed to explore the stage properties, to play the piano, to roam the catwalks and imagine the ballet below him, to people with sounds the orchestra pit and envision the black notes tripping across the pages of his unwritten opera. He foraged on leftover fruit and stale bread he found in the cafeteria, oblivious to the quality or taste, doing it solely because his body required it.

Erik kept his gaze averted from the old man and his voice. It was safer to stare at the row of ordered ivory keys. The only movement he made was to glide his fingers soundlessly across them as if stroking a cat.

"You must be the one causing the stir."

"I'll get my things and leave," he responded in a flat, expressionless tone.

The man put his hand on Erik's shoulder and pressed him back gently to the piano bench. The firm pressure of the man's hand surprised Erik, who in reaction turned to look up at him. He was a tall, distinguished man whose age Erik judged from his gray hair and the slightly bent look to his knuckles to be anywhere between sixty and seventy. Erik lowered his face at the renewed gasp he heard his unexpected audience emit on seeing both sides at once.

"Remarkable. Please forgive me. Not only do I interrupt you as you were making the most lovely music, but I react so incredibly badly to your … unfortunate scar. Please allow me to introduce myself. I'm Signore Costanzi, patron and manager of this establishment."

Erik saw the hand held out to him, but was overwhelmed by a sudden wave of emotion that threatened to bring him to his knees. Perhaps it was the lack of food and the exhaustion of days filled with dreams, perhaps it was the constant heartache he felt for Megan and François, perhaps it was the fact that he expected no kindness from human society. Although he controlled himself as best he could and clasped Signore Costanzi's hand, the gentleman discerned his turmoil but politely ignored it.

"Please, could you tell me where you heard the melody you were playing before? It's enchanting."

Erik's fingers fluttered over the keyboard playing out the motif he'd been working on for the last few days.

"Yes. That's the one."

"It's mine."

"So you're a composer as well as an accomplished musician?"

Erik didn't respond at first, but looked quizzically at his hands flexing them several times as if surprised to find them functional. He kept his face averted. Instead of answering, he started to play again. From the simple motif he branched out—eventually forgetting the old man—into variations, adding complex accompaniments until he reached an epiphany after which the piece had to recover the sweet simplicity of the naked melody once more. He sat back and let out a tremendous sigh, satisfied with the direction the piece had seemed to demand.

"I sincerely hope you've written that score down somewhere?"

Erik tapped his head. "It's here."

"If I were to ask you to repeat it, you could? From memory?"

Erik nodded.

"But it seemed as if you were just composing it as you went along!"

"Yes."

The old man sat and considered for a moment.

Erik rose from the piano and without a backward glance climbed the stairs from the pit to the stage and circled back toward the wings.

"Wait."

Erik paused just before disappearing off stage and turned slightly toward the voice.

"Your name. You never gave me your name."

"Pierre. Pierre Fusco."

"Where are you going?"

"To collect my things."

"Are you living here in the opera house?" The old man had heard rumors of some spectral creature haunting the lower rooms. Theater people were so incredibly superstitious that he had not given it a second thought. However, now he realized that his opera house indeed had a resident. When Erik didn't respond, Signore Costanzi went on. "Well as far as I'm concerned you need not leave. I would also like to make you a proposition."

Erik straightened suddenly in surprise, but didn't turn around. He preferred not to show his unmasked face again to the stranger. Suddenly he knew he must be cautious. He had had his fill of "propositions." He was happy not to collect his few belongings to find somewhere else to live although the prospect of someone—anyone—knowing where he was disturbed him. Yet he would leave if the proposition the old man offered was not to his liking, something he assumed to be more probable than not.

"What I would like to suggest to you is that you work as a musical consultant for the company. I would also pay you for any original compositions. You do know how to write music?"

At that, Erik whirled around and grimaced at the old man. "Of course!"

"I didn't mean to offend, I assure you."

After what seemed to the old man an incredibly long pause, Erik spoke up. "No one can know of my presence here."

"Agreed. That's not a problem. I can even furnish you with a key. I don't know how you've managed to come and go so freely, but it might make it easier for you. Do you have any other conditions?"

"No one is to come down past the storeroom marked with the letter 'D.'"

"Agreed. Now how much should I pay you?"

Here Erik hung his head as if overcome with some woe and didn't answer. Puzzled by his reaction, Signore Costanzi climbed the stairs to the stage and approached, stopping several meters from his new acquaintance.

"May I ask what the matter is?" He spoke gently. It occurred to him that he had stumbled upon a very strange creature. This Pierre was obviously deeply disturbed, perhaps even mad. Even if he were a genius, he was living a bizarre life hidden away in the cellars of the theater. He seemed to know no one. The barest hint of an accent gave away his foreign birth, but his Italian was flawless.

"Why didn't you call for the police?" asked Erik as if this were the most important question, much more important than his retainer.

"I don't know. Why? Should I have? You weren't doing any harm. On the contrary, you were playing like an angel."

"An angel ...," interrupted Erik with a slight laugh.

"Can I help you in any way? Are you in serious trouble?"

"Why aren't you afraid of me?" Still he used the same tone as before, intently interested in the answer.

"Again I ask, should I be?"

"No."

Signore Costanzi waited for the intruder to continue, but Erik only stood staring at the old man. Finally he confessed, "I have money, but I can't use it very easily."

When the old man didn't seem to understand, Erik lifted his hand to his face.

"Oh, I see. You perhaps need someone to help you make transactions? I suppose it isn't comfortable to deal with the public. People can be quite cruel."

"Yes."

Although it was a simple answer, the old man recognized a note of bitterness in the tone.

"I tell you what, Pierre. May I call you that?" Erik gave a slight nod of his head. "I will pay you monthly, but I'll handle the money for you, and you will let me know what your needs are. Would that work for you?"

"Will you also help me post some letters and make sure that I receive any letter that comes?"

"Yes."

All of a sudden, Erik became quite animated. "There's a horse that I left with a stable in the area. Can you check on him? His name is Charlemagne."

Struck by this strange request, the old man hesitated, but when he saw the gleam in Erik's eyes intensify into anguish at his lack of response he agreed to check on the horse.

At that, Erik left the old man on the stage ruminating over the strange deal he had just made with the specter that had been haunting his theater for the past weeks. He asked himself the same question Erik had asked. Why? Why was he drawn to this disfigured man? Why didn't he draw back in revulsion and fear? Well, he had seen a good deal in his lifetime and was not easily frightened. He also knew sadness and solitude. He had been alone for some years now since his wife's passing on. They had had only one child, a son, and he had died, too. Henrico had loved music, studied at the conservatory, dreamed of a life as a composer. He had been taken too soon, still a relatively young man, like this one.

Raoul had received the note from the Phantom. Never had he been so shocked to hear from anyone. Christine had also received several urgent notes from Meg explaining the bogus crime, Erik's escape, a strange message from a stable in Rome about Erik's horse, as well as her plea for help. At first Raoul meant to ignore the letter from Erik. He had done far too much already, risked everything to assist the man when he helped him escape in the first place to Italy. But, of course, Christine would never have forgiven him if he had not. So he had made arrangements for Meg and the Phantom, helped to establish them outside Pianosa, and then washed his hands of the whole unfortunate episode. It had been over three years ago, nearly four, he and Christine had two lovely children, a beautiful and peaceful life together, and he refused to get embroiled yet again with a man who had once been his rival. For even though he had helped Erik escape hanging, he couldn't ignore the fact that Erik had murdered innocent people in his mad obsession to possess Christine. The two of them had made a pact, and Raoul had never expected to see or hear of the Phantom ever again. Now a letter had arrived in which it was evident that the Phantom was once more in hiding. Didn't this prove that the man would always be poison? There was no way that Erik could become part of society.

Christine forced him to listen to Meg's tearful letters detailing the injustice perpetrated against her and her husband. In an effort to hide the fact that he was indeed moved by the account, he said in a callous and off-handed fashion that Meg was better off without the Phantom (he tended to avoid calling him Erik, for he insisted on cautiously remembering how dangerous the man could be). It was a small mercy that he had escaped once again, and perhaps it would be best if he stayed away forever. The look on Christine's face showed him the error of his ways. It stung to see her so concerned for another man's fate, and he tried to convince himself that it was because she thought of Meg as a sister and that she was a truly Christian soul who pitied the monster. But didn't she remember that Erik had almost killed him?

So although he had preferred to avoid getting involved, he sent the money as Erik had requested. Christine took it upon herself to answer Meg's desperate notes informing her that she and Raoul had heard from Erik and that he was safe, hidden somewhere in Rome. Nevertheless between the two of them they worried that something must be done for Meg and the child. They couldn't be left alone in such a state. It was one thing when Meg had been able to count on the support of the community, but now it became apparent from subsequent notes, each written on the heels of the other, that the community had turned its back on her as well. They blamed her for bringing into their midst a criminal, and those who were vilest in their attitudes conjectured that a man who wears a mask must have even darker sins to cover than the theft of a valuable jewel from a lady.

Raoul glimpsed Erik through the crack left in the partially opened door as he waited for Costanzi to announce his arrival and his need to speak with him. He was glad that the old man had given him time to prepare himself to face the Phantom. It had been years since he had seen that face, but his memories and the occasional nightmare could not rival confronting it in the flesh. He discerned through the slit in the doorway that Erik reached for something and brought it to his face. Evidently the old gentleman was quite used to the Phantom's deformity. He seemed not the least affected. Raoul still didn't understand how Meg could … He brushed the thought away as he examined a narrow slice of the room. It was far less opulent than the bizarre lair in the Opera Populaire.

Raoul remembered being amazed at the richness and excess of those underground chambers. Erik had lived in a world of stolen props from the stage, and the effect of a wild accumulation from the operas staged at the theater left one dizzy with the impression of standing in the opium-inspired dreams of a romantic poet. In contrast, here Erik slept on a humble cot pushed against the wall. The space around him was marked off by piles of boxes and crates. There was but a spare table, a chair and stool, no mirrors that Raoul could see from the vantage point where he waited.

Raoul's attention was drawn back to Erik as it appeared that Costanzi was about to come fetch him except that Erik held him back momentarily. It touched Raoul a little to see his rival straighten his shirt and put on his vest and coat as if wishing to make an appropriate impression on his guest. He was relieved to see the mask in place on the Phantom's face. Of course when Christine and Meg had insisted that he go in person to Rome to find him, with nothing but a postmark, Raoul had suggested Erik might not be pleased to see him. Instead he had proposed they write. Meg reminded him that the authorities were watching and a note posted to Rome from her home would be a direct clue as to her husband's whereabouts. (It struck him how easily and naturally she referred to the Phantom as husband.) The Italian police had no reason to suspect the Chagny family of involvement in the unfortunate episode of the necklace, and Raoul could easily explain his trip to Rome as a matter of business. Reluctantly, he agreed to go to make sure Erik was well. Whatever else he planned to do, he knew he should keep to himself to avoid useless argument from the women. Someone had to be rational and keep a clear and steady mind on the problem. The Opera Ghost was once again in hiding. Megan and François were in an intolerable situation. They had asked for his help, and he would do what was reasonable to protect the woman and the child from the Phantom's fate.

"He's ready, Count Chagny." The old man seemed genuinely worried, but Raoul wasn't sure for what or for whom. He watched Signore Costanzi retire before he pushed the door open and stepped inside. Immediately he felt claustrophobic from the lack of windows and the close proximity to his old rival. As he glanced around the room, Erik's eyes followed his gaze to see the room perhaps as Raoul was seeing it. Neither man spoke for several moments. The silence was strained until Erik grabbed the straight-backed chair and dragged it across the floor leaving it somewhere between them as if inviting Raoul to sit. This freed Raoul finally to take a first step.

"We should get to the point," he said in the voice that he used to discuss the issues at the estate.

Erik's emotionless expression gave way to a cautious, inquisitive appreciation of his one-time opponent. Raoul had matured since their last meeting. He had always struck Erik as hopelessly young, but now there was something dry and hard about the man as if he suffered under great responsibilities.

"The first thing we must do is …" Raoul started to lay out his plan for them but was interrupted.

"Meg and François? Tell me they are well! Tell me. How are they?" Erik's entreaty was undeniable, and Raoul chastised himself inwardly for not starting with these reassurances. Suddenly it struck him—uncomfortable as it was to have any empathetic connection to the Phantom—how painful Erik's situation must be for him. He thought of Christine and his son and daughter, but he must be practical. Someone had to be.

"They are safe. Christine and Mme. Giry are with them."

"Madeleine?" Visibly Erik relaxed as if relieved of a great burden or sorrow until Raoul spoke again.

"Once she realized you were gone, she insisted on joining her daughter and grandchild."

His voice carefully neutral, Erik responded, "I'm glad. Meg shouldn't be alone."

"She won't be. Erik, you need to be aware of something." It was a relief to Raoul to say the man's name at last. After all, he had to call him something.

Just as Raoul was about to set out the major points of the plan, Erik interrupted him again. "Did she send for Charlemagne?"

"If you continue to interrupt, I won't be able to tell you what we've decided."

"Decided? We?" Erik tensed and quieted apprehensively.

"Yes. Plans have to be made."

"What plans may I ask?"

"For Meg and the boy. There are decisions that must be taken."

"Meg and François are my family. What decisions have been made for my family without consulting me?"

Raoul noticed the edge to Erik's voice. He had to proceed cautiously. "It would be easy to make mistakes drawing the police down on you. A case in point is that horse."

"Charlemagne."

"Yes. He's been placed in your name—Pierre Fusco—and boarded at the same stable for the year. The farrier will receive regular payments and understands that you will visit as it suits you. We couldn't have anyone from Meg's estate retrieve the animal. The police will know it's your mount, the one you escaped on, and trace it straight back here. How would Meg explain its sudden reappearance?"

Erik considered Raoul's reasoning and realized he was right. It galled him to know that he might have put them all in jeopardy. Reluctantly, he thanked Raoul.

"Except for the priest and perhaps a handful of local people, everyone has turned their backs on your family. They won't have anything to do with them. There's even been some violence."

"What? Who?"

"Nothing serious."

"I'll kill them. If anyone hurts my wife or child, I'll throttle them with my bare hands." Here was the monster that Raoul remembered. Erik's eyes were wide with fury, and his teeth clenched in a grimace that frightened even with the mask in place.

"This is exactly the kind of reaction I'd expect from you and why we've decided to take Meg and François back with us to Paris. They'll be safe and …"

"You can't. You can't take them, Raoul. They're my family. If you take them to France, I'll never see them again." Fury struggled with both panic and incredulity.

"Perhaps that's for the best," said Raoul quietly, knowing that he was on the edge of a dangerous situation. He watched Erik closely ready to defend himself if necessary. The Phantom was tall and gaunt, thinner than Raoul had remembered him. Even so Raoul knew how strong he was and was glad he had had the foresight to sequester a tiny revolver in his vest pocket just in case. He would use it if he needed to.

Erik couldn't believe what he had just heard. He stared at Raoul silently. He noticed his rival's hand edge close to his vest pocket and recognized that he must have a firearm concealed in his inside pocket. It didn't frighten him. He didn't hear the next several words as Raoul continued to map out the plan to pack Megan and François off to Paris within the fortnight. The count was saying something about Victor and Elise and how well the three children played together. Erik's heart was pounding in his throat, and he was having trouble catching his breath. He wondered how Raoul could calmly suggest that Megan and François would simply become part of his household, his family, for that was what he meant to do, to steal them away just as he had stolen Christine and his very life away from him so many years ago. François would grow up thinking of Raoul as his father. Meg would live like a maiden aunt among them unless they eventually convinced her to put her marriage aside and remarry.

He couldn't avoid the tremors in his voice as he insisted, "You can't take them from me. Bring them here. Bring them to me."

"What? To live in the cellars here with you? Do you really want them to hide the rest of their lives like you will have to do? Think, Erik. If you love them, give them a life, especially your son."

Unable to think rationally, overwhelmed by the shock of considering the loss of Meg and his son forever, unable to understand Raoul's plan as anything but cruel revenge, Erik begged, "Don't do this to me! Raoul, don't take them away from me! Don't take out your revenge against me in this way. Meg loves me."

Losing his patience, Raoul retorted, "What are you talking about? I'm trying to help you and Meg. I've dropped everything to come and help you. Do you think I want to be here?"

Erik sank disconsolately to the cot. "You've taken everything away from me. You took Christine. Now you're taking Meg away, too. I can't lose everything. François is my son, my flesh and blood. I didn't do anything to deserve this. Not again." All pretense of control disappeared as Erik collapsed in upon himself.

Raoul, stunned and speechless, watched Erik. He had never thought Meg's marriage to the Phantom a good idea. For one thing, even now he was sure Erik was still obsessed with Christine and always would be. For another, he was a criminal. He was unpredictable and volatile. How was Raoul supposed to reason with him? Clearly the best solution was to take Meg and François back to Paris where they could be safe. Erik was intelligent. Eventually he'd have to see reason.

"Is it the separation that you fear or the fact that your family would be under my protection?"

Erik didn't answer immediately. Slowly he raised his eyes to Raoul and studied him. Indeed, he realized that just the presence of Raoul in the enclosed space of his secret room brought back flashes of anger, jealousy, and loss. If someone else had come and offered asylum to his family, would he have reacted in the same way or would he have been grateful knowing that Meg and François would have a chance at happiness even if it had to be without him? When had he begun to think that he could lead a normal life, that he had a right to something beyond his own prison walls? He had his music. Signore Costanzi promised him sanctuary. He could lose himself again in the compositions. He could train himself again to be alone. He tried to imagine it. He had to. He must.

Raoul saw the battle Erik must be waging. Erik opened his mouth to speak several times only to shake his head and clench and unclench his fists. He alternately glared at Raoul as if contemplating ripping his throat out and looked away at some imaginary point on the wall with which he seemed to converse. Finally, a very low murmur rose from Erik's averted face. Raoul had to lean in close to hear him. "… they would be well taken care of, I know. Paris is home. She's young. She could …" Erik stopped, his lips clamped tightly shut. Before Raoul could begin to speak, Erik looked directly into his eyes and asked urgently, "Meg agrees? She has agreed to this plan?"

Raoul hadn't expected this question, although he should have. Of course he had not even discussed his plan with Meg or even with Christine. It simply was the only option that made any sense, and he was sure that he'd be able to convince Meg that it was the right course of action. As he considered his response to Erik's question, he knew that anything short of a yes would prolong the man's resistance. On the other hand, if he lied, it might be enough to push Erik to make the right decision. Which was more important? The truth or the safety of the innocent victims of Erik's ill fated destiny?

"It's imperative to Meg to protect your son." He swallowed hard knowing that this was the truth, but it was not the truth that Erik's question sought.

Erik slumped forward in resignation.

"Monsieur Chagny, I think you'd better go for the time being. Could I call on you at your inn later?" The voice came from behind Raoul.

Costanzi must have been listening outside the door. He had spoken peremptorily, and Raoul accepted the suggestion. He was moved by Erik's reaction. But this whole affair had confirmed for Raoul that Erik must make his way alone. Meg and the child must be rescued. It was the kindest thing that Raoul could do for the man, perhaps the only thing anyone could do for the poor creature.

Raoul rose to leave. Erik had doubled over, his face buried in his hands and pressed against his knees. His whole body trembled, and Raoul was pained to hear a low, muffled groan of sorrow rising from him. Costanzi drew close to the Phantom and softly placed his hand on the man's back. Just as Raoul turned the corner to walk down the hallway, he saw Costanzi pull the grieving man into a compassionate embrace.

"Tell her to be reasonable, Christine!" Raoul was beside himself. Meg was wailing; Christine stood by her whispering soothingly as she threw darts at him with her eyes. Even Madeleine, who had not really forgiven Erik for running off with her daughter, sat near Meg wringing her hands at her daughter's hysterics.

"I should never have written to you! How could I deliver Erik into his enemy's hands?" Her face was covered in tears, her eyes red and puffy, and the look she gave Raoul was one of pure hatred. Christine drew back in momentary shock at her friend's vituperation against her husband.

"Meg, you must listen." Madeleine spoke up just as Christine, too, was about to intervene. "Raoul has come to help. What's most important, even to Erik, if he weren't selfish …"

"Selfish?" How can you say that about a man who has had nothing real to call his own until now? You of all people, Maman!" Then she whirled on Christine, seeking solidarity, only to note the flushed expression on her face as well. "You, Christine, would you condemn him again to solitude? I'm sorry but you've chosen a cruel and hard man to share your life with. If you were in his situation, Raoul, and Christine came to Erik to ask for help, he'd risk his life to bring you back to Christine's arms."

"What kind of a life can you have with him? Always hiding, always running? Life with him will always be dangerous. You'll condemn your son to be an outcast, too. Erik lived like an animal for years. He spent most of his life scurrying around in the shadows. Erik will never belong in our world, Meg."

Christine groaned at her husband's unfortunate directness. Meg's mouth fell open, and all the blood rushed from her face. Her mother grabbed her to steady her just as she threatened to collapse.

"Raoul?" asked Madeleine, hoping to restore some civility, "you said that this man, the manager, seemed to have befriended Erik?"

"Yes, he actually seemed genuinely fond of him, and I think it was mutual."

"And that surprises you, doesn't it?!! You can't imagine anyone befriending or loving him!" Meg challenged sarcastically.

"Well, after all he's a murderer, Meg." Raoul was fast losing his patience with them all. Raoul hadn't meant to go into details, but once he started to explain the plan and Erik's reaction, everything came spilling out. He even tried to lie just a bit to soften things when Meg pressed him on how Erik was holding up, but she kept at him until details slipped in that Meg was quick to catch. From that moment on, she had been ranting at him.

"Please, stop it, both of you!"

Madeleine looked for help to Christine, who in a soft voice asked her husband, "You said he was distraught to hear your plan. Was he otherwise well?"

Raoul's hesitation was all Meg needed to know the truth.

"Take me to him! Take me to him now!"

There were no more tears spilling over the rims of her eyes. The hysterics had ended, and pure determination had taken their place.

CHAPTER 16

❀

Meg

for wither thou goest, I will go; and where thou lodgest, I will lodge: thy people shall be my people, and thy God my God: where thou diest, I will die, and there will I be buried.

Bible, Book of Ruth

Christine convinced Meg that Raoul had to rest before returning to Rome. They departed two nights later with only a full moon to guide them down the road until they were well beyond the turn off for Rome. If anyone asked, the servants would explain that the Count and Countess de Chagny had decided to spend a holiday in Rome, leaving the children with Meg and her mother, Mme. Giry. Christine would stay indoors only going out with a hood and cloak to mask her face and hair so that the authorities would assume she was Meg. Word was sent to Father Antonio, saying that Meg was indisposed and wouldn't be coming to the church for a couple of weeks. Annetta and the children went without her to weed the gravestones and help the priest with the cleaning of the saints. Madeleine went for provisions to Pianosa and made a special purchase of candy that Meg liked and made sure the customers who milled about waiting for juicy tidbits of gossip heard her. She experienced the unkindly treatment her daughter had been exposed to since Erik's escape first-hand on this very occasion when behind her she distinctly heard a matronly woman snicker about theater people and their loose morals. She restrained herself from confronting the little enclave of self-fashioned respectable citizens. Instead she smiled disarmingly at the store clerk—who was admiring the cut of her bodice and lingering on the soft curve of her long neck—and swept out the door with her best ballerina flourish.

In the street she recognized from Meg's description the tall man who swaggered along the store fronts as Giovanni. He was with several friends of the same age, all of them looking as if they had nothing but time on their hands. Upon seeing the carriage from the manor and the graceful older woman who handed the driver the packages, Giovanni had also recognized her. Meg was simply a younger version of this stunning woman who carried herself with the grace of a cat and the pride of a lion. Madeleine paused only one moment to return the young man's invasive stare; that was all it took for her to know who and what he was.

Madeleine and Christine lavished their attention on François, taking this opportunity to get to know him better. He had cried disconsolately as his mother took her leave of him, and Christine thought perhaps Meg would relent and stay with the child. But Meg's resolve was iron. She had always struck Christine as so small, so fragile in appearance, so sweet in temperament, that she was amazed at the courage and strength she now showed. To love Erik, to love him as Meg did, required a strength and determination that Christine painfully realized she herself lacked. Meg was determined to fight for her right to be with Erik; she would fight for their right to love each other in the face of hopeless odds.

Christine watched the little boy play with the lead soldiers on the piano bench and studied his face. All children are beautiful, and her own were seraphic, but she couldn't take her eyes off François. He was a version of Erik whole and unblemished, strikingly beautiful and strangely alluring. She could see in the child's face his father's eyes, the turn to his sensual lips, the wide forehead, the expressive brows, and what would become a strong jaw and chin. Although Victor and François were about the same age, François looked nearly a year older than her son. He was tall, strong, with a poise that was almost unnatural.

"Aunt Christine, do you want me to play for you?" He was morose and had not wanted to go see the puppies with Elise and Victor, but this new idea dispelled the cloud and brightened his eyes with anticipation. Without waiting for an answer, François pushed the bench close to the piano, placed the large encyclopedia on top, and climbed up so that his fingers could reach the keyboard. He began to play from memory with the skill and passion of a much older child. It was clear that he had Erik's talent as well. The melody reminded Christine of a song Erik used to sing for her!

"Don't cry, Aunt Christine. I'm sorry. My father plays it better than I do."

"You play beautifully, just like your father." She hugged him to her breast, wishing he was hers. Madeleine came up behind the two of them and patted Christine on the shoulder. She had raised Christine since she was very young. When Christine's father had died, Madeleine had assumed responsibility for the child and brought her to live and train at the ballet in the opera house. For Madeleine, Meg and Christine were sisters; both of them were her children.

"François, why don't you go see the puppies now? Elise and Victor are with them in the garden. I'll take care of your Aunt Christine." He wiggled out of Christine's arms and ran to the garden, his former sadness forgotten.

"What is it, Christine?"

"Were we cowards? Was I? Why couldn't I have loved him the way he needed to be loved?"

Madeleine couldn't believe she was hearing Christine correctly. Her heart had leapt into her mouth, and she couldn't refrain from clenching her fist over her breast in surprise. "Cowards? No, ma petite. Meg has always been special. I didn't realize she was so taken with Erik until it was too late. The price of loving a man like Erik is quite high, ma cherie. You were wise to make the choice you made."

Christine smiled sadly at Madeleine; she was like a mother, the only mother she had ever known.

Hesitantly, Madeleine asked, "You do love Raoul, don't you, Christine?"

When Christine didn't immediately respond, Madeleine grabbed her hand and squeezed it hard. "Be careful, Christine. Don't risk your happiness or Meg's."

"I love Raoul, but I've never been able to get Erik out of my mind, or my heart. Seeing Meg, seeing how much she loves him, how she's willing to fight for him, brought it all back to me. The way he moved, his eyes, his intensity … Perhaps if I had …?"

"Stop. You won't do yourself any good doing that. It's easy to regret decisions not taken. Think how that intensity of Erik's you now find so attractive frightened you!"

"But that's the point. I let fear overwhelm me."

"And Raoul?"

Christine lowered her eyes and spoke in a whisper. "He promised to protect me."

"Christine, listen to me well. Meg and Erik truly love one another. I've resigned myself to this. You must control these feelings or they will destroy you all."

"Prepare yourself. He's somewhat bedraggled. I haven't been able to get him to come out for days, ever since the Count de Chagny's visit. He barely eats. He mostly sleeps." Signore Costanzi glanced inside the dark room and held the door open so that Meg could enter.

Raoul started to go into the storeroom with Meg, but she stopped him. He insisted on keeping the door ajar just in case. Too anxious to see Erik to argue with Raoul, she slipped inside the dark room with the light of the one candle she held in her hand. She called out to him softly and listened for a reply that didn't come. There was no sound; it was as if everything were wrapped in cotton. She advanced toward the back of the room—careful not to go beyond the dim crescent illuminated by the candle—where she expected to find Erik's cot. She came upon a small table with a lantern and stopped to light this as well. The glow from the lamp extended farther through the blackness until it reached the cot where Erik, dressed in a simple shirt and dark breeches, lay with his face toward the wall.

Holding her breath, she looked for some sign that he was alive. Whether it was a trick of the fluttering lamplight or not, she eventually thought she could see his chest rise and fall as he breathed. She called out again to him, and this time he stirred. Slowly he twisted on the bed in the direction of her voice, his eyes still closed as if refusing to wake up. She sat on the edge of the cot and caressed his face with one hand as she gently shook his shoulder with the other. His eyes fluttered open and fixed on her in gradual recognition. He reached up and wrapped his arms around her, squeezing her almost painfully. Slowly he relaxed his grip on her.

"Meg? Have you come yet again to rescue me?" Although he smiled at her, and his tone was light, almost chiding, there was yearning in his words. He wanted her to remember those first days when she had followed him to the underground vaults in Paris, days when he had slunk away like a wounded animal to die alone in the dark. She knew that he was more moved by her presence than he wanted her to know, that this episode had seemed to him as hopeless as the other. And that he had felt nearly as lost as before.

"I couldn't stay away. I followed you once to the edge of hell; a trip to Rome seems like a holiday."

He smiled at her more broadly and drew her down in another kiss, tender and long. He ran his hands across the landscape of her body that he loved so well as if to remember it through his touch. For just a moment, she pushed away from him. She called out to Raoul and Signore Costanzi, who still stood vigil on the other side of the door, that she and her husband wanted to be alone. She refused to return to his embrace until she heard the click of the latch as the door closed. Then she slipped her hands along her husband's chest and pressed her body against his as she whispered to him that she loved him and would always love him and would never be separated from him again by anything short of death itself.

"Raoul plans to take you and François back to Paris where you'll be safe. You can start a new life."

His voice floated down to her as she lay naked leaning across his body, her thigh casually draped over his groin, her breast and hip pushed against his side, her face on the plain of his shoulder and chest. Soft, warm, and drowsy, she was loathe to answer.

"We won't go with him, Erik," she murmured. The words flowed along his skin, like breezes over a landscape. She closed her eyes in hopes of falling back into the gentle dream she had been having when he woke her.

"Raoul says everyone shuns you and our son. If nothing else, we have to think of François." His voice was tight as he spoke. "Raoul's a good man. Christine is like your sister." His hands roamed up and down her back, sweeping under her blond tresses to the back of her neck and gliding down to the rise of her buttocks. She melted against him nuzzling her face in the dark hair along his chest. In spite of his caresses, she sensed the tension in his muscles, the denseness of his flesh, as if he were readying himself to meet disaster.

The drowsiness dissipated, and she listened intently to his heart pounding beneath her ear. It had stepped up its pace. Erik's words were rational and cold, but his body told her how hard it was for him to tell her what he thought was necessary.

Wide awake, she raised her cheek from his shoulder and answered, "I can't leave you. I won't. If we have to move a hundred times, I'm determined to make my home with you."

"I can't ask you to lead that kind of life. I won't have it for my son, either. We must be realistic. We tried; it didn't work." He hoped that he sounded convincing.

"No, it won't work in the countryside. We can't stay in the manor. But here in Rome, we could disappear. You and I belong in a city! I could work again. François could go to school. You could give him music lessons. You could write, compose. This is the heart of opera, Erik. It would be as if we had gone home." She saw the glimmer of hope, a hint of excitement in his eyes. There had to be some way for them to be together and be safe.

Erik didn't speak for a long time as if he were considering the options. He continued to stroke her skin in an effort to calm himself as well as her. Almost in a whisper, as if the thought were so fragile it couldn't withstand reality, he confided to Meg that Signore Costanzi had told him that construction of a new opera house was to begin the following year. It was to become the official opera house of Rome, Il Teatro Dell'Opera. Slowly the details of a plan emerged.

"He's shown me the design. I've asked to be involved in the construction. I can make sure that there are rooms constructed, rooms and vaults similar to those in the Opera Populaire, where we could hide if we needed to."

Meg looked away from Erik, her hopes dimming. Erik rushed to ease her doubts. "The underground rooms would be there in case we needed them. In case *I* needed them," he explained. "Signore Costanzi has asked me to reside with him in his home. He has no one, and he's very lonely. He wants the three of us to make his home our home."

"Maman can come to live with us, too?"

"Yes. If she wishes to."

"Then we should close the manor and join you here in Rome as soon as possible."

"Meg, think carefully first. If you come here to Rome, there's no guarantee that something like this won't happen again. I can't protect you; I can't give you the life you want. It can never be the way you imagined it." Erik turned to his side to face her. He took her face in his hands and examined her eyes, her expression. He thought about the past days since the police had accused him of stealing the diamond necklace. He remembered his panic when he had come home and found them waiting for him. It was only when Raoul came to the Teatro Argentina to speak with him that Erik realized that the police didn't know that he was the Phantom and that they were arresting him on new grounds, a crime of which he was completely innocent. "I won't be able to live like you and François. You might be able to lead a normal life, but I may need to remain hidden or at least in the shadows. Signore Costanzi is a powerful patron. He'll keep my secrets; he'll keep me safe from the mob. I can be productive. He's given me a way to have my music, but I may have to live much as I lived before. Can you bear that? Can you bear to live married to a phantom?"

She wasn't able to mask the tears that swelled in her eyes. They weren't for her or for her son. She had asked too much of Erik. She knew that now. He wasn't asking her to live in the bowels of the opera house. This wasn't the fate that might have met Christine if she had chosen to stay with the Opera Ghost. But nor was it the fairy tale life Meg had painted for the two of them as they journeyed over the border from France to Italy. There would be sacrifices, but she would lie in his arms at night. She would be surrounded by his music. He would be safe. She would love him.

Seeing the answer in her eyes, Erik urged Meg to come close until their bodies locked together once more, sealing their new pact.

"M. de Chagny, I have spoken at length with Pierre, and I believe I can help him build a new life here. He is a musical genius and is already working for the Teatro Argentina. The new theater we are building might be under his musical direction."

"Do you know who Pierre really is, Signore Costanzi?"

"Do you, M. de Chagny?" challenged the older man. "I know his real name is Erik. I'll have to accustom myself to calling him that. I also know that he's had a turbulent, perhaps even dark, past. Whatever he was then, he is not that man now. The man I know is one who can offer the world a tremendous gift. He is kind and extremely vulnerable. He wants what any man wants, a life and someone to share it with. He doesn't want to disappear as if he never existed. Is that so hard to understand?"

Raoul listened to the gentleman as if he were talking about a different man. Then he realized that perhaps this was the case. And yet, to be fair, much of what the old man said had always been true, even of the Phantom.

They had been together for over three hours, and Raoul paced impatiently. Signore Costanzi simply smiled discreetly at Raoul's rudeness, knowing that the time was being well spent. When Erik and Meg finally joined them in the manager's offices behind stage, a lovely blush had returned to Meg's cheeks, and she held Erik's hand in her own as if he might disappear at any moment. Erik, too, seemed confident, more relaxed than the old gentleman had ever seen him. Yet when his eyes fell upon Raoul, they turned dark and cautious.

"Meg, we must be getting back. If we leave now, we can cover at least ten miles before dark." Raoul gathered his gloves without a look toward the reunited lovers and started for the door.

No one had moved. Signore Costanzi looked at the Frenchman as if he were mad. Meg smiled at Erik before addressing Raoul, "I'll be ready to go in the morning. Erik and I have plans to make. When we get back home, I intend to close the house and …"

"Yes, I know. It's all been discussed. We will leave for Paris as soon as possible."

"No." Erik spoke for the first time. Meg's smile disappeared as she saw his eyes harden. She squeezed his hand, and they softened immediately. "My family will come to Rome to be with me."

"Bravo, Pierre, I mean Erik." Costanzi was delighted that his idea had been accepted by his new musical director and friend.

"That's absurd. At least let me take François. He'll be well educated and brought up in a loving environment."

Erik jerked forward before Meg could calm him. "You will not take my son!"

"How can you seriously think you can be a father? Until a few years ago you lived in a circus cage or the underground vaults of the opera!"

In his anger and desire to get to Raoul, Erik pushed past Meg. She tripped over the leg of a chair and fell with a sharp cry to the ground.

Both men rushed to her, but Erik stopped when Raoul lashed out yet again at him. "And you think you can be a father! Indeed!"

The pain that crossed Erik's face nearly caused Raoul to regret his harsh words. However, he believed they were essentially true whether or not Meg and Erik wanted to believe them. Meg pushed Raoul's hand away and rose to her feet unassisted and uninjured by the fall. She ran to Erik and grabbed him close to her, turning him away from Raoul, whose gaze he had painfully sustained. She whispered something in his ear. He shook his head several times, but she held on to his arm and whispered more fervently into his ear. He remained with his back to Raoul as Meg stepped forth and addressed him.

"François is our child. If you no longer want to help us, we understand. Regardless, I am going back tomorrow morning and packing my things and my child and coming to live with Erik. We won't be living in the storeroom. Signore Costanzi has asked us to share his home. If my mother wants to come, she'll be welcomed. You, unfortunately, will not be." This last statement was forced out in a voice on the edge of tears. "I won't have anyone around my son who so despises his father."

Raoul was shocked. He didn't know what to say. He felt profoundly miserable, and a good deal of this feeling was bound up with shame and guilt. Before Meg and Erik left, he forced his voice to work. "Meg, I'm sorry. It's of course your decision. I'll escort you back tomorrow and help you with whatever matters I can."

She smiled back at him even though she regretted that his apology in no way included Erik. The only response from Erik was his back as Raoul walked out the door.

Giovanni had been spying on Meg for weeks since her husband's escape. Seething inside from her rejection, he no longer considered her a worthy marriage prospect. Indeed much of the gossip around town had been fanned by him and his friends, Carlo and Giordino. Yet he was obsessed with revenge. It wasn't enough to see Meg's discomfort when the citizens of Pianosa looked askance at her and the strange man she had married. It wasn't even enough that she and her husband had once more been separated. Soon he imagined other men would come sniffing at her proud skirts. She thought she was too good for him, but he would show her the mistake of spurning his attentions. He would show her what she was.

The arrival of the Chagnys had made it difficult to approach the house. He could no longer risk climbing to the second story to watch Meg in her bedroom. There were too many people around, too much activity. Fortunately he had just found out that the Chagnys had taken a holiday trip to Rome. Indeed they had departed several days ago. No one knew when they'd return. Meg was practically alone again. There were only a handful of servants, Meg's mother, and the little boy in the manor. This might be his only opportunity.

God how Giovanni wanted to tell his friends about the necklace! Never had he felt such a thrill of delight as when he put the mask on and flew past that old dowager. He would never forget the look on her face or that of the bystanders as he ripped the necklace free from her neck. The mask made him feel impervious. He regretted having to drop it outside the house for the police to find. The necklace was of less consequence than the mask for him. The mask had given him power, power to do whatever he wanted without consequences for himself. The necklace would only have given him more of what he already had, money. Sneaking up to the second floor and planting it inside the library desk had been almost as thrilling as the theft itself. Meg and her husband had been in the garden, mere moments away. Anyone might have entered the room and found him there. How would he have explained his appearance on the second floor? It would have been very suspicious. But no one had discovered him, and he had slipped away as easily as a ghost.

Now it didn't matter for he was sure both Meg and her husband knew exactly who had stolen the necklace and planted it among their things. He had made a formal visit shortly after Erik's escape only to find Meg barring the door and calling him a thief and a liar to his face. It did no good to accuse him, no one would believe the word of a foreigner like her—a former performer in an opera house in Paris—over that of a native son from an important and respected family. And after a momentary feeling of panic, the fact that Meg knew him to be the cause of her troubles actually made the whole escapade even more delicious to Giovanni.

Each day it became harder not to tell Giordino and Carlo that he was the masked thief that had stolen the necklace right from underneath everyone's noses.

The three of them had been drinking since dinner, and Carlo was looking a bit green when Giovanni suggested they pay a visit to the Giry whore. What kind of woman ties herself to a man like that, a man who has to wear a mask so that he doesn't frighten little children? Giordino smirked suggestively and elbowed Carlo who grunted bleary-eyed as if in sudden discomfort. It took little persuasion to convince his friends that the Giry woman deserved to be taught a lesson. She had teased Giovanni, strung him along over the past months, like any French slut, pretending to be above them all. A woman couldn't treat a man like that and not expect to pay. And pay dearly she would.

All the way to Meg's manor, images of the blond beauty, naked and begging him for mercy, flashed across Giovanni's mind's eye. He'd show her how unworthy she was. Her body was the only thing of any value to him now. The sound of her begging for mercy would only enhance his enjoyment. So beautiful. So deceitful. He might cut her face so that she would be a better match for the disfigured man she had perversely chosen over him.

The men soon came upon the dark house. It was well past midnight, just a few hours from daylight. Carlo relieved himself against the front door giggling so loudly that he shook uncontrollably and drenched his own shoes as well as the door. Grimfaced, Giovanni watched as his friends stumbled about in the dark. They would be of little use. Giordino hinted that they might set fire to something, perhaps the stables. That would certainly cause a stir! Giovanni barked at him to stay put. He warned both to be quiet and wait for him.

He had other fires on his mind, fires that only Meg's body could put out.

Signore Costanzi had spent hours trying to convince Erik to wait until Meg and his son returned from Pianosa; there was no need for him to risk being arrested by traveling back to the country manor. At first Erik listened calmly; however, he never intended to heed the old man's warnings. It had been agreed, Signore Costanzi reminded him yet again, that Meg and Raoul would return for François. There the Chagnys would help Meg close the house and make the arrangements for the relocation of the household to Rome. Erik had indeed listened as Meg and Raoul went over the details, one of which was that Erik remain safely hidden in Rome. Nevertheless he never once agreed that he would wait; he simply didn't say that he wouldn't. There was no way that he could let Meg out of his sight again. He would follow them, silent and unseen. He knew there was a risk, but he couldn't stay behind doing nothing.

He still didn't trust Raoul. What if he changed his mind again and took François against Meg's and his wishes? Meg wouldn't be able to live separated from her child. She would be forced to go after Raoul and Christine. Erik knew that he wasn't thinking rationally and that Meg would probably be able to reassure him, dispel his fears, were she here. But she was in a carriage on her way back to Pianosa, far from him. She had gone, and Erik was left alone with his fears.

Erik listened with stoney silence while Signore Costanzi enumerated the reasons that he should wait. Then he took his leave of his new patron and set off for the stable to prepare Charlemagne for the journey back to the villa.

Knowing he would move more swiftly than Raoul's party, Erik veered off the path on several occasions only to catch a glimpse of the carriage either a bit ahead on the road or lagging just behind. As he drew near Pianosa, he felt himself drawn irresistibly toward the town. It was late. In the back of his mind, he imagined that Giovanni might yet be about with his friends, either gaming, drinking, or whoring. Meg's cautionary voice whispered in the back of his mind that he should avoid any contact with Pianosa and especially with the young Italian who had stolen the diamond necklace and planted it at the villa.

Until Raoul told him the details of the necklace and Giovanni's role in its theft, Erik had assumed that there could be only one reason that the police had arrested him. In his panic, he imagined that the Parisian police inspector Leroux, the man who had tortured him and brought him to trial and execution, had somehow tracked him down and was determined to drag him back to the gallows in Paris. He had been certain the armed men were taking him to his death. But then again it hardly mattered what the crime was. He would never survive another imprisonment, even if the sentence were light. He would die before anyone locked him away again in a cell.

Giovanni had destroyed their future in Pianosa. What most angered Erik was that the young Italian had destroyed Meg's dreams. As unrealistic as he thought them, Erik had suffered a great deal to keep Meg's dreams alive, and this man had cruelly made them impossible. In the back of his mind, Meg's voice asked him what he planned to do if his path should cross Giovanni's tonight in the streets of Pianosa. Why was he going into town, knowing that he might come upon his enemy? He didn't listen to her voice, although he knew he should; he didn't want to consider consequences. There were some things in his nature that he simply couldn't control no matter how much he wanted to live up to Meg's ideal image of him.

CHAPTER 17

❁

The Light

> *Ulysses, taught by labours to be wise,*
> *Let this short memory of grief suffice.*
> *To me are known the various woes ye bore.*
> *In storms by sea, in perils on the shore;*
> *Forget whatever was in Fortune's power,*
> *And share the pleasures of this genial hour.*
>
> Odyssey, Homer, Alexander Pope

Erik took the fork to Pianosa, curious to see the town that had shunned him and his family, the town he had barely come to know before it cast him out. In the back of his mind, he admitted that he yearned to run across Giovanni, the man who had nearly ruined his life. He told himself that he would only observe him. Any act of revenge would effectively seal Erik's fate.

He first passed the gaming hall where many a young gentleman won and gambled away minor fortunes. Then he set off for the less respectable areas of town where drink and cheap women were plentiful. Outside one such establishment, a friend of Giovanni's nearly stumbled over someone else who had passed out in the street. He kicked the unconscious youth viciously with his boot and laughed calling back to someone inside the doorway. The man on the threshold of the bordello stepped out under the gaslight in the street. He was tall and broad shouldered with dark hair. Erik straightened in his seat in anticipation as he recognized Giovanni, his wife's spurned suitor. The young Italian swayed slightly as he joined the friend in the street bringing him close in a conspiratorial embrace.

Erik's hand caressed the hilt of his rapier, but he forced himself to sit and watch. Charlemagne pawed the ground sensing Erik's tension. How easy it would be to spur Charlemagne forward, draw his rapier, and bury it in the young Italian's gut. Another of Giovanni's friends came out into the night air and joined the conversation. Erik knew he could easily dispatch all three, but Giovanni's friends had done him no harm that he was aware of. As likely as not, one of the three would manage to raise the alarm before the deed was complete. Erik congratulated himself on his cold reasoning. Meg would have told him it was simply wrong, but it helped Erik to have more practical restraints than that.

The friends mounted their horses and trotted out of town taking the road north. Erik's senses were on alert; they were headed in the same direction that he would be taking to return home. Erik followed quietly at a discreet distance. The three men were rowdy. It would be a miracle if they became aware that they were being followed.

When they arrived at the manor, Erik circled behind the stables and left Charlemagne tethered nearby. The coach horses were already bedded; Meg and Raoul must have arrived an hour or more before. All the lights in the house were off, except for one that remained lit throughout the night near the front entrance of the manor. One of the drunken men was pointing toward the stable, but the one he recognized as Giovanni stood motionless staring up at the balcony window that opened from his and Meg's bedroom.

Suddenly it was as if he were seeing through Giovanni's eyes as the young man was climbing the trellis outside the balcony to the second floor. Even as Giovanni stared up at Meg's window, Erik left the dark stable, ran quietly to the back of the house, and slipped inside.

As Erik made his way up the backstairs, he heard the scream. Abandoning any attempt to be quiet, he ran toward the cry. It was coming from Meg's room. He burst inside to find his wife sitting up in the bed holding the sheet to her throat as she watched Raoul struggle with the intruder. In the faint light from the open window, Erik could make out the glint of a knife blade as it plunged down and came up again, not once but twice, in rapid succession. He threw himself toward the fighting figures just as Giovanni was about to plunge the dagger down yet again. Raoul stumbled back, Erik taking his place. The dagger came down in a wide arc, but Erik stopped it before it struck flesh. His fist squeezed Giovanni's arm and shook the blade from his hand.

The sudden glow of candles and the sound of a panicked scream distracted both men momentarily. Out of the corner of his eye, Erik saw Christine rush to Raoul who lay stretched out and motionless on the floor. Disarmed, Giovanni struggled uselessly to get away from the masked man's vice-like grip. Erik twisted Giovanni's arm until it was pulled painfully up behind his back. Applying constant pressure on the limb, Erik pushed the intruder toward the edge of the balcony. He leaned Giovanni over the railing until the young man's center of balance dragged him head first over the ledge. The only thing saving him from toppling to the ground was the fact that Erik was still holding him. Below, Erik was delighted to see that several servants had rushed out and restrained Giovanni's two drunken friends.

"Tell them! Tell them who stole the diamond necklace," hissed Erik as he dangled his enemy's body precariously over the ledge into the night air.

"I don't know what you're talking about. You did! Everyone saw you!"

Erik released his grip just for an instant and Giovanni lurched forward toward the ground. He caught the young Italian again, straining to hold the man's weight—nearly the same as his own—and to keep him from crashing head long against the hard paving stone below.

Giovanni screamed in terror and pleaded to be pulled up to the safety of the balcony.

"Tell them!"

"I will! I will! Just don't let go! I did it! I stole the necklace!"

"Details!"

"I ... I took a mask from François. I waited until the night of the ball."

"Why?"

"Witnesses. I wanted witnesses."

"Go on. My arms are tiring."

"Oh God! Don't let go! I put on the mask so they'd say it was you. I made sure several people saw me. I grabbed it off her throat."

"Then?"

"I'm falling! Hold me!"

"I think you're holding back on us. The whole story, Cimino."

"I slipped it into the desk in the library."

"Exactly?"

"The ... the drawer on the right."

"You're quite heavy, you know."

"I did it while you were in the orchard. I dropped the mask outside for the police to find. That's all. That's all I can say. Now, please pull me up!"

"Why?"

"I told the truth!"

"Yes, but you need to listen to my questions more carefully. Why did you do it?" Hearing no answer, Erik allowed his grip on the material of Giovanni's coat to loosen ever so slightly. In a new panic, the man babbled incoherently for several seconds before finally managing to utter what Erik was waiting for.

"She refused to marry me. I was angry."

Erik pulled the young man to the balcony where he sank to his knees unable to stop his body from shaking. Then Erik turned toward the scene by the door. For one moment, he stood fixed to the spot as his eyes lit on Christine. He hadn't seen her for nearly four years. They had told him that she had died in childbirth. No matter how many reassurances he had gotten that this was a lie, he couldn't shake the image of her dead body lying cold and pale in the crypt.

She was pressing cloths to the wounds in Raoul's shoulder. Meg, too, was by the wounded man's side, but her eyes had been trained on Erik the whole time. She held her breath as she saw her husband observe Christine.

His former pupil, the woman who had obsessed him and led him to mad acts of passion and violence, was beautiful, a warm golden light in the darkness.

Erik forced his eyes away from her to the reclining figure of her husband. Raoul was bleeding profusely, his face the color of ash, but he was breathing and conscious. In response to Erik's look of concern, Raoul smiled faintly.

"You were supposed to wait in Rome so that I could solve all your problems for you and be the hero."

"I've never been patient," Erik replied in a matter-of-fact tone. Stooping he pulled Raoul's uninjured arm up and around his shoulder and helped the man to his feet. Raoul was too weak to stand, so Erik picked him up and carried him the short distance to the bed. Meg called to Giuseppe to send for the doctor and the constable. When Erik heard the latter instruction, he turned nervously in her direction.

"I must go." Erik cursed inaudibly under his breath and moved toward the door. Meg rushed to bar his way. She stood, her back against the doorknob, as if she could physically keep him from leaving.

"No, no more running. Giovanni's confessed. The charges will be dropped."

"Do you suppose the constable will believe his confession, a confession dragged from a young man being held by his feet over a ledge? Meg, I've had false witnesses speak against me before. Why would this time be different?"

"Because this time you're not alone. This time you have all of us to speak up for you." Raoul's voice was weak, but firm.

"Have you been avoiding me?"

Erik looked up from the shrubs he had been examining to see Christine. She was dressed in a simple pink dress with a burgundy shawl draped around her. Her hair lay loose over her shoulders in curls. He would not have thought it possible that she was even more beautiful than he had remembered her. Married life and children had given her form a richness and bounty that took his breath away. His eyes scanned the length of her and only on reaching her eyes once more was he aware of the intrusiveness of his glance, for her cheeks were tinged a deep red. He didn't answer, but he indicated the bench as if inviting her to sit in the garden with him.

"You were always on the quiet side unless you were singing or giving me instructions." Her tone was light as if they had been lifelong friends.

Erik stared down at his hands as if puzzled by their existence. She felt his discomfort. She, too, was nervous, but she had promised herself that she would have this conversation before she and Raoul left for Paris. Erik's entire household was ready to depart for Rome, and it was time for her and Raoul to end their visit and return to Paris. Even though the authorities had officially apologized to Erik for making a false indictment, their attitude was cold, brusque, and resentful. Erik insisted that they go through with the original plan to close the manor and relocate to Rome. In a large urban center, he felt he could be less visible, more at ease. The beautiful manor and its vineyards were an impossible dream. In Rome, he had gained a powerful patron, Signore Costanzi, and this would make a huge difference in their lives.

As Erik thought of his imminent departure, he also considered that of Christine and her family. She, too, had farewells on her mind. He had spent the better part of the last week avoiding her, unsure as to whether or not it was necessary. He feared Meg realized this as well, for she had been curiously quiet and even a little distant. Christine's skirts rustled seductively as she sat down beside him. He remembered their last farewell on the border between France and Italy and how close they had been. He had felt her breath on his face as he waited to know if there was any hope of her loving him the way he loved her.

"Remember your promise to me?" he suddenly asked.

Surprised, Christine wasn't sure to what he was referring.

"You promised me that you would be happy and never regret your decision to be with Raoul. Have you kept it?" He turned toward her on the bench. She felt the pressure of his leg against hers, and her pulse increased in response. His eyes were serious and dark, reminding her of those days when she had been his pupil and he had demanded her complete obedience.

Could she answer that question truthfully? she wondered. Her eyes hesitated, and he caught the edge of doubt immediately. She started to speak, but he grabbed her hand in his and pressed it to his chest. The look on his face was one of pain.

Before she could reply, Erik began to speak.

"You are dear to me, Christine. I would do anything to see you happy." When Christine made as if to speak, he placed his finger against her lips to silence her. "You were my gift to the world. I would dearly love to know you were singing again in public, but you've chosen to share your gift—our gift—only with those you most love. I need you to understand something that I have only just recently learned through many painful lessons. Meg is the gift you have given *me*. You were right to leave me. I would always have thought of you as my creation; you would never have had your own soul, your own destiny. Meg has come to me like rain to a desert. She is a gift, and I love her more than life itself."

Obscured by the thick growth of vines and flowering shrubs, Mme. Giry watched and listened. She had come upon the two of them—Christine and Erik—their voices quiet and intimate, their bodies close, and she couldn't turn and leave. But after a few moments, she drew back into the shadows of the house, slipping through the half opened door. She had heard enough.

Erik helped Raoul into the carriage. The injury had healed enough for him to travel, but it was still annoyingly sore. The two men had come to a kind of peace in the last days.

After the incident with Giovanni, Erik had kept mostly to himself, communicating only with Meg and his household. Raoul's recuperation had necessitated a delay to the Chagny's departure, and Meg lingered over details to stretch out the chance to be with Christine. So since the women and children were occupied with various errands and duties, Erik more and more often found himself alone with Raoul. One afternoon while they sat stupidly silent for several hours in the same room, Raoul finally remarked on some bit of news from Paris. Although Erik had never had any interest in society or politics, he found himself listening to the reasoning Raoul employed as he discussed the issue that so disturbed him. The questions Erik chose to ask demonstrated that his lack of interest was not due to ignorance or incomprehension. Soon they were arguing about representative government and the rule of the mob, as Raoul called it. At a particularly intense moment, the two men had stood jowl to jowl bludgeoning each other with their arguments.

Raoul dictated that government must guarantee the wellbeing and follow the will of the majority, to which Erik proposed the question of what would happen if the majority were wrong? What guaranteed the individual's rights? An individual that society had eschewed? Abruptly the voices calmed. Yes, Raoul saw his point. Erik knew the force of the majority decision all too well.

Soon they were talking excitedly on other afternoons about the best care for horses, breeding practices, the benefits of natural fertilizers for crops, weather patterns, and the best soil for roses. Meg and Christine were delighted to see the two men converse so warmly and comfortably. Raoul had even agreed to accompany Erik to the construction site to check on the progress. He listened as Erik discussed the final concerns for the school building with Bruno, Simon, and the other men. The workmen paid close attention. Erik suggested that Bruno take over the supervision of the project. With a touching gruffness, Bruno grasped Erik's hand in a firm sign of appreciation. Raoul couldn't help but be impressed. Later the same day, Erik brought down the plans for the new Teatro Dell'Opera to be built in Rome and explained to Raoul the absolute marriage of utility and aesthetics in the choice of design and materials.

But Raoul would always know that it was the startling realization that his own children accepted Erik unconditionally. Raoul had chanced upon Erik one afternoon chasing François, Elise, and Victor in the garden. At first Raoul thought his children were actually frightened until Elise lay crumpled in the grass screaming at the top of her lungs and reaching out for Erik to pick her up and twirl her around for the third or fourth time. At night before bedtime, he found out that Erik sang all three of the children a special song, a different one for each of them, and promised that Christine would know the words and melodies and sing for Victor and Elise when they were once more at home.

So it was with a strangely warm feeling that the two men gave their farewells to one another. They said but the essential: Goodbye and have a safe trip. But there was a fondness behind the words that was new and unexpected to everyone, but especially to themselves. Meg kissed each of the children and grabbed Christine in a tight and tearful embrace before letting Erik hand her 'sister' to the carriage. Only when Christine was seated next to Raoul did she lean out the window and offer her cheek to Erik who kissed it softly. Then they were gone.

Meg watched the carriage disappear down the road. Erik had turned away already and sauntered off to the stable. When she joined him, she found him leaning against the black stallion, rhythmically patting Charlemagne's crest and whispering to him. Her mother had told her she had nothing to fear from

Christine. Madeleine wouldn't explain how she knew this to be true, but she insisted that Erik's love was true and strong and solely hers.

"You'll miss the noise of those children. I know François is pouting; he's hiding in the orchard with the puppies so that we don't see him cry."

"He shouldn't be afraid to cry. If we didn't cry sometimes, our souls would dry up and little by little blow away like dust."

"Do you feel like crying?" She gingerly touched his shoulder.

He wrapped his arms around her and whispered that until she came to him he had felt a little sad. She stretched up on tiptoe to reach his mouth for a kiss, but he bent his knees and lifted her so that she was held against his chest, her feet several inches off the ground. Feeling a bit silly, she insisted he let her down. A sly grin on his face, he eased her slowly to the ground, enjoying the feel of her as she slid along his body. He then bent and kissed her, lingering on the soft moist sweetness of her mouth.

Placing his hand on her stomach, he grinned at her. "If it's a girl, I would like to name her for my mother. Her name was Laurette. It means little angel."

"How did you know?" Meg started in wonder, placing her hand over his.

He smiled against her mouth and kissed her again before answering.

"I can tell. I know your body, Meg. It speaks to me, tells me things, teaches me."

She giggled and kissed him on his lips and on the edge of his jaw where she stopped to nibble at his beard with her teeth.

Her blond hair lay like sunshine round her face. Several loose strands, lifted by a gentle breeze, brushed across his face and shoulders like protective rays.

"My light in the dark," he whispered as she settled against him. "I love you, Meg."

978-0-595-45454-9
0-595-45454-2

Printed in the United States
85261LV00004B/40-42/A